DISAVOWED

BRIDGET E. BAKER

For Tessa
You are effortlessly fierce, you are infinitely kind, you are my
Chancery at heart

❧ I ☙

For six thousand and five hundred days, my mom took care of every single thing that went wrong in my life.

When Shamecha threatened to attack, she eradicated their armies and leveled their military bases. When my hair tangled into a snarly, unmanageable knot, Mom delicately combed it out. When an assassin shot a dart at my leg, she batted it away, and then removed the assailant's head from his neck slowly, so he suffered for placing me in danger. Not that I knew about the torture—that would have distressed me. When I was hungry, Mom handed me a bag of goldfish —the rainbow kind, because I preferred them to all the others.

I closed my eyes on a fluffy down pillow every single night knowing that I was safe, treasured, and valuable.

Until Mom died.

Although my maternal safety net vanished, my belief that others would help me persisted. I trusted that my family and friends would buoy me up, sacrifice for me, guide and direct me. The faith Mom instilled in me, the optimism, it didn't evaporate like water on a hot pan. So I relied on my sisters, my friends, Mom's confidantes. And on an ancient prophecy.

I was a total chump.

One of her allies poisoned Mom right here in our palace. That should have been enough to cure me of my desire to trust right there, but I hoped that he or she fled. Like a child, I hoped that I was no longer at risk, not here, not in my home. Thanks to my optimistic stupidity, the same villain abducted my older sister Melina right out from under my nose. After butchering every one of her guards.

"How can we have no idea who did this?" I ask.

Balthasar runs a hand through his hair. "I can give you a list of who it isn't. A huge contingent of us weren't even on the island when this happened, and many more had only just returned." The idea that anyone would defy my mom's former Chief Security Officer and my Warlord this way baffles me. In nine centuries, Balthasar has never known defeat, other than Mom's assassination.

"Gather every guard who has watched that villa in the last few days, and compile a list of people who *were* present. I also want to know who could have modified the guard placement around Melina's cottage." I close my eyes. I'm no closer to rooting out the traitor who killed my mom today than I was on the day she died. And if Melina's accusation in the security feed is correct, the same person just killed twenty-four more people on my watch. And he or she did it *alone*.

"Technically, the Chief Security Officer should be doing this," Balthasar says.

I slam my hand down on the table. "He's in the infirmary, because I blew up my friends. I think you can step in for the time being."

Balthasar's eyes widen.

I drop my voice to a whisper. "Just do it, okay?"

As badly as the sheltered, scared little girl inside me

wants to trust someone, when I look around now, I don't see allies.

I see threats.

I see risks.

I see liabilities.

Even Balthasar, my mom's brother-in-law, is suspect. After all, he returned to Ni'ihau just before I did. He might have had time to butcher those people himself, and if anyone has the capacity, it's him. But why would he want Melina's people dead? What does he stand to gain from her disappearance?

I wish I knew what motivated the people who have surrounded me my entire life.

My six thousand and five hundred days are nothing compared to their several hundred thousand days, for Balthasar and Alora. Even those close to my age, like the twin sister I've wasted years hating, the fiancé I love to kiss but struggle to trust, and my best friend who concealed a secret almost my entire life are hard to comprehend. And how can I trust someone I don't really know?

Although, the one person who has told me the least about himself may be the person I trust most. At least Noah's honest about how little he tells me. But I haven't seen him since I reunited the stones and blew all my close friends and family to kingdom come. He might not even be alive. I shudder at that thought, which in turn makes me wince, at the pain it causes in the unhealed wound in my side.

"Whoa," Balthasar says. "What happened to you?" His fingers barely brush against the injury.

I leap away. The pulsing in the place where Adika scored me with her sword beats like a second heartbeat, heavier when I breathe, but constant, unending. I glance down to see what tipped him off.

There's a hole through my shirt and my pants, showing

the wound itself. Both things were completely fine when I flopped out of the ocean and onto the sand, because they kept clinging to the gash just above my hip. With a little effort, I don't grit my teeth when I cover it with my hand. My side is sticky with a mixture of blood and something else. "It's no big deal."

"Wait." His eyes widen as he takes me in. "You're still injured from the blast? Why hasn't it healed?"

I shake my head. "It's not a big deal," I repeat. "And it's not from the blast. When I was fighting Adika, she sliced me. There must've been something on her blade, or that's what Edam thinks."

"Edam!" Balthasar bellows. "That idiot is lying in bed in the infirmary while I do his job for him. Meanwhile Job's hovering at his bedside for a little blunt force trauma to the head, and his queen is actively *bleeding* from a wound she received *yesterday?*"

"It barely even hurts." As long as I don't breathe. Or move. Or think about it. "And I meant to see Job about it immediately, before. . ." I gesture at the screen where we just watched my sister being hauled away by someone who is likely also Mom's killer.

"You just took a little break to destroy a chunk of the island first." He grunts. "And then this load of bricks fell on your head. I get it."

"It's one thing after another lately."

"Well, now you've seen the video, and you're headed straight to the infirmary." Balthasar takes my forearm in his hand. "March, missy." He tugs me out of security headquarters and into the main hallway. The Motherless who found me on the beach straighten up and fall into step behind us.

I practically stumble along behind him, my feet pumping to keep up with his much longer stride.

"You should have told me right away," Balthasar says. "Your health always comes first."

"Compared to the twenty-four people who just lost their heads, this really isn't that big of a deal," I say. "Adika doused her blade in some kind of poison that prevents blood from clotting, probably."

Balthasar's head ducks lower, his voice low in my ear. "It has been quite some time. No matter what she used, it should have healed—and I'm guessing by the look on your face, the holes in your clothing are new."

He's right, but I can't handle any more terrifying admissions right now.

"Are you okay to walk?"

I yank my arm away. "I'm perfectly fine, and I won't have you creating some kind of panic."

"Your majesty." Frederick jogs down the hall, the Motherless parting like curtains welcoming the morning sun.

"Frederick," I say. "Good to see you." Except, I can't help wondering whether he might be Nereus. He and Mom were quite close, and he has watched over me tirelessly since her death. But what if he killed her and this whole devoted act is just a cover up? He certainly could have poisoned Mom—he had access. He also remained behind on Ni'ihau while I flew to Europe.

And three minutes ago, I was suspicious of Balthasar.

Frederick frowns.

Because I'm standing like a statue in the hallway, glancing from Frederick to Balthasar and back again. "We're going to the infirmary to check on Edam," I say, silently pleading with Balthasar to concur.

"Right. The Security Chief needs to be up and running," Balthasar says.

"Of course." Frederick motions me forward and falls into step beside me, but on the opposite side of Balthasar.

Oh good. My entourage is growing. "I'll be fine in my own palace." But even I don't believe that lie. Mom, then Melina. . . who's next?

5

"We're simply happy you've returned triumphant," Frederick says with a smile. "Larena wanted me to let you know that Gregor will be visiting your room shortly to find out what kind of setting you'd like for the stones. I hear the two of them have merged into one?"

I nod tightly. "That's correct. Tell him I'll return there as soon as possible."

Frederick bows. "I'll leave you in Balthasar's care, then." He turns to face the six Motherless trailing me. "Hayden, Porter, you two will report to Robert immediately. He'll dispatch the proper attendants per the schedule. The rest of you will stay with her until the assigned guards arrive. I appreciate your help until we've properly integrated her return."

As impatient as I am, I do appreciate that he's paying attention to details. They might keep me alive, if I can figure out what's wrong with me.

Edam's voice carries so well that I hear him several yards before we walk through the door to the infirmary. As usual, he's strong and confident, but abnormally, he's also acutely irritated.

"You can't keep me here," Edam says. "I need to find Chancery."

"She's with Balthasar," Job says with almost no inflection in his voice, as if he's said the same thing a hundred times. "She's fine—and I'm almost done with my final check. You sustained a pretty severe—"

"Actually, she's not fine," Balthasar says. "And that idiot should have been telling you that."

Edam's eyes meet mine and my heart flips. "You're not fine?" His brow furrows. "The poisoned blade?"

Job chokes. "What's this about poison?" He's probably a little gun-shy about it, what with Mom being poisoned.

"We don't know what's wrong, exactly," I say.

6

Edam stands up, brushing Job away. "It's still not better?"

I shake my head.

Edam crosses the room in a few steps, sliding effortlessly past Balthasar, and sweeps me upward. His arms slide under my back and knees and he carries me to the bed he just vacated. "Something on Adika's blade has prevented Chancery from healing." His steady hands carefully shift the edge of my shirt that I tugged down out of the way, pausing when he notices the hole in my shirt and pants. "What happened here?" He leans closer, his eyes intent.

Job clears his throat. "Unless you've been studying evian anatomy in your free time instead of, say, lifting weights, I think I might be better qualified to figure this one out."

Edam startles. "Right." He steps to the left, allowing Job to examine me, but staying close enough to touch me. His fingers brush my cheekbone. "I'm sorry."

I'm not sure why he could possibly be apologizing.

"Yeah, yeah," Balthasar says. "You're both so terribly in love, blah blah. If you have this in hand, Job, I'm going to return to the security office and start doing this lovesick puppy's job." He points at the Motherless. "You four, wait outside." They jump and file out in front of him.

Edam doesn't even huff when his former boss leaves. I'm proud of him for ignoring first Job's, and now Balthasar's jabs.

"What does he mean, doing your job?" Job asks.

I shake my head. "Let's just say there's been a lot going on, and I need to catch Edam up on some things."

Job prods at something and my insides contract.

"Ouch," I say. "Careful."

He shakes his head. "I've never seen anything like this. It happened yesterday, right?"

I nod.

"It should've healed. I'm going to need a few samples."

I sigh. "That's fine."

"Do a better job than you did with her mother." Edam's voice practically bristles.

Job frowns. "This is a topical injury. Enora ingested something that caused her harm."

"Potato, po-tah-to. Figure out what it is and fix it," Edam says.

"Are we going to have a problem?" Job asks.

Edam laughs then. "I'm sorry. I get snarly when she's hurt, apparently." He squeezes my hand. "I'll try to be less hostile."

"It's kind of your default setting," I say.

Edam smiles. "I suppose it is."

"That's okay," I say. "You're kind of hot when you're prickly." Actually, he's hot all the time, but I'm not about to say that in front of Job.

"From what I hear, you two haven't even set a date yet. It's easy to get ahead of yourself when you're young and in love, so maybe simmer down a little."

Since he's the only physician for the Alamecha royal family, he'd be the first to know if I got pregnant. Which I definitely do *not* have planned for a while. I open my mouth to tell him not to worry when it hits me. I've been focused on who might have known about Mom transferring the throne to me, and I've contemplated who might have been upset about my reaction to the stone.

But I've been ignoring a huge clue.

Job crosses the room with a small set of tweezers, a needle, and several specimen containers. "I'm going to have to take a few samples. It won't be comfortable."

"It's fine," I say. "Go ahead."

He's right, it's not fun, but it's nothing to a stab, slice, or whack with a sword and that's standard fare for me. After he closes the last container and sets it on the counter, I pounce. "Job, Mom was pregnant when she died."

8

He turns toward me slowly.

"And I know you did the autopsy."

"Okay."

"But I don't recall ever seeing a report on the identity of the father."

Job's mouth drops open.

And for the first time, I wonder whether it's him. "Can you tell me who it is?"

He shakes his head. "I don't know."

"How can you not know? Wouldn't you have identified paternity of the child, if only to notify the father?"

"If he knew she was pregnant," he says, "he'd have known the baby perished with the mother. And if he didn't know, it's because she hadn't told him. I prefer not to violate her trust by disclosing anything she wouldn't want shared."

"But I need to know. What if that had to do with her murder?"

His eyes widen further.

"Why didn't we look into this sooner?" Edam asks.

I shake my head. "There's been a lot going on, but I should have thought of it before. I feel terrible that Mom's investigation has taken the back burner to this stupid prophecy."

"Your Mother didn't think the prophecy was stupid. She changed her heirship because of it, I'm positive." And Job is the one who told me about her last words—reinforcing her actions with the heirship documents in selecting me over Judica.

But what if Job didn't test Mom's baby. . . because he already knew it was his? I shake my head. "I hate to do this, but we're going to need to—"

"I'm not entirely sure that a test will reveal the paternity at this point," Job says. "But even if there's enough tissue from the small fetus left to test, we would also need to have the father's DNA on file, or we won't be able to identify a match."

"I'll make every single person on the entire island submit to a DNA test, if that's what it takes," I say. "Because I will have my answers. Patience and lax investigation may have cost me another family member. I'm done waiting and hoping like a dope."

Job nods. "Let me send these samples off to be analyzed. I have a few ideas, but I need answers on this ASAP." He steps out of the room and I hear him talking to his apprentice, Tristan.

Could he be putting me off? Delaying to make time to plan a way out of the paternity test? My nostrils flare. Job as Mom's secret boyfriend? Could it be?

When he steps back inside, he motions for me to get up. "No time like the present. Let's go down to the family crypt."

Or. . . maybe he's not delaying.

The walk down to the crypt below the main palace is two hundred and thirty-six steps. I count every single one, because each of them jars my injury. But I don't whimper, and I don't whine. By the time we reach the bottom, guilt surges in my chest. I haven't been down here to pay my respects to Mom—not even once since the funeral. Probably because, to me, Mom is much more present in her study, or her library, or her secret vault, not down here in the final resting place of her inert body.

But when Job unlocks her vault and opens the solid door, I step closer. I duck my head to make sure, but it doesn't alter what is right in front of me. Or rather, what isn't.

Mother's vault is empty.

"Whose job is it to provide security down here?" I ask.

"Job has the key," Edam says.

Job swallows. "I don't believe we've ever dealt with security breaches down here." Job meets Edam's eye. "You don't provide any guards or patrols for the crypt, I assume?"

Edam shakes his head. "I've never heard of evians grave robbing—and certainly not here inside the palace."

It's a desecration. Who would take Mom's body? And why? "Where are the closest cameras?"

Edam points toward the main entrance. "At the top of the stairs."

More than two hundred steps up. "Could her body have been moved from one spot to another?" I ask. "Or misplaced? How many vaults are there?"

Job sighs. "I'll certainly check, Your Majesty, but I doubt you want to stand here while I open hundreds of these." He gestures at the rows and rows of small doors. All royals are eligible to be interred here, should they choose.

Many of them want to be placed alongside the monarchs of Alamecha, which means there are a lot of vaults to open. "It's certainly worth a look, however. If I were trying to hide the body, moving it into another vault, especially an occupied one, would be the simplest way to do that."

The wound in my side throbs. "No, I don't, or at least, not right this minute."

Edam puts a hand on my shoulder. "You both have other things to deal with that may be more pressing."

Job's eyes dart to my injury. "Locating your mother's body will be my top priority the second we've solved your persistent injury, Your Majesty. Certainly your present health is more urgent." When Job closes Mom's vault, it clangs with an eerie echo. "Also." He drops his voice to a whisper, as if the dead might be listening. "I think we need to assume that Enora wasn't misplaced. I think this makes it much more likely that the identity of the father of her child might be linked to her death."

A chill runs down my spine. Other than our quest to identify the paternity of her baby, why would we come looking for the body again? Nereus, or someone else, knows the paternity, and they're working against us. It could be Job, who would've had an easy time moving Mom's body since he has all the keys. The fact that he didn't think about pulling a sample to determine the father of Mom's baby when she was murdered seems. . . negligent at best, guilty at worst. He and Mom were close. He could be the father, in which case, I shouldn't allow him to conduct the search, and he certainly can't be allowed to look through any of these vaults alone.

Although, most anyone could have worked around the lack of a key. I squat down and look at the keyhole, searching for scratches or any indication it has been tampered with, the motion tugging on the wound in my hip painfully. I see no signs, but I'm no expert.

"Edam, I want guards watching the crypt—and a camera in this room. No one may enter without my permission for any reason, including guards and all security personnel. I'll search the vaults myself as soon as I have time."

Job's eyes widen. "You can't do everything yourself."

But I don't trust anyone else to handle the important things, not even Edam, not entirely. "I'll return to my room until you figure out what can help me. While I'm waiting, I'll focus on a problem I can fix—securely mounting this new stone."

"You don't trust me." Job blinks. "You think I moved Enora's body."

I fold my arms. "You might be the father of her baby, for all I know."

Job's face hardens. "I'm sorry you think I might hide information from you like that, but I understand."

I march up the stairs, Job and Edam on my heels, each step sending a stabbing pain into my side. Once we reach the main hallway, they fall in on either side of me, with my guards splitting to walk in front and behind. Job peels off first, headed for his lab. Edam takes my hand then, but it doesn't reassure me. I feel disconnected from my own body, so unsure of who I can trust, who I can believe. Unsure, even, of my own feelings.

When I reach my doorway and Edam continues onward, it's almost a relief. I duck into my room with a sigh. I need some time to think through everything and everyone, to decide who to trust. There must be someone. Two of my guards take up their position outside my door, and two follow me inside to ensure the room is clear. Allsted and Javer will take up a post outside the back door that opens on my courtyard.

But my room isn't empty.

Both men reach for their swords before I can stop them. "It's fine," I say.

Judica jogs across the room and hugs me tightly. "You're okay, and you still have the stone." Normally a hug from my reserved, almost severe, twin would lighten my heart.

But today, pain lances from my hip down my thigh, and I bite down on a groan.

"What's wrong?" Judica pulls back. "Are you hurt?"

I wave the guards through the back door before I shake my head. "Not really. Just an injury from Adika that hasn't quite cleared up yet."

Judica's brow furrows. "From *Adika*?"

"She coated her sword with something. Maybe I should call Moses." Our brother was sold to Shenoah and was married to Adika's Heir, Vela, right up until Adika killed her own daughter for betraying her to me. "He may know what she might have used." I pick up the phone in my room and dial. While I wait for him to answer, I explain. "Even if Moses knows nothing, Job's looking into it. I'm sure he'll have an answer on what's delaying my healing soon." My call goes to voicemail, probably because it's the middle of the night there. I could call the main line for Shenoah and ask them to wake him, but his life is hard enough right now without getting no sleep. I hang up.

Judica sits down on a wingback chair. "That's terrifying. And also, I want to get some of it for our next battle." Her eyes sparkle.

My twin hasn't changed a bit. There's some comfort in that. A knock at the door reveals Gregor, here to devise a setting for the modified staridium. His head nearly brushes the doorway into the room, the enormous muscles in his forearms flexing as he lugs a box full of specialized equipment.

"How tall are you?" The words rocket out of my mouth.

As a child, I never felt I could ask without being unbearably rude. But now that I'm queen...

Gregor's mouth turns upward into a half smile. "Seven feet, six inches."

"That's a little disappointing," I admit.

His eyebrows rise.

"I mean, there are humans who are at least that tall, right?"

"I'm tall enough that even here, in this fabulous palace, my height is irritating. Shower heads are too low. Door-frames are a frequent nuisance, and impertinent children hassle me."

I can't help giggling. I like that he's mocking me, even though I am who I am. Like he just doesn't care. "I hope you're not referring to me."

He shakes his head solemnly. "I wouldn't dream of it." Gregor crosses the room to Mom's desk and sits. He points at the other chair. "I'll need to see the new stone to determine what can be done with it."

"It's not quite double the size of Mom's. I think a ring will still suffice." I pull it out of my pocket and set it on the desktop.

Gregor leans closer, his hands at his side.

"I'm not my mom. You can pick it up. I know you won't try and steal it."

Judica steps closer. "And if you did try, towering giant or not, we'd mow you down."

Gregor laughs and picks up the stone. "It's a real honor to be touching this. It's . . ." His eyes widen at the stone. It flashes, but only faintly. "It's a miracle. It has no fault lines visible to the naked eye." He looks through his loupe. "And even magnified, I can't see any place where this was recently rejoined. It looks like one single, seamless stone."

"What are my options for a setting?"

Gregor places the stone back down on the desktop.

have family I believe in, and friends too. I can't do this alone. So I need to take a leap, and then place someone in charge of ferreting out the information I need. Mom had a lifetime to develop relationships and contacts. I didn't even try until a few weeks ago, and now I don't have time to spare. In my heart of hearts, I think I was wrong about you the day she died. I think you loved Mom too, and I don't believe you had a hand in her death." I sit on the edge of Mom's bed and pat the spot next to me.

She sits.

"I'm sorry, Judica. For accusing you. For driving the initial wedge between us when she died."

Judica shakes her head. "I was mad with grief and beyond sense with jealousy."

"As I would have been in your place." I fold my hand over hers, smashing the letter inside her fingers. "This is your chance. I must trust someone to always be with me, to be on my side, one hundred percent honest. I want that to be you. You understand me, and you knew Mom, so I've given you a get out of jail free card. It's hard for an evian to commit suicide, but it can be done. Poison, explosion, carefully prepared beheading. If you want to kill me, you can. In some ways, it would be a relief, and you could step into the role you've prepared your whole life to fill."

Judica crumples the letter. "You're ridiculous. I can't kill you right now. No one would believe this handwritten note. And if I was the one working against you, I'd wait to move until you had gathered all the stones. That makes my failure to take this—what did you call it?"

"A get out of jail—it's from a human game Lark and I used to—" I shake my head. "Never mind. Then I'll offer this instead. I don't mind abdicating to you. You can have the throne. I don't even want it—now, or after I join the stones."

Judica wraps an arm around my shoulders. "I know you

don't, and I can't even fathom that feeling. I want to rule. I want to tell everyone what to do. I burn with a desire to set things right. I'm constantly irritated because I know that I can do things the best way possible, and everyone else is screwing things up. I would love to take over the entire world." She flops backward on the bed and her voice drops to a whisper. "But your reticence is likely why God selected you. It has been generations since any leader of an evian family *loved* and *trusted* first and foremost. I'm not sure if any other queen has been motivated by a genuine desire to help people—all people. And perhaps he placed me here with you by design as well, to watch your back."

"Mom thought so."

"Well, she was a very smart lady." Judica bites her lip and blinks repeatedly.

I miss her too. Desperately.

Judica sits up and clenches her hands by her thighs, my dumb letter dropping to the floor. "I don't need your jail card, and I don't need to kill you or have you abdicate so I can take the throne. I've learned a lot about myself in the past month. I'm so proud of you, Chancy." She clears her throat. "And you can trust me, because I know I can trust you. Any other monarch, Mother included, would have ordered me to take Melisania's deal the second she offered it. I'll have a hundred years with Roman, if I even want them all, and then I can do my duty to the family. It's a small price to pay for peace. My hand in marriage, in exchange for you ruling another family?" She clears her throat. "But you have always worried about the people you love. You always look for a better way. So I'll do whatever you need me to do. I'll hunt down Nereus, and I'll execute anyone who deserves it. You can sleep well at night, knowing it was my call each and every time, not yours."

"I'm not trying to force you to do my dirty work," I say.

"And nothing can shift the weight of such decisions from me, not really."

"I know that," Judica says. "But if I could, I'd take it."

"Wow, who thought we'd ever be this obnoxiously caring?" I punch her arm. "I mean, the last time we shared breakfast, you stabbed my hand with your fork."

"You were unbelievably smug," Judica says. "You deserved it."

She might even be right. "Still, I prefer this to the threats and glares."

Judica scrunches her nose. "Not me. In fact, you're lucky there aren't any forks lying around. Life is all about balance."

I roll my eyes.

"Speaking of." She stands up and begins to pace. "I know you don't want to hear this, but I think Nereus may *be* Melina."

I laugh. "You haven't seen the video."

Judica stops and pins me with a glare. "I have seen it. I saw it the second I landed. Balthasar's freaking out."

"You think Melina answered the door. . . for herself. . . and then killed twenty-four of her own people, after which she, what? Had someone drag her outside and pretended to resist?"

Judica shakes her head. "Aline, her wife, wasn't among the dead. Think about it. It's brilliant! Aline leaves, then she comes back, and Melina answers the door. They kill their own people, and then Melina pretends it was all done by some Nereus person we can't see."

"Aline left?" I ask. "When?"

"She left for a 'jog' a few moments before the hooded figure shows up. What better way to sell the story than to kill her own people, including her brother-in-law? It's a pretty major commitment, but far, far stranger things have happened. Then Aline drags Melina away, everyone thinks they're dead or missing, and our nefarious sister has free rein to skulk all over an island she knows like the back of her hand, enlisting the aid of her evil henchmen on the island to do whatever she wants. When she finally resurfaces, she can point the finger at anyone she wants, and you'll believe her."

Could Melina have moved Mom's body?

"You're taking a button and sewing a shirt on it," I say, "just because you want it to be her."

Judica shakes her head. "That's not my only theory, but it's a strong one."

"You didn't see her in Austin," I say. "She cares about her brother-in-law and her people. She wasn't desperate. I was meeting with her when I returned. I think it's much more likely that—"

"I did see her in Austin—a side of her you haven't seen. You think it's more likely that someone terribly deadly snuck past our defenses? Remember, it also has to be someone Melina knew and trusted, if it wasn't an act. And then they destroyed twenty-four evians without any resistance before marching back out."

I gulp.

"On the other hand, Melina's people probably wouldn't resist her if she attacked them. Just think about it, Chancery. Consider it, that's all I'm asking, and I'll keep my mind open to anything else that makes sense."

"We have a lot of evidence to parse through," I say. "No one has analyzed the crime scene, but I'll consider your ideas as we do. You should probably also know that I think the father of Mom's baby might lead us to Nereus—and when we went to pull a sample to do a DNA test, Mom's body was missing."

Judica frowns. "You've asked—"

"Edam is posting guards, and no one but me is allowed down into the crypt, yes."

A banging at the door startles me. "Come in," I say.

Judica's hand goes to her hilt, in spite of the guards stationed outside. Looks like we're all a little on edge.

Job bursts through the door. "It's coagulative necrosis."

"Excuse me?"

"I've isolated the issue. I didn't even realize that something like this existed." Job's eyes flash, and he talks even faster than normal. "Adika found a bacteria that aggressively secretes alkali cells when it's in a humid, warm environment, like your body."

"I don't speak nerd," Judica says, "in spite of a basic proficiency in biochem. Dumb this down."

Job shakes all over like a dog. "If she had coated the sword in a basic substance, not basic as in simple, but as in *acidic* is the opposite of *basic*, then it would have burned through your flesh quickly and eventually stopped. The wound would have recovered almost as fast as normal."

"Okay. Like drain cleaner, for instance, would have burned my arm, and then gone away?" I ask.

"Right," Job says. "But Adika found a *bacteria* that secretes alkaline cells, and they reproduce in your wound, essentially releasing these cells non-stop, which is why it probably hurts quite badly."

"This doesn't sound promising," I say.

"Oh, on the contrary, it's fascinating. Truly revolutionary, in fact." Job steps closer, his eyes intent on my wound.

Judica huffs. "What's the treatment? That's what we want to know."

"And how soon can we implement it?" I ask.

"Oh, right, duh." Job straightens his shoulders. "Unfortunately, the only way to repair the damage is to remove all of the infected tissue rather aggressively. You'll then need to regrow what has been—" Job clears his throat. "Cut out."

"That sounds. . ." Judica forces a pained smile. "Absolutely awful."

"I would strongly recommend that Your Majesty allow me to put you into a medically induced coma for this procedure, and we shouldn't delay. The longer we wait, the further the bacteria will burrow."

I think about the time I cut off my own nose and shudder. A coma sounds better than simply biting my lip while Job saws on the side of my body. I'll need someone I trust absolutely by my side to watch over me during the coma. Job certainly isn't that person.

"I sent for Edam," Job says. "I figured you'd want him—"

As if on cue, my fiancé flies through the door, his eyes wide. "Balthasar says Job needs to put you into a coma?"

I nod. "Job just explained that to me, but you have a lot to do. Melina is missing, and apparently Aline too. I shouldn't keep you from that search. Also, I hope Balthasar conveyed that locating Noah is a top priority."

Edam steps closer. "Troops are searching for them right now, but you're my priority, always."

"Guarding my physical body isn't as important as making sure the entire palace is safe. I'll take Judica with me. She's more than capable of ensuring no one stabs me while I take a forced nap."

Edam's eyes betray the truth. I trust Judica more than him, and he knows it.

"And, while we're discussing tasks, I need you to issue and begin execution of a new decree. Every citizen of Alamecha will be required to provide a sample of their DNA. It can be provided any time during the course of the next week. I'll be forming a database so that we can determine who may be involved in recent criminal events. Submission to this testing isn't optional. Anyone who objects or stands in the way of the collection will be arrested. And along the same lines, Judica has another title to add to her growing list. She's my new Inquisitor, with the attendant power to follow any and all leads to Mom's murder and Melina's disappearance in my name."

Edam doesn't argue. He simply bows and exits.

His lack of any objection tells me he knows that I could only choose one person for this task: the person I trust most. And it's not him.

3

"Edam's a top priority," I whisper. "The first person you clear." We're walking down the hall toward Job's infirmary, my guards only a few paces ahead and behind.

Judica's eyes widen. "Edam in particular won't appreciate me prying into his personal life."

"He already hates you," I say. "It's not like he will hate you *more*."

My twin barks a laugh. "That's true. I'm beginning to think this might be the best job I've ever had."

"It's the first job you've ever had."

Judica glares at me. "I'm on the Council. I was Heir, and I still am."

I roll my eyes. "Fine. You're highly experienced for this brand new position which has never before existed."

"The idea of having the power to do whatever I need to do in order to locate information with zero concern about upsetting people for the first time in my life—"

I choke. "You were concerned about upsetting people before?" Because I did *not* see that. If pre-Mom's-death Judica was considering public relations ramifications, I

Judica will root out the traitors, but until she does, I will trust my support system to do their jobs. "Let's do it." I cross the room to the bed he has set up in the center. The tall metal stand next to it has two bags of fluid hung on it, tubes dangling from each.

"Humans are regularly put on IV drips," Job says. "But your body will require a far higher dose than a human's would to keep you under. Luckily, this isn't the first time we've needed to sedate an evian, so the numbers for this are pretty well established based on your weight." He points at a scale.

I dutifully stand while Tristan tinkers with the top of the scale to assess my weight. "Why don't we have digital scales?"

Job shrugs. "I prefer to use the old school ones. Power goes out, equipment malfunctions, but the weights always work."

Fair enough.

Judica hovers next to me. I'm almost surprised she's not wringing her hands.

"You're just trying to see my weight," I joke.

She inhales quickly. "Not at all." She frowns. "But you weigh less than I expected."

"Gee, thanks." We'll have to work on her sense of humor. "Good to know."

"I'll talk to Edam about modifying your weight training to increase muscle capacity. Perhaps that can be a segue into the questions and investigation you tasked me to complete."

Oh my goodness, she's serious. "We can discuss it afterward."

"Are you ready?" Job asks.

I climb onto the bed and lie down.

He takes my arm and shifts it slightly before plunging a small needle into a vein on the inside of my elbow. He tapes it down carefully. "I'm going to begin the flow of a medicine in your arm that will put you to sleep. You may be confused or disoriented at first, since you're accustomed to being in complete control of your body. Rest assured that you're in good hands, and Judica and I will take good care of you."

I hope he's right. I hope his are *good* hands.

He pushes on a small clamp wheel on the tubing and cold liquid flows into my arm. I sit up, and Job shakes his head and gently presses me back. "The medicine is strong and will work quickly. Please sit back for me. I'll need to place a tube down your throat once it takes effect so that you won't stop breathing during the procedure. It's not pleasant, so I'd rather do it once you're asleep."

"Okay."

Job leans closer. "You should be out by the time I count to. . ."

His words grow fuzzy, and I blink, but the room still darkens. And then nothing.

It feels as if only seconds have passed when I awaken, but the room looks entirely different. Judica isn't around, and neither is Job. Edam stands at my side. I clear my throat and shift in the bed. I realize his strong hand is in mine, our fingers interlaced. "Why are you. . ."

"Men are out looking for Noah," Edam says. "Judica's forcing everyone to submit to a DNA test, but she cleared me first and assigned me to keep an eye on you while you recover."

I sit up abruptly and yank the tube out of my arm. "Why was that still in?"

"Job said extra fluids and nutrients would help your body heal more quickly."

I pull my hand out of his and press my fingers against my side. Nothing but smooth skin. I collapse back against the pillows on the bed with relief. "It worked."

Edam smiles large enough to create dimples on both sides of his mouth.

I slide my hand back into his and squeeze.

"I have been counting the seconds until you woke up, watching as your body incrementally regenerated." He shakes his head. "There was something almost soothing about it, an evian body at work, but even so, let's agree never do this again."

"Totally." I smile this time.

"Did you know Job kept the parts of you he removed?" Edam's breathing hitches. "He wants to recreate those little beasties. Says it would be a good line of defense in battle."

"Sneaky and underhanded," I say. "No thank you. I'll make him dispose of them."

"I told him that already, and he said he would at least need to work up a better solution—in case anyone else pursues the same biotech."

I sigh. "Being a scientist must be horrible."

Edam shrugs. "He chose it."

"He did?" My eyebrows lift. "When?"

"Job was your mother's executioner for six centuries. The best she'd ever had. You didn't know that?"

Evian executioners don't simply axe traitors. They're frequently sent to locate and return with the sentenced individual first. It's a respected and demanding job, but I doubt if it's a very sought after one. "I had no idea."

"He hated it, but Enora needed him. I don't know the details, but I know he finally did something for her that was hard enough that she released him and allowed him to pursue the scientific studies he always preferred. But he's got quite a talent for finding people, and for thinking like a villain to do it."

So many things I don't know, even for the people I know well. At least I wasn't wrong to trust him to heal me, apparently. I swing my legs off the bed and stand. Not a twitch, not a twinge. I'm as good as new.

"You know," Edam says. "There's no reason for us to be in *such* a hurry."

My heart speeds up.

"I've reworked the guard rotation. I've got men looking for Noah. Judica's doing her job."

"You mentioned that."

"Guards are watching the catacombs."

He steps closer, and I sit down again. Edam braces his arms on either side of me, and heat from his body radiates toward me. His face lowers, and his arms contract, and suddenly I'm staring into his eyes. "It has been such a rush since you agreed to marry me that we haven't even talked about it."

I gulp.

"I want to make sure this isn't a simple reaction to Noah—you aren't marrying me because you feel betrayed by him, right?"

His clear eyes press more than his questions. His fingers splay against the mattress, brushing against the side of my thigh in the process.

"I made this decision myself," I say. "I chose you."

His eyes light up. The corner of his mouth hitches upward slightly. "Then you won't mind if I ask *why.*"

"Of course not." I lean forward slightly and press my lips to his.

His entire body shifts then, his arms curling around me like a hand scooping water from a stream. His mouth is warm against mine, insistent. My heart soars, my brain spins.

Edam's arms lift me up, and he sits down, settling me onto his lap. His hands shift, one of them into my hair, tugging me gently closer, cradling my cheek. The other arm wraps around my back, his hand encircling my waist. I never want to leave this place I've found against his side.

But Edam pulls away slowly and shifts me to a space next to him on the bed.

My brain is raspberry jam.

My heart is an overworked racehorse.

My lungs are a vintage car motor.

"What?" I clear my throat. "Why did you stop?"

"I didn't ask you whether you're attracted to me." His gorgeous, full lips purse. "I already know the answer to that."

He scoots over another inch and I want to follow him, but pride keeps me in my place.

"I asked *why* you chose to marry me now. Finally. What changed?"

"I don't—" Pain blossoms in my lungs. It feels as though someone has thrown a chest full of gold coins on top of me. Or like an arrow has punctured my heart, preventing it from beating. My lungs contract, but I can't breathe. I try to inhale and wheeze instead.

Wheeze is the wrong word.

When I try to suck in a deep breath, it's like I'm trying to vacuum a swamp. My lungs slurp, and watery snot fills my chest.

Edam grabs my forearms. "Chancery. What's wrong?"

I shake my head and the room spins. I can't form words. My fingers tremble and grow cold. The room darkens, and I'm no longer with Edam. I'm somewhere dark, so dark, and cold, so cold. The pressure on my chest grows, encompassing my entire body, like I'm deep underground.

But I'm wet. Every part of me is wet. I try to scream, and salty water floods my mouth and nose.

My lungs aren't full of snot. They're full of salt water. The pressure is the weight of the water. Maybe I never resurfaced from the blast. Melina wasn't taken, and her people weren't killed. Was all of it a hallucination? In reality, am I dying? Down here, deep in the ocean, in the dark, in the cold, with no one to love me or hug me or even miss me. . .

I'm utterly alone. I am dying alone.

When the realization hits me, I surrender to it. There's nothing I can do, so why try?

But I don't die, not yet. My brain has no oxygen, my body is clearly trapped, but I'm still alive. I force my arms to move, marveling that they can, and discover that a pole has punctured the right side of my chest, pinning me to the ocean floor. How long can an evian survive under water without being able to breathe? I don't know. And I have no idea how long I've been here already.

Something pulls on me, tugging me upward. I'm being saved! Someone has come for me! As I float toward the surface, the pressure lessens, the pain abates.

No! Don't leave me! Don't leave me alone! I'm sorry, so sorry!

As I'm pulled upward, I realize the plea is distinct from my own thoughts. It's distinct from my mind and desires. And then light slaps me in the face. Bright, blinding light. Sounds, so many, many sounds. People saying my name. I expect ocean waves and sand and the setting rays of the sun.

"Should she be this groggy?" Judica asks. "Maybe we should've waited until everything had regrown."

As if her words call it into being, fire burns along my side, where Adika's monstrous little bacteria were eating at me. My hands spasm, curling into fists, my nails biting into my palms, but eventually I regain control and bring them against my side. A huge chunk of my body is missing.

"Her major organs have regrown and are intact, and the rest will heal up faster once she can eat and focus on healing them," Job says.

My mind spins out, stray thoughts spraying the walls of

my skull. Edam and our conversation, being trapped underwater, the panic, the dread, and then this agony. What's going on?

"Where are we?" I groan.

Job reaches behind me and shifts the bed, lifting the top of it and raising me eight inches. I blink and blink and look around. I'm in the infirmary, just where I was when he stuck the tube in my arm. "You did the procedure?"

"Of course I did," Job says. "And it went as well as we could have hoped. I had to remove more of you—"

Judica coughs.

"Doesn't matter. It's all healed, and once the muscle and skin of your side has regrown, you'll be as good as new."

"Was Edam here?" I cough. "And should my throat be this scratchy?"

"Your throat will heal soon," Job says. "The intubation can be rough, and your body's prioritizing. But don't worry, there's nothing else that should slow your healing. No more nasty bugs of any kind."

"And Edam?" I ask.

Judica frowns. "You told him to keep working."

I lift one eyebrow. "He hasn't come to check on me?" Maybe his voice during the procedure prompted the vivid dreams.

Job shakes his head. "No one has been here, other than my assistant Tristan and your sister Judica. And me, of course."

It felt so real. Was any part of it real? I narrow my eyes at Job. "What did you do before you became Mom's physician?"

Job's mouth drops open. "Excuse me—are you asking me?"

"No, what did *Judica* do before becoming Mom's doctor." I roll my eyes. "Yes, you."

"I haven't thought about that in a while." Job sits back. "I was Enora's executioner. For centuries."

"Six centuries?" I ask.

Job nods. "You've been searching your mother's old records?"

"No," I say. "Never mind."

"Are you alright?" Judica asks.

"Fine." I sit up the rest of the way and focus all my attention on the wound in my side. The wound that didn't bother me in the slightest while I slept in Job's medical coma. It takes several agonizing minutes, but the skin regrows and all evidence of the ongoing misery disappears. I can't even imagine being human and taking weeks and weeks to recover from a simple slice or break.

My side now looks exactly as it did in my dream, when Edam sat at my side, asking me uncomfortable questions.

About Noah.

"Has anyone found Noah?" I ask. "While I've been asleep?"

Job shrugs. "We haven't heard anything."

"How long did this take?"

Job stands. "No more than an hour, from when we put you under until now."

I swing my legs off the bed and yank my poor, devastated, hole-ridden shirt down over my healed torso.

"You should probably incinerate that shirt immediately," Job says. "It probably can't do you any harm—without an open wound, I doubt the bacteria can reproduce, but you never know."

Right. "I will." I walk toward the door, Judica following quietly. Before I leave, I spin on my heel. "How long could an evian last on the bottom of the ocean? Let's assume they're deep, like way down, where it's very, very cold and the pressure on their body was significant."

Job's eyes widen. "Why?"

I shrug. "Do you know?"

He grunts. "Not precisely. We certainly haven't tested it, but I've heard reports of recoveries after considerable time without oxygen, when the body is kept cool enough. So the temperature might actually help extend life."

Don't leave me. I'm sorry.

Noah isn't the only person who owes me a major apology, but he's missing and something about that plea made me think of him. I can't explain it, but it sounded like him.

"Noah may be stuck on the bottom of the ocean." I open the door. "And if he is, I mean to find him before it's too late."

❧ 4 ❧

"You think he's on the bottom of the ocean?" Balthasar's voice isn't incredulous. He doesn't raise his eyebrows. He doesn't even tilt his head. But his eyes dart toward Edam's, and I know.

He thinks I've lost touch with reality. I don't even blame him. If I hadn't had that vivid—dream doesn't seem like the right word. Vision?—I wouldn't believe me either.

"I believe he is extremely cold, and trapped by some kind of pole or something, deep underwater. Yes."

"And you know this because of a dream you had?" Edam shows not a scintilla of the frustration he must feel.

I exhale. "I'm aware of how it sounds, and that's why I asked everyone, other than the three of you, to leave."

"You were there, Judica," Balthasar says. "Did you notice anything? Trumpets sounding in the background, maybe? An angel in the window?"

Ah, finally, the sarcasm I expected.

"There aren't windows in the infirmary," Judica says. "And no. I noticed nothing at all while Chancery was in the medical coma, which was exactly the point. Her body didn't experience the horrible pain and trauma from the procedure Job performed. If this was a message, it was for her alone, clearly."

"You believe me?" I hate the hesitation in my voice.

"I believe you're the only person alive who can use those stones." She points at my finger. "Er, the stone, I guess."

Flashing on my finger, bigger, but otherwise the same.

"I believe God chose you. So sure, a message telling you where to look?" She shrugs. "I've heard and seen stranger things—this week, even. But I also think it's distinctly possible that your mind's recalling something about that blast that you subconsciously interpreted as Noah heading out to sea. We checked the closer areas already, knowing it was a possibility. The mind is an amazing thing—I wouldn't rule out the possibility that it's a message from you to you, which is also valid."

"Either way, it looks like we're going to be investigating this possibility further." Balthasar brings up a map on the main security screen. "This shows the bathymetry—"

"You're making that up," Edam says.

Balthasar scowls. "It's the term for the topography of the earth underneath the water, taken by multidirectional sonar. So no, I'm not making a play on my own name." He points. "In these darker places, the earth underneath the water is low enough that the water would be very cold. If we indicate the blast location. . ." He gestures for me to show him.

I mark the bluff on the map.

"We can create circles that focus on the deeper zones of the ocean and sweep them in expanding circles."

"I'll divert our search teams to underwater rescue," Edam says.

"The teams were looking for Melina?" I ask. "Or for Noah?"

"Both," Edam says. "I didn't have enough people to send

two different sweep crews. I tasked them to be on the lookout for anything and everything out of the ordinary."

"Does everyone know what happened to Melina and her people?"

Edam shakes his head. "They know Melina and Noah are both missing. I wasn't sure what additional details you wanted to share."

"I think it's fine to disclose that Melina was taken by someone, and that Noah hasn't been seen since the blast."

"We better not waste any more time." Edam prints off the page that shows the circles around the blast site.

"I'm coming," I say.

Judica stands. "Absolutely not. You just woke from a procedure where Job cut out a huge chunk out of your body, and you're empress. Did you hear where I said you're the only one who can use those stones? The only one God speaks to?"

I roll my eyes. "A chunk I've already regrown, and I'm not going off to war, which you let me do twice already. I'm following my fiancé to help locate one of my supporters. And if it really was a vision, I might remember something that could help." I stand up and march toward the door. "I'm not asking permission. I'm ordering. You'll begin your new duties while I'm out there. Get me my core group of people ASAP."

"Core group?" Balthasar asks.

"Judica's my new Inquisitor. She'll conduct an investigation into every person on the island if necessary, beginning with a group of scientists who will be taking DNA samples from every single evian in Alamecha."

Balthasar lifts his eyebrows.

I step toward him, my voice low when I say, "Mom's killer will be brought to justice. Nereus will be revealed, and this family will be brought to order. And if I have to behead half my Council to make that happen, so be it."

Balthasar grunts. "You were supposed to be the sweet one, the kind one, the one we could guide and advise." He laughs. "Your mother is beaming up in heaven."

I really hope she *is* in heaven. I've begun to wonder.

Edam motions for me to exit first and taps a com on his ear. My guards fall into place in front of and behind us as we walk down the hall, Edam giving directions efficiently. By the time we reach the beach, four motorboats are waiting, all of them manned with a captain and four divers. Edam and I climb into one, and he raises his voice and says, "Four boats to handle the four quarters I've divided. We will start at the closest spot and work out in uniform sweeps. You've each been given the largest underwater lamps we have."

"You have gear for me?" I ask.

Edam frowns. "Your best bet is to wait on the boat with me. If they find him, you'll be close. We will all be in communication via the radios. I'll know the second they find something."

I don't argue.

Larena races toward us from the palace. What now?

"Your Majesty!"

I don't sigh. I don't grimace. "Yes?"

"Moses has called twice. He says it's urgent." She waves a cell phone in the air.

Edam cocks one eyebrow. "He didn't call you directly?"

I smack my head. "I lost my cell in the ocean. He could have called me over and over without any success." I hold out my hand for the phone.

"Chancery?" My brother's voice is ninety-nine percent panic. My heart sinks.

"Yes, I'm here."

"I've been calling for an hour."

"What's wrong?" Please don't be anything major.

But I know it is. Why else would he hound me?

"There's been a revolution. Small scale and disorganized, but our leadership here is in such disarray that it was a near miss." He drops his voice to a whisper. "Nearly two hundred royals are currently awaiting trial for treason."

"What losses did we sustain?"

"Several dozen of Shenoah's royals, mostly those under a hundred years old, refused to fight alongside their family members and joined me—some of them died. A few of the troops you left. Only fourteen casualties on our side, thanks to the defectors. One of them, Peter, risked a lot to warn me. But it's ugly, Chancery. Really ugly." His voice is barely loud enough for me to hear. "I can't hold them all for long, not safely. They're going to break out and cause more issues."

By issues, he means deaths. I swallow hard. I need to be there with him when he tries them. I need to show the people of Shenoah that I'm not Adika, that I care about them.

I need to win them over.

But Mom's killer is loose here. My friends and family are betraying me. I'm surrounded by enemies. Mom's body is missing. Two families are allied against me openly. I have four more stones to secure. My sister's missing, her people dead and her wife at large. Something snaps inside my chest.

God wants me to be merciful? Kind? I'm supposed to recast the mold and repair the damage? How am I supposed to do that alone? I haven't eaten in. . . I can't recall. Haven't slept in a bed in at least two days. Noah might be stuck on the bottom of the ocean, thanks to me, and if God is warning me, why isn't he giving me time to do anything about any of it?

I can't fly to Europe or Africa, not now. Which means I'm backed into a corner. "Moses, I can't come. It'll be several days before I can. I'm so sorry to ask this of you, but. . . you're going to have to try them on my behalf. Outwardly base your decision on something—some kind of evidence. But you'll need to weigh each person based on your knowledge of them. If you think mercy will turn them, show mercy." I close my eyes. "But if you have to execute each and every one of those two hundred rebels, do it. Yourself. And tell them it's *my* decree." We can't afford any more rebellions, not right now.

My brother is silent for a moment, a long moment. I wonder whether the line has cut out. "Thank you."

For giving him the power to do what needs to be done. "I believe in you. Show mercy when you can, but do what you must." Utter destruction. It feels like it's already here. I hope this is the right call. *Oh, God, please, let this be what you want of me*, I silently pray. "I'll call you as soon as I have a new phone. I'm in the middle of something time sensitive right now, but as soon as I can, you and I will talk about the direction we need to take."

I hang up and hand Larena her phone.

Larena's head is bowed. "I apologize for chasing after you like that." Larena has silently and efficiently run the entire island for as long as it has been our home base— more than a century before I was born. Even so, I know virtually nothing about her, or why Mom trusted her to coordinate all the sensitive administrative details of our lives.

"Thank you for your devoted service. I appreciate you racing out here with that. Truly."

"This isn't a good time, I can tell," she says. "But." She glances at Edam.

"What?" I ask. "You can say it."

"Franco has been trying to manage it without bothering you, but I believe we have reached critical inroads."

What now? "This is something to do with the humans." As my head of governance, Franco manages all issues regarding the humans' ruling shell—managing the humans the majority of mankind believes make all the decisions.

"Some months ago, a new virus emerged in China. Wuhan, to be precise."

A chill runs up my spine.

"Early reports suggested that it could and would be contained."

"But there's no ruling family in China to see to that."

"It spread," Larena says. "And it appears to be spreading more every day. Our early models didn't reflect an accurate contagion level, or the impact it would have on humans."

"Evians are unaffected?" I ask.

"Of course."

I inhale and exhale slowly. "So it hasn't been a priority."

"Their stock markets are not doing well, but we don't worry overmuch about small adjustments. It's a long game for us, after all. But it has gone beyond that. Quite a few humans have died in China, the middle east, and Italy, which again, wasn't our concern."

"Until yesterday."

She swallows. "And now it's spreading into America and the UK."

"People are dying?"

She nods. "Quite a few."

Edam clears his throat.

"When I return, I want a meeting with Franco. Tell him I asked for it. Don't detail your interference in any capacity. In fact, we need a Council meeting to address all that has happened. Let them know to be on notice. I'll meet with him first, and I expect hard numbers, modeling of what he's preparing to combat the impact to our people, and a defense of his actions in concealing this until now."

Larena bows. "Yes, Your Majesty. It's a privilege to serve."

Right, right. "Let's go," I tell Edam.

Minutes creep by slowly in the boat, the sun beating down on us from above. Sweat runs down the back of my neck. The divers resurface periodically to report that there's nothing to report. I check my watch every three minutes.

None of which helps.

A million things demand my attention, but here I am, crippled with fear that Noah is pinned on the bottom of the ocean.

"Why?" Edam asks softly. So softly that the pilot at the front of the boat doesn't shift a hair. He's far enough away we can't even hear his heartbeat, not on the back of the boat.

"Why what?" I ask.

"Why have you come so unfurled about Noah's disappearance?"

"I'd be just as upset if you were missing," I snap.

Edam's eyebrows pull together. "I'm your fiancé. I hope you'd be *more* upset."

"Of course," I say. "Of course I would." I take his hand with mine. "I'm sorry. It's like I'm carrying a hundred tons around and staggering under the weight. I need someone I can say anything around—someone who isn't interpreting whatever I say the wrong way."

Edam's eyes soften. "Of course you do. Please forgive me. I'm that person, I swear it."

"I'm scared," I admit. "I haven't caught Mom's killer, and now that same person has killed Melina's people and taken her. Moses is barely hanging on against local rebellions. I have no idea who I can trust, or what I'm supposed to be preparing for—what is this utter destruction? What's facing us? Why did the stones react to me?" My throat closes off and tears threaten. "I'm such a baby—not at all equipped to fill my mom's shoes." My voice drops to the barest whisper. "The only thing I'm doing perfectly, uniformly, is failing."

Edam shakes his head and yanks me against his shoulder. "I want to mow down anyone who threatens you. I want to eviscerate everyone who scowls in your direction. I've never felt like this, and it scares me too. But I know you, and I know God does too. Which tells me that you will sort this out. I know you will."

I breathe in and out, the familiar smell of steel, sweat and resolve that accompanies Edam centering me somehow. "Thank you."

"And it's why I'm happy to submit my DNA to Judica, and then I'll patiently undergo any and all interrogations that she wants. She can have my phone, my computer, my login codes. I'll surrender it all. You already know the worst things about me. You know the deepest, darkest secrets in my life. The only thing I haven't told you yet is how jealous I get sometimes, but I'm working on that daily. Because I love you, and I have faith in you, and you deserve more than me, but I am here—and I will improve."

"I needed to hear that."

A diver surfaces. Then two more. Sixty seconds later, the last diver from our team reaches the boat. "We've cleared the entire area," Todd says. "There's no sign of wreckage, and no sign of any life other than marine."

I close my eyes. Have I been wasting everyone's time? Did I send Moses to handle my dirty work alone for no reason? Maybe I can video conference in as a show of support. "Head back," I say. "Now."

Edam calls the other boats one by one. They've all cleared their sections. I try not to sink into despair. Am I losing my mind?

After issuing the command to return, the boat picks up speed. We haven't gone far when my ring flashes and the wells in my head. . . vibrate. I can't think how else to describe it. "Stop!" I shout to the captain.

But it will take too long.

Noah's below me. I know it. I don't think or ask permission or anything else that will waste time. I leap over the back of the boat and into the water before anyone can stop me. The warm water slaps my face harder than Judica could. I ignore it and swim downward as fast as I can, feeling the wells in my head. When I swim to the left, they still. To the right, they buzz. I head down to the right.

Light dissipates. The temperature drops in shelves as I paddle and kick downward. Pressure builds in my ears. And yet, down I go.

My hand is barely visible in front of my face the first time my body tries to force me to take a breath. I suppress it and keep on kicking. Something brushes against my leg and I nearly scream, forcing out all the remaining air in my lungs. I choke a little and blow air out my nose to regain my equilibrium. Salt water floods my nasal cavity anyway, and my eyes sting.

I push onward, my eyes adjusting to the utter lack of light and the sting of the salt. The stone on my finger is pulsing, but the light is so erratic and the waves and odd angles send it skittering in unpredictable directions. When a shelf of cold water surrounds me, I know.

I'm close.

The wells in my brain hum. He's here. I know he's here. I wish I could call for him. It hits me then, that I might be able to call out after a manner, and create some light too. I reach into the well from Mom's stone, the first one, and I dip my fingertips inside, figuratively. I pull them out, shove the energy together and push it downward as hard as I can. A pulse of energy leaves my body, but the water immediately extinguishes the fire. A quarter second of light, followed by nothing.

I hold my hand out in front of me, as steady as I can. The flashing from it provides flickers of light, not much, but enough to see why the divers found nothing. An entire chunk of the island, complete with an upended tree trunk, lies on the very bottom of the ocean. It's far, far too heavy for me to move it.

At least, it should be. I beeline for the trunk, a black squid zipping across my path. I startle and nearly drop my hand, but I continue onward. As I near the trunk, I dip into the other well of power, the new one. I empty the whole thing out, prepared to blast the entire area away. Then I worry that such a large impact might hurt Noah. I pull back and send a large pulse, as large as the one that sent my friends flying backward before, directed toward the trunk.

I follow it up with another fireball to try and illuminate the entire area briefly. It blinks out as fast as the last, but I make out the shape of an arm. It has to be Noah's. I paddle toward it as quickly as I can, squinting and blinking rapidly to try and make it out in the brief flashes that punctuate the sea water. But when I reach for it, my hand circles something squishy that burns. I release the anemone and fumble along further, my legs barely pumping anymore. My head pounds. My ears scream for relief. And my hands shake. Evian or not, I was clearly not made to withstand this depth without equipment to aid me.

Finally, I reach Noah. My hands fasten on his arm. I tug as hard as I can, but he doesn't budge. I'm sure he has long since passed out. I'm headed there fast myself. I force my hands forward until they encounter resistance and realize that while I shifted the pile of rubble to the side, much of it fell back downward.

He's still pinned.

I prepare another blast and center my hands over Noah's torso, shoving downward with as much force as I can muster. We shift again, and my body begins to float upward, dragging Noah up with me.

Black dots begin on the edge of my vision. My body demands I take a breath. I can't do it. I can't.

But I do anyway. I'm wracked with coughs, salt water flooding my desperate lungs. I release Noah, unable to control my limbs any longer.

Before I pass out entirely, I pull out every last speck of strength, all the power in Mom's well and release the biggest fireball I can—upward. Please, Edam, please see it.

The entire world disappears in a blink.

5

Roaring in my ears. Warmth against my cheek. Painful chafing of my hands. I sit up abruptly and open my eyes, blinking rapidly at the blinding light. My throat is too raw to talk, and my eyes burn, but my heart pumps steadily. The pounding in my head and the roaring in my ears abates, slowly. After a few more blinks, the stinging of my eyes subsides, and they focus on the deep, cerulean blue of the eyes a few inches from mine.

They're full of concern.

Dark golden eyebrows arch over them. Powerful hands stop rubbing mine and squeeze instead. The tension in Edam's shoulders relaxes. His voice is deep, husky almost. "You're trying to kill me."

My voice is scratchy, almost alien-sounding to my ears. "Not at all. I never have to worry about my warrior." I squeeze his hand back. "I was trying to save poor Noah." I straighten and look around. "Did I succeed?"

"He's alive, we think," Edam says. "We dragged that poor guy up from the hole you blasted him out of. I have no idea how you knew he was there. A tree branch punched

49

through his chest cavity. He had crabs in places you don't want to know about."

My heart stalls. "He's injured and oxygen deprived?"

Edam stands and helps me up, wrapping an arm around me so the swaying of the boat doesn't knock me over. "You were only out two or three minutes. Not much damage to you, it appears. We're powering toward Job as quickly as we can, but even in those minutes, look."

I finally process the image before me. The divers have cleared the back seat of the boat, and Noah's lying across it with a blanket over his torso. His usually copper skin is pale with a bluish tinge. "He looks horrible."

"Move the blanket," Edam barks.

Todd peels the blanket back, and I prepare myself, but it's not quite as bad as I expected. Noah's shirt is shredded around an eight-inch diameter wound on the right side of his chest. Blood burbles from it, and I cry out.

"No, that's good," Edam says. "It was all blue when we pulled him out—no blood oozing at all." He wads up the blanket and applies pressure to the top of the wound. "It means he's warming up and healing."

He's right. It might look awful, but color is actually returning to Noah's face. "Is there anything else we can do?"

Todd throws his hands up. "With what?"

"I don't know," I snap. "A blood transfusion, maybe?"

"We don't have those kinds of supplies," Edam says. "But I radioed ahead and Job—"

When Edam cuts off, I turn toward the front of the boat where the shore rapidly approaches. Job's in the sand with a gurney, next to a stand with tubing and bags hung on it. I love Job. I want to stay near Noah, but I'm in the way. I back up so Job's crew can load him onto the bed. Job attaches a tube to his arm with a needle near his elbow.

"Is that what you used to put me under?" I ask.

"This is an IV," Job says. "Intravenous therapy. You can send medicine into someone like I did to keep you in the coma earlier, or you can send nutrition and energy, which is what Noah's body needs if it's going to heal from this. The fact that he's already healing as he warms up is very promising."

"And the wound to his chest?" I ask.

"It's bad." Job prods the area, pulling debris away, cutting fabric, disinfecting. Noah doesn't move at all. "But look!" He leans nearer. "He's breathing."

I don't need to lean close to know he's trying to breathe. The watery rattle coming from his chest isn't confidence inspiring. "Should it sound like that?"

Job shakes his head. "It shouldn't, but the fact that he has started is promising. He should—"

Noah begins coughing, and Job shifts his body so that his head is sideways. He does it just in time, because Noah begins to spew pink fluid from his mouth immediately.

"Is this normal?"

"There is nothing approaching normal about being underwater for hours." Job calmly pats Noah's back while he coughs and hacks.

I can't keep watching and doing nothing, so I look downward and notice that the wound in his chest is closing up. In fact, the wound is now less than an inch across. "Look!" I clap my hands. "He's healing." Tears streak down my cheeks.

It feels like the first good news in a week.

Job smiles at me. "I think we're past the worst of it. If he's sitting up and coughing, I think there's still brain function."

"As much as there ever was," Edam mutters.

"Still kicking puppies I see, Edam?" Noah collapses into more coughing.

But I'm delighted. If he's there enough to make fun of

Edam, Noah's going to be fine. I shove past Job and wrap an arm around Noah's shoulders.

"I'm still having trouble breathing," Noah says.

My heart accelerates. "I'm sorry. I shouldn't have shoved Job out of the way."

"Not at all." Noah's mouth curls into a smile. "I certainly don't want him to resuscitate me."

"No?" I ask.

"It's done mouth to mouth." He reaches out and touches my lips. A shiver runs up my spine.

I nearly drop him, and he deserves it. "Oh shut up."

"You're ridiculous," Edam says. "Don't make me cut you up moments after you're finally healthy again."

"Ah, old man, I must still be weak yet. I'm actually almost happy to see your stupidly pretty face."

"Same back at you," Edam says. "You gave us a real scare."

"I knew you thought I was pretty."

Edam scowls. "Don't make me punch you."

Noah's smile doesn't even look very pained. "That blast when you joined the stones." Noah whistles. "Was anyone else injured?"

"I spent five minutes with Job poking at me," Edam says.

"So you really spent an hour?" Noah asks.

Edam laughs. "Something like that."

Noah looks at Job. "Can I yank this thing out yet, or what?"

Job leans over and pokes at his chest. At least he has a sense of humor. "I'd recommend allowing the entire bag to process. But what do I know? I'm merely a physician for people who won't listen to one. Mostly, I poke at ungrateful patients and storm off in a huff."

Noah whispers so loud I'm convinced they could hear him at the palace. "Dude, I'm trying to look tough in front of the girl who just saw me dragged up from the depths of the ocean."

"She didn't watch you get dragged up," Todd says. "She was unconscious."

"I'm sorry," Noah says. "Who are you?"

"I'm the diver who rescued Her Majesty. After she leaped from the boat without warning, dove three thousand feet down, and used her royal ring to shift a ton of rubble and rescue you."

"Wait," Noah says. "You were in danger?" He manages to raise one eyebrow and scowl at Edam at the same time. Kind of impressive, actually.

"No one expected her to jump off the boat," Edam says. "This one's not on me. I've been dying to ask her how she knew you were down there at all. We had already swept the entire area."

I can't explain it. If I say that I felt a tugging or a humming or a buzzing from the power wells in my brain, *everyone* will think I'm bonkers. Or worse, Edam will think I'm saying that I have some kind of cosmic connection to Noah. I can't handle any more drama right now, not of any variety.

"It was the stone." Noah points at my finger. "It warned you."

My mouth drops open. "Why would you say that?"

Noah shakes his head. "I can't say more."

His idiotic promise to his family. I'm beginning to hate knowing that he knows things that he won't tell me. "I have a lot to do." I stand up. "Now that I know you're safe, I'd better get to it." I march away, Edam scrambling to catch up.

"First you're diving into the ocean—with no warning—to save him," Edam mutters. "And now we're giving him the cold shoulder and racing away like he's the enemy. Want to clue me in on the play?"

I sigh and force myself to slow down. I wrap an arm around Edam's waist, and his arm wraps around my shoulders perfectly. It's exactly what I need. Someone I'm virtually certain supports me in every way. "His cryptic comments just tick me off, that's all. He knows more than he'll tell me, and I can't figure out why."

"If he's on your side, and he certainly acts like he is most of the time, why not own it?" Edam shrugs. "I can't work it out either."

"I was terrified he was dead, Edam. I don't know what that means, and I don't want to hash it out right now. But my disgust with this is real, too. I want you to know how much I appreciate knowing that you're on my side, all the time."

Edam doesn't say a word the rest of the way back, which is exactly what I need to prepare for my next battle. The one against my own Council. Larena is standing outside the Council Chamber, arms folded across her chest.

Exhaustion rolls over me like a wave, threatening to do what a gazillion tons of ocean water couldn't—pull me under. I stumble on the smooth marble floor. Edam's arm pulls tighter around me. "This can all wait. You need to sleep."

"I need a shower. I need food. I need sleep. But not until after I bring my Council into line. Not until I've checked in with my brother. He just survived a coup, not many hours after I left him to rule in my stead."

Edam stops, his arm effectively halting me too. "You are the ruler of a third of the world. Maybe more. But you're not omnipotent. You're not omniscient. You need rest, or you will collapse. You can't save anyone else from a heap on the floor."

"I just had an hour-long nap," I say.

"A medically induced coma during which Job hacks several pounds away from your insides is *not* a nap."

I shrug. "It'll have to do. Please help me accomplish these last things so I can sleep longer."

Edam scowls, but he doesn't argue.

"I'm going to shower," I tell Larena when we reach her. "Send Franco to my rooms in five minutes."

She hands me a thick file, bobs her head and says, "Yes, Your Majesty. I'll gather the others here when I send him."

"Actually." I gauge the weight of the file. "Make it fifteen minutes. Thank you."

I trot down the hall. The faster I move, the less exhausted I feel. I can't quit now, no matter how badly I want to lie down and close my eyes. Edam takes up a position outside with my guards. I shake my head. "You can come inside."

His eyes widen, but he doesn't argue. Before I shower, I sit down at Mom's desk and look over the file. "Edam. Look at these." He leans over my shoulder but doesn't say a word.

It's grim. Four hundred thousand cases tested positive in the United States alone, and it has been notably behind the curve on testing. Over eighty thousand humans have died so far, worldwide.

Italy's mine now, and it's horrific there. And China's been on lockdown for ten weeks. I hope Noah's family is alright. Since they seem to be evian, I'm sure they're fine. But still. The deaths are predominantly older humans with underlying health conditions, but not all of them.

The projections for the future infection rate are abysmal.

I stand up and drop the file. "You can keep reading if you want. I'm no longer sure a shower will help, but I'm going to try."

Edam stays in the office portion of my rooms while I shower and change into clean clothing. Somehow, being clean brings me a second wind. I wish it could clear the fog from my brain, but some things can't be helped.

I shove through the doorway into the office. "If I say anything especially thick, put your hand on my knee and squeeze. I'm too tired to think of a better signal." I laugh. "Can you do that?"

Edam smiles. "I'm always happy to put a hand on your knee. But I'm so tired myself, I'm not sure how much help I'll be."

"Let's make this quick, then." I point at the door. "Invite Franco inside." I sit on Mom's desk chair and sling my arms up on the armrests, my hands resting casually on the ends. My ring is flashing brightly, as if it can sense my mood.

"Your Majesty." Franco bows deeply. "Congratu—"

"Why didn't you apprise me of the pandemic before now?"

He coughs.

"This SARS-CoV-2, COVID-19, whatever you want to call it, it's killing *my* people. If you meant to conceal it from me, why haven't you at least begun to mitigate the impact?"

"Humans." Franco tilts his head and lifts one eyebrow. "Only humans are dying. Like all these viruses and bugs, evians are entirely immune."

I stand up, but I don't scream like I desperately want to do. "Humans are my people too."

He splutters.

"And it was your job to keep them safe and to keep things running smoothly." I swallow. "It's *April seventh*, and this emerged in China in November. It didn't occur to you, when you took over this position more than *two weeks* ago, to let me know that it's a problem?"

"It was already in the United States when your mother passed away," he says. "A thousand or so cases, and thirty deaths, I think. She knew about it."

I close my eyes and count to ten. "But you and I never discussed it. I knew nothing about it, and your response, judging by this—" I point at the pile of papers. "Has been woefully inadequate."

"Pandemics are difficult on the economy, but this one is almost exclusively killing the older, sick humans, the ones who are a drain on the entire system. In many ways, it's actually a mercy to both them and to us."

I slap him.

His entire cheek flushes bright red, and his eyes flash angrily.

"I ought to execute you for utter and complete negligence—and that's the best thing I can assume about the job you've done."

"No one expected anything like this," he says. "Past viruses have been contained."

"And this one, why is it different?" Edam asks.

"For one thing, it's much more virulent. It lasts longer and appears to be far more communicable among the humans than past illnesses. For another, it's deadlier. But mostly," Franco says stiffly, "it spreads at an alarming rate. If we hadn't ruled it out as a military movement, I'd almost say it was released with purpose."

My eyes widen. A virus that only eliminates humans, and the weak ones at that. Nereus? Could it be? Was Mom's death only one prong in a coordinated attack? Have I been entirely blind, not even realizing the world is under attack?

"Am I to be placed on trial?" Franco's nostrils flare and his heart races.

"Not presently." He may be guilty of nothing more than prejudice against humans, which wasn't even frowned upon until I took over. Well, that and idiocy. While that may render him a lousy selection for my Council, execution might be a little hasty. "We are all attending a Council meeting right now. Before we go, I want to hear your plan to mitigate this and protect our humans as much as possible from here on out."

He nods. "We did issue a shelter in place order, or at least, we encouraged the states to do so. I have other plans in place, and we're making great strides already. From what our experts tell me, we had two options to pursue. There was a third—to contain it like we did with past outbreaks—but by the time I took over, that already seemed unviable."

"What are the two options?"

His brow furrows. "The first, with a virus this communicable among humans, is to do nothing. It seems to be impacting the already ill and elderly most significantly. The idea is that the virus will tear through the population, most of whom will be just fine. The economic suffering will be sharp and then recover quickly. However, the loss of life may be steeper. But herd immunity will develop quickly, and it will essentially knock the effectiveness of the virus back from then on. I would liken this first option to jumping into the cold ocean water instead of easing in incrementally."

"But if this kills people, won't hospitals be overwhelmed, worsening outcomes?"

Franco's face drains of color.

"Please tell me you didn't choose that option."

"The second option has dramatic downsides as well. It involves quarantining the ill and the sick, because the virus sheds before symptoms. And some people are asymptomatic. We essentially had to lock down nearly everyone in the country. Even the humans hated this option, most of them."

I shake my head. "So we are stuck, pants half on? Not really doing option one or two?"

He clears his throat. "Something like that. No solution is perfect. Humans are fragile creatures, easily injured. The idea with that second option is that less people will die because the spread will slow and the very ill won't overwhelm hospital resources. It does seem to be working. New York had a very bad day, but other places are plateauing."

"What was your plan?" I ask. "You clearly didn't mean to botch things this badly."

"I planned to split the difference." His mouth hardens into a grim line.

"What does that mean?"

"In the UK, I chose option one. And in the United States, we implemented option two with varying degrees of success. The other impediment I didn't contemplate was how selfish humans are. Sick humans went to bars and parties, knowing they would infect others. Some reported to work at jobs where they cared for the elderly, knowing they had been exposed, because they needed the money. The results were bad across the board."

I grit my teeth while Franco outlines the problems with both approaches and then details testing, immunization, protection for healthcare workers, and treatment plans.

"Please tell me you've halted option one in the UK."

He nods. "The cost was determined to be too steep. Also, insulating the at-risk segments of the population proved more difficult than expected."

"And what are we doing to help the humans who are suffering from the impact of staying home? I assume their job losses are impacting their families *and* the local economies."

"I put together a stimulus package over a week ago to ease the burden in the worst segments, but it will take time to distribute it." His heart slows a bit, but not by much.

"You may keep your job for the time being. We'll readdress this in a week. If I don't see significant progress, you may yet be on trial. Edam, can you oversee this for me?"

Edam nods. "Of course."

"It's not exactly 'security,' but I doubt anyone else wants

to deal with it. And roll Alora into all of this, as Exchequer General."

"Right." Edam steps toward the door.

I follow Edam out, Franco at my heels. The entire Council is waiting when we arrive, even Noah, who I didn't expect. He can't possibly be my human liaison anymore. I don't bother dickering over his presence or extending the usual pleasantries either. "We have a lot to discuss, and I'm exhausted."

"We need to select a date for the celebration." Alora beams. "For your engagement, as well as your successful attack against Shenoah."

My mouth drops. "A party?" I shake my head. "You think I'm here to discuss the details of a *party*?"

Eyes shift around the table, no one willing to meet mine other than Judica, Edam, Noah, and Larena.

"Moses called me not even an hour ago to inform me that there has been a revolution. He put it down, barely, and is trying and executing those who orchestrated it *right now, while we stand here*. Nereus has captured Melina after killing her entire contingent. My mom's body is missing. Noah was buried under a ton of rubble, three thousand feet under sea level. It's a miracle he's here at all. And if that's not reason enough, there's a virus raging through the world we're supposed to be governing. Our citizens cower in their homes, hoping they won't *die* from something they can't even see while their alleged leaders are mostly entirely oblivious. What would our theme for the *party* be? Shrouds? Coffins? Perhaps blinged face masks."

"I'm sorry," Alora says. "I didn't mean to—"

"Actually, there's something we can do about that. We can begin to help out." Why didn't it occur to me before?

"Help out with what?" Franco asks.

I square my shoulders. "A member of my inner circle has

60

betrayed me—likely one of you. I intend to find out who it is and remove their head from their neck."

"You're kind of bouncing from one thing to the next." Inara stands up, her palms flat on the table. "Did you call us here to yell at us?"

"Not at all." I point at Judica. "I called you here to announce to you, before the rest of the world hears the news, our new normal." I glance at my twin. "Did you suitably vet anyone who can perform the tests?"

She nods tightly.

"Perfect. Then invite them inside. No time like the present to begin. Every citizen of Alamecha will donate a quart of blood. A tiny portion of that will be used for DNA testing. We will keep the DNA of every one of you on file so that when we begin analyzing our evidence, we won't have trouble identifying Nereus and taking him or her down. The rest will be donated to the humans to help cure those afflicted of this SARS-COV-2. It's the least we can do."

"Judica is—"

"Wait, what—"

Suddenly the members of my Council are stumbling all over themselves to explain why this is a terrible idea. I hold up my hand. "A small donation of blood is inconsequential. You'll all recover quickly. And Judica is my new Inquisitor. Effective immediately, this gives her the same power I have to do *literally anything* she deems necessary to pursue Nereus and anyone else who stands against me. She will investigate and execute whatever she needs with my full approval and support. We will not live in fear any longer. We will not be paralyzed by a desire to keep everyone happy. You will submit or you will leave Alamecha immediately, never to return. Am I clear?"

"Is that all?" Larena asks, lips pursed.

"Oh, not even close," I say. "I need to keep this quick,

since I have trials and executions to attend yet. But, before I do, a few housekeeping issues. First, set up the idiotic party for one week from today, in Rome."

Franco chokes.

"What's wrong now?" I ask.

"Italy is one of the places hardest hit with the virus."

For the love. "Where would you recommend? I promised Moses I would return within the week to set up a regent and establish a core group of leadership within Shenoah. Would San Marino be better?"

Balthasar and Edam lock eyes and both shake their head in unison.

I throw my hands up in the air. "Where then?"

"We can't secure any location within Shenoah that quickly," Balthasar says. "Not with any reasonable level of comfort."

I sigh. "Fine, we'll let Moses know it will have to take place here. We'll call it a joint engagement/Shenoah and Alamecha family merger party. We should have plenty of blood to inoculate any humans impacted by this decision, and we'll have Job coordinate with Franco to distribute the rest to the worst cases in New York, Rome, and wherever else the outbreak is bad. We'll invite all the royals from each of the families. And when we send the invite, we may as well send out a formal declaration of Alamecha's updated demands. Or we can call it a decree from the Queen of Queens. I don't much care."

"Queen of Queens?" Balthasar asks.

"Even so." I look at Larena. "Better take this down." When she doesn't move to grab a pen or pencil, I turn slowly to face my older sister. "Or would it be you, Inara, who handles this? You're Steward." I shrug. "I don't much care."

Everyone stares at me blankly. Rage burns through me. Perhaps my own Council has forgotten why they're here. I grab a fistful of ink pens from a cup in the middle of the table. Then I toss them in the air and shove with the power from Shenoah's ring, sending them all flying outward toward a dozen startled evians.

"Write. This. Down."

Everyone scrambles for paper. Inara yanks an ink pen out of her forearm and heals up the puncture wound, which is more satisfying than it should be. I should feel horrible for throwing a tantrum, but I don't.

Maybe there's more Judica inside of me than I realized. "First, royal children will all select their own spouses, male or female, right alongside non-royal evians and humans. Obviously, there will be no more sales of children under any circumstance. Second, females are no longer preferred in any capacity. My youngest child will rule, whether it's a boy or a girl. Every single law will be rewritten to reflect this, for both humans and evians. Male and female are different, but neither one is better than the other. It's long past time for males in our society to receive protections, and the females among the humans to be similarly safeguarded. We allowed them to be subjugated to keep the humans easy to manipulate, but it's wrong. It has done unbelievable damage over the millennia. No more. Third, humans are valuable. They will not be mistreated by us, not anymore. A bill of rights for all subjects, evians and humans, will be constructed. Lark will work with me on this. Humans and half-humans are every bit as valuable as evians. All laws governing jobs and positions will now be based on performance criterion, not genetic profiles. And finally, all citizens of Alamecha and Shenoah will join in the search for the Garden of Eden. It's beyond time that is located."

My entire Council is scribbling down what I've said, but I wonder how many are doing it to avoid making eye contact with me. Only one person boldly meets my gaze.

Noah.

What am I going to do with him?

He smiles at me. "You grow more magnificent every day."

And that's my cue to leave. I need to make an appearance at Shenoah's court.

❦ 6 ❧

My brother picks up on the first ring. "Chancery."

"I don't know how long I can stay awake," I say. "But I want to support you. Can you patch me through to some kind of screen or something?"

"We're prepared. Can you switch to a video feed?" Moses asks.

Leia, one of our IT experts, nods and I tap the buttons on my phone that transfer the call to a video input.

"Is it working?" I ask.

Moses' face appears on the large computer screen on Mom's desk, er, my desk. It's very strange, with the way the video feed works, that I am able to watch most of the room, including the screen on which my own face is displayed. "Thank you."

Leia leaves.

"Thank you, Your Majesty," Moses says, "for making an appearance at these proceedings." He steps backward and turns to face the gathered crowd. "Your Empress, Chancery Alamecha, is live with us. She will pass judgment on the next few cases herself, for as long as she can spare."

My throat tightens, but I don't flinch. "Proceed."

Moses gestures and two Motherless bring a short, heavily muscled evian forward, metal cuffs binding his hands and feet. "This is Boris ne'Adora ex'Shenoah. He is married to Katika Shenoah, third daughter of Hera, eleventh daughter of Sethora, nine generations removed from Eve. Katika has been named by four of the rebels with spearheading the revolution." Moses extends his sword toward Boris, whose shoulders tighten. "You are charged with high treason against your Empress, Chancery Alamecha. It is further charged that you killed two individuals who stood to defend her rule here in San Marino: Ilyena Shenoah who bravely stood against her own cousin's uprising, and Clinton ne'Lenora ex'Alamecha, a Motherless, a sworn servant of Chancery herself."

Boris lifts his chin.

"Do you deny the charges?" I ask.

Boris spits at the screen on which my face is displayed.

"I'll take that as a no," Moses says. Before I have time to reply, Moses swings his mighty broadsword around in a circle that removes Boris' head from his shoulders. Red spray arcs across the room and splatters on the video recorder, covering my screen with a crimson haze.

My jaw drops and I can't breathe.

"Who's next?" Moses' sword arm lowers and hangs at his side. My eyes take in something they hadn't processed before, thanks to my complete exhaustion and the nature of the tiny video screen. He's covered in gore. "I think it's about time we had Katika up here." His eyes blaze. "Because it's my *sister* who she tried to take down. My sister, who is the first and only evian ruler I've ever been proud to serve. The first ruler the staridium stones have ever reacted to—the first ruler who has ever ruled by *right*. I ordered every single Shenoah citizen present in this city to be at these proceedings because I want you to see the consequences of standing in opposition to Chancery Divinity Alamecha."

Oh no. He's losing it.

I'm not even sure I blame him. He was handed the reins to the sixth family, a family he had recently fled after his wife was murdered by her own mother. And then he had to put down a bloody revolution.

I should never have left him in charge. This is my fault.

The same two Motherless who held Boris tug the chains attached to the hands and feet of a small, dark haired woman until she stumbles into the center of the throne room. They haven't even cleared the corpse of her husband. The pool of blood from his body expands at an alarming rate. Her wide eyes stare blankly at Moses. I don't recall her calling out when he died. Perhaps she wasn't yet in the room.

"Katika Shenoah, third daughter of Hera, eleventh daughter of Sethora, nine generations removed from Eve, you are charged with high treason for killing four members of Chancery Alamecha's government, and for planning and spearheading the attack against me, against my sister's rule, and against the new world order. How do you plead?"

Her voice is as blank as her gaze. "Does it matter?"

"It matters to me," I say quickly. "How do you plead, Katika?"

Her head whips toward the screen. "Your brother has slaughtered twenty-three of my supporters, Your Majesty. I beg mercy."

Moses' lip curls. "You ask for mercy? Your mother knew Chancery was the empress of prophecy. She had every chance to relent. She employed terrorist tactics in which she slaughtered thousands of humans. She murdered my *wife* in front of me. She then tried to kill my sister, which would have resulted in the utter destruction of the world prophesied by Eve herself. And now, after the balance has been restored, after your Great Aunt has been deposed, you saw an opportunity for a power grab and you took it, unconcerned about the cost. Unconcerned about the impact on your people. *You* killed twenty-three of your own people. Don't lay that at my feet."

"This isn't a trial," Katika says. "This is a massacre."

"We aren't a merciful people," I say. Every voice in the room falls silent. They all swivel to face the screen. "My mom taught me that from a very early age. Every mistake is met with an equal or even occasionally disproportionate response. My brother is absolutely right that Adika declared war on me, but it only took place after I threatened her birthright."

Moses frowns.

"Adika acted in the way I expected her to behave, based on her training, her history, and her past experience."

I pause and meet the eye of as many of the audience as I can, in this bizarre medium.

"I am nothing like Adika," I say slowly. "In fact, I am nothing like the ideal many of you believe evians *should* be. My goal is not to dominate. It's not to destroy." I lift up the ring on my hand so they can all see the new stone. "You know I took Adika's staridium stone. What you don't yet know is that not only does it react to my call, not only does it bow to my command, it is rejoined with my mother's stone and now made entirely whole."

Moses takes a step closer. I accommodate him and move closer to the video camera. "If you were here, you'd be able to see, as my jeweler did, that my mom's stone and Adika's stone are seamlessly rejoined. You can't see where one ends and the other begins, not anymore. Today, not even an hour ago, I issued an edict. It details a lot of changes. These will be very difficult for you to process. They may not feel right. They aren't what you've been raised to believe. But I need us to find a better way."

I tilt my head. "Oh, Moses. My sweet, warrior of a brother. You were torn from your family when you were only weeks old. Then your wife was robbed from you, from us, far too early. You protect, you serve, and I love you for it. But rage and destruction have never been my path."

I hold up my ring and the flashes in its surface pick up speed. "My path is one of healing. Which is why I am going to pardon every single one of you who will come forward now. Bow, apologize to me, and to Moses, and to his strong, dedicated, devoted men. Swear you will protect and serve. Swear it on my name, on my ring, and as citizens of neither Alamecha nor Shenoah. Swear it to me as a descendant of Eve. We all have that in common."

Katika's shoulders square, and she doesn't hesitate in dropping to her knees. "I am sorry, Your Majesty. I wish I had met you. I wish I understood." Tears well in her eyes. "I am sorry for what I have done to Moses, as well. You will never regret pardoning me, or my people."

I very well may regret every single thing I'm doing right now. I may simply be exhausted and delirious. I hate how Moses is looking at me—as though he's a puppy and I've just yelled at him for peeing on the carpet. "I'd like it to be clear that Moses was absolutely right, under the law, and under my mandate, to execute every last rebel. He witnessed and endured your attack first-hand."

Katika swallows hard.

I meet her eyes. "Will you actually be able to forgive him for his actions today, knowing your own behavior precipitated it?"

Katika stands up and holds her hands palm out. "I am willing to offer myself as a sacrifice for my people, if that will help you forgive them. They followed my lead."

"I don't want any more killing. Humans are dying the world over right now, thanks to a virus we haven't yet sourced. I'm disgusted with the death and violence. What I need is supporters. Swear to me, now. Make me believe it."

Katika kneels again, and she shouts her oath. "I, Katika Shenoah, a ninth generation daughter of Eve, swear on the mother of us all that I do pledge my life, my sword, and my resources to Chancery Alamecha. I vow that I will support her against all foes, now, tomorrow, and for the rest of my life on earth. Further, I offer of my own accord that I personally support her vision as far as I understand it. Evians have long needed a course correction. Boris and I—" She chokes up. "We saw an opening and we took it. We didn't understand."

My ring flashes brightly, and I decide to try something. It probably won't work, but if it does. . . I look at the two unlit torches on either side of the empty throne. "I accept your vow," I say. "And I am sorry I am not there myself to do it."

I think about the room on the screen in front of me. I was there not long ago. I imagine the weight of the stones, the smell of the cypress trees outside, the solid, cool feel of the tiles under my brother's feet. "I accept your apology as well." I reach into Mom's well and lift my hands. I throw sparks at the torches and they catch fire on the screen. My heart soars and my hands shake.

Moses' eyes widen, and he drops his sword. It clatters loudly against the tiles I was just imagining.

Murmurs spread around the room. Before I have a chance to speak again, people all over the room drop to their knees. Katika shouts, "Chancery Alamecha."

The citizens assembled repeat my name.

Katika says, "I Katika Shenoah."

Hundreds of citizens shout their names.

Katika says, "I swear on Eve herself."

In unison, the kneeling citizens repeat her words again.

"To pledge my life, my sword, and my resources to Chancery Alamecha."

I'm utterly exhausted. That's probably why tears well up in my eyes. I wipe them away as quickly as I possibly can.

"I vow to support her against all foes now, tomorrow, and for the rest of my life," Katika shouts.

Hundreds of voices shout together.

"We will follow your brother's commands," Katika says.

A hundred voices shout that, too.

Katika's laugh is shrill. "No idiots, that's not part of the vow. That's my promise to Her Majesty."

Laughter, like a balm, fills the room. The fury seeps from Moses' face, replaced with wonder.

"And when you're able to come here," Katika says, "we will make our vows to you personally."

I nod. "I need to sleep now, desperately. But I am planning to celebrate the joining of our families next week. My Steward will communicate the details. I believe we will be hosting all of you who are able to travel here, in Ni'ihau."

"I would be honored to come," Katika says. "Or if your Regent prefers, I'll stay here. Locked up, if he prefers that."

Moses shakes his head. "I think this concludes today's trials. I'll call you shortly, Chancy."

I nod and wave and end on the video call. The screen goes black. I sit down in Mom's desk chair and lean back, my eyelids heavy. I could go to sleep right here, sitting up.

A sharp rap on the door feels a hundred miles away.

"Your Majesty?" Inara asks.

"I'm tired," I say.

"There are reports that you're in San Marino right now."

I can't quite suppress a laugh. "I'm right here, Inara."

I drag myself up and walk across the room. When I open the door, Inara's face is more perplexed than I've ever seen it. "One of my agents just called to tell me that hundreds of Shenoah citizens just vowed to serve you? And you lit two sconces with fireballs?"

Edam's head pokes around from the other side of Inara. "Fireballs?"

I shrug. "That's all true." I yawn. "But I'm right here. I did that on a video call. And now I need to sleep. Can someone else take Red Bull so he doesn't wake me up?"

Inara grabs him by the collar.

"Thanks." I slam the door in both their faces and barely get my tattered shirt and boots off before dropping onto Mom's bed. I fall asleep the second I close my eyes.

⚜

The sun beats down on me from above. Sweat trickles down my brow.

"You're so young and stupid." Adika ducks and swings upward, her sword biting into the side of my body.

"I'm young." I dance away, playing for the moment I need to heal my side. But it doesn't heal. My limbs shake and slow. "Your sword's poisoned," I slur. I shake my head to try and clear my vision.

"And stupid." Adika showcases beautifully white teeth when she smirks.

A dagger thunks into my chest, slicing my heart nearly in two. I stumble backward and fall onto the ground on my backside, air fleeing my lungs.

Adika stalks me. "I don't play fair. I never have. Expecting justice from the world and taking unnecessary risks is the province of the innocent."

Kirabo jumps to the top of the wall above me and to the left. She threw that dagger. Two minutes ago, I was saving Edam and Balthasar. I was winning. Now I'm about to die and Edam and Balthasar may already be dead. But

72

wait, I'm not alone. Noah's here. I know he is. Something tells me he will save me.

I cry out, "Noah! Help me!"

But no matter where I look, I'm alone.

Adika's sword cycles around, the blade connecting with my neck. And worst of all, when I die, the world dies with me.

❈

I sit upright in bed, sweat covering me head to toe. The world is dark outside, only a few stars winking at me through the window. I cross the room to my bathroom and take a quick shower. I'll sleep better now that I'm clean. I pull on white training gear, clean and soft, and climb back into bed. I'm not sure how long I slept, but it wasn't nearly long enough.

But every time I close my eyes, Adika's there. Laughing at me. Sword held overhead.

I finally walk across the room to the door and throw it open. "Edam?"

"He's asleep," Frederick whispers. He tosses his head toward my fiancé, asleep on the marble floor.

My heart contracts. I kneel down and shake him awake. He leaps to his feet faster than I'd have thought possible, whipping a dagger from his boot. "What's wrong?"

I place a hand on his shoulder. "I need you."

His eyes soften immediately, thawing from Defcon three. "What?"

My words are the barest whisper. "I can't sleep."

Muscles in Edam's jaw work. "Judica hasn't cleared me yet."

And that's when I realize that I don't care. I thought I only trusted her, but maybe that wasn't quite true. "It's fine."

His lips part slightly and I want to touch them, run my finger across his bottom lip. I want to pull him against me. With four guards watching us, I don't. I simply step back.

But Edam comes along, tugged into my room by an invisible connection. Once he has stepped past the threshold, he slams the door shut behind him without looking. His eyes never leave mine.

"Can't sleep?"

I shake my head.

"Nightmares?"

I nod.

His hands cup my face, pulling me toward him, his lips covering mine roughly.

Claiming me.

I spiral downward, collapsing entirely against his hard angles. I am melting ice cream. His mouth is warm and hard against mine, somehow centering me and disintegrating me at the same time.

A groan from deep inside his chest sends a shiver down my spine, and I pull back enough to see him. Without sunlight streaming in from the windows or any lights turned on in the room, I can barely make out his sharp features. But I know them by heart.

His eyes follow mine, sparking in the low light. "I was beginning to think you had changed your mind."

"About?" I ask.

"Me." His hands circle my waist and lift me up. And he carries me effortlessly to the sofa a few feet away.

"No." I should say more, reassure him. I should tell him that my fingers longed to touch his lip, to run down the planes of his chest, and spread across his abdominal muscles. I should explain that when I close my eyes, I see his face, his eyes staring at me exactly as they are now. But my words aren't working right now, so I kiss him instead.

And then I sink deep into oblivion. Healing, strengthening oblivion. His arms encircling me, his heat against my chest, his scent all around me. Nothing can harm me when Edam's close. Nothing. The world is full of beheadings, and traitors, and danger, and fear, and fury. But not this room, not this sofa. Not Edam's embrace.

Until he pulls back and air rushes to cool my skin where his mouth has abandoned me.

"What?"

"You couldn't sleep." His voice is a low rumble against my hand where it rests on his solid chest.

"Now I don't want to sleep."

"But your body needs rest." He pulls back further.

I fist his shirt in my hand and yank him closer. "What I need is you."

A smile spreads across his mouth, revealing perfect, pearly teeth. "I'm not going anywhere, and I won't lie. I needed to hear that, but there's no rush, not between you and me." He leans down and kisses me softly and withdraws again. "Tell me why you couldn't sleep. We will fix that first. There's time for *this* once the world is sitting on its axis again."

My heart hammers in my chest. Confusion, frustration, and tenderness battle for control. "I'm not even tired."

His hand brushes my temple. "You've slept four hours at most. You're exhausted. Why did you wake?"

"I had a nightmare." I shove away from him and begin to pace. "Adika was taunting me back in San Marino, and then she killed me."

His eyebrows rise. "You actually died?"

I nod.

"Because. . ."

I shrug. "I couldn't stop her."

"But you didn't stop her." Edam's voice is soft.

I shake my head. "I didn't."

"Noah did."

I keep my heart steady, but it's hard. "That's true. But in my nightmare, he wasn't there."

"Was I there?" Edam's body is frozen, not shifting a hair, his voice carefully modulated.

"No."

"But you didn't miss me, you missed him."

I shake my head a little too hard. "I didn't miss him. He wasn't *there* when I needed him. You always are."

"But not in this dream, I wasn't."

"No."

He crosses the room to the enormous bed in the center. He points at the pile of pillows. "Lie down. I'm here now, and I'm not going anywhere."

A wave of exhaustion rolls over me, and I don't argue with him. I pad across the floor to the bed and climb in. He throws the blankets over me and tucks me in.

"Wait," I say. "Where are you going?"

"I'll be right here," he says. "On the carpeted floor. It's a huge step up from marble, believe me."

I laugh and sit up half way. "Please sleep right here, by me."

So he does. And when I fall asleep this time, I don't dream of anything at all.

7

When the first rays of the sun wake me, a heavily muscled arm is wrapped around my waist. Butterfly flutters in my chest mirror the fluttering of my lashes as I snuggle deeper into the blankets. When Edam shifts, I realize he's already awake.

"Morning." And he knows I'm awake.

"My mom would flip out." I shift around until I'm facing him. At the sight of his achingly square jaw, sprinkled with golden stubble, I can't suppress the smile that steals across my face. "But I rather like the sight of you right here with me when I open my eyes."

"You're not bad either." Edam props himself on one elbow and touches my face reverently. "I could do this for a thousand years and never tire of your smile."

I turn my face into his hand and close my eyes.

"No more nightmares?"

I shake my head. "You?"

"I'm only really afraid of one thing," he says. "And when you're right next to me, my brain knows it."

I shift back and shove a pillow behind my head. "You have nightmares?"

Edam laughs. "Not really. I'm not sure what it says about me, but my dreams tend more toward delusions of grandeur."

My eyebrows draw together. "You're king?"

He shakes his head. "I'm mowing down anyone who attacks you, effortlessly, and you're watching with a doting smile on your face."

"So your dreams are basically your everyday life?" I smirk. "That actually is funny."

"Or, you know, sometimes when I sleep, I'm doing this." Edam pushes himself up easily, the muscles in his arms rippling, and lowers his face slowly toward mine. As his deep, sky blue eyes near mine, the world around me fuzzes. He becomes everything.

My heart stutters as his mouth meets mine. My arms wrap around his neck and pull him even closer. "I'm not tired at all this morning."

A guttural purr from deep inside his chest sends a shiver from my toes to my nose. But he doesn't kiss me. His lips hover just a hair's breadth away from mine. "Chancery Divinity Alamecha."

Something crawls its way up my spine, a burning desire I've never experienced in my life. "Edam—"

He kisses me then. Slowly. Heavily. As if we're holding the world at bay, one kiss at a time. And I realize that we are. As the thought strikes, concerns pile up around me. Mother's body is missing. A traitor is here with us. Noah is who knows who. I'm at war with two families. My brother has PTSD. My sister is missing. And a virus is tearing through the humans I'm supposed to be protecting.

Utter destruction.

Edam rolls to his side with an exaggerated sigh.

I sit up. "What?"

"Where did you go?" His lips are pursed, but his eyes are bemused, thankfully.

"It's not you," I say. "You're like a double chocolate brownie with gelato and whipped cream. And nuts." I poke him.

He sits up. "No caramel sauce?"

I slide up next to him and put a hand on his chest. "But my life is a gasoline drenched dumpster fire right now. Everything keeps piling up, worsening by the minute. I can't turn off my fears. They just crowd in closer when I try."

He leans toward me until we're nose to nose. "I know you can't, and I love you for caring. Truly."

Edam climbs out of bed, and I follow suit.

"I'll go check on whether we've made any progress with the search for Melina," he says.

But when he opens the door, Judica's waiting for me.

Her eyes widen, taking in my mussed hair, my training gear that I obviously wore as pajamas. Her eyes immediately track toward the bed.

"It's not like that," I say.

She brushes past Edam. "None of my business."

I sigh.

"But I thought you might like to know that based on our analysis of the video, we're virtually certain that Nereus is a woman."

I grab the doorframe that leads into the bathroom. "That's good news."

"Is it?" Judica raises her eyebrows.

"I'm going to meet with Balthasar," Edam says.

I wave in acknowledgment, and he closes the door.

"I did not expect that." Judica's compressed lips give away her suppressed enjoyment of my discomfort.

"I told you already—nothing happened."

"He didn't sleep in here, right next to you?" Judica looks at the rumpled bed.

"Okay, then something happened. But not, like, anything . . . monumental."

"Last I checked," Judica says, "you said you trusted no one on earth, except for me. But last night, you slept. . . with Edam next to you all night."

She's right. The muscles in my shoulders relax. I was so busy trying to convince her that I hadn't acted in a way of which Mom wouldn't approve that I lost sight of something even more significant: I trust Edam. I'm not ready to discuss what that means, so I ignore it and move on.

"How do we know Nereus is a woman?" I ask.

"Based on the body shape and movement. Pretty reliable software that analyzes hip width and height. That sort of thing."

So basically, we just know. "Okay. Well that cuts our list in half."

"But we still need to figure out who fathered Mother's pregnancy, and whether that might be related to her death in any way."

I nod. "I agree. And why her body is missing, and we need to locate Melina."

Judica shakes her head. "She's gone. This island isn't large. If she was still here, we'd have found her by now."

"So you think she left by boat?"

Judica sighs. "I think she's either dead, or she had an accomplice who helped her leave. Boat, helicopter, who knows? But continuing that search is a waste of resources."

I don't bother arguing. We'll reassess at the next Council meeting. "Have we made any progress on locating Mom's body?"

"You are searching the crypt today, right?" Judica asks.

I nod.

"Balthasar says they'll be tracking other avenues, in case it left the area entirely. The incinerator has a log, for instance."

"Clearly if someone was burning Mom's body to destroy evidence, they wouldn't log it," I say.

"But if there are more ashes than are accounted for by the bodies and weight. . ." Judica's face is pale.

Ugh. "Let's hope that's not what happened." Because if she's been incinerated, there goes our chance to pursue the baby-daddy idea. And also, just. . . I shake my head and frown. "As if seeing her poisoned wasn't bad enough."

"I get angry sometimes," Judica says.

"About what?" I kind of thought anger was her default.

"That we couldn't stop it, what happened to her. That it all happened to us." Her voice drops to a whisper. "That she left us."

"You hide it so well," I say. "That sometimes I forget you're just like me." I hug my twin, and she doesn't even resist.

Judica straightens and clears her throat, clearly uncomfortable about the show of affection. "Also, I've been thinking. The individual outside Melina's door was female. But for all we know, Melina was misleading us—as I mentioned before, I think it might have been Aline. That means I need to systematically dig through the background and motivations of every Alamecha citizen just as I planned to do before. We've tested a hundred and eleven individuals in the past twelve hours while you slept—and let me tell you, they are not delighted to be donating blood for humans."

"It's not even an inconvenience to them," I say. "How selfish are we, that we can't give up a little time. . ." Speaking of time. "Did you say while I slept? You've been testing people? Did you sleep at all?"

"I was planning to check the crypt next, for Mother's body. The guards won't admit me. They said you gave specific orders that only you are to be allowed."

I smile. "I did. I'm glad someone listens to me."

"We could go now."

"Except you didn't answer me. Have you slept at all?"

"I slept the entire plane ride."

"Which was at least twenty hours ago now." I put one hand on my hip. "I will check the crypt. You will sleep. And if you don't—"

"You'll sic your odd little puppy on me?"

"Oh nothing like that. Red Bull is adorable. That would be a reward."

"Then what?" Judica asks.

"I'll tell Roman."

She gulps.

"I can handle searching for Mom's body alone. You go sleep now. I'm not asking."

"If you don't need me for that, I was talking to Marselle about—"

"Judica."

She scowls. "Fine. Three hours."

"Four."

Noise outside my door distracts us both and we turn. The door is so well soundproofed that it's hard to make out what's going on. Judica waves me back and opens the door, one hand on her sword hilt.

"She'll want to talk to me," Balthasar says.

"She's not to be disturbed by anyone who hasn't been cleared yet," Frederick says.

"And I suppose that's you?" Balthasar's eyes flash.

"I have cleared Frederick," Judica says. "After taking his blood sample and noting his DNA in our system without any objection. I also interviewed him for the better part of four hours."

"You have?" I ask. "That's great news."

"Well you can bloody well clear me next," Balthasar says. "Because I need access to Chancery—"

"Her Royal Majesty," Frederick says.

Balthasar rolls his eyes. "None of that matters. What does matter—"

"Just tell me," I say. "What's wrong now?"

"One minute, I'm analyzing the video," Balthasar says. "The next, it's gone."

"What video?" But a sinking feeling in my stomach tells me I already know.

"The one of Melina being dragged away." Balthasar's hands curl into fists. "It makes no sense. I had watched it a few moments before, searching for micro clues—"

"It can't be gone." Judica pushes past me and storms into the hall. "You're not exactly a tech guru. You probably cleared your cache—"

"It's gone," Larena says behind him. "We called in McGregor, Hessian, and Corina. None of them could find any record of it in any part of the server. Someone wiped it utterly clean, and they did it right under our noses."

"Still think I need a nap?" Judica mutters.

"More than ever," I say, my words sharper than I intended. "You need to be at the top of your game. Frederick will follow me to the crypt, and we will search for this clue and hope it's not too late."

Marselle jogs down the hall toward the impromptu gathering that's taking place in far too open a spot for my liking. I don't groan or shout. Instead, I set off for the crypt. "Everyone back to work. Marselle can share her newest revelation with me as I move."

Frederick leaps into place next to me, two of his guards falling in behind us. Judica practically spits fire at me with her eyes, but she stomps away toward her room. I don't know or care where Balthasar and Larena go next. I do hope Judica makes Balthasar the top of her list when she wakes.

"Your Majesty," Marselle's words are barely louder than a whisper.

I slow slightly so she can match my steps. "What is it?"

She purses her lips. "Angel has been spotted."

My heart accelerates. "Where?"

"Near the same marketplace where Nereus acquired the poison that killed your mother."

I stop dead in the hallway, my bare feet squeaking on the marble. I look ridiculous, padding around barefoot in rumpled training gear, but I don't even care. Not right now, not while we're finally getting somewhere. "She must have realized she missed something. She's trying to cover her error. What could it be?"

"I'm not sure yet," Marselle says.

"There must be something from before, something that gives away her identity conclusively," Frederick says.

"We missed something?" I ask.

Marselle's mouth looks grim. "Maybe. She evaded my scout, but I've sent five teams to search for whatever we might have missed."

"What about apprehending her?" I ask. "And when was it? Could Angel have gone from here to there?"

Marselle shakes her head. "She was spotted days ago. But the scout who saw her was killed. We only know from a recording—" Marselle snaps her mouth shut. "Doesn't matter. She was there several days ago, and we are only now hearing about it. But we're working the lead to her and searching for anything we might have missed."

I close my eyes and exhale. "It's too late. If she went and left un-apprehended, she's already corrected whatever she went to do."

"Not necessarily," Marselle says. "She was interrupted by the presence of my operative. We didn't catch her, and it has been some time, but she may not have finished. We may yet discover whatever she was trying to hide."

I nod. "Good, yes. Thank you."

Marselle bows slightly and turns around.

"Wait."

She freezes.

"Make sure Judica moves you near the top of the list to clear. I want no doubts about your loyalty, since you run my entire network."

"I'd be very convincing at covering my lies if it was me," Marselle says.

"And that's why you'll give Judica complete access to everything," I say. "Your phone, your body, your person, everything. I need to know I can trust you."

"You must really trust Judica." She lifts one eyebrow.

"I have to trust someone," I say.

Marselle takes my hand and squeezes. "I'm very sorry, Chancery. It shouldn't be this hard. Your life, I mean." She inhales slowly. "You've grown so much, and so much misery still lies ahead of us. I vow that you can trust me, but I'll do anything I can for Judica to help you believe me."

I nod.

As distasteful as it is to tell every single person in my life that they're a suspect and they must bare all their secrets to me, searching dozens and dozens of crypts which house decaying corpses is worse. Like, way worse.

After we've checked the very last one without any sign of Mom's body, I want to take a shower in rubbing alcohol, burn out the inside of my nose, and then curl up in the corner and bawl.

"The oldest ones smelled the best," Frederick says. "I guess it makes sense, but I hadn't considered it before now."

I wish I didn't know what decaying bodies at a dozen different timeframes smell like. At least I didn't shower *before* coming to do this. "I want to be cremated."

Frederick laughs.

"I'm not kidding."

"Well, if your mother had been cremated—"

"There'd be nothing to look for, I know."

Frederick shrugs, and I realize he's a decent candidate for the father.

"How close were you to Mom?"

His eye twitches.

"Did you ever kiss her?"

His eyes widen and his pupils dilate. His heart accelerates. He shakes his head. "I did not."

But I wonder whether he wanted to. "Did Judica already ask you all this?"

He nods. "She did."

I breathe in a sigh of relief. I'm Red Bull to her Death. If Judica says he's good, I can let it go. "Alright."

"You're supposed to be training with Edam and Balthasar in a handful of minutes," he says.

"To learn to use my new powers." I grunt. "How exciting."

"To everyone but you, it is. You need to decide whether you'll allow your subjects to watch. They're dying to see you in action."

I might be as excited as everyone else, if I hadn't blown Noah into the depths of the ocean and badly injured Edam the last time I tinkered with it. "Not this time," I say. "But once I've figured out exactly what I can do, they'll be welcome. Can you pass that along for me?"

Frederick nods.

On the walk back to my room, my brain compiles a list of things I need to do. Read and study in Mom's sanctum. Review a list of my supporters and discuss with Judica her plans for vetting them. Prioritize who she should assess first. Confer with Franco regarding the plague and its impacts. Ensure he's taking aggressive enough measures to contain it. Review things that have been falling by the wayside as a result in governance and the integration with Shenoah. Meet with Moses to discuss ways to win over the sixth family's royals, and finalize our steps for improving the situation for every citizen of their family, human and evian both. Work with Franco and Inara and Maxmillian to discuss the implementation of the new decree, codifying the equality of humans and the rights of the Motherless. Continue the hunt for Nereus and Mom's missing body. Develop a plan for subduing or convincing Melamecha and Lainina. Hammer out the details of Melisania and Analessa's surrenders.

Figure out exactly what the utter destruction is and how to prevent it.

And those are just the highlights.

By the time I reach my room, I want to shower and then dive under the covers to hide for the next ten years. I settle for the shower and putting on clean, pressed training gear.

I'm headed for the door when a ringing begins on my desk. I pull up short and spin around. My phone died in the ocean. I walk slowly toward the desk and look at the source. A new iPhone. The caller ID says 'Analessa.'

Looks like my phone has been replaced. No matter how badly I'd like to screen this call, I need to pick it up.

"Hello?"

"Chancery, darling, I received your newest decree along with your party invitation."

"Oh." I wait for her to tell me what she wants, but she doesn't say anything else. Finally I ask, "Are you coming?"

Analessa tsks. "That depends entirely on you."

"How so?"

"Your decree, my dear."

If she doesn't quit calling me darling and dear, I'm going to jump through the phone and strangle her. I wonder whether I could shoot a fireball into her room. . . "I don't know what you mean." Perhaps she's going to demand I rescind it.

Her voice is flat, all charm and teasing gone. "You declared that the heirs of Empresses may be male or female. The youngest child."

Oh. My heart picks up speed. My palms begin to sweat.

Because Edam is younger than her, by a fair margin. My decree makes him the Emperor of Malessa. I consider the ramifications for a split second before deciding it's not worth the fight, the casualties, and the fallout. "I see your confusion. Obviously this would be going forward, so as not to destabilize the current power structure. But even beyond that, Edam, as my pledged Consort, wouldn't be eligible to rule Malessa. No one is contesting the legitimacy of your rule."

"Hmm."

"Is this going to be a problem?"

"As long as you don't make it a problem, it should be fine," Analessa says.

"I have every intention of allowing you to continue to manage Malessa under my supervision," I say. "Just as we agreed."

"Very well," Analessa says. And then, as if I've thrown a switch, her charm reboots. "I so look forward to seeing you in a few days, sweet Chancery. Until then."

She hangs up.

❧ 8 ❧

In spite of my clear instruction, several clusters of people are gathered in the training room when I arrive. My gaze cuts toward Frederick.

He shrugs. "I told Edam."

"Those four are assigned to train here the same time as us." Edam points.

"And I'm entitled to see how it's going. It might be crucial to our war strategy," Balthasar says.

"Same," Inara says. "But for political maneuvering." Her hands are laced behind her back, her eyes full of innocence.

"And you?" I turn toward Alora and Marselle.

"It's important to managing my assets?" Marselle offers.

Alora laughs. "You're all ridiculous. We're here because we want to see what you can do."

"That's why I'm here," Noah says.

"I figured you'd be hiding as far from here as possible after what happened the last time," I say.

"Glutton for punishment," Noah says. "That's me."

I raise my voice so the dozen people present can all hear. "When I joined the staridium, an explosion propelled me far off shore, sheared a cliff face off the island and into

89

the ocean, and buried Noah under a ton of rubble on the bottom of the ocean. I'd recommend that you clear out while I work on learning to use the power."

No one wavers.

Edam steps closer. "You're a historic prophecy come to life."

Inara clears her throat. "In time of great peril, when the lives of women and men shall fail, the Eldest shall survive certain death to unite the families. She comes in a time of blood and horror, in a world overrun with plague and warfare. She shall command the stone of the mountain, be it small or large. Its power shall destroy the vast hosts arrayed against it. With the might and power of God, the Eldest shall destroy all in her path and unite my children as one. Only through her blood can the stone be restored to the mountain. Together, with the strength of her strongest supporter, she shall open the Garden of Eden, that the miracle of God shall go unto all the Earth to save my children from utter destruction."

"I plan to record what I witness and share it with generation after generation," Alora says. "Can you fault us for being willing to risk the danger? You've survived certain death, three times, by my count. And now you're commanding the stone of the mountain, small and then larger. I mean, it's pretty. . . monumental."

"And you flung me into the ocean," Noah says. "But you saved me, too."

I groan and climb into the sparring ring.

Edam leaps in behind me. "We begin today as we always do. Her Majesty observes melodics, and she warms up with standard forms." He signals and Balthasar keys one of the harder warm-ups into the main computer, Shostakovich's Symphony No. 5 in D Minor. Sweat has beaded on my brow by the time it concludes, and I don't know whether I'm simply drained from the past few days, or whether the presence of an audience wears on me. Certainly, the weight of that prophecy does.

When Edam and I move on to actual hand-to-hand, he takes it ridiculously easy on me. After his third slow strike, I slide underneath his guard and punch him square on the nose. I used to cringe when I heard a bone break, but I can't quite keep the smile off my face as blood flows down his lip and chin.

He wipes his face on the shoulder of his training gear and beams at me. "Ready to step it up, I see."

I shrug. "Can't look like a cream puff in front of all these people."

By the time we're both quite a bit more blood spattered, Edam calls a halt. "Time for a little two on one, I think."

Balthasar swings up and into the ring so quickly my head spins.

"Oh." I didn't expect him to participate.

"I think it's time I take a more active role in your training," Balthasar says. "When time permits."

Perfect. Because one intense, semi-sadistic perfectionist directing my combat skills wasn't enough. "Sure, great."

Balthasar trained Edam, and they worked together for so long, I'm not even surprised when they operate like a four-armed, four-legged war machine. After a sequence of punishing blows to my face, I snap.

"Enough!" One tiny pull from the new staridium well and they both fly backward against the ropes.

Edam beams.

Balthasar's expression isn't even smile adjacent. He's a cat, mouse in his paw, about to take a bite. He's a wolf, tearing into the haunch of a deer. He's positively triumphant. "That was. . ." He leaps to his feet. "Do it again."

I do. This time I don't wait for them to batter my face

before sending them flying backward. By the time Edam halts our efforts, I realize that several members of my audience are filming, their eyes wide. Great. Now the world will know.

Which might be for the best. So far, only Analessa has reacted to my decree and invitation, and her reaction wasn't super supportive. Maybe a little reminder of who I am and what I can do will encourage the reticent.

"Okay," Edam says. "I think we need more opponents to get a feel for what you can do. I'd love to see whether you can push outward in a circle, for instance."

Noah leaps into the ring without waiting for an invite. "I'm happy to help," he says, "but are we sure she should be using the power so often?"

Edam shifts slightly so that his body squares off against Noah's. It's subtle, but he's sending a message: He's in charge. "Oh, you're probably right. The last time I got a new weapon in my hands, I did nothing with it. I figured when I was in the middle of a battle would be a good time to learn."

"No reason to get so testy," Noah says. "I'm simply asking if we have a good feel for the cost of using the staridium."

"What does that mean?" Balthasar asks. "The cost?"

Noah tilts his head just like our calculus teacher at Trinity did. "Everything has a price. Surely you know that."

"I beg to differ," Edam says. "When you own the world, many things don't have a price. And Chancery owns the world."

"How do you mean?" Noah asks,

"Name something," Edam says. "She can eat whatever she wants, for instance. No price to her."

Noah shakes his head. "Untrue. We're evian, so sometimes you forget the price—or it seems inconsequential—but it's still there. Anything she consumes is something no one else can eat, and it requires time, resources, and effort. It takes Lark's dedication and supervision to ensure that it's safe, and it takes a taster, be it a dog or a guard or a boyfriend, to ensure that it won't harm her. Beyond that, every bite has a caloric value. She's active and healthy and evian—so those calories melt away. But if she lay in bed, doing nothing, and ate and ate all day, she would gain weight, just like a human. Don't mistake small payments for no payment at all."

"He's babbling," Balthasar says.

Noah shakes his head. "Do you know where Chancery's new power originates?"

No one answers.

"What about you, princess? Do you know?"

I think about the wells in my head. "I think it's coming from the stones. They provide me with a certain amount of power—and they're limited to that amount. The power refills at a rather steady rate after I use it. I appreciate your concern, but I think Edam's right here. There appear to be no negative ramifications to my use of the staridium."

"You're training, in order to prepare to use them in a larger capacity," Noah says. "Is that a fair assessment?"

I shrug. "Maybe."

"And let's assume that as your skill, your ability, increases, you'll use them more and more. Take my analogy. Eating a handful of cookies before bedtime may have no noticeable impact on your physiology whatsoever. But eating a truckload?" He shrugs. "That amount of lard in your system, the lack of protein as you gorge on sweets, in large quantities, it might have significant consequences. That's all I'm saying."

"You don't think the power comes from the stones?"

Noah shakes his head. "Actually, I don't. If it was the rocks themselves, they would gift power to everyone who touched them. No, I think it's your power somehow, princess, and they're mere focal points or something akin to that. They may amplify the power inside of you, but I believe that ultimately comes from you. Which means using it more and more, without any real understanding of where it's coming from, could be problematic. Dangerous, even."

Edam steps closer to Noah. "You think that by training her, I'm endangering her?"

Noah rolls his eyes, for all the world like a human teenager. "I'm saying, genius, that you might want to do a little more testing than just 'try to fling us in a circle' before you start amping up her usage."

"She may put herself or the rest of us at risk if she can't use her abilities to their full potential," Edam says. "It's in the prophecy that she controls them. Have you thought of that?"

"I'm going to save you some time and a headache too, probably," Noah says with a half grin. "If you've thought of it, I've definitely considered it, analyzed it, weighed and made a logical determination. Because I'm ten steps ahead of you. Just assume that from now on."

A muscle in Edam's jaw works.

"Okay. Well if you've thought of it," I say, "then what was your analysis? Because I am with Edam here. I think that preparation now, determining what I can do, is worth whatever nebulous threat of excess lard looms in the future. At least, without more information."

Noah inhales deeply and opens his mouth. No words come out. He swallows and opens his mouth again, but still, nothing. Finally, he coughs. "Look, think about the past. You figured it out on that jet, princess. And then again, when we were headed over to save this one in Europe." He jerks his thumb toward Edam. "When you've needed the special brand of power from the staridium, we've figured out how to get you to do what was necessary."

"We?" Edam asks.

Noah smirks. "Oh, that's right. You haven't been there during any of those dire times. It's been just me and the princess, saving the world twice over. Maybe if you'd been there, you'd realize she doesn't need your help in doing what she was *born* to do."

"I don't need help from anyone else to save the world from the plague of Noah's nonstop mouth," Edam says. "I can do that without any stones at all."

"Okay," I say. This is devolving quickly. "I think he was—"

"Your boyfriend is challenging me," Noah says. "And I accept."

I should have hidden in my room. "This isn't a good idea—"

"I see no reason to wait," Edam says. "I'm ready now."

"Look—" I say.

But Balthasar grabs my arm and shakes his head. "They need to get it out of their system. Let them."

"First blood," I say.

Edam laughs. "First *major*."

I march across the ring until I'm standing inches away from my fiancé. "Do not kill him," I whisper. "Do you hear me?"

Edam's eyes sparkle. "I make no promises."

I put my hand on his chest. "I want you to make me a promise. Do not get carried away. Make your point and then stop."

He groans. "Fine."

Good. I climb out of the ring and stand next to Balthasar. It hasn't escaped my notice that citizens are streaming through the doorway, their eyes eager, their fingers tapping out more texts.

Good grief.

"I'll count you off," Balthasar says. And then he does.

95

Everything moves far faster than it does when I'm in the ring. Time seems to slow when I fight, as if every second has multiplied somehow. But this fight, it's like it's in fast forward. And why is this challenge hand-to-hand? Ugh, because they're men and that's the most agonizing way to reach first major. Edam lands a blow on Noah's cheekbone, shattering it, I'm fairly sure. Noah spins around, covering his retreat with an impressive back kick I didn't expect. Men don't use kicks often enough, in my opinion.

It doesn't buy him much time, but it's enough. When he turns back toward Edam, his face is healed, faint purplish bruising the only evidence of which cheek was smashed. Edam plays with Noah for a few moments, their interchange resembling the one on the jet, when Noah came out as evian.

But then Noah says something to Edam. I'm too far away to understand exactly what, but something about his sister.

Whatever it is, it pisses Edam off, and the entire gambit shifts. Edam's blows fall harder, faster, sharper, and with increasing frequency. Noah kept pace before, but not now. No one can keep pace with this. And yet, Edam's still measured in his ferocity. He breaks Noah's right foot.

Noah hobbles back, but his sluggish reaction allows Edam to break his left arm. And then his nose. And finally his leg.

Is this really necessary? It's like instead of finishing it, Edam's running Noah through a meat grinder. I open my mouth to object when Balthasar takes my hand. "They need to work this out."

"But they aren't," I say. "Edam's just tenderizing him."

"This is how men work things out," Balthasar says.

I shake my head. "No, it's not. Men can—"

He squeezes my hand. "Some men may talk things

through. And Edam may be able to do that with you. Eve knows that Noah could talk the hind legs off a donkey. But you're asking Edam to deal with having his rival around, supporting you, advising you, hovering around you. Forever. And it's harder because Edam respects him, however grudgingly. Let him do what he needs to do to come to terms with your friendship with Noah, or whatever it is. Interrupting now won't help either of them. Trust me."

So I watch, my nails digging into my palms, while Edam pulverizes Noah—like rapid fire torture, only Noah's not about to spill his guts figuratively.

Only literally.

And then, it happens. Edam breaks both Noah's kneecaps at once, and Noah falls to the arena floor. He can't possibly heal the damage quickly enough, so it's time. Edam has to break his spine, and this will all finally end.

Edam drops to one knee as a matter of simple logistics. His arms reach for Noah's neck, his hands twisting.

And in that moment, something strange happens. Something that leaves me blinking, confused.

Somehow, Noah shifts, almost imperceptibly. Edam snaps his neck, but at the same moment, Noah smashes Edam in the nose, driving up and into his brain.

Both men fall to the mat.

I swing in and rush to their side, unsure who's in more eminent danger. Broken neck, nose smashed upward and into the brain.

In my entire life, I've never once heard of a challenge to first major ending in... a draw.

But as I watch, both men heal their injuries at almost the same time and climb to their feet, like the world's most macabre synchronized swimming performance.

"I defeated him," Edam says.

"Sure you did, old man," Noah says. "And now you can

tell me exactly how your brain smells. So that's a new skill for your resume."

"What is he even talking about?" Edam asks.

"If you two are done beating your chests and throwing fecal matter, I'm done. I've got a list longer than my arm of urgent tasks." I spin on my heel and storm out of the room.

Edam falls into step with me by the time I reach the hallway. "Don't be mad."

I ignore him until I reach my room. I yank him inside and close the door. "Never again," I say.

Edam's eyes flash. "Never defend myself?"

I shake my head. "Never attack one of my supporters because you're jealous."

"Jealous?" He fumes. "You think I attacked him because I'm jealous?"

I close the space between us and grab the back of Edam's head. "Didn't you?" I yank his head down to mine and kiss him. His anger quickly shifts, and his arms wrap around me, pressing me so tightly against his long frame that I can barely breathe.

Not that I need to.

Edam releases me. "I was jealous. I have been for weeks now."

My hand slides down from behind his neck, to his shoulder, and down his arm to his hand. I lace our fingers together and look at them clasped in front of us. "We're getting married."

His voice is as small as I've ever heard it. "You *sensed* him leagues under the ocean. You dove away from me and nearly drowned yourself to save him. God sent you a message to save his life—a vision." He chokes. "I can't compete with that."

"I didn't pick any of that," I say.

He doesn't say the words, but I know he's thinking the same thing as me: I didn't choose to marry him, either.

It was forced upon us both, and as much as I care about him, I may never know how things would have gone down without Analessa and her entire family hanging over our heads. But I can't change that, and I won't risk another war, not when all I have to do to prevent it is marry someone I clearly care for deeply.

I can't tell him what he wants to hear, so when Lark knocks at the door, Edam makes an excuse and leaves.

"What's wrong?" I ask the second we're alone.

"Judica cleared me," she says.

"Uh, that's a good thing," I say. "But it's hardly a surprise. You were near the top of the list for a reason. As my chef, I need to be sure that you're doing your job."

She waves her hand. "Right, right, it was mostly just questions about how upset I am for my mother's death, that sort of thing."

I sit on the edge of my bed. "And?"

Lark sits next to me, closer than anyone else would sit. She throws an arm around me. "It was my mom's fault. She should have trusted her friend. Like I trust you."

"Life sucks all around right now," I say.

"And we both need our moms, but they aren't here."

I sigh. "Yeah, we're all alone. It's totally unfair." I lean my head against her shoulder. "Did you know that for a while there, I wondered if you might hate me?"

Her arm drops. "Why?"

"It would be normal for you to blame me for Lyssa's death. I mean, I kind of forced the fight, and then my mom killed yours."

"Enora didn't have much of a choice," she says. "I see that now. Mom backed her into a corner, and she couldn't spare me *and* Mom. Enora knew Mom would choose me, and that you would too. It took me weeks to see that, and I won't lie and say it doesn't hurt, but that's like blaming the butcher, not the rancher, for the cow's death."

I raise my eyebrow at her bizarre metaphor.

"Or whatever." She laughs. "The point is, you love me, and you loved my mom. You did everything in your power to help us, and I would never blame you."

"But something is wrong," I say. "Or you wouldn't be here outside of meal time when you know I'm drowning in problems."

"I could be here to check in on you." Lark frowns. "Have I really been that lousy a friend?"

"You were giving me space, not making demands. You're the best kind of friend." I tilt my head. "But just tell me what's up. Trouble in the kitchen?"

She shakes her head. "No, but I gave my DNA sample yesterday, and I donated blood."

"Okay," I say.

"And I went back today to donate again, and they won't take my blood."

I frown. "You donated yesterday."

"Right, and I figure if I donate every day, then I can help more humans. I may only be half evian, but I heal well enough to regenerate my blood. And mine will help the humans, I know it will."

Actually, if the full-blooded evians had half her heart, the world would be a better place. "But they won't take it? Like, maybe they don't have enough time?"

She shakes her head. "They said they don't think I can regenerate quickly enough, and if I donated, I'd be endangering myself. But I think they just don't believe my blood is good enough."

Lark has spent her life among evians being taught that humans are trash, but now she wants to take her time and give of her body to help them. It's one of the reasons I love her. And I'm embarrassed I didn't think of it sooner. "Come with me."

By the time I'm done "chatting" with Judica's medical

staff, they're already changing the signs to welcome voluntary donations from any and all residents of Ni'ihau.

"Thank you," she says.

"No," I say. "Thank you, for trusting me to set things right, and taking the time to make it happen."

"One day," Lark says, "more of your people will understand. We may all be different, but we really are in this together."

❧ 9 ❧

"Y ou're absolutely positive?" I ask.

Edam nods. "I weighed and measured it myself."

"There's an extra body's worth of ash?"

Hugo clears his throat. "It's not actually ash," he says. "That's a misnomer."

"It is?" My eyebrows rise.

Hugo shakes his head. "What's left at the end of the cremation is this." He opens a container that's full of gray-ish-white chunks and lumps, chunks that strongly resemble bones.

I grimace. "Are those—"

"Bones. Yes, after the soft tissue, hair, organs, and skin have burned away, the dried bones remain."

Gah. "But people scatter the ashes from containers afterward. I've seen that, on human television shows at least. Is this a human/evian difference?"

"Have you seen a blender?" Hugo asks.

I may never drink a milkshake again.

"It's much larger, of course, and stronger too," he says.

"Intended to process the bones into something more palatable."

I really did not need another food comparison. "And you're saying that you didn't notice that an entire body had been processed and blended right here?"

"It only takes two to three hours to cremate a body," Hugo says. "And as you can see, we have a number of empty tubs that are not monitored. There's usually very little call to supervise or secure remains. We also very rarely have cremations. We mostly have the facility because your mother decided she didn't want to outsource the few that we did have."

"Who's that?" I point at the box.

Hugo smiles. "These bones are false, used to show someone who's considering the course they choose to take for their relative, if they request to see the process of what we do." He offers the box to me.

I shake my head. "So how many cremations have taken place here in the last month?"

"There would only have been two," Hugo says. "Lyssa, who was executed for treason and not entitled to a typical burial, and Nihils, whom Judica killed while you were—er, during a training." His eyes dart from me to Edam and back again.

"Would have been?"

"In the past few days, I've been tasked to perform cremations on nearly all the individuals killed in conjunction with your sister Melina's disappearance."

"Twenty something, then?" I ask.

"Seventeen. As I understand it, Larena did her best to contact the families of everyone who passed, and she asked if they'd like the bodies shipped, or if they'd prefer that cremated remains be sent. Most opted for cremation."

"What about evidence?" Edam asks. "Wouldn't they have kept them around in cold storage for that?"

Hugo shrugs. "I'm not consulted about—"

"I approved the disposal," I say. "Two days ago. We did keep several of them in cold storage, but it seemed unlikely we'd gain a lot from retaining all of them. Not enough to justify delaying their families from grieving."

"And when did you notice that the weights were off?" I ask.

"Edam came yesterday," he says. "He started asking about the process, and I explained that the remains usually vary from six to eight pounds after they've been processed."

"Blended?" I scrunch my nose.

"Yes." Hugo gulps. "But when I began weighing them this morning, to prepare them for shipment to the appropriate families, several of them weighed nearly nine pounds. I pulled out the log and saw that somehow, weight had been added to a number of containers after the remains had been processed. If I had simply copied the weights we originally recorded, I would never have noticed."

"Wait, someone added ashes to all seventeen?" I ask.

"No," Hugo says. "To seven of them, it appears. If they had been more patient, we might not have noticed. Had the weight of one been distributed to seventeen separate containers, I might have written it off as an accounting error—or if they had selected to distribute extra only to the smaller weighted containers. But I've almost never seen more than nine pounds of remains after processing. That, combined with Edam's questioning, made me look closer."

"But if you identify which seven had extra material—"

"We've done that," Edam says. "And that gives us a time window. The processing, at least, had to happen after those seven, but likely before the others—and be spread over the remains available at the time."

"If we hadn't noticed Mom's body was missing—"

"He might not have gotten sloppy," Edam says. "These

might have been shipped out and we'd never have figured it out."

"To be clear, we have withdrawn samples from each to be DNA sequenced, but we still won't know for several days whether it *is* in fact the remains from Her Majesty that have been added."

"Thank you, Hugo," I say. "I appreciate your help."

"Edam ordered that we prepare the samples," Hugo says. "And I have them for you right here." He indicates a box. "Judica and her team of scientists will know what to do with them."

Edam walks me out, and once we reach the hall, my guards fall into step around me. Ten of them. "Why are there more guards today?" I lift my eyebrows.

"We have another stop to make. I thought we might need some backup for it."

"We do?"

"I pulled the video feeds from the relevant times, and there's one person who was coming in and out of the crematorium at the right times. Only one person."

I bite my lower lip. "Not Hugo." He seemed so awkward and so nice. Please not poor sweet Hugo.

"Not Hugo—that guy is there far too often, but I assume he would have been less forthcoming, less eager to figure out why the weights were off. Or he could have told me that nine pounds is within the typical parameter, which he didn't. No, he's the one who helped me figure it out."

"Then who?" I ask.

"Job's assistant, Tristan."

He would have had access to Job's crypt keys, too. My heart accelerates. "And we're going to question him?"

Edam nods. "I thought you might like to be present."

"I would, yes."

I make a conscious effort not to race, and I moderate

my heart rate. For the first time in weeks and weeks, we may be closing in on an answer to Mom's murderer.

Edam stops in front of a door and tosses his head to order the guards to move to either side. He knocks.

Tristan opens the door, his eyes widening as he takes in the group. He throws the dagger so quickly that I barely realize it's flying my direction.

Javer throws up his hand, the dagger slamming into his palm.

Edam kicks Tristan in the chest, and he flies backward into the back wall. He shoves the blade of his sword against Tristan's throat. "I could kill you for attempting to kill Her Majesty and not feel a pang of guilt."

"But then you'll never know why I did it." Tristan doesn't look concerned or guilty or scared. He looks smug.

"Why did you do it?" I ask.

"What are you asking about, exactly?" Tristan raises one eyebrow.

I speak past gritted teeth. "Why did you steal my mom's body and cremate it?"

Tristan smiles. "Past debts."

"Debts to whom?" I ask. "Who made you do it?"

"No one makes me do anything," he says. "I serve voluntarily. I serve to cleanse the bloodlines."

Edam releases him and spins him around toward the wall, presumably to bind his hands.

But Tristan gets one hand free and sticks something in his mouth.

"Wait," I say.

But it's too late. He has swallowed it.

"Call Job," I say. "He can't kill himself. I need to question him!"

Javer, injured hand and all, sprints down the hall, but by the time Job arrives, nothing can be done.

"Search his belongings," I say. "Find out everything we

can about him, about who he might have owed, about who he could have been working for or with."

While Edam and Judica focus on tracking down everything they can about Tristan, interrogating Job and everyone else who has worked with him, I throw myself into my training. After an arduous warm up, with sweat rolling down the side of my face, I say, "I need to do some damage today."

Balthasar nods. "I totally understand. How about we try some hand to hand?"

My mom was married to his brother for centuries. Alora and Inara's uncle, my . . . almost uncle? Balthasar has always been a legend. Something about breaking a legend's kneecaps improves my mood.

"Why are you so upset?" Balthasar asks. "Shouldn't you be pleased? We're drawing closer to answers, finally."

"Are you happy?" I ask. "That he died so easily, so quickly?"

"Tristan was a pawn," Balthasar says. "Pawns go down all the time. What we need is the person pulling their strings. That's the person I want to draw and quarter, and then heal up, and repeat. Over and over." Something about his musing distracts him.

Which is how I land a solid shot to the face, shattering his nose. I freeze. "Will it make you feel better, do you think?"

"What?" Balthasar asks. "Healing this? I hope so."

I shake my head. "Inflicting pain on the one who took her from us."

He frowns. "I don't know. Maybe."

Somehow I doubt it.

"Your Majesty," Javer says.

I spin on my heel. "What?"

"One of the patrols found something you might want to see." Javer gestures.

A tall guard with a hooked nose and dark hair steps forward. His arm is wrapped in a towel. "I spotted a tiger shark feeding near the north shore. This was floating next to him in the water." He jerks his head.

Javer holds up a hooded sweatshirt. It's shredded in places, but it's still easy to make out what it was. A dark hoodie with bright florescent orange bands around the wrists and neckline. I've seen it before—it's part of the video feed that wasn't deleted leading up to Nereus attacking Melina's people. Aline was wearing it when she left for a jog.

I swing off of the platform and cross the room. "Are you alright?" I stare pointedly at the guard's wrapped arm.

"I will be fine soon enough. We decided to capture the shark," he says. "We weren't really prepared to do that, and we had to kill it."

"Why?" I ask.

The guard swallows. "It was eating something."

I close my eyes.

"And when we cut open its belly, we found remnants of what it was eating." The guard looks back, and another guard steps forward.

I think her name is Cina. She holds up a bag with something in it.

I step closer and squint.

It's a finger.

"Do we know whose finger that is?"

"Not yet," the guard says.

"Well, we better figure it out." I march with the finger and the sweatshirt all the way to Job's lab.

He's being interrogated by Judica and Edam, but they stop mid-sentence when I walk into the room.

"Do you think Job had anything to do with Tristan?" I ask.

Judica frowns. "We haven't finished yet."

"Right, I get that. And you can finish, but I have something urgent and I'd rather not wait until you're done. Do you have any reason to believe that Job knew what Tristan was up to?"

Judica shakes her head. I fill them in on what we've found.

"I should have Aline's DNA sequence on file," Job says. "Enora kept close tabs on Aline and Melina both, especially since Aline did most of the traveling."

"Since Mom banned Melina from going anywhere," I say.

Job nods.

"Test it. How long does that take?"

"Days," Job says. "And that's actually only if we fast track it. I assume you want this bumped to the top of the list. You don't want all the other DNA sequencing on samples we've collected to be done first?"

I sigh. Why does everything take so much time? "Yes," I say. "Bump this to the top."

"You should prepare yourself," Judica says.

"For what?" I ask.

"It might be Aline's," she says. "Or."

It might be Melina's. "I know."

❧ 10 ❧

"**N**o attacks anywhere?" I ask. "I know we threw the party together fast, but it has been four days. They could have done something by now."

Balthasar shakes his head. "I expected at least one of them to strike before the party."

So did I. "Maybe they're reconsidering their position."

"Melamecha and Lainina aren't stupid." Balthasar paces back and forth. "They refused your invitation for a reason. They know this isn't a simple celebration of destroying another family—and they know something like this has never happened before."

"I didn't destroy—"

Balthasar ignores my protest. "They either need to press their positions now, before you've shored up alliances with Malessa and Lenora, or they'll be forced to wait and see how that shakes out. Since there hasn't been an attack yet, we can assume it's the latter. Which means they'll have emissaries reporting back on what happens tonight."

I gulp.

"You'll be concluding any formalities necessary to bring

Analessa and Melisania over to our side, yes?" Balthasar frowns.

The Council has been pressing hard, but Balthasar has spearheaded that pressure. I suppose it makes sense. If negotiations break down and Lenora doesn't come to our side peacefully, it's Balthasar who pays the price. "I need to talk to Judica. I promised her time—"

"Judica's smart. She's strong, and she always does what needs to be done."

That's exactly what I'm worried about. Doing whatever Alamecha demands has been her lot in life, but I don't think what has been is always what should be. "I'm not convinced it's the right path. Trading away something that doesn't belong to me doesn't feel like the right way to unite the families."

"One woman's hand in marriage in exchange for ruling an entire family and obtaining another stone?" Balthasar lifts his eyebrows. "We're definitely on the right end of the bargain."

I sigh. "Which means, of course, that it's not the real reason Melisania agreed." I sit down and prop my elbows on the pristine table in Balthasar's spartan war room. "No, she's joining us because she sees that it must be, and she's carving out as much power for herself as possible in the new regime."

"And one of her main demands is a permanent familial union," Balthasar says. "Access to your heir, your Inquisitor, your twin. It's not an inconsequential demand, and you need to accept it at tonight's party."

"Speaking of," I say. "I need to approve final details with Lark and Larena and then get dressed."

I stand up and walk past Balthasar toward the door. He grabs my hand. "Please be prudent tonight, Chancery."

The hair on my arm stands up. "I will not force my sister to give up all hope of happiness—"

Balthasar shakes his head. "I would never dream of dictating affairs of state, Your Majesty. That's not what I mean." He drops his voice. "But your Inquisitor hasn't yet cleared even a tenth of the residents of this island, and she isn't even one hundred percent sure that the ones she has cleared don't mean you harm. No matter how much time is spent and how much digging is done, none of us can ever really peer inside the head of another person. We can't know their true motives."

The tension leaves my shoulders.

"I'm not in charge of security anymore, and no matter what you may fear, I'm not bitter about that. I appreciate that a single person can't do everything. I also believe Edam is competent and capable." Balthasar releases me. "But you need to let him take care of you. No charging off without guards. No unnecessary risks. I barely survived your mother's death. I'm an old man, Chancy. I can't lose you, too."

I bob my head. "Nothing rash, I promise."

"Thank you."

Judica, Edam, Lark, and Larena are all waiting for me right outside the door. It finally occurs to me why Mom never seemed flustered by anything. She was pounced upon daily, hourly even, by one problem after another. Eventually, it's so constant that it hardly suffocates you at all.

And almost nothing surprises me. Not anymore.

"No," I tell Larena. "I don't mind the change to the color schemes. And no, dogs will not be allowed for anyone but ruling monarchs and their heirs. No one else can bring pets of any stripe."

"I absolutely will not allow my guards to be temporarily bumped to twelve. Six is fine," I tell Edam.

"Yes, if you're worried, change the menu to cooked oysters," I tell Lark. "No sense in the weaker bloodlines complaining that the raw oysters were some kind of litmus test to determine worthiness."

After I've resolved all the other issues, only Judica remains. "What?" I lean against my doorframe. I'm frankly surprised Judica waited so patiently. She usually insists I address her first.

"There's been a mix up," she whispers.

"Excuse me?"

She glances around, her eyes pausing on the guards within earshot.

I push through the door and wave her inside. "Come inside." It's not like I need fourteen seconds of privacy, after all. Once the door is closed, I put my hands on my hips. "What's wrong?"

"I think your gown was delivered to my room."

I cross the room to my closet and peek inside. Varvara left my gown in the very front, on a mannequin. The skirt of the stunning Marchesa is made of a cross between crepe and tulle, the gown a stunning mix of cream and pink fabric combined. It cinches at the waist and flowers climb from the bust on the right upward, to the single sleeve on my left shoulder. The flowers vary from a dark burgundy to the palest pink, and there's a similar bunch of flowers on my left hip as well, which perfectly imbalances the one shoulder. To tie it all together, burgundy ties cross in an 'x' over the waist and knot in the back. It draws the eye and offsets what would otherwise have been too much pink.

I turn back to face Judica. "Nope, mine's here."

"The one delivered to my room is. . . pink." Judica's eyes are wide.

"Right," I say.

"Maybe you misheard me." Judica clears her throat and raises her voice. "The dress Varvara left for me is pink, as in a watered down, feminine version of red."

I laugh. "I know it is."

Her eyes widen further, impossibly.

"You hate it."

Her eye twitches.

"That's fine," I say. "I chose it out of deference to Mom, since she couldn't be here, and then I forced them to make a second gown exactly the same as mine—for you." Again, as a nod to Mom, who always wished we would have any desire to match whatsoever. Apparently we still don't.

Judica blinks rapidly.

"But if you'd rather wear something else, it doesn't hurt my feelings."

"You wanted me to match you?" Judica's hands are clenched into fists at her side.

I shake my head. "I don't want to upset you, truly. It's totally fine."

"Is this to confuse anyone who might try to kill you? Are we not telling anyone which of us is which?"

"Huh?" I ask.

"I'm supposed to be your double?"

I laugh. "What's wrong with you? Did your brain go haywire?" I shake my head. "No, look, I'm not trying to use you as a meat shield. Mom and I used to match all the time, but I knew that wasn't really your thing. It was a stupid idea, okay? Forgive me. I should have realized you'd never want that."

Judica inhales quickly and rushes toward me, pulling me against her chest for a hug.

"Oh." My breath catches in my throat.

"Thank you," she says.

"You're my sister," I say. "I love you, and I always will."

"I miss her every day," Judica says into my hair. "But some days, I feel so guilty."

"Why?" I pull back so that I can see her face.

"Because I am so much happier now that she's gone.

Her death." She shudders. "I thought it broke me, but maybe it really just broke the ice around my heart."

"Oh, Judica." I take her hands in mine and squeeze. "I'm so happy that you've found joy, and Mom's just as delighted as me. She's smiling down on us from heaven, and that won't change, even if you don't want to wear pink."

"I do," she says. "I mean I don't but for tonight, I really do."

I wipe away a stray tear and beam at her. "Even better. And listen. I've looked at this from every direction. No matter how I evaluate it, I don't think we need you to agree to Melisania's terms. Control over your choice of spouse just isn't going to be a make or break it deal. So I'm going to refuse that component."

I recognize the light in her eyes. It's hope. "Don't ever feel guilty for finding happiness, not around me."

She steps back and bites her lip.

"Go, get dressed. I'm going to be doing the same."

She bobs her head and shoots out the door.

Varvara arrives less than five minutes later to do my hair. We opt for piling it high, with a few matching flowers interspersed to tie it in with my gown. Finally, she places Mom's favorite tiara into the tumble of curls above my head. Edam's waiting for me outside in a black tux with a burgundy tie. He looks as handsome as always, my heart skipping a beat when I see him. When he lifts his hands and smiles in appreciation at my gown, I notice that topazes wink in his cufflinks.

"Nice touch," I say.

He tosses his head at the ring on my hand. "Not quite the same as the staridium, but at least people will know I tried."

I hold out my hand and he takes it, shifting so that our fingers interlock. "You always try. It's one of the things I adore about you."

"Adore?" Edam quirks one eyebrow.

"I had an idea." I breeze past him and into the hall.

He follows me out and offers me his arm.

"Maybe we should announce a date for our wedding tonight."

Edam stumbles and stops.

I beam. "For next week."

He shakes his head. "Are you serious?"

I shrug. "We need to lock down that ring."

Edam frowns.

I swat his arm. "If you like me, then you really should put a ring on me, after all."

"Excuse me?"

"Never mind. It's just a song. But why wait, right?"

"I guess." He starts walking again.

"You're excited, right?" After the number of times he's told me he can't wait to marry me, I expected a little more joy. "I've been talking to Varvara about dresses. We've got it narrowed down to two."

Edam stops and spins me around until I'm facing him. "I'm not excited, I'm ecstatic. I would marry you tonight. On the beach, on a plane, in the dungeon. I'd marry you in board shorts, or training gear, or a strait jacket." He shakes his head. "I don't care where, and I don't care when. I do, however, care about *why*. I don't like feeling that you've been forced."

"Does it really matter how we got here?"

"I guess not," Edam says.

I decided to dispense with the formal entry and announcement for tonight, since we'll be having a formal dinner with plenty of announcements near the end. Even so, when Edam and I walk through the ballroom doors, conversations halt, heads turn, and everyone already present stares.

"Welcome," I say. "I'm delighted you could all make it."

I scan the room, meeting the eyes of everyone in turn. Lark's moving toward me from the back right, looking more concerned than I had hoped. In the back of the room, I notice Moses, arm in arm with a very beautiful woman. Err, widow. The very beautiful widow whose husband Moses decapitated last week. I'll need to look into that more as soon as possible. I was hoping they could find a way to work together—but I did not expect them to get along quite this well.

As if he can read my thoughts, Moses catches my eye. "We need to talk," he mouths.

I nod. "Soon," I mouth back.

He bobs his head. Hopefully he can't see that I'm dreading the conversation. After all, he wouldn't ask to talk to me about something great, so it's bound to be bad news.

Lark reaches my side. "Chancy," she says. "We may have a problem."

I lift my eyebrows.

"We have over a hundred guests who didn't RSVP, and I only made enough extra food for fifty. Angel's notes suggested that figure."

A food shortage? That's her concern? "Make a few huge pots of macaroni and cheese," I say. "It's delicious, and it's quick, and that'll teach them to be rude."

Her eyes widen.

"And if anyone complains, let them know you did it on *my* orders."

The corner of her mouth twitches.

"And you can be the one to serve it to them. I dare one of them to complain."

Lark smiles. "I wish I could be out here the entire night. You are so spectacular. But in case I miss the big announcement. . ." She leans closer. "Congratulations! Can you even imagine what you'd have said about all this a year ago?"

Even two months ago, I was gushing to Lark about Edam with no real belief I'd ever spend more than five minutes talking to him. "If only we hadn't waded through so much heartache to get here."

Lark's smile slips off. We've both lost our mothers, our paths, and our future. "But we've done alright with what life threw at us. I couldn't be more proud of you." She glances at the masses of people who have milled this direction, all of them eager to chat with me. "I'd better get to the kitchen. It takes a while to boil that much water."

"You've come a long way, too," I say. "I'm positive your mother is bursting with pride up in heaven."

Two hours for mingling before dinner felt excessive to me, but Inara, Larena, and Alora all agreed.

"It won't be nearly enough time," Alora said.

And they were right. I don't have a single second's break —but Alora intervenes about an hour into the pre-dinner block.

"Her Majesty needs to drink something." She gestures for me to follow her toward the edge of the room where there's a drink station.

Edam's debating the merits of a war strategy I've never heard of, but the second I shift away, he stops midsentence. Clearly he's my Chief Security Officer right now, not my fiancé. "You're going?"

I shake my head. "Only right there." I point two dozen feet away, "I'll be back in three minutes."

He eyes me, and then Alora, and then the guards who shift and glance his direction, obnoxiously mirroring my every move. Finally, he nods.

I do not widen or roll my eyes. Too many people are watching.

Alora says, "He's just doing his job. Admirably, in fact."

"I know that, of course, but I swear, everyone acts like

I'm a monstrous weakling, utterly incapable of defending myself from a paper cut."

Alora laughs. "Or they act like you're surrounded by enemies, the subject of a prophecy, and the only individual alive who can prevent utter destruction."

"Sure," I say. "Or that." I order a glass of watermelon juice and wait patiently while two of my guards taste it.

"You don't have to wait as long if you have your dog taste it," Alora says.

I glance down at Duchess, sitting politely by my feet. "Red Bull is too big a mess to behave himself in company," I say. "And if I'm being honest, I haven't been able to use either Mom's dog or mine for tasting."

"Not since Cookie."

I swallow. "I'm sick of other people being punished for me, abused for me, dying for me."

"Life certainly isn't fair," Alora says. "But if you had overheard some of the conversations I just did, you'd realize that people already love that about you. Your subjects feel that you care about them and their well-being. You may be the most beloved ruler Alamecha has ever had."

And if Judica can't find Nereus soon, perhaps the shortest lived as well. "Thanks for the reprieve, but I'd better dive back into the fray," I say.

"Wait," a male voice behind me says.

I spin around.

Moses.

His arms wrap around me and I sink my face against his chest. "I'm so sorry I left you there. I shouldn't have asked that of you, especially since I knew how much you were hurting after Vela—" I choke. So much pain, so much death, so many people gone since I touched that stupid stone. "I should never have put so much on you."

Moses releases me. He sits down in a chair near the wall and pulls one out for me.

Alora touches my arm. "I'll reassure Edam that you'll be back the second you've finished talking."

"Thanks." I take the seat next to Moses. "I have about four options for your replacement. I think we should discuss the pros and cons and select one sometime tomorrow."

Moses frowns.

Oh no. "Or tonight. We can decide tonight, if you need that. I saw Katika with you, and I can only imagine how hard that must be."

"Actually." He sighs. "I can't explain it, but Katika and I have been grieving together."

"Wait, *together*, together?"

Moses' eyes widen. "No, nothing like that. I know it sounds strange, but we both lost a loved one by force, in a way out of our control, but also in part due to our own decisions—our own gambles." He pauses and looks at the wall. "I think she understands how I feel, and why I did what I did. I don't think she blames me. And something about seeing you on the phone, watching what you're capable of, well, she's nearly a zealot, Chancery. I think she'd burn her own hair off before speaking a single word against you."

That's a little horrifying. "Okay, what's wrong then?"

He leans toward me. "Katika had quite a network of individuals who answered to her."

"Okay."

"One of the largest groups that came to her aid when she put together the ill-advised rebellion call themselves the Sons of Gilgamesh."

"Sons of *Gilgamesh?*" I ask. "Like, the Sumerian king?"

"The one who supplicated Utnapishtim, the immortal survivor of the flood, to grant him eternal life."

"Uh, okay."

"This group is big," Moses says. "And they recruit heavily among disenfranchised, banished, or displaced evians of all varieties, pushing purity of bloodlines and the corrupt nature of the leaders."

"In Shenoah?"

Moses grunts. "In all six families, if Katika understood correctly."

The immortal survivor of the flood. And Nereus is the God of the Sea, whom Herakles wrestled in pursuit of knowledge. Coincidence? I clearly need to find out more.

"I wanted to offer myself," Moses says. "I'm Motherless, and I'm far from you, over in Europe. If I intimated that we'd had a falling out, they might approach me. I could try and find out what their goal is, and who their leader is— and their endgame."

It's a brave offer and a kind one. Although I trust Moses to support me to the bitter end, I'm not entirely certain he can handle the stress I've already heaped upon him. I shake my head. "Bringing me the information was enough. I'll work with Marselle to develop an approach. Thank you again."

"And about ruling Shenoah, I know you're worried about me." He sighs. "I totally understand why, but I really do want to help. I think, the rebellion aside, it has been really good for me to have something important to do. It helps me to add value somewhere."

It helps him not to feel worthless, like he suspected he was most of his life. I understand that sentiment all too well.

"I'd like to continue at least in an interim fashion, if it's alright with you. Maybe give me a week before you reevaluate."

"Well."

"I also think your selection of me has been a huge

rallying point for the Motherless and for other evians who have long felt neglected and overlooked. I've had hundreds of other men petition to join the Motherless."

"They want to pledge to you?" I ask.

He barks a laugh. "Not me, no. They want to fight for you. It was bold of you to declare that you'd accept us and that you were changing the world. But you didn't just say it. The very second you had a huge position open, and four sisters nipping at your heels, you gave control of that placement to *your brother*. For the first time in six thousand years, a male is ruling one of the families, even if it is only in your name."

A rallying point? Because I'm doing exactly what I said I would do and treating him as an equal? Are things really that bad? "Alright." I stand up. "We'll reevaluate in a week." I lean closer. "It's not about me wanting to replace you. It's about doing what's best for my brother. I care for you. The world may see the position you're filling as a badge of honor, but I know what it really is—a target on your back and an anvil strapped to your chest."

"I wish I could do more." Moses' hand goes to the hilt of his sword. "But for now, I will do every last thing I can."

That's what worries me.

I cross the room, angling toward Edam. From the corner of my eye, I notice Judica, in her bright pink dress, an exact replica of mine, staring intently at Roman. His dark arm is wrapped around her shoulders. He's telling her something urgently, but it's not making her happy. She shakes his arm off, and her face hardens.

I need to talk to Melisania. I'm sure Judica's preparing to do something noble, and Roman's upset about it. I glance at the clock. Dinner is in fifteen minutes. Not much time to chat with Melisania. I scan the room, finding her in the far back corner. I'll never get all the way over there without it being patently obvious I've trekked over to talk

122

to her. So much for casually bringing something up. It'll devolve immediately into a straight up negotiation.

When I reach Edam's side, I realize who he's talking to —Marde. Melisania's Heir—the heir I'll be displacing with any kind of peace deal.

"—until then, anyway," she says.

Until when?

"Your Majesty." Marde curtsies.

"I'm glad you could come tonight," I say. "Are you having a good time?"

She nods. "I am."

I can't think of a single way to subtly ask her how she feels about her mother's offer. But subtlety has never been my forte. A sledgehammer it is. "Are you upset about the offer your mother made me? To surrender Lenora's sovereignty in exchange for a handful of assurances?"

Marde's eyes widen. "You really are as blunt as they say."

I shrug. "I suppose I never learned to hide what I think and feel successfully. . ."

Her deep brown eyes meet mine. "It's refreshing."

"I displaced my sister. I know it's a difficult thing to endure."

Marde's lips compress.

"I won't even blame you for hating me."

She snorts. "You're easy to hate." Her eyes dart beside me to Edam. "You have the perfect fiancé. The strongest, most impressive family. Your rival fell in behind you—tamed from a feral cat into a domestic one, if what everyone says is true, by your kindness. As if that's not enough, you recently waltzed in and took over another family, just like that. Something that hasn't happened once in thousands of years."

I don't bother arguing.

"But here in person, you're so disarming." Her lips twist.

"If it helps, she didn't want any of it," Edam says.

"Well." I take his hand in mine. "Except perhaps the fiancé."

"I wanted it," Marde says. "I still do, but I'm not deluded. Mother's barely a hundred years old. I won't be her youngest heir, and I was always going to be displaced, barring some horrible catastrophe I would never want. Mother has been a good parent, and she's a good ruler. If you can do even two-thirds of the job that she's done—and you prevent the destruction that's coming, then. . ." She shrugs. "I promise not to hate you forever."

"Fair enough," I say.

"I'm sure that's a huge relief to you," she says.

I bob my head. "It is, actually. It's hard to make enemies everywhere I go just by breathing."

"Mother has been very impressed," Marde says. "It's all I hear about, really."

"I was surprised she brought you," I admit. "Typically the empress and heir don't both attend large events outside of their control."

"Unless the empress no longer needs the heir, because she's about to be replaced, for all intents and purposes, by your twin." Marde shrugs. "And at least I can attend parties, and soon my life will be my own for once, to do what I choose."

It's my opportunity to ask, finally. "How would your mother react if Judica didn't agree to marry a member of your family?"

Marde's eyebrow arches. "Mother spoke to Judica herself and didn't feel that she objected to the idea. Was she wrong?"

I open my mouth, but before I can speak, motion to our left draws my attention. Judica has drawn a sword and it's resting against some guy's throat.

"Uh," I say, "excuse me for a moment."

"I just love your twin," Marde whispers.

I trot across the room, Edam at my side.

"What's, uh, what's going on?" I ask.

Horatio Lenora, Melisania's nephew, swallows slowly. He eases backward, putting half an inch between his throat and Judica's sword.

"Judica." My tone is a little sharper this time, since she hasn't answered me yet.

Her head swivels in my direction, and the end of her sword wavers, nicking Horatio's skin.

"Are you planning to release him? While he's still breathing?" I ask.

"He insulted me," she says.

I lift my eyebrows. "Did he?"

Horatio clears his throat, his eyes so wide they're making mine hurt. "I told her—"

"Hush, you," Judica says.

He gulps.

"Release him," I say firmly.

Judica blinks and looks around, seemingly only just taking in the number of people watching her. She lowers her sword, thankfully.

"We will not be fighting any challenges tonight," I whisper. "Certainly not over some alleged insult."

"He said I looked. . ." She drops her voice. "Lovelier than the most breathtaking flower." Her hiss carries.

Laughter spreads across the room, erupting in small pockets.

"I hardly think that qualifies—"

"He knew I wouldn't want to be compared to a useless—"

I put my hand on her arm. "Put the sword away."

She does, slowly, glaring at everyone around us.

"Do you think there's any chance you're a little overly sensitive, seeing as I'm giving Melisania my answer tonight?

He might have been trying to express interest, or even, horror of horrors, pay you a compliment."

Her lips purse.

"For many women, myself among them, a compliment regarding our appearance isn't an insult. It makes us. . . happy."

"Most women are idiots. I did nothing to obtain the face I have. Saying it's beautiful tells me nothing about who I am. Not to mention that comparing my features to a *flower* makes no sense."

"He did say lovelier than a flower, not similar to a flower — you know what? Never mind." She's even more of a porcupine that usual. "Alright, at least make me this promise."

She cocks one eyebrow.

"No more swords across any more throats tonight. Can you do that, do you think?" I swear, sometimes I feel like I'm tutoring a toddler.

She folds her arms across her chest. "Did you talk to Melisania? Is she going to drop the requirement that I marry her son?"

"I haven't actually—"

"It's fine if she doesn't," Judica says. "Truly."

A jingling bell. Dinner time. Which means my time to prepare Melisania for my partial refusal is gone.

❦ 11 ❧

I glide from the ballroom into the dining hall, my eyes taking in the final product. A dozen long, rectangular tables, each with seats for forty, and all adorned with floral arrangements that complement the blooms on my dress. Pale pink hedge roses drip and trail, with sprays of white, cream, and ivory roses, lilies, and plumeria—and enormous, deep burgundy roses punctuating each arrangement at odd intervals. I walk up the middle of the room, toward the front. None of the long tables have seats on the end, except the thirteenth.

It rests at the very front of the room, and there's a massive throne placed at the head of it. My motto is carved into the back, and the center of the letters has been stained much darker than the rest. *The smallest light still vanquishes darkness.*

I sit on it reluctantly, and Edam sits to my right. Analessa wastes no time settling on my left, her Consort Daniel next to her. I try to think of a single word he's ever said in my presence and can't think of one. Not that he has much chance with Analessa around.

Melisania and her Consort Albert settle just past Edam.

She smiles and inclines her head. "What a beautiful spread, Chancery, and on such short notice. I can hardly wait to taste dinner."

"With Angel unaccounted for and a half-human in the kitchen, I wouldn't get my hopes up," Analessa says.

I wish I could tell Lark to serve her macaroni and cheese. "Human chefs are as good as evian ones," I say. "And possibly much more trustworthy."

"You still haven't caught your mother's killer?" Analessa feigns innocence.

"He or she is proving to be quite adept at subterfuge," I say. "And I'm the first to admit that's not my strength."

"What exactly are your strengths?" Analessa asks. "Other than reacting to staridium rings."

"Being chosen by God, you mean?" Melisania asks.

Analessa clears her throat. "Exactly. I misspoke."

"As her ally, I'd think you'd already have compiled quite a list of her strengths. I certainly did, before I drew up my offer of surrender." Melisania sips her bubbly apple juice.

"Oh?" Analessa asks. "Is that what took you so long?"

Melisania sets the delicate flute on the table. "I don't take bait, as you should know by now. But back to the list you need to hear, it's quite lengthy. After all, she's only been empress for a few weeks, but she has already conquered another family—one that declared war on her. She sparked and then welcomed a flood of powerful refugees, our strongest men in fact. They fled our courts and joined hers—after which they pledged themselves, *sua sponte* I might add, to guard and protect her personally. She has turned whole contingents of my people toward her way of thinking. When I loaded up to leave, my jet flew over hundreds of gathered citizens expressing to me their agreement with her sweeping measures regarding gender and genetic equality via large signs. I've had more missives and calls and visits on the matter than I could possibly share. Your own brother never leaves her side. At a baseline, that level of support and follow through evidences that she's bold, consistent, and has an uncommon level of integrity. I think those are under-valued qualities that have been lacking for quite some time, which is likely why our people are surging forward in support."

"Surging forward?" Analessa meets Melisania's eyes for a moment before she raises her glass and surveys the entire room. Every seat is now filled, every eye turned toward our table. "Quite well said. I propose a toast, to Chancery Alamecha, Queen of Queens, wielder of the stone of Eve. May our alliance never die."

"Speaking of alliances," I say in a much lower tone than the two of them have been using, "I need to speak to Melisania."

"Perfect timing," she says, "since I'm right here, and always eager to speak to you."

"I've given your offer of surrender a lot of thought, and I am willing to agree to every single term—with one modi-fication."

Melisania's face is far too smooth—far too calm.

"My sister Judica has met—"

"Your sister," Judica says, "is prepared to do as Melisania has requested. I agree to spend the requested time in Lenora and to marry one of your sons."

I close my mouth with a click. I glance from where Judica is sitting entirely too stiff in her seat next to Roman, who won't meet my eye. Have they fallen out? What's Judica doing this for?

Melisania bursts out in laughter. "Judica's in love with someone. Judging by her behavior, it's her escort to this very party. Roman, is it?"

"Yes, Your Majesty," Roman says.

"Oh, never mind the titles and formal nonsense."

Melisania narrows her eyes. "You love her, do you? Prickly demeanor, sword swinging and all?"

Roman inhales sharply.

"I'm not insulting her, you understand. Lenora appreciates passion in all forms. But I need you to tell me one way or another. Do you love her?"

Roman clears his throat. "Love feels like an insufficient word to describe what I would sacrifice for Judica Alamecha."

"I just love this more than I can say." Melisania stands up and holds up her hand. "Chancery Divinity Alamecha, if your delightful, horrifying, obstinate twin will agree to spend the same amount of time with me, I'm prepared to hand this ring over, as well as my rule of Lenora. I only wanted to make sure that you weren't passing me over. The last thing I meant to do was create a situation that will foment discord among your family or sour our relationship before it begins. I'll waive that one term, gladly." She removes her ring, the stone darkening to black, and holds it out to me, pinched between her thumb and forefinger.

I glance at Judica. A tear rolls down her cheek, and she doesn't even wipe it away. "Thank you," I say to Melisania. "We won't soon forget your flexibility or your kindness." I reach out and carefully take the ring, not touching the stone. I place it in front of me at the table.

"You won't put it on?" Melisania asks.

"The first time I touched Mom's ring, I set her closet on fire. When I joined these two—" I hold up my hand. "I sheared thirty tons of rock off the back of the island."

Melisania's eyebrows rise.

"I thought I'd wait until after dinner, at least."

She laughs. "That might be for the best." Melisania turns toward Judica. "Well, with as anticlimactic as all this has been, you could at least kiss the boy."

"After all that," Analessa says, "I think we deserve something spectacular."

Judica gulps. Knowing my sister, PDA is far worse than, say, being flung into a pit of vipers. It's probably worse than the threat of execution.

I clear my throat. "It would hardly be appropriate—"

Roman stands up and pulls a box from his pocket. It's far too large to be a ring box. In fact, I'm not sure how it fit in his pocket in the first place. "Judica, my warrior, my friend, your life has changed this year. More than either of us could ever have imagined. Many of those changes have been hard on you."

I'm shocked my twin isn't reaching for her hilt or slamming Roman up against the wall.

Judica's sitting utterly still. Entirely calm. Her eyes fixed on Roman.

"You were always the scariest boss I'd ever had, and the most stunningly beautiful. But when life tossed you against the rocks." Roman shakes his head and swallows. "I can't explain it, really. Somehow, it exposed the iron beneath the iron." He sighs. "I'm not great with words. But I want to tell you how much you dazzle me. You are the singular joy in my life, and I—" He opens the box to reveal a dark tiara, set with onyx stones, and adorned with tiny swords. "I thought a ring would be boring, or maybe remind you of—" He clears his throat.

He really stinks at this.

"I don't know, this just fit. You may not be empress of Alamecha, but you're empress of my heart, and you always will be."

Cheese alert! Oh my goodness, Judica must hate this.

Except Judica isn't squirming and embarrassed, or even angry. No, her eyes are rapt with. . . could it be joy?

She sets the tiara on the table and attacks Roman,

kissing him so fervently that I turn away to give them a modicum of privacy.

Except no one else in the room is looking away.

And Judica and Roman don't seem to care.

"Well," I say. "That was an exciting few moments. Apparently my sister is engaged, and also, Lenora has surrendered. Alamecha is pleased to accept the surrender and delighted to welcome our new ally into the fold. For all intents and purposes, most of the day to day operations won't change, as I will rely on Melisania to manage things much as she always has, with competence, dignity, and care."

And. . . everyone is still staring at my sister, who is making out rather loudly five feet from me.

"Also," I yell, "congratulations to my sister, who is clearly very pleased!"

Judica and Roman spring apart. Her face flushes as I expected it to in the first place. She stands up abruptly. "I've lost my appetite." She spins on her heel and walks out the door. Roman bows to me and follows her out.

So much for looking older and more regal than our age. I wave for Lark to begin, and servers place salads in front of each guest. Roman and Judica return before they've cleared the entrees, and if Judica's hair looks a little messy under her new and somewhat unorthodox onyx tiara, well, everyone seems as pleased about her newfound joy as me.

As soon as dessert is brought, I stand up, ready to make our big announcement. "I want to say again, how happy I am that all of you came to celebrate the joining of Alamecha and Shenoah, as well as the addition of Lenora. It has been a difficult few months for Alamecha, with the loss of our monarch, and my reaction to the ring. I never sought for more power, but sometimes the best things in life are not something you choose on your own." I glance at Edam. I may not have chosen to marry him like this, at this time, on my own, but the thought brings me joy anyway. "So it is with great excitement that I announce—"

Edam stands so abruptly that his chair scrapes across the marble and clatters to the ground.

"What's wrong now?" I whisper.

Edam shakes his head slightly. "All of you will have seen my queen's recent proclamation. As the Queen of Queens who was prophesied, she has begun gathering the families. She will prepare us for what is coming and protect us all from utter destruction. My sister Analessa has offered to surrender to Chancery, but one of her requirements is that Chancery marry me."

Low murmuring doesn't surprise me. If the people gathered didn't already know that, they aren't very well connected.

"However, Chancery Alamecha has no need to accept the offer tendered by Analessa Malessa."

"Excuse me?" Analessa asks.

"She has no authority to bind Malessa at all." Edam crosses his arms. "Because as the youngest child of Senah Malessa, I am the rightful ruler of the entire family. And I surrender to Chancery without condition, without requirement, and without delay. And if Analessa disagrees with my decision, as my Heir, she's welcome to challenge me."

Oh, no.

❧ 12 ☙

Analessa springs to her feet and draws her sword. Her Consort, Daniel, does the same. As do more than a hundred Malessa citizens around the room. Which, of course, prompts all of my allies to stand.

Edam and I are probably the only people in the room without our swords drawn.

"You swore to me," Analessa says, her eyes flashing, her blade shining in the incandescent lights. "You lured me here under false pretenses."

"I didn't," I say. "I'm not going back on my word."

"You aren't?" The wobble in her voice tugs at my heart. "Because my brother has no right to challenge me. I don't recognize it. I flatly refuse to recognize it at all."

"Which is an act of war against me, to refuse my proclamations." What a tangle. She trusted me, and she believes I betrayed her. In her mind, I lured her here only to yank the rug out from under her. "I had no idea Edam intended to say any of that."

"If you don't accept her Royal Majesty's declaration, you don't accept her," Edam says. "You no longer hold the cards here."

I should have invested in a muzzle, but as I didn't, I ignore him. "I was standing up to announce our wedding date," I say.

"I will not be forced into a wedding," Edam roars. "Not when I'm the rightful heir to Mother's throne. An heir you sold, an heir you then went out of your way to turn into a traitor."

No piece of dirty laundry left unaired today, for heaven's sake. "Edam, Analessa, please sit down, both of you."

No one listens to me. Some Queen of Queens I've turned out to be.

A movement to my left catches my eye, but before I have time to do anything about it, someone hurls a dagger at Daniel's throat. Blood gushes from his neck, pouring down the front of his tux. I follow the trajectory to where Noah's seated at the end of the table. "He was about to do the same thing to you." Noah points at Daniel's hand just as it releases its hold on a wickedly jagged dagger.

"Look," I say, "It's not time for—"

But it's too late. The swords were already drawn. I should hardly be surprised when five hundred and fifty gathered warriors begin swinging. I step onto my throne and dip into the new well. I send a pulse through the entire crowd. "Sit down."

Half a dozen of them drop their weapons, and many more cry out. But they all freeze.

"Sit, or I'll graduate to fireballs."

A thousand eyes widen.

"Trust me, you don't want me to do that. Burns are miserable to heal, and these are worse than usual, I hear."

Everyone sits.

"Analessa, am I to understand you don't recognize Edam's claim to your throne?" I ask.

She agrees with me. Colorfully.

"Fine—"

"And there's no chance I'll surrender to you now," she says. "Since I can't trust a word you say."

It pains me, but there's no other way. She won't surrender, she won't fight Edam, any other path leads to a skirmish here, in the palace, a slaughter of my people and hers. "Analessa Malessa, as far as I know, you don't challenge my claim to Alamecha's throne. That means I have a right to challenge you to a duel to the death, monarch to monarch. Should I win, you will rule Alamecha, Shenoah, and Lenora. However."

"If you kill me, you can cut this ring from my finger."

"Even so," I say.

"I won't agree unless you remove that first." She glares at the staridium on my finger.

Melisania makes a choking sound. "You can hardly expect—"

Analessa's face contorts. "I'm a good fighter, but I can't deflect fireballs or kinetic blasts. If she keeps it on, I may as well kill myself now. If I'm doing that, I'll take as many of you as I can with me, thank you very much."

She's too upset to notice her people's heads swiveling toward her. She's losing their support. I could probably press the issue, and they wouldn't fight us long.

But the death toll would still far exceed one. And one is all that's at risk if I fight her. Plus, at a certain point, I either believe God wants me here, or I don't. If He doesn't care, then my life matters no more than any others. If He does, He can do His part to keep me safe. "I agree." I pull the ring from my finger.

Judica and Inara fall in on either side of me.

"Here," I hand my joined staridium to Judica. "And you take this one." I snatch the band of Melisania's ring from the table and hand it to Inara. "Don't stand too close to one another, or anywhere near Malessa's people."

No one else argues with me, not even Edam.

136

"I choose pointed melee weapons," Analessa says quietly.

"What?" I whisper. "What does that mean, pointed melee weapons?"

Judica groans.

"Spears," Inara says, "Or pikes, I suppose. And you also get to choose a shield."

Isn't a pike like fifteen feet long? Why would anyone choose that? Unless she's exceptionally good with them. Or maybe she's chosen this madness because I have no idea what to do with them. When my hand begins to tremble, I still it. No sense in showing anyone else that I've made a tremendous mistake. "I'll go to change now."

Balthasar catches my eye.

"Prepare the arena. I expect a substantial audience."

He meets my eye for a moment, and I can't tear mine away. "Be careful," he mouths. "Please." Then he salutes me and says, "I'll see it done, Your Majesty."

I never knew my dad, but Balthasar is probably the closest thing I've had. An uncle to Inara and Alora, and a dear friend to Mom until the end. I wish I could talk to him briefly, if only to find out whether he has tips. And why can't I? "Actually, belay that order. Edam, you prepare the arena. Balthasar, please accompany me to my room."

His eyebrows draw together, but he nods. Judica and Inara walk on either side of me, and Balthasar follows. Once we've reached my room, I wave everyone inside. "I'll change in the bathroom. But tell me, Balthasar. Anything you can think to tell me about spear fighting." I grab my clothes and duck into the bathroom stall, pulling the door nearly closed.

"It's primarily a weapon used by beginners," Balthasar says. "It develops upper body strength, but it's a stabbing weapon. That means the kill shots are to the—"

"Face," I say, "throat, and groin."

"Right," Balthasar says. "But since you'll have shields—"

"Focus on the head," I say, "because she can't block that and see me at the same time."

"She'll try to disarm you by breaking your spear with her shield," Balthasar says.

"Good to know," I say. "Do you have any recommendations for weapons, or am I going to be stuck using general practice gear?"

"I have a beautiful shield." Inara frowns. "Not, like, a pretty shield. What I mean is, it's lightweight and extremely hard."

"I can substitute a dagger for a shield, can I not?" I walk out of the bathroom, ready to go.

Balthasar shakes his head. "It's permitted, but that's a bad idea. The shield is as important as the spear. Maybe more. The amount of damage a stab from the spear can do is tremendous, and with the length of the spear, you want to force her to try and attack your face."

I also want at least one weapon that I know how to use. "The longest daggers allowed are how long?"

Balthasar smiles now. "That's the Enora in you. Eleven inches is the longest. Any bigger and it's considered a short sword."

"She's accustomed to attacking others with spears and shields. But will she know how to fight against a dagger and spear?" I shrug. "Maybe it'll even the playing field."

Judica's face is tight, her eyes stormy. "This isn't a game. It's not a playing field. It's a *dying* field."

"And you have no idea how badly I wish you could take my place," I say.

"Marry Edam right now," Balthasar says. "He'll destroy his sister."

White hot fury rises inside of me at the thought of marrying him. I shove it away. No time to contemplate my reaction or my avoidance of him, not right now. "I need to do this myself."

"Okay, mini-Enora." Balthasar pulls a long, black metal dagger from his boot. The hilt is two men, both of whom have their hands on the other's throat. "Here, take this. It has served me well for a very long time."

I touch the edge and it slices my finger without a hint of pain, which tells me it's deliciously sharp. "Thank you."

"I have a spear," Judica says. "It's nothing special, but it's weighted well."

"You got it on your fourteenth birthday," I say.

She smiles. "I did. You got your horse, and I got a new spear."

I got a pony, and she got a weapon. And here we are, me fighting to the death for the family throne, and Judica engaged to the man of her dreams. I would never have believed this six months ago.

"I'll meet you all at the arena. Balthasar, go with Judica so no one can jump her and steal that stone."

"Why'd you pass it off so early?" Judica asks.

"It felt like the right move to defuse the impending fight," I say. "Did you see how many people were trying to kill each other?"

"We would have destroyed them." Balthasar doesn't even look smug.

"But how many would have died?" I ask.

"None of them are you," Inara says. "You need to learn that you're valuable. You can't keep acting like a pawn when you're the queen."

"Not you too," I say. "I can't handle more insubordination."

Her smile is crooked. "It's not insubordination when I offer my opinion in private."

She has a point. "Duly noted. And now it's time for me to go. Judica? Go grab that spear double quick."

Streams of citizens clear out of my way as I walk toward the arena. Edam is there, and Noah too. In fact, my entire Council is there, except Balthasar and Judica.

"Are you ready?" Analessa asks.

"Are you sure we need to do this?" I ask. "I already told you that I had no idea Edam would claim that."

"Will you rescind your order that all children, male and female, can inherit?" Analessa asks.

I shake my head. "I'll make it clear that it only applies going forward, as I should have clarified to begin with."

Analessa tilts her head. "I meant to wait to kill you until you'd gathered the other families for me." She sighs heavily. "But I may as well do it now. Taking out two won't be a problem when I control four."

"What about the prophecy?" I ask.

She laughs. "What about it? It could be interpreted a million different ways. Those things have always been useless. Could it be any more vague?"

So she never meant to honor her word. I should have guessed.

I move toward the arena, stopping to examine the spears in the weapons rack. *Hurry up, Judica.* I finally settle on a pale wooden spear with a shiny stainless head when Judica bursts through the back door. She strides toward me, spear clasped in her right hand, the staridium susurrating on her hand. Once she's only a few feet away, she tosses it to me. I swing up and into the arena, spear in one hand, dagger in the other.

"No shield?" Analessa scoffs.

I shrug. "Some of us are more bulletproof than others."

She lifts one eyebrow. "I suppose we'll find out."

Edam jumps onto the side of the ring. I worry Analessa will stab him, but she doesn't. Her lip does curl as though she's smelled rotten eggs. He counts us down and we're off.

Analessa wastes no time stabbing at me, her six-and-a-

140

half foot spear shooting toward my ribs. I deflect it clumsily with the shaft of mine, but it takes a chunk out of the side. Whoops. Analessa circles and jabs again.

I deflect better this time, without weakening my own weapon. I consider what she knows of me—my youth, my inexperience, my reticence to harm others. What's her plan? She probably intends to either eliminate my spear or my dagger or both, and then close in. I inhale through my nose and exhale slowly through my mouth, quieting the chaos around me. The murmurs, the shouts, the shifting, the nervous laughter. The sound of weapons and posturing and threats. The crowd is restless, unhappy, on edge.

None of that matters, not in this moment. Not to me.

I relegate the white noise to the background and I *listen* for Analessa. Not her jabs and her parries, but her emotions. She's walled them off, apparently. She's young, relatively speaking. Two hundred years old, but she's only been ruling for twenty or so years. She exudes confidence like a natural musk, but is it real, or is she posturing? Is she scared?

She will die, or I will. She has to be terrified.

So why can't I see it? I listen for her melody, and finally I begin to make it out. Staccato, sharp, disjointed. But not worried. "You're not afraid of me." I don't bother asking. I can tell, absolutely.

"You can't even control your own people." Analessa smirks. "Melisania called you bold. She said you inspire dedication, but you promised me one thing and your fiancé reneged on your behalf, without your knowledge, much less your permission."

I grit my teeth. "The strength in people lies in their agency, their ability to make choices. When you take that away, you've weakened the world, the family, and the governing body, in that order."

Analessa pulls back. "A body can't survive with fifteen

heads, much less five hundred. Not everyone can rule. And if you try and hold everyone equal, you'll quickly learn that's a fool's attempt as well. No one is *equal*."

"I disagree," I say.

"You're faster. You're smarter. You're *better*." Analessa stabs at me again, but at the last minute she snaps her knee and jabs upward, stabbing me in between my lower ribs and pressing her advantage.

I bring my dagger downward as fast and as hard as I can, taking full advantage of this chance. Balthasar didn't fail me—the dagger blade tears through the spearhead. It doesn't snap it entirely, but it shears a chunk off the edge.

Analessa yanks it back like I dealt her a flesh wound instead of the other way around.

I lift my spear and press on her while she's retreating. She bats me away easily, and I hear it. In the dismissiveness of her gaze, the carelessness of her defense, the relaxed posture of her feet.

She's not afraid of me because she doesn't think I can possibly bring myself to kill her. Even if I am able, she doesn't think I'm *able* to do it.

Maybe she's right. I heal the wound she dealt me quickly, but I can't shake the fear that her confidence has ignited in my chest.

Judica. I spared her, and I have been so grateful that I did it. It was the right call, no matter how wrong it seemed to the world. And then Noah. He betrayed me, but I couldn't force him away. And Melina. And then Adika. The list goes on and on. I've spared them all.

Am I merciful? Or just not strong enough for this kind of life? Does it matter, if I can't do what must be done? If I can't wrest the ring from Analessa's hand, will my mercy mean anything?

Do I even want to kill her?

She won't stay her hand like Judica did. She won't serve

me like Noah or Melina. Like Adika, she wants to end me. Her spear jabs at me, and it's like time slows and warps around me. I've shattered the left side of her spearhead. A huge, jagged chunk is missing, destroying the balance, but it can still slice, maim, and kill.

Like that spearhead, am I flawed? Is there an important chunk of me missing? A burning feeling floods my body, like lava, but lighter, brighter. It strengthens my limbs, it bolsters my resolve, and it eases my horror at the task that lies before me. I would never have killed Analessa, *never,* but it has been forced upon me. I can hate everything about it, but there is no other path. And I can do what it takes, just as the jagged, broken spear can fulfill its task, imperfect or no.

"We may not all have the same skills," I say. "But we all have value. And that's the point." I go on the offensive then, for the first time. My spear jabs, and she parries. But this time, I don't try and press any advantage. Because her harmonic line founders. It's time.

I hurl Balthasar's violent dagger at Analessa as hard as I can, and it flies steady and true.

And lodges in her throat.

It's not a kill shot, but it's a debilitating one. And eerily similar to the shot Noah took at Daniel not half an hour before. I leap across the space that separates her and ram my spear into her shield, twisting and yanking it away from her. I throw it out of the arena, and shove on the handle of my dagger, forcing downward, shoving her to her knees. I grab my dagger, removing it from her throat, watching transfixed while blood spurts from the wound I made.

Before she can begin to heal the damage, I wrest her own, bloody, spear from her hands. It's slick from head to shaft with my blood. Blood she spilled in an attempt to kill me.

"I don't want to do this." I stand over her and raise my

voice. "This is not my way. This is not a triumph. But sometimes, it's better for one person to die than hundreds, thousands, or even millions in a protracted war. So today, I'll do what I must to bring justice and safety to the world."

Analessa's throat is healed, and her eyes flash. But I'm holding her spear, and I don't care what she thinks of me, not anymore.

She doesn't know the first thing about Chancery Alamecha. I flip her spear around and stab it straight down, severing her spine between C7 and T1. I force myself to watch until the light fades from her eyes. I may hate myself forever, and tomorrow, I may not be the same girl who walked into the ballroom tonight, but I can do what is asked of me. No matter how distasteful, no matter how dire. I am not defined by the expectations or dismissiveness of others.

I reach down and yank the staridium ring from her finger. I hold the black stone over her head. "I, Chancery Divinity Alamecha, hereby claim sovereignty of Malessa by right." I look around the arena, but no one meets my eyes, not Noah, not Judica, not Lark or Frederick, not Balthasar, and especially not Edam.

In some ways, although I defeated Analessa, it feels like Chancery Divinity Alamecha died tonight.

❧ 13 ☙

"**A**re you going to put it on?" Someone in the audience asks.

"Yes, put her ring on," another voice urges.

"The ring," someone says loudly.

The ring, the ring, the ring. The onlookers take up the chant quickly. A hunk of rock, a blasted, cursed piece of rock that forced me to kill a radiant daughter of Eve. I hate that prophecy to the marrow of my bones. I hate it for forcing my hand, for warping the world around its procla-mation. I wish Mom had destroyed it before I ever saw it.

Or that Edam hadn't done what he did.

Or that Nereus hadn't killed my mom.

Or that I had been able to talk Analessa into scaling back.

The senselessness of her death washes over me, but instead of cleansing me, I feel filthy. I feel polluted. It makes me furious.

I don't trust myself to speak, so I shake my head instead. It's a simple movement, but they all fall silent.

Between my thumb and forefinger, I'm holding Analessa's ring. A staridium stone passed down from Eve to

Mahalesh, and Mahalesh to her daughter Malessa. And on and on, through Edam's mother Senah.

It was fought over by Senah and her twin, Denah. Hundreds of thousands died during the Hundred Years War because of this stupid rock. I'm gripped with a compelling desire to hurl it as far from me as I possibly can. I *hate* it. These stupid black rocks and Eve's horrible prophecy have ruined every day of my life.

Put the ring on, they say. The gathered crowd wants confirmation that I'm the chosen queen, the one who should be ruling. They want the carnage, the ugliness, the horror to *mean* something. But all I can think about is that utter destruction. A looming threat I know nothing about. I'm entirely unprepared to protect anyone from it, much less everyone. I consider Shenoah. Humans within its control were being executed en masse until I showed them the power of the stones. Evians were being executed for rebellion. The citizens of Shenoah and the leadership were at odds, but my control of the family halted the unrest, at least temporarily.

As much as I dread the spectacle, a display today might prevent similar bloodshed in Malessa now that their leader has also died because of me.

I hold the ring out. "Judica."

Judica jumps into the ring, slipping on the bloody pool expanding around Analessa. She doesn't even acknowledge it's there. Oh, how I wish she had been the one to react to these stupid rocks. But the joined stone barely flickers on her hand.

"Take this." I hand her Analessa's ring.

"But—"

"We want to see—"

"No! Can't you—"

I hold my hand out. "You're all welcome to follow me outside. But you will follow at your own risk. When I

146

added Shenoah's ring to Mom's, the blast was such that many of us were hurled into the ocean." I gesture for Judica to give me Mom's ring back, and she does. I slide it back on my finger with a profound sense of relief. The wells in my head refill, and I'm prepared for any outside attacks again. "I will join these new stones at the far north edge, on Lehua Overlook Beach."

I don't take time to change my clothing—perhaps the image of the blood of their justly defeated monarch will dissuade the people of Malessa from attacking or protesting. I swing down from the raised platform and walk toward the exit, the gathered evians scrambling to clear a path. It could be to avoid bloodstains on their fancy clothing,

But I doubt it.

By the time I reach the door, Judica's walking on one side of me, and Inara has fallen in on the other. She tries to hand me Melisania's ring.

I shake my head. "Not until we reach the far end of the beach. I don't want to risk crumbling the entire palace down around our ears." Balthasar, Edam, Noah, Frederick, Ibrahim, and Gregory all fall in step around me, on top of my assigned six guards.

As if they've heard some kind of whistle the rest of us can't, more Motherless turn corners and evacuate doorways. By the time I exit the palace to the north and begin the path toward the beach, I've accumulated dozens of guards.

And hundreds of other evians are moving toward the beach. Many of them are my own family. Many, many more are not. I recognize nearly every one, including Moses, Marde, Lark, and Marselle. All people I care about. It's no surprise my heart races. My hands tremble, and the angry pulsing of Mom's stone intensifies, as if it can sense my agitation, my anxiety.

Or maybe it merely senses the presence of two more compatriots. Melisania's ring on Inara's finger and Analessa's on Judica's hand both pulse slowly, calmly, reassuringly.

Finally, my feet hit sand, the millions of grains churning underneath me. It's so dark that I can't see Lehua, but I know exactly where it rests. I keep walking until I'm a few feet from the water. I kick off my shoes and proceed until my toes are hit by a wave. I finally stop and turn around. Chains of people walking toward me stretch from where I stand all the way back to the palace. There's no way they'll all be able to see, much less hear.

But they'll be able to tell their children and grandchildren that they were present.

I extend my hand to Judica. She removes the Malessa ring from her finger and holds it toward me. I glance slowly from the left to the right. Then I take it from her hand and slide it onto my left hand. I sense the new power immediately. It's cleaner, somehow, brighter. Like sunshine in liquid form, shimmering in the corner of my mind. I close my eyes and focus on it entirely. I dip into it and inhale, throwing my head back. It feels as though a pulse of menthol shoots through my entire body, cleansing me of exhaustion, residual combat aches, everything.

But nothing else happens.

When I tap into the power and push outward, still nothing. "It's flashing," Judica says.

I shrug. "I can feel it, but it doesn't seem to do anything."

"Maybe move along," Judica says. "Since there's not much to see."

I laugh. "I didn't promise a performance."

"You did say that the last time you blasted everyone into the ocean," Inara says.

"That was a warning," I say.

"Or, for a whole society that has been uniformly taught that there's no magic in the world," Inara says, "it was the promise of a miracle."

I hold out my hand impatiently. "Fine."

Inara bites her lip. For the space between one heartbeat and the next, I worry she'll refuse to return the Lenora ring. But it's just paranoia. She slides it off her finger and drops it into my palm. "I hope you can deliver on your promise."

I lift one eyebrow. "To provide a miracle?"

"To save the world."

Right. Nothing major. Just, you know, everything. And I need to do it without even knowing the source of the threat. An overwhelming urge to slap Inara courses through my entire body. I suppress it, of course. It's not her fault this has been dumped in my lap. It's not even really her demanding this impossible task. She's merely giving voice to the pressure I've felt for weeks and weeks.

I slide the ring on my index finger, glad that Melisania's fingers are thicker than mine so that it fits on a less conventional finger. I close my eyes and wait for the feeling, of a new well of power.

It never comes. But slowly, consistently, the other pulsing spots in my head. . . grow. I slide the ring off.

They immediately shrink back down.

"What's wrong?" Judica asks.

I slide the ring back on and pivot on my heel so that I'm facing toward the water. I squint until I can barely make out the form of Lehua in the distance. It's less than a mile from here, a barren, rocky eruption formed from the dormant Ni'ihau volcano. I gather up the entire contents of my, now larger, first energy well, and I throw my hand outward. Somehow the motion helps me focus.

The fireball that explodes out of my body tears through the sky, flooding the sky with bright red light. It pulses as it courses through the air, and my heart pounds in my chest. In the dark, I didn't aim it very well.

I meant to hit the center of the water in the crescent in front of it.

The enormous fireball slams into the Lehua Rock Light, incinerating it instantly. I shudder at the damage I've done to the gorgeous lava rock island.

But the idea of harnessing this much boosted power to level an attack at an enemy—the disgust I felt at killing Analessa is nothing compared to the recoil I feel at the idea of unleashing this. The damage I could inflict with this is catastrophic. I wonder, not for the first time, whether I might *be* the utter destruction. The world might be better off if someone like me, someone who can use these stones, doesn't exist at all.

I turn around to face the gathered audience. I blink twice, three times, to give my retinas time to heal from the blinding light. Once I open them wide enough, I notice that starting a few rows back, the people gathered in front of me are kneeling. And in another second, the row behind them kneels. In a bizarre, rolling motion, away from me, more and more evians drop to their knees.

"Oh, stand up," I say. "Don't be ridiculous."

None of them respond—they don't even move.

"Stand up!" I tug the Malessa ring from my finger and remove the black dagger I borrowed from Balthasar from my waistband. I hold them up above my head. "The real danger last time came from combining the stones. You need to be standing, eyes on me, prepared for whatever may happen." I drop my hands and pry the stone loose from the simple setting. It pulses where it sits on my palm. The closer I move Analessa's stone toward my larger ring, the more furiously it pulses.

"Like last time," Noah says.

I meet his eyes and nod. "Just like that." When I blew him to kingdom come and he spent hours underwater.

"It's fine," he says. "It won't be exactly the same."

"How do you know?" I ask.

He shrugs. "I don't. But it's hardly helpful to tell you to brace for killing half of us, and we're not standing on a cliff this time, so that's got to help."

I slip the Malessa stone into my pocket. My heart hammers in my chest as I pry out the Lenora stone and slide it into the pocket on the other side of my pants. Finally, I pry the last stone out, the large one. I examine it carefully. It's roughly the size of a large grape, but it's not round, or smooth-sided either. On one edge, there's a jagged line, like the edge of a serrated blade. On another, there's a curve and a dip, like a roller coaster with a lip at the bottom. Across the top, it's totally smooth, like the glass pane of a window.

I pocket it and examine the other two stones, one in each hand. I don't want to join the two new ones first and then combine the two—that would risk two cataclysmic events. Ugh. Maybe I should simply keep them all separate. But as I bring my hands closer, the stones pulse frenetically, and a racing, soaring, limb-tingling feeling surges in my chest.

They must be joined.

Which is when I realize that there's a part on the edge of the Malessa stone, a bump that juts out like the top of a Lego. It would just fit inside a hole on the back of the Lenora stone. And if I did, the two pieces would exactly fit inside the roller coaster curve.

I place each stone carefully on my palm, only a tiny space separating them. With my free hand, I remove the first stone from my pocket. I rotate it until I've located the curve.

And before I have time to contemplate or fret or worry, I shove them all together.

This time, unlike the last, no pulse erupts. No one is sent flying to the ground. But I feel something, a pounding that begins at the base of my skull. Careful to maintain my grip on the stone, I grab the back of my head with both hands and fold inward.

"What's wrong?" Judica asks.

"Are you in pain?" Inara asks.

"What's going on?" Noah asks.

Before I can answer, it's like the wells inside of my head explode, power spraying all over the inside of my brain. My arms begin to shake, and then my legs. I can't explode anyone, I can't sheer off chunks of the island, so I send the power down, down, down. I funnel it all, as deep as I can. So many people around me, so much danger. I must keep them safe.

And I can't drop the stone.

Even when I curl up on my side, my arms gathered around my knees, the stone remains clasped in my hands. But from the side of my body, I feel it. A thrumming, underneath me. Underneath us all.

I freeze. "Can you feel that?"

Inara, Judica, Alora, they all crouch down by my side.

"Feel what?" Edam asks.

"It's beneath us." My eyes widen, and the pain dissipates, the power wells forming again, but larger this time, larger even than they were when I was simply wearing the Lenora stone. The first well is connected to the fireball/EMP power from Mom's stone. The next well is the kinetic power I haven't used much, from the Shenoah stone. And the third is . . . I don't know what. Four stones, and only three wells of power.

But bigger ones. Maybe the Lenora stone boosts the others somehow.

I shake my head and shove to my feet, the stone still firmly clutched in my right hand.

A rumble high above and behind us all, followed by a sound like a hundred tree trunks snapping, forces everyone's head around behind them.

Toward Mount Pānī'au.

A bright red flash, followed by a plume of black smoke has me sprinting toward the palace, which stands between us and the newly active shield volcano. As they did after the challenge with Analessa ended, evians melt out of my way. Edam and Noah and Balthasar vie with Frederick, Gregory, and Moses for a position at my side.

I don't pay any attention to that.

I have to keep this volcano from wiping out the palace, and all the people inside. I'm nearly to the palace when a plume of smoke explodes from the top, followed by a red streak of lava pouring down the side of the mountain. It's not directly headed for the palace, but far too close for comfort. Instead of ducking inside, I circle around the west end and head for the mountain itself.

Strong hands grab my forearms. "We should be evacuating," Edam says, his voice low and urgent.

"I have to shift this flow." I yank one arm out of Edam's grip.

"With what, princess? A few fireballs?" Noah's skepticism stings. Because of all people, he has always supported me.

I shake my head. "This is happening because of this." I shake the staridium lump in my hand. "And it's going to stop it, too, just like I used it to save Noah before." I wrench my other arm free and stumble forward, toward the lava.

Balthasar clears his throat. "I hate to argue, especially in light of your extreme confidence, but what if you're wrong?

You'll have placed yourself right next to a threat from which we cannot protect you."

"Balthasar trained me by forcing me to walk on hot coals." Judica bumps my side as she passes me. "I'll walk with you as far as I think we can safely go, and I'll haul your stubborn butt back if you try to go further."

I gulp. "Fine." This time when Judica and I begin jogging toward the mountain, no one stops us. And in spite of their complaints, Noah, Edam, Balthasar, and Frederick accompany me. "No." I stop and point at Edam, Frederick, and Balthasar. "You three need to manage the chaos back at the palace. Help the visitors to leave, and help the residents to get on boats, if they'd like, or at least to relocate toward the water." I brace myself to argue the point, all the while lamenting the forward progress of the lava.

But they merely salute, spin on their heels and jog back toward the palace.

Judica and I run until we've reached the base of the mountain. My lungs burn as I inhale smoke and ash. Judica stops, and I follow suit. "No closer." She coughs.

I nod.

"What's the plan, exactly?" she asks.

I shake my head.

"You have no plan?" Her eyebrows climb.

"Not per se," I say. "But I have telekinetic powers and a fire ability, sort of. And I caused this. There must be a way to fix it."

"I'm not trying to be argumentative, but I don't think you really caused it," Noah says. "I mean, your joining of the stones set it off, maybe, like the reunion had a power signature that triggered this reaction, but I'm not sure—"

"Shut up," Judica and I say at the same time.

Noah's mouth snaps shut.

I squint and peer as well as I can past the smoke, and ignore the heat rolling toward us in waves. I probably can't do anything about the eruption, but if I can redirect the lava flow to make sure it doesn't head our way. . .

I focus on the top of Mount Pānī'au and try to sense the flow. Nothing. I focus on the crater that has opened up in the earth, on top of the domed volcano. Noah said that the pressure from the formation of the joining of the stones had to go somewhere. Like the power from the ring went somewhere... and I think about it. He might not be wrong.

But it might still be my fault. Because last time I fired that energy off, in the same way I used the telekinetic force in that second bucket, it flung half the cliff face into the ocean, and my friends along with it.

This time, in my fear, in my desire to protect the gathered crowd, I funneled it downward, into the heart of the earth. And now all that power, that force, that roiling energy had nowhere to go but into the core, powering it upward, along the path of least resistance, where there had already been eruptions in the past, eruptions that created this very island—Mount Pānī'au.

I groan. "My fireballs won't help."

A stream of lava shifts and turns toward the palace. I dip into the Shenoah well and pull hard. My heart skips a beat, and then another.

"Stop," Noah says.

"Why?" I ask. "What else can I do?"

He clenches his fists. "I don't know, but I can't believe this power is just floating around in the air. And I know it's not coming from those inert rocks."

My eyes widen. "You still think it's coming from *me*?"

He shrugs. "Maybe."

He's worried that somehow I'm putting myself at risk. The lava streams downward, popping, melting, boiling. No matter where it's coming from, the staridium power is our only hope. I pull on every single drop of that power and shove it toward the stream of lava, pushing it away from us and out toward the ocean.

And it works. As the stream pops and jounces and sears its way down, an invisible wall shifts it slowly sideways until it joins the other flow, the one that's already steaming and hissing its way into the ocean.

I gulp.

"And now what?" Noah asks. "You're going to stand here forever, shoving any lava that might hit the palace into the ocean?"

"Yes," I say. "If I have to, I will."

Noah shakes his head. "It's only a building, princess. Evacuate."

I inhale and exhale, my breath jerky.

"He's right," Judica says.

"No," I shout. "He's not! He doesn't understand."

Judica touches my hand. "But I do." Her eyes are wide, filled with tears.

It's our *home*. A sob wracks my chest. "Every single memory I have of Mom—" I shake my head. "So I'll stand here. And I'll do whatever I have to do, because it's not just a building. It's my only home."

Noah's arms wrap around me. "I understand."

He doesn't argue with me anymore, but he does bolster me with the strength of his arms. I shift another stream of lava, this one much harder to move than the last. And when a third streams our direction, my hand shakes. The well is only half full from the last big push. I'll need to wait momentarily. I let the lava flow a little further down than I have in the past, but it's not too near us, not yet.

A huge eland screams and bounds our direction from the bush above and to our left. It barely reaches us before it collapses, one leg and the side of its body melted. Mom never should have brought all of the exotic animals to the island a few years before I was born, but they have thrived, and here we are.

I looked into Analessa's eyes and ended her life. But this, I can't stomach this. Not now, maybe not ever. The smell rolls over me then and I curl inward, my right hand clenching around the stone, my left collapsing into a tight fist. What good is having all this power if I can't halt the destruction right in front of my eyes?

I've never felt more powerless, not since I watched my mom's still body, unable to do a single thing to help. Powerless to heal, to repair, or to turn back the clock.

But a pulse in my head beckons to me, as if that useless well that did nothing actually does something. I plunge into it, and shove the power toward the eland. And faster than an evian could heal, the burns recede. New flesh replaces the burned, charred, stinking mess, and hair grows on top of that. The eland scrabbles against the rocky ground for a moment and then shoves itself upright.

It looks at me for a brief moment, and I almost see recognition in its eyes before it bounds away. Toward the palace.

"It's a healing power?" Judica asks. "The first ring? The one that did nothing?"

I shake my head. "It's not healing." I struggle to explain. "Healing is something I can do with it, but it's not what it does, not precisely. As an evian, I can already push on parts of my body and they repair. This was. . . different."

"Because you can heal other things," Judica says. "That would feel different."

"It's not that," I say. "Or I don't think it is."

Before I can stop her, Judica removes a knife from her thigh sheath and slashes her arm. "Try."

Oh my word. She really is only half sane. I focus on her forearm and scoop a bit of power. I salve it over her arm, and the wound closes. Faster even than she could have healed it.

"See?" She lifts one eyebrow.

"It's more than that," I say. "It's like I'm setting things right again, broken things, damaged things." And that thought hits me like a sprinting eland to the face. Setting things right. Like a huge, uncontrolled bolt of energy that has unsettled the earth's core. A power blast I should have sent outward, toward the ocean, or upward into the sky. A bolt I caused to destroy the integrity of the earth's core in my ignorance.

I set my feet and swallow.

"No." Noah's eyes flash. He shakes his head vehemently. "You don't know if it will work, and you could hurt yourself badly. Don't do this. You can build a new home, anywhere. You can buy time to allow them to remove your most precious possessions—but let this play out on its own."

How does he always know what I'm planning before I plan it? "I stopped the missiles. You supported me then. I defeated Adika."

"I was always there to help," he says. "But I can't do anything for this. If you released enough energy to cause a *volcano*, how are you ever going to set that right? And who's to say it won't just shift, causing something worse, somewhere we can't just leave?"

I gulp.

Mom, lecturing me over a bite of eggs. Mom, patting the sofa next to her. Mom, brushing my hair. Brandishing a sword. Cutting me a slice of cake. Tossing her head back and laughing. I'll never see her again. I'll never touch her arm or hear her voice. But I won't just flee from the home she made for me. I won't just throw in the towel on saving our island.

"I have to try," I whisper.

A tear rolls down Noah's cheek. "Promise me that if it's

too much, you'll stop. You'll let me carry you off this island and evacuate."

I bite my lip. It won't be too much.

"Promise," Judica demands.

"Fine." I turn toward the point of Mount Pānī'au. I pull on the well, the much larger well thanks to Melisania's stone—the booster. And I let the well refill while I hold all that power in my mind, my eyes watering, my mouth dry, and I pull again, draining it down to the very last drop, and I focus on the center of the volcano. I focus on removing the anger, the heat, the fury that I funneled downward. I must cool the livid core.

It works. Somehow, I absorb the heat, I consume the fury, and the volcanic activity recedes. It's almost enough. I just need a little bit more. I pull the last tiny bit, the dredges at the bottom of that well of power, and smooth them over the wound in the surface of the earth, and the world blinks out.

🦋 14 🦋

There's a machine beeping next to me when I wake. I blink against the light, adjusting slowly. Why is it so bright in here?

"Hello?"

"Chancery," Inara says. "Thank goodness."

I clear my throat. Everything about me feels fuzzy. "What happened?"

"You used that—" Inara points at the rock still clutched in my hand. "And you singlehandedly sent a volcano dormant."

"I never let it go?" My eyebrows ache.

Inara laughs. "Even unconscious you had such a death grip on that rock that we decided to let you hang on to it. Here, let me tell Job and Judica that you're awake."

I grab at her with my free arm, catching nothing but air.

"What?" She smiles at me.

"It stopped? Really? No more lava?"

Her smile grows until it's practically brighter than the overhead fluorescent lights. "You were absolutely unbeliev-able. I think you can rest easy knowing that no one else will be attacking us any time soon. Or at least, *I* wouldn't pick a fight with a supernova."

"Judica and Noah are both fine?"

Inara's eyebrow cocks. "Both fine, yes. And you appear to have recovered, too, but I'll feel better once Job can confirm that."

I sink back against the pillows. "Right, of course. Sure."

My big sister brushes my hair from my face and leaves the room. I glance around and realize the beeping is coming from a machine, and a tube is going from my arm to the machine. Like when Job put me into a coma. I yank the tube out and watch as my skin heals up immediately.

Good to know I still heal, at least.

Two hundred people burst through the door, all of them talking. Or maybe it only feels like that many. Eight or ten pour through, at least, surrounding my bed. My poor, tired brain struggles to make sense of them while they're all talking over one another.

"Chancery, you're awake," Edam says.

"You went way too far," Noah says.

"That was the most amazing thing I've ever seen," Judica says.

"Mom would be so upset with you, passing out like that," Alora says. "You need to be more careful."

"Now step back and let me examine her." Job grunts.

"I haven't even seen her, what with you lot crowding around." Balthasar shoves Edam to the right and Noah to the left and pushes through.

"Does she look alright?" Frederick asks.

"And at what point will I be allowed close enough to her Royal Fanciness to give her a hug?" Lark bounces on her toes, her face appearing over the back of Alora's and then disappearing in alternating fashion.

I laugh. "At least no one is upset I'm awake."

"Quite the contrary." Edam leans against the side of my bed, taking my free hand in his.

Job circles around and lifts my arm up. "Push against me." He shoves my arm down, and I resist. "A little weak, perhaps, but I imagine a few solid meals and she'll be as good as new. I see that you've already liberated yourself from the bonds of the nutrition replenishing IV." His eyes berate me, but I don't care.

I force myself upward and stretch, dislodging Edam's hand in the process. The hurt in his eyes stings, but I don't take his hand back, not here, not now. "I think I'll rest better in my own room." I swing my legs over the bed, noticing the dark brownish-maroon stains on my pants and shirt. Killing Analessa feels like something that happened a week ago. "How long was I out?"

Job glances at the clock. "Three hours? Three and a half?"

The middle of the night, and I'm so hungry I could eat an entire eland. I lean around Alora until I see Lark. "Can you bring something to my room?"

She nods. "Anything. I'm just so happy you're alive."

My internal monologue triggers the memory, and the smell of the burning eland flesh turns my stomach. "I want carbs, lots and lots of carbs."

Lark jogs toward the door. "That I can handle."

Everyone fusses and fusses, but finally I escape. I'm opening my bedroom door when Edam catches up.

"Can I talk to you?" His eyes meet mine, his soulful eyes, the eyes that I hoped would look at me exactly like this for years.

I nod.

He follows me into my room. "I'm sorry." The words burst out of him before the door has even closed.

I shake my head. "I don't want to talk about this right now."

"I know you're tired. I'll wait. But when you're ready to talk, so am I. I just needed to tell you that I'm sorry."

Words. He's offering me words. "I *killed* her, Edam. I stabbed her with a spear. I ended her life, and watched the light leave her eyes." I hurl the staridium across the room and it thunks against the carpet. "You did that to me, and it changed me. It hurt me. It was so senseless, so unnecessary."

"I know. If I could take it back, if I could undo it—"

"But you can't. There are no take-backs in life. You know that as well as anyone. You saw my mom die, and you lost your mom. Things can't be undone, and you didn't even talk to me about it beforehand."

He squares his shoulders, but his eyes are broken, shattered beyond repair.

"What?" I ask. "What did you think, what did you *hope* would happen? Because if you think that it's fine with me that you didn't mention your plan, that you hatched this plot to, I don't know, wrench Malessa from Analessa's control." I tighten my hands into fists. "Did you hate not having your own title? Do you want power that badly?"

Edam stares at the ceiling. "Do you not know me at all?"

"I guess not," I say. "Not if you'd burn down everything we had, just to. . . I don't even know!"

"You." He chokes. "You are the only thing I have ever cared about, ever since I got to know you well enough to realize—"

"How did that have anything to do with me?"

"It had everything to do with you!" He walks toward me and then stops short. "You were *forced* to marry me. You would have done it to save a single person, with as kind as you are, but to spare a war? You couldn't have done anything different than what you did. I may as well have marched you to the altar with a knife to your throat. You've

163

always done everything in your life to save other people, but this isn't such an easy thing. And then the window opened. Your proclamation, it set the world right, and I realized that you shouldn't have to marry me just to have what I would freely give you, what I should already have had."

"I loved you," I say.

"Loved?" Edam swallows and turns around slowly. He starts toward the door.

"Stop," I say.

He freezes, but he doesn't turn.

"I am angry, Edam. Furious doesn't begin to describe it. Knowing what you know about me, you set events in motion that forced me to *murder* someone. Someone who was voluntarily giving me everything I needed already. Someone respected by her people. Someone whose countries were completely settled. And now there will be rebellions and recrimination and hatred. Every single time I close my eyes, I'll see her, proud, an ally, a strong, capable leader. Lying on the ground." I close my eyes, the vision playing behind my eyelids even now.

Edam doesn't mention that she meant to betray me. He doesn't defend himself at all. And I find that my anger isn't muted by reason, by logic, or even by his lack of response.

"I ended her life. I speared her, severing her spine. I can never erase that memory, thanks to my perfect evian recall. I can't surgically remove it, and even if I could, I wouldn't. The hatred I feel for myself, the disgust, the fear of who I've become, it's all earned. I did it. I own it. I *am* transformed."

"I am sorry," Edam says softly.

"What?" I ask.

He turns around, eyebrows furrowed, lips parted.

"What did you think would happen?" I ask. "What was your best-case scenario?"

"I thought I would fight her," he says. "I thought that I would be the one murdering her, and for me, that's nothing new. That's already who I am. I've killed, often, and exceedingly well."

And that's when I realize that we have more problems than I even knew. "Killing her changed me, Edam."

"I know it did," Edam says. "And I know that's my fault. I didn't mean to hurt you or change you—I meant to spare you. I loved you before, and I love you still. But I wonder whether you see the real me. Because killing my own sister wouldn't have kept me up at night." He closes his eyes. "You're so good, so light, so *you*." He opens them again. "I've never deserved you, but I think now you see that too. So I won't argue with you or try to convince you. And I'll be who I am, a weapon at your side, a shield before you, a dagger in the heart of your enemies. And if that's all I am, I can live with that. I just hope that one day you can forgive me. It wasn't my plan to burn *us* to the ground." Edam's eyes well with unshed tears. "If you only believe one thing I say, let it be this. I couldn't start a life with you on a foundation built from brokered deals and peace treaties. If you marry me, I want you to do it because you can't imagine being with anyone else, because you see who I am and you still love me for it."

I don't try to stop him when he leaves.

My heart aches from the effort of being still, but when Lark arrives with a mountain of muffins, I collapse into sobbing. She doesn't ask me a single question, because she understands. She pats my back, and then she sits with me while I consume my weight in baked goods. Eventually I collapse against the pile of pillows on my bed. "Today felt like a hundred days crammed into the skin of one day."

"You're such a poet," Lark says.

I lob a pillow at her. "Poets are overrated. I prefer clarity."

"Oh?"

"Like, for instance, if I were writing a prophecy, there would be no Chosen this, Eldest that."

Lark smirks. "What would you write?"

"I'd say, "Four thousand and two years after I die, a year being three hundred and sixty-five days, a girl named Chancery Divinity Alamecha will be born. Her mom will love her so much upon sight that she'll decide not to kill her after all. And then this rock her mom has will set off a fire when she touches it, and she will be tasked to take all the stones from the other greedy rulers. If she doesn't, ants will turn against humans and destroy them on the winter solstice in the year 2020."

"Ants?" Lark laughs. "That's the best you've got?"

"What do you think?"

"Solar flare, nuclear bomb, famine, and now I suppose volcano too. Also, maybe dragons."

"Dragons?" I ask. "Seriously?"

"It's more likely than swarms of killer ants."

"We actually *have* ants on Earth," I say. "Geez."

"I know we do, because I step on them out there in your courtyard. In fact, I had to squish a bunch that have built a huge pile near that really long root under the banyan tree. You know, the one in your mom's courtyard." She grimaces. "Or, I guess it's your courtyard now."

The banyan tree above the bunker. The bunker Mom showed me—that I almost forgot about, or more likely, that I blocked. I bolt upright. "Oh no, the bunker."

"The what?" Lark asks.

"It's this underground safe house Mom had built. Only me and her, and I think maybe Judica, have access to it. I'm hoping the volcano didn't damage it."

Lark frowns. "It didn't even reach the palace."

But the ground trembled. I felt it. A few good shakes

and that entire thing might have cracked. I should check it out, seeing as I'm almost the only one who can.

Like an arrow to the eye, it hits me. "Melina."

"Excuse me?" Lark asks.

I shake my head. "Judica thought all along that Melina set the entire thing up. She believes that Melina killed her own people, had her wife drag her out, and then pinned it on Nereus so that she could hide here on the island and move around unchecked. I discounted the entire theory, because where on earth could Melina hide on this tiny island that we wouldn't find? She couldn't escape and there's nowhere else." I swallow slowly. "And we found her girlfriend's sweatshirt, and I assume any day we'll have confirmation that Aline was eaten by tiger sharks."

Lark stands up. "But you think that maybe Melina had access to this underground hideout?"

The hair on my arms rises. "I don't know. Maybe. It was keyed to take Mom's Heir. Would she have changed it, after Melina left?"

Lark frowns. "Well, in the morning—"

I leap up and cross the room toward my back courtyard. "I won't be able to sleep." And it's not like I can call Edam back to help me. He's not my security blanket, not anymore.

"Oh," Lark says. "You're going now?"

I turn around. "Should I not?"

She shivers. "No, I mean, that's great."

I lift one eyebrow. "What?"

She offers a half smile. "It's just. . ."

"Yeah?"

She gulps. "It's really dark. You're going down into a hole in the ground? In the early morning?" She shivers again.

I laugh. "Oh please, you big baby."

"At least take that." She points at the staridium where it

lies on the carpet in the corner. "I mean, and a sword or whatever. Just in case."

"Large spiders?" I ask.

She frowns. "You haven't been down there in how long?"

I shrug. Since before Mom died. I recall my last memory in there—working with Mom to master my ability with her stone. "It's fine. Honestly."

"You suspect your sister might have murdered her own people and may be hiding down there," she says. "That sounds fine."

I laugh. "It's more of a conspiracy theory. I mean, if Aline is dead, then Melina probably is, too. Nereus probably removed her, tortured her and—" I choke up. I've been thinking this, of course, but admitting it aloud. . . I close my eyes. "It's more like I'm hoping she's in the bunker."

"But if she is, then she's a sadistic murderer."

Lark's right.

"Maybe I better come with you just in case," she says. "Unless you don't want a half-human defender. I can call your guards."

If it's dangerous, and if Lark was injured. I can't deal with losing her. "You have to work again soon, right? It's. . ." I glance at the clock. "Nearly four in the morning."

She rubs her eyes.

"I'll take guards with me, I promise." I squeeze her hand. "But it has nothing to do with my faith in you and everything to do with your work schedule and the likelihood that I'm being paranoid."

She sighs. "The more you do, the closer you get to uniting the stones, the more dangerous things become. Can you feel it? Like there's an ax dangling over our heads just waiting to drop?"

I know exactly what she's feeling.

"I was kidding about the tsunami, solar flare, nuclear

bomb thing, but Chancery, something is coming. If we just knew what it was, I would feel better."

I think about Moses' intel on Gilgamesh—that might give us more information on what's coming. If they have any idea. But who to send? Someone I trust, but someone who they would believe could stand against me.

It hits me then. The perfect person. "Lark, before you go to bed, can you ask Edam to come to my room?"

"Uh, sure?"

I ignore the question in her tone. Not enough time to unpack that baggage right now. I'll completely break down again. "Thanks."

She's not gone five minutes before there's a knock at my door.

I swing it open. Edam's gorgeous face is filled with hope. Like I've decided in the space of an hour to forgive him. Ugh, maybe calling him here was a mistake. "Come in."

He does, although clearly that wasn't the reception he was hoping to receive. Watching the guarded look steal over his features stings.

"I have a favor to ask."

"Anything," he says.

"I can't." I swallow and start over. "I may not understand."

"I meant it when I said anything," Edam says. "You don't need to be nervous. If your favor is 'slit your throat so I won't hurt every time I look at you,' I'll do it."

Okay. This isn't helping. I turn and look out the window. Maybe if I can't see him. . . "I need you to act like you're angry with me. Like you're upset at our breakup."

"Our breakup."

My heart shudders. Our breakup. Is that what this is? "I don't know what I want right now," I say. "But I need this to be a breakup, and I need you to put out feelers for a group. It's working against me, or at least, it helped organize the rebellion in Shenoah. It's apparently present in every family—mostly from people who support the purity of the evian line. They call themselves the Sons of Gilgamesh." I spin around.

Edam's eyes are wide, his shoulders slumped. "I'd rather slit my throat," he says, "than act like I hate you."

Ah, Edam. "I know."

His mouth turns downward, like he's tasting something terrible. "But I'll do it."

"Thank you," I say. "My biggest problem right now, other than Shamecha and Adora, is figuring out exactly what the prophecy is predicting will happen. I'm hoping that digging into this insurgent group might help me figure that out."

"I need your permission."

I shrug. "For what?"

"If I find the leader, and they mean you harm, I'll eliminate them. All of them."

I inhale. "Edam, that's not safe. You can't go in and try to destroy an entire multi-family group of rebels."

"Why?"

I step closer, drawn to him like a magnet pulled toward iron. "It sounds, I don't know, kamikaze."

He lifts his eyebrows as if to say, 'so what?'

"I can't have this discussion with you right now," I say.

"So I don't have your permission?" He sighs. "To eliminate your enemies?"

"No, because it puts you at risk."

His smile is sunrise after the darkest night. It's the first breath of oxygen after a near drowning. "You do still care, even if it's just a little."

"I care so much it might crack me open," I whisper.

A muscle works in his jaw, and his hand reaches toward my face.

If he touches me, I'll crumple. I'll disintegrate.

But before his fingers brush my skin, he drops his hand. "I'll do anything you ask, Your Majesty. Now, forever."

"Maybe a little less on the pledges and devotion," I say. "Since you hate me."

"I'm not sure how convincing I'll be." He steps backward. "But I'll try."

"Stick to grunts and scowls," I say. "I imagine you'll be alright. Less is more. A simple complaint here, a grumble there."

"Why do you think they'll approach me?" he asks.

"You're in charge of my entire security team," I say. "If they really are working against me, they'd be stupid not to snatch up the bait."

He nods. "I will miss you."

"You'll still see me every day," I say.

"It won't be the same."

He's right. "I'll miss you, too."

After he leaves, it feels like a good time to shower, and once I'm clean, I feel more than ready to walk down into the darkest depths of the earth. It matches the state of my heart. I grab the staridium hunk and pocket it. I don't grab my sword, but I do strap on a thigh dagger. Then I sneak through the back door of my courtyard.

Of course, there are two guards stationed there, guards I told Lark I would bring with me. I swear under my breath.

"I'll be here in my courtyard," I say. "No reason to be alarmed."

Linus looks at Giorgio.

"Just follow me." I purse my lips. "And keep anything you see quiet." At least Judica cleared them both a few days ago.

They both follow me without a single word of complaint. I approach the banyan tree, its roots a tangle of spaghetti noodles. Viney limbs dangle from the canopy. I shift the large rock that covers the keypad as quietly as I can, and then key in Mom's password. Once the door slides out of the way, I motion for the guards to follow and climb down the steep ladder to face the main entry screen.

After a retinal scan and a password reentry, I access the main security profile. Only two users are currently validated. Enora and me.

I should delete Mom's access. After all, she hardly needs it. My finger hovers over the 'remove user' button, but I can't bring myself to do it. I close it out and enter the bunker, leaving the door cracked.

"If you hear me shout, if you hear anything at all," I say, "come after me."

Both guards nod.

I walk on, unspeakably depressed that the only other person who could enter will never breach my safe space. In fact, in light of that, the bunker doesn't feel very safe at all. Because what brings me joy, peace, and comfort can't be found in a hole in the ground. Being alive isn't the same thing as living.

I walk inside quietly, slowly. The lights click on, their fluorescent hum at once unnerving and reassuring. It sounds just as it did before. When Mom brought me here.

"Melina?" I call out, just for kicks. "Are you down here? Hiding out? Plotting and scheming? Are you a murderous villain?"

I've rarely felt as ridiculous as I do right now, calling for my probably dead sister in a hole in the ground. A place no one else can even enter. I sit down on a chair in the entry way and open up all my senses. I can't hear any heartbeats. I can't sense anyone else. And nothing looks cracked, damaged, or destroyed in any way. Utterly undisturbed by the drama from earlier.

I turn to leave, noticing the pile of discarded devices.

Two flip phones and an iPod. Mom and I brought them here and worked with them, trying to hone my ability to destroy only targeted electronics. Working to perfect my abilities—because Mom believed I was destined for greatness.

And now I've killed two empresses and made one single ally. I've flooded Alamecha with refugees. And it seems inevitable that we'll be at war with Adora and Shamecha soon.

"Oh, Mom. Why?" Tears flood my cheeks, hot and fast. "Why did God want me? Literally anyone else would be better. You would have done a fine job. Judica, even Melina, who was taken right from under my idiotic, blind nose." I shake my head, tears dropping onto my shirt. "I'm not a warrior. I'm not a brilliant strategist. I'm a bumbling idiot, feeling my way around with guesswork and hunches. I alternate between wanting to hide down here in a hole and run away forever. I spent a week after you died imagining I might never return. And today, I created a *volcano*, because I have absolutely no idea what I'm doing."

But Mom doesn't have any advice for me. No one does, not really. So after a good long cry, I dry my tears and I exit, sealing the door closed behind me. And then I climb up the ladder and reposition the rock. I thank my guards.

And finally, I go to sleep for the night just as the sun begins to rise, alone, scared, and entirely unqueenly in every way.

❧ 15 ❧

If Mom had died the way she should have, from old age, with advance notice, after telling me goodbye, I can imagine what she'd have tasked me to do.

"Start at the back of the library," she'd have told me. "Work your way forward. That way you'll learn the history of our people, the true history, right from our ancestor's mouths, or hands as it were, yourself."

I'd have done it too.

I walk down the aisle between the rows and rows and rows of books. I'm only six generations removed from Eve herself, and as the first family, even Eve's writings, the originals, are here. Although, technically, they're copies of copies at this point. But we *had* the originals, before they disintegrated from age. I slide out one of the slimmest tomes from that early period. The words are in Adamic, but I translate them into English easily. Translating into Adamic from English and back again was one of my earliest lessons as a child.

The role of mother seems insignificant, in so many instances, compared to the other tasks set before us. Giving birth to a child is messy, unglamorous and in many instances, also tedious. Beyond that, all of my children replicate it without much effort.

And yet, doing it properly, raising children with a balance of discipline and love—it's a mixture of science and art.

Oh how I wish I had learned better, faster, and without the need to experiment on my own. I've made a right mess of things, and I'm not sure any of it can be undone. It's so hard to remake a thing once it's already been made. Impossible, really.

I snap the book closed. I'm not here to pretend that Mom died in the ordinary course. I'm not here to peruse the wealth of knowledge at my fingertips, or philosophize about parenting and discipline. Even the thought of raising a child makes me shiver with unease. I have no idea what it takes to be a good parent. My mother had all this knowledge and even she managed to pit Judica and me against one another and banish our older sister. No, I'm here for answers to the pressing questions before me, the questions that threaten the world. The sons of Gilgamesh. Utter destruction. A plague tearing its way through the population of humans. Utter destruction. The threat posed to me by Nereus. Utter destruction. How to rule all Eve's children, not just those we've separated out as worthy.

How to change the minds of the most bigoted people in the world. How to shape our surroundings into a place that's worth saving.

I spend an hour digging through journals, and I learn a lot, but none of it is imminently relevant.

I slump in the corner and drop my head in my hands. *Think, Chancery, think.* Nereus. God of water. Gilgamesh, allegedly sought immortality from a survivor of the flood. The greatest precipitation event in history, but not quite as world-encompassing as the religious humans believe. Mom mentioned it occasionally—it took place not long before Mahalesh died. I scan along her journals for the last few recorded. It takes me a good half an hour, but I find it. The passages describing the months leading up to the flood.

It hardly seems possible that in only sixteen hundred years, Mother's blood has become so corrupted, but it's undeniable. It saddens me, as it does many others, to see the children of Eve so. . . degraded. It takes them weeks to heal from a simple slice of a sword. They die in childbirth, of all things. They struggle to understand basic languages, simple mathematical concepts. They can't run quickly or lift things adeptly. My heart sorrows for them, for what they could have been—but they've squandered their strength. They've had children and children and children, without any thought to what would happen to successive generations.

I abhor their method thoroughly, but even I can see that we might be better if the Sons of Gilgamesh have their way.

I drop the book.

The Sons of Gilgamesh.

I swallow. What have I sent Edam to pursue? How long has this group been around? I crouch to the ground and pick it up again.

But I won't allow them to do it lightly. I await a sign from God. Without His approval, I will not move against the degraded and diminished children of Eve, no matter how debased —no matter how low they have fallen.

The journal ends, and I scrabble to grab the next.

The flooding hasn't been limited to certain regions. No, nearly every city and nation across the globe has been subjected to deluge after deluge, as if God himself wishes to wash the Earth clean of the unworthy. It's the sign I've waited for. I hope I am not misreading it. They're so insistent, and I find that I struggle to know how to react in the face of such certainty.

So I granted their request.

They've released it, this illness they discovered. They say God placed it here—a disease that eliminates the weakened of Mother's children without touching those of us with pure blood. The degraded one can't withstand it, and it passes from one to the next like fleas on vermin. Within days, or even sometimes hours, the illness floods the organs of their bodies, much like the rain pouring down around us. Their organs rupture, their lungs fill with fluid, and they perish. Is it kinder? To watch them all die together, to cleanse the Earth in the way God seems to want? It will clear the path for those of us with pure blood to rule with a clean slate, but are our hands clean or stained beyond repair?

I don't know anymore.

But when I lay my head down at night, my mind is overrun with nightmares. The degraded children of Eve scream my name in a thousand voices, a hundred thousand. Am I never to have any peace? I hope it will end soon. And after the last one is gone, and I record the events that have taken place, I'll spare my ancestors the details of the misery, the disgusting mess of it all. No, if this was God's will, it hardly seems helpful to outline the many atrocities of it, the utter and complete destruction.

The Earth was cleansed as he intended—it has been renewed, and that's what our children will enjoy. It's my legacy.

The account stops there. I snap the book closed. The flood was really a lot of rain and a plague? Why didn't Mom ever tell me that? Do the other empresses even know?

I think about the plague ravaging the humans now. The Sons of Gilgamesh. Nereus, god of the ocean. I close my eyes. Is it happening again? Unlike Mahalesh, I will never believe that humans are worthless and must be eliminated. I shudder at the thought. Mahalesh may be my ancestor, but she can't possibly have been guided by any kind of God I could follow. And clearly the purity of bloodlines does nothing to ensure the right view of the world.

My job must be to prevent a repeat of this. And now I worry anew about this recent plague. Could it be another illness orchestrated to wipe out the earth? How can I stop something if I don't even know where it's coming from? Now more than ever, I need to find Nereus and the Sons of Gilgamesh. I need to puzzle out a connection.

I must identify my enemy—and prepare for battle.

I wish Mom had scanned all of this in so I could digitally search it, but of course, once it's digital, it's accessible by anyone who can hack a system. But right now, it could all be destroyed in a fire. Plus—I have a tendency to believe that extra knowledge will help more than it will hurt. But without having reviewed everything myself, there's no way to know what exactly may be in here. Ugh, no easy answers.

I finally emerge, prepared to demand hard data on what exactly is going on with this SARS-COV-2.

Inara is waiting for me. "There's news."

Judging by the grim set of her mouth, it's not good. "What kind of news?"

She hands me two letters. They're unopened.

"You can't even know what it is." I glance at the addresses. To Chancery Alamecha. From Lainina Adora and Melamecha Shamecha. I groan. "No one surrenders via letter."

She shakes her head.

I tear them open. Identical declarations of war. Fantastic. "But it's hardly a surprise," I say.

Inara shrugs. "Neither is the fact that there have been consistent waves of refugees flocking into Italy, and into the United Kingdom. And even fleeing here."

"Wait, more Motherless?"

"Some of them, but many of them are merely opposed to your rivals for a variety of reasons. Or they support your radical positions."

"I need to find someone I trust to oversee their integration into the various communities into which they are traveling."

"Or," Inara says. "You could turn them away. It's a dangerous precedent to set, caring for people, easing them into their new situation. If you take on a monumental task like this, you may never be free of it."

"Dangerous or not, war creates refugees, and I've set this in motion. I won't turn them away."

"Very well," Inara says. "I'll compile a list of people I believe would be up to the task."

"Thanks," I say. "And now I better get over to my training session."

Inara frowns. "About that."

"Yeah?"

"Edam asked Balthasar to take over your training for a while."

I blink.

"I think he's. . ." Inara looks at the toes of her dark brown boots. "Breakups are hard." She looks up sharply. "He offered to help Judica—which makes sense. He's pretty good at interrogating people."

Judica? He's working with my twin, whom he hates, rather than training me? But then I consider what I asked him to do. What better way to signal that we're on the outs, so that someone might approach him? He's still got a seat on my Council. He's still working hand in hand with top brass—the Inquisitor, even. So he still has influence and power, but we aren't together. Maybe it's part of his plan.

Or maybe he's actually avoiding me.

I hate it either way. But I understand both. "That's fine," I say. "I'll meet Balthasar there." Inara leaves, and I change, my enormous ring catching on my shirt when I pull it down over my head. I suppose I'll get used to it, but every single time I look at it, wider now than my finger, taking up far, far too much space on my hand, it reminds me how much things have changed since I tried on Mom's ring, that day in her bedroom.

I scrawl out a note to Franco, demanding a number of technical details about the virus, as well as my daily update, and hand it to a guard before heading for the arena. I've barely gone ten steps when I hear my name.

"Chancery," Balthasar says.

I turn around. *What now?*

"Our session is going to have to wait." He frowns.

"Why?"

"It's best if you come with me."

I fall into step beside him, and we continue past the training arena.

His steps are larger than mine, but he shortens them so he's not rushing me. "We've been incrementally processing the evidence in the—" He clears his throat. "In the cottage."

The devastation, he means. "Okay."

"Job has been coordinating the efforts, given his unique background."

"What does that mean?"

Balthasar freezes. "He acted as your mother's executioner for hundreds of years."

I nod.

"Those were all performed as beheadings, Your Majesty."

Ah, so he would be familiar with the power required, the resistance that might exist, and the speed at which it could be performed. "And combined with his medical knowledge. . ."

Balthasar nods. "And Judica had preliminarily cleared him."

"Wait," I say. "Preliminarily?"

Balthasar shrugs. "All her clearances have been preliminary. She said her investigation is ongoing, and she's clearing people to work, but she hasn't yet cleared anyone one hundred percent."

I snort. That sounds exactly like something she'd say. "Go on."

"As you know, Job cleared the bodies one by one, sending them to be disposed of and remains sent to their families. But after he finished with the bodies, determining the same individual had killed them all in exactly the same way, he began to direct the analysis of the crime scene. He shut the entire investigation down this morning when he found something strange."

"And it is?"

Balthasar shrugs. "He won't tell me. Apparently, I haven't yet been preliminarily cleared."

I laugh.

He shakes his head. "It's not funny to me. A thousand years of service, almost, and here I am, as likely a candidate to have. . ." His entire face twists. "Killed Enora." He chokes. "If Judica's investigation turns up the murderer—"

"When," I say firmly.

"Fine. When we find the murderer, I request." He stops and turns to face me fully. "Not request. I beg your permission to carry out the punishment. I have several creative ideas of ways to prepare them for death." His eyes cloud over.

Judica may not have cleared him yet, but I can't imagine a world where Balthasar killed Mom. I doubt Frederick could have done it either. They're actually, along with Job, my top contenders for the role of Sotiris' father. "Did you and Mom ever. . ?"

Balthasar coughs until his face turns red. "Are you asking if I ever kissed Enora?"

I open my mouth. Kiss? "Uh, yes, I guess that's what I'm asking."

He swallows. "She was married to my *brother* for centuries. They are the two people I loved more than anyone else on earth."

I'm going to note that as a no. "Okay." Also, Judica is not getting enough credit for interrogating these ancient people. They have history upon history that I can't even imagine. Balthasar has been alive. . . I do the mental math. More than fifty-two of my lifetimes. I don't ask him anything else on the walk over to the cottage.

He takes my silence as an opportunity to grill my guards. Apparently, he doesn't believe they've been trained to appropriate standards and is holding extra sessions for them after their assigned hours.

The cottage comes into sight, but I stop a few dozen yards away. "Balthasar."

"Your Majesty?"

I sigh. "You don't need to call me that, as I've repeatedly mentioned. You seem to be working extremely hard to make sure that my guards are twice as capable as they need to be."

He opens his mouth to talk, but I'm not done.

"I appreciate everything you're doing, more than you know, but I wonder whether this fervor is motivated by the wrong thing."

He folds his arms across his chest. "And what do you think inspires me?"

"Mom's death wasn't your fault."

His hands drop to his sides. His pupils dilate.

"It wasn't your fault Enora died." It feels like it might bear repeating. "It took me a long time to accept it wasn't my fault, and even now, I still struggle occasionally with the same guilt. But it will eat at you until you let it go, and it will consume you if you allow it."

Balthasar swallows heavily. "Fine."

"Don't kill yourself because she died," I whisper. "I still need you."

He wraps one arm around my shoulders and begins walking toward the cottage. "I'm not going anywhere."

Noah jogs up just as we reach the front porch. "Mind if

I tag along? I heard from Judica that there's been some big piece of evidence."

He's talking to Judica now? Maybe she's thawed since discovering that he's evian—although she is still "investigating" him, whatever that involves, in conjunction with Alora's investigation. Apparently Judica's applying pressure to both to hopefully yield some helpful information. I can't blame her. They're clearly connected somehow.

The cottage looks entirely different on the inside than the last time I entered. The furniture's gone, the bodies thankfully are too, and there are small carts with swabs and cotton balls in jars in each room.

"What's the new development?" I ask.

Job bows. "Welcome, Your Majesty. I'm delighted to see you looking entirely recovered. And the volcano remains dormant." He blinks. "It really is a miracle. I wish I had less going on here and I could spend more time examining it myself."

I lift my eyebrows.

"Right," Job says. "The news." He spins on his heel and crosses the room.

I follow him toward the fireplace.

"If you sit on the brick here, you can look up into the flue."

"The flue?"

"Well, technically the entire escape is the flue," Job says. "It's the tube through which the heat escapes."

I sit on the brick and turn, looking upward at the damper. There are papers shoved up inside it. "You didn't pull them down?"

Job shakes his head. "I'm assuming this cottage was regularly cleaned. This may be something Melina held as important. I thought you might want to be the first one to see them."

My hands shake as they reach upward.

Job clears his throat.

"What?" I ask.

He hands me a pair of gloves.

Duh. I put them on and carefully shift the damper and remove the papers. I set them on the brick hearth, spreading them out slowly. They're photographs of some kind of archway. Or perhaps a sequence of archways.

"It's ancient Sumerian." Noah tilts his head. "Or perhaps Amorite?" He leans closer, his breath shifting my hair slightly.

"Do I even want to know why you can read Sumerian?" I turn my head slightly.

Noah's dimple shows up on one side of his cheek.

I love his knowing half smirk. "Care to take a stab at what it says?"

He points. "I think that symbol means healed. Or maybe repaired."

I lift the image toward him.

"Gloves," Job says.

Noah pulls on a pair and takes the image from me.

Which is when I glance downward at the rest of the papers. "Oh, wow, it does mean healed, I think. Look."

I lift up the next page, which contains handwritten notes. Balthasar and Job both lean closer, nearly crowding Noah out.

"Someone else was also a student of the ancient languages," Noah says.

"I guess so." I wonder whether it was Melina, and if so, why she hid it. "What exactly are we looking at? Does anyone know what the archways are from?"

"I assume these are the gates around the Garden of Eden," Job says. "And this is the prophecy rumored to be written upon them. It's supposed to be a companion to the prophecy you read before."

The one that proclaims me as Eldest. The one that

threatens utter destruction. My eyes scan the handwritten notes hungrily.

My children, the pure and precious, a task I give you, a price for your power. The strength of my children will fail but will also be restored or all shall perish. The Eldest ascends, against mighty and furious enemies, with the help of the lost. The family lost and the family youngest, opposed before but together in the end. After the lost is found, the Eldest must trust and together lost and Eldest will enter the garden. Only death shall renew life and must be freely given or all will end. The rift must be healed before the bisection in convergence of the ringed with the largest and smallest in the seventh generation or the time is past and the end begins, never to renew.

Great, more nonsense. The lost? My hands tremble, so frustrated I want to shred it into bits. Why? Why are these all so obtuse?

"It's the timeline," Balthasar says. "That sets the boundaries for the destruction predicted in the other prophecy."

I focus on the words again. "Something about the bisection in convergence of the ringed with the largest and smallest in the seventh generation. . ." I shake my head. "Why not just give an exact number of years? Why does it always have to be so hard?"

"Astronomy is more precise than reliance on the record keeping of men," Noah says. "Besides, maybe Eve didn't know the year. Maybe she worked with what she had."

An urge to slap him grips me. "You seem to know everything. Why don't you just tell me what it means?"

Noah frowns. "I'm trying to help any way I can."

"Are you?" I ask. "It doesn't feel that way to me. Tell me what you think that last line means."

"The bisection in convergence. . . I'm not sure. But the ringed is likely Saturn, and the largest is Jupiter. It could be referring to the convergence between the two planets, which only occurs once every twenty years or so and is due this fall sometime."

Job whips out his phone. "December 21, of this year."

"Whoa," I say. "Does that mean we have a timer on this? I've got nine months to save the world?"

Job shrugs. "Maybe so."

I gulp. "That doesn't seem too dire. I can work with that."

Noah peers at the image. "Assuming this is accurate."

"What does that mean?" I ask.

He shrugs. "I mean, these images, they look like they're in a cave or something. What would the archways leading into the Garden of Eden be doing in a cave?"

I snatch the image out of his hands. He's right.

"And wouldn't the inscription on the Garden of Eden be in Adamic?" Noah asks.

I frown. "So this whole thing may be some kind of trick, or a red herring."

"Melina hid it," Balthasar says. "And whatever Judica may believe, I don't think she was trying to fool us. I think this is probably legitimate. Which means that might be an accurate timeline."

"It's not legitimate," Noah says. "Believe me, I know because—" He chokes, but manages to spit out a few more words. "I've—seen—" He falls to the floor, his knees drawing up against his chest, shudders wracking his entire body. Foam drips from his mouth and his body flails like a fish on shore.

He's seizing.

I drop to my knees in front of him and cast around for a stick, a spoon, anything. I've never seen an evian seize, but I've seen plenty of humans on television shows and movies. We need to protect his tongue. Or I guess we would, if he couldn't heal any damage to it immediately. I settle for simply cradling his spasming head in my lap. "Relax. It's okay." I stroke his hair in a way I hope is soothing, but my heart rate has spiked, and my hands are clammy. This is not normal, and I have no idea what's going on. I look up sharply at Job.

"His heart is racing," Job says. "He's definitely experiencing a seizure."

"You are indispensable in a crisis," I say. "Thanks for stating the obvious. Now, *do your job*."

Job crouches down, clutching Noah's arms and legs, trying to still them. It does nothing.

"Have you ever treated anyone who was seizing?" I ask.

"Trauma, sure. Partial beheadings. Severed spines that aren't healing properly because a foreign object is still lodged somewhere, absolutely. Poisoning, fetal distress, all yes. But seizures?" He shakes his head.

"Move, then." I pull Noah closer and whisper in his ear. "It will be okay, Noah, I swear." I think on what he was doing when this started. He hadn't eaten or drunk anything. He was holding the same papers I held, with gloves over his skin. He was telling me he had seen. . . the archways into the Garden?

Has Noah seen them? The real ones? Does he know where the Garden of Eden is located? As Noah's body begins to relax, my brain kicks into high gear. I worry that steam might be pouring out of my ears. I think furiously. He's from China. I've assumed he was part of a family comprised of rejects, exiles, and refugees.

But what if he's not?

I *felt* him beneath me when he was drowning. I had a vision, for heaven's sake, telling me to save him and where. I've always felt drawn to him. And he has been helpful, insightful, almost unbelievably so... He tried to prevent me from working with the stones—alleging that they might not be the source of the power, concerned that somehow using them might harm me. Why would he think that?

Noah's still trembling, only half alive, his skin abnormally pale. Was he convulsing because he tried to tell me something he wasn't supposed to tell me? Why did I feel drawn to him? Why have I always believed him? Trusted him? Felt some kind of kinship I couldn't explain?

Mom's voice echoes in my head. "The records report seven stones," she said. The hairs on my arms rise. *Seven*.

A suspicion rises in my brain. I can't contain it, but I can't interrogate Noah with an audience. I can't be one hundred percent sure of Job, or Balthasar either, I suppose. Not one hundred percent.

Once Noah's trembling has finally subsided, I stand up. "Job, make copies of all of this and distribute them to the Council. Tell them not to share it yet. We need to convene a meeting to determine our next steps. We're at war with Shamecha and Adora. It's time we prepare to defeat them, and this might help us develop our attack plan and timeline."

With my help, Noah stands.

"And you're coming with me," I say. "You've got some questions to answer."

❦ 16 ❧

Noah doesn't argue with me during the walk back to my room. Not a single joke, not a quip, and not even a sarcastic remark. Job may have cleared him to leave with me, but I'm not so sure he's alright. I wish I could give him more of a break to recover, but even if we have until December, that's not much time to unite the families and figure out how exactly to stop a group I know nothing about.

And I feel as if I'm actually on to something, finally.

I push through the doorway to my room and refuse to allow the guards inside. Noah follows, his eyes darting left and right nervously.

"Calm down, Noah."

"No one expects the Spanish Inquisition," he says.

"Huh?"

"Never mind."

Now that I'm standing across from him, alone, my suspicion feels. . . nearly delusional. "Earlier, when you started to. . ."

"Convulse?" Noah asks.

"Was it because you tried to tell me something that you couldn't share?"

Noah stares me in the eyes. His are nearly indigo in this moment. "What do you think?"

"I think you're on my side," I say. "But I've been angry with you. I've trusted you, mostly, but never all the way. Never like I could trust Judica, for instance."

"Or Edam?" Noah lifts one eyebrow.

I inhale sharply through my nose. I can't think about Edam, not right now. "You haven't been willing to share anything about your family, or what they're doing in China, or what their goal is."

He nods.

"And even now, you won't tell me?"

He shakes his head.

"What if I ask you something?" I ask. "Can you say yes or no?"

He shrugs. "You can try."

"I think your family isn't a bunch of misfits," I say.

He swallows.

"I think they've been hiding for a very long time."

"Hiding from whom?" Noah asks.

"From all of us," I say. "From Mahalesh's daughters, from Shenoah, from everyone who matters."

Noah doesn't answer.

"And?"

"You didn't ask me a question."

I sigh. "Is your family a bunch of refugees?" I ask. "Are they comprised of evians who have left other families or been banished or escaped?"

Noah smiles. "Yes."

I swear under my breath. "Really?"

"Really," he says. "They are."

But his smile. He's not defending, he's not posturing.

"Did your family form solely from outcasts, exiles, escapees, and refugees?"

"No." A smile spreads broadly across Noah's face. "Hey, that worked."

My heart takes wing. "They've been around for thousands of years."

"Is that a statement?" Noah asks.

I groan. "Have they been around for thousands of years?"

Noah bobs his head.

My hands begin to tremble. I step closer, my heart accelerating. Has Noah truly been on my side all along? Is he bound by something I don't understand? "Are you unable to tell me anything?"

"I tell you a lot of things." Noah steps closer still, his eyes darkening.

I never really paid attention to how much taller Noah is than me. He seemed so. . . fragile. So breakable, even, before I knew he was evian. And since, he has grown, expanded. He has a presence now that he never had before. I think about his ability, one I've now tried to replicate over and over without success. I reach out and touch his forearm. It's warm, solid, and wrapped in solid muscle.

"You." I swallow. "You feel more solid than you did before."

He nods.

"Yes? You're bigger?" I pause. "Have you been lifting weights?"

He laughs. "No."

"Then what?" I ask. "Training with Edam?"

His laughter is sharper this time, angry almost. "I didn't need his help."

This nearly feral Noah is new to me, but he doesn't scare me.

He thrills me.

"Does your family have the seventh stone?" I ask.

Noah opens his mouth. He takes my hand in his. He clears his throat, but he doesn't speak.

"Can you say yes?" I ask.

He shakes his head.

And without warning, without time to even think about it, I grasp his shirt at the collar and tear it apart, as hard and as fast as I can. At first I blink and blink and blink at his beautifully dark chest. It's larger than I suspected, bulkier, but then my eyes focus.

On the dark cord I've seen around his neck. A cord that holds a flashing stone against the skin of his sternum.

"You," I whisper. "You have the seventh stone."

Noah's eyes bore into mine, intent, serious.

"That's why I felt you," I say.

"It saved my life," Noah agrees.

"And it allows you to look any way you want?"

Noah gulps, my eyes transfixed on the muscles in his throat. And then he shifts, like a mirage. Suddenly it's not Noah the evian holding my hand. It's skinny, human Noah. I drop his hand and stumble backward.

"You can't—the reason—I don't—"

"It's a lot," skinny human Noah says.

I breathe in and out and in and out.

"I want to explain," Noah says.

"But you can't," I say. "Because somehow, your family has kept you from sharing information."

He nods.

"Can you at least tell me what you call yourselves?"

Noah opens his mouth, "My name isn't actually Noah at all." He coughs. "It's Sh—" His skin turns white and he falls again, and somehow in the fall, skinny, human Noah is replaced with strong, tall, evian Noah. The convulsions last longer this time, but eventually, they abate. I stroke his hair until his color begins to return.

"I'm sorry," I say. "I'm so sorry."

He closes his eyes. "It doesn't seem to kill me. I wonder if I can write things down."

"Let's rest a bit before we try that, shall we?" I ask.

"You haven't taken the stone yet," Noah says.

"I'm not a thief."

"You are the Eldest," Noah says. "I believe that."

"You didn't give it to me."

He closes his eyes.

"You can't."

"I can't."

"If I take it from you, what will happen?"

He sits up. "I don't know. Hopefully nothing."

"Did your. . . Who gave you the stone?"

He lifts his eyebrows.

"Right. Did your mom give it to you?"

He shakes his head.

"Your dad?" I think back on the imposing figure who stopped on Ni'ihau.

Noah nods.

"Is it yours, or do they expect it back?"

He laughs.

Gah. "Does your dad expect you to return the stone?"

"Absolutely, he does."

"And he runs your family?"

Noah's face crinkles up.

Something's wrong with the question. I think about what I know of Noah, the respect he has for me, for women in general. "Your dad runs the family, sort of, but with your mom by his side?"

He smiles. "Yes."

"So your family is pure evian, which means you're like

193

me, only a few generations removed. Are you seventh generation?"

He beams. "I am."

Wow. "And your dad sent you here because he knows the prophecy." Alora. She introduced us. "You've known who I was then, all along. Is that right?"

He shakes his head.

"But you suspected."

"We did. It seemed likely, what with the 'Eldest' moniker."

I have so many questions, and no idea which ones he can answer. "I don't even know where to start," I say. "But most of my questions have to do with the Garden and the full prophecy and what's coming."

He sighs. "Most of which I probably can't answer."

"It kills me that you can't," I say.

"I'm not going anywhere," he says. "We have time to try and figure this out. And my dad and mom really do support your efforts, if we can just work out the details that are getting in the way."

"Like the fact that I turned their spy?"

Noah frowns. "I was never a spy. I was tasked to connect with you—because—"

"You can't say why."

He growls. "You have no idea how obnoxious it has been."

I scoot closer and lean my head against his shoulder. "I've been blaming you, for not really being on my side."

"I would hand you this stupid rock right now, if I could."

I imagine fighting Noah to steal the stone from him. If trying to tell me a few basic answers sends him into convulsions, what would happen if I wrested it from his control? "I don't even want it," I say. "At some point, I'll meet your family. If your dad gives me his blessing, we'll work something out."

"My dad's not the creampuff he seemed when he flew out here."

His horrifying human father act was a creampuff compared to the real guy? My eyes widen. "I could tell he was a tough negotiator, even then."

"And it hasn't endeared you to him, that I've switched allegiances."

"Well, if they aren't opposed to me," I say, "then why are they so mad you support me?"

"I was supposed to b— b—" He chokes and seizes again.

When they stop this time, he's pale, and his hands continue to tremble.

"Don't push it again," I say. "It hasn't killed you so far, but. . ."

He frowns.

"But if they tasked you to do something with me, maybe bring me to them, maybe guide me, and instead, you cut off contact with them and you simply support whatever I do. . ." My hand flies to my mouth. "Oh my goodness. You've basically been—"

"Disavowed?" Noah laughs. "Yeah, that's right. Disavowed, disowned, and probably, if they ever get their hands on me again, destroyed."

"I'm so sorry, Noah. I feel like this is my fault."

"No." He shifts so that his eyes lock on mine. "Never apologize, not to me. You're radiant. You've navigated the most complex maze of half-truths, complicated ancient prophecies, avarice, prejudice, and violence that any empress has ever been hit with. Truly. My dad should be here right now, bowing, and begging your forgiveness for not crawling on his knees to help you at the very beginning."

"You didn't say that to him, did you?" I whisper.

Noah tucks a stray hair behind my ear. "I might have."

I close my eyes. No wonder his dad hates me. When I open my eyes, Noah's closer than before. Close enough that the heat from his breath warms my cheeks. Close enough that I can see tiny flecks of silvery grey in his eyes.

Close enough that with one little shift, I could kiss him.

Which is no big deal. I mean, I've kissed him before. Several times, in fact. But it's different somehow. This isn't skinny, human Noah. This isn't a game, pretending that I could care for someone different. This isn't flirting with the enemy, with a possible spy. This isn't a gangly, somewhat awkward and unsure teenager.

No, this Noah is solid. He's steady. He's strong, and he's fierce, and he makes my heart sprint toward the finish.

"Noah, I—"

When his face drops an inch and a half and his mouth closes over mine, I'm sundered.

Split.

Shattered.

Remade.

Noah defied his family for me. He rebelled against vows that physically bound him to silence. He risked everything that mattered, everything that makes him who he is. For me. To protect me, to guide me, to support me.

The reservations that surrounded my heart, that kept me safe from the cocky, sarcastic kid, my qualms at allowing him close, at trusting him near me, evaporate. Smoke. Vapor. Gone.

And I crawl toward him, my right hand reaching up to cup his jaw. It's bristly, it's square, and it shifts as he smiles into our kiss.

He groans then, his hand moving to my waist, tightening as if to say *mine*.

Yes.

My hand drops from his jaw to his chest, where I ripped his shirt, my fingers running down the length of his perfectly sculpted pec. He inhales sharply, and I pull back.

"You have no idea," Noah rasps, "how badly I wish I wasn't about to ask this. But I need to know."

I gulp.

"Did you and Edam really break up?" His eyes are wide, vulnerable. "I've tried to stay light." His breathing is shallow. "I haven't been demanding. I understand that your life is hard enough. And I actually like the guy, not that I'll ever admit that to anyone else."

"Yes," I say.

Noah's smile cannot be contained. His head dips down, his lips lowering to mine again.

I block them with my index finger. "And no."

A wrinkle appears between his eyebrows. I want to smooth it away, but he deserves to know. And Edam, well, I don't know what he deserves. "We did. I am angry with him." I wince. "Unreasonably angry, perhaps."

Noah collapses back to the floor. "He betrayed your trust."

I lay next to him, and our fingers intertwine. "He did. I know that sounds a little silly, but if we're supposed to be a team—"

"He should have told you that he intended to challenge Analessa, not spring it on you. He had a right, considering your decree, but I could tell you were shocked. And Analessa." Noah sighs. "Sounded like you two had discussed the possibility, and you told her it wasn't going to happen."

"Exactly that," I say. "He made me look like a fool, like my future consort doesn't even respect me or honor my wishes."

"I think he was trying to find a way to court you without forcing you," Noah says. "Which I totally understand."

"But he peed the bed."

Noah's laughter is immediate, pure, unadulterated.

"So yeah, we broke up," I say.

He falls quiet.

"But I still—"

"You love him."

I close my eyes. I imagine his face in my mind's eye. "It's messed up," I whisper.

"Because you feel something for me, too."

I try to withdraw my hand, but Noah won't let me.

He twists and pops up on his elbows so that he's looking down on me. "It is, a little bit. But before you beat yourself up about it, think about your life. You had seventeen plus years of preparing to spend the next few decades with your mom, after which you figured you'd retire to somewhere predominantly human, like Alora did. You had to learn to be someone who wouldn't threaten Judica, or she'd double down on her plans to kill you. You fantasized about the freedom and novelty of human culture, admiring your sister who did that for real. Then bam, suddenly all of your plans are out the window." He reaches out and traces my eyebrows one at a time. "You've been on a roller coaster the last few weeks, and you've managed not to hurl so far. But is it any wonder that part of you, the part that wishes for the crown, that wants to make Enora the Merciless proud, the avenger of the humans, wants to stand with the ferocious, pedigreed, perfect Edam at her side?"

"You sure are smart," I say. "Then what part of me is responsible for this unspeakably strong pull I feel toward you?"

His dimples both break out this time. "Oh, that's easy. It's the parts of you that like unbelievably good looking, dark, handsome strangers. The mystery, the humor, the skill." He flexes his bicep. "I mean, I'm the whole package. Who can *really* compete with that?"

I swat his arm. "I'm being serious."

"So am I," he whispers. "Which is why I'll explain a little more. You've always mistrusted Edam, almost as much as you liked him. First, he dated your sister. Then you find out he was working for Analessa all along. Sure, he changed sides, but he took his sweet time telling you about it. You caught him—he didn't confess. And then, when you finally believe in him, he pulls that stunt."

"But you're part of a secret family and you've been concealing a staridium stone that no one even knew existed."

"True." Noah presses his hand to my forehead. "But you know here, and here." He moves his hand to press on my sternum. "That I would never betray you. I never have, not once. I've told you every single thing that I could, the very second I could conceive of a way to tell you."

He's right. He has.

"And that's what makes me right for you. In New York, when you needed a friend, someone to make you laugh, someone who would love you whether you picked to live among the humans or to fulfill your destiny, that was who I was."

I roll my eyes. "You would not have flown away with me, hiding out from everything."

There's no joking in his eyes when he says, "I would do it right now."

"You wouldn't," I whisper.

"Try me," Noah says.

I swallow. "I couldn't let all those people die."

"And that's why I love you," he says. "But I'm not as gloriously caring as you. I'm far more selfish. I always have been—but for once I found something that eclipses my love of myself."

I laugh. "You did?"

He holds my gaze. My stomach flip flops. I reach up

and trace the line of his lips slowly. His heart skips a beat, and he bites my finger.

"Ouch," I say.

"You liked it."

He's right. It's the mixture of attack and defend in Noah that draws me to him. He'll never hurt me, but he won't hold back either. That's the real difference between human Noah and this one. He's whole now, and he's dangerous, and he challenges me. Always.

He shoves backward and stands up. "But until you see it, until you know it, burning down deep inside, I won't cause you to collapse like a dying star. I will never do you harm."

"Are you saying you won't kiss me?"

Noah yanks me up to my feet and kisses me full on the mouth. He pulls back, his lips moving against mine. "I would *never* say something that stupid."

I smile. "What, then?"

"I'm saying." He buttons up the two button survivors on his shirt.

I try not to gawk at his gorgeous skin through the gaping holes.

"That all this—" He gestures at his chest. "Is off limits until you know what your heart wants. I'm saying, take your time, and until you know what you want, I'm here. Like I'll always be here. No matter who or what you choose. Because from the second you showed up at Trinity, all nervous about whether you fit in with a bunch of humans, I knew. You were empress of a sixth of the world, and yet you were also an indescribable mix of unsure and ferocious. Retreating from harming others, and attacking in their defense."

"I had no idea what I was doing then, and I don't know much more now." I pop a hand on my hip. "But it sounds like you just want to take care of me, which is a stereotypical male response."

"Take care of you?" Noah snorts. "Please. I'd guard your back, but you don't need saving. You're the most capable person I know. Unlike every other ruler I've met, you're also honest about your limitations. That's the real reason that from that moment forward, there has been no one for me but you."

❧ 17 ❧

I still need to train. And to talk to Franco about the virus—how it works biologically, if they have an idea of its source, possible solutions to slow the spread, progress on a vaccination. I need to meet with the Council to discuss the declarations of war, our attack strategy, and on and on and on.

"Whoa, what happened to you?" Noah asks.

"Same thing that always does," I say. "Overwhelmed at how badly I'm falling behind."

Noah looks at the small table at the corner of my room where my breakfast tray is still resting. He picks up an empty plate.

"Are you hungry?" I ask.

He shakes his head and begins to spin a plate on his finger. "See how easy that looks?"

I tilt my head. It does look easy what he's doing, effortlessly spinning a plate on his index finger. "I'm sure you just make it look easy."

He shrugs. "You could do it. It's simple balance."

"Okay."

He picks up another plate with his free hand, still

balancing the spinning plate on his index finger. "That first plate represents the normal business of ruling Alamecha. You were trained, overtly or not, by your mother from birth. You could do it. It might wobble or slow or go a little too fast, but you'd be fine. You'd work out a balance and a rhythm and you'd spin the heck out of that plate."

He flicks the fingers of his left hand to set the second plate spinning on the index finger of his left hand. Now he's got two plates spinning on two different hands. They're not moving the same speed, but he keeps them moving on his index fingers with small, quick movements from his other fingers. "Now, that second plate, that's Shenoah. You took it over recently, with no evian precedent to do something like that. No one has ever tried to rule two huge, disparate families at the same time, and you're doing the best you can. When one plate wobbles, you adjust. You're doing great."

I shake my head. "It's not only that."

He grins. "No, it's not. I wish I had the skill that one of my dad's friends has. Or you know, some of his props." He sets one plate down on the table, and then the other. "But for our discussion, imagine that I had sticks in my hand, and I had plates spinning on a few of them. I could balance one on my knee, one on my nose."

"Okay." Where is he going with this?

"You have dozens of plates spinning right now," he says. "Can you spin them all at the same time?"

Compression bands tighten around my heart, and I shake my head. "That's the problem. There's only one of me."

Noah wraps an arm around my shoulders. "There is only one of you." His expression is full of something—not pity, not chagrin, not regret. Then I recognize it. Empathy. Compassion.

"That is a nice analogy," I say. "But I don't see how it helps me."

"You do what you'd do if you were performing with plates," Noah says. "You spin the one that's about to fall."

"I don't want any of them to fall," I wail.

"Of course you don't, but you're only one person," Noah says. "Ask for help and prioritize. There is no real balance, not life, not in death. Life takes and takes and takes and then it's over. So until then, you spin and spin and spin." He lifts my chin. "And you point me and Judica and Edam and Moses and Alora and Balthasar and Marselle and Inara at any wobbly plates and we'll spin them for you."

"I can't—"

"You can," he says. "So let's start listing plates. I'll help you figure out who can spin them." He sits down in the wing chair near the window.

I take the one next to it. "Fine. So, we need to decide what to tell everyone about you."

"What do you want to tell them about me?"

"You act like it's so simple," I say. "Like I can tell them anything I want."

He smiles. "Chancery, you can. You're empress. I'm your subject by my choice."

I leap to my feet and start pacing. "But there are consequences. Your dad, if I out his family, will be furious."

Noah shrugs. "Or maybe he'll be relieved."

My heart seizes. "Or maybe he'll have you executed!"

Noah crosses the space between us in one step. "He won't," he says. "He's hard, and scary, and powerful. And he loves me. And I happen to be right next to the most powerful woman in the world. Plus, I'd like to see him try. I can escape from anywhere, remember?" He taps his chest.

I squint. I see nothing there anymore. No bulge, no cord, nothing.

He chuckles. "Habit."

Suddenly, the stone winks back into view.

"I keep it hidden, always," he says. "Too many people know what staridium looks like. It has become second nature at this point."

"Wait, does that mean. . . Do you know something about how it works? Does it pull power from me like you said?"

"I don't know. Like you, I'm the first person in our family that it has ever reacted to." He beams. "Hey, I said that without repercussion."

My eyebrows rise. "So, wait. Can you say anything now?" Hope rises within me.

"Mahalesh also had a son, to whom she gave the last stone, the smallest stone." Noah pauses, blinking rapidly. "His name was—"

And he's convulsing on the floor, foam frothing from his mouth.

"We really need to figure out what subjects are taboo," I say, as his convulsions fade.

"I'd really prefer not to fall into one of these fits in front of the Council," he whispers.

"The Council?" I ask. "Or Edam?"

"Both?" Noah's smile is weak, but it's there.

"I'm not telling anyone," I say. "Not about your family, not about the stone."

His eyebrows draw together. "How will you explain my seizure earlier?"

I shrug. "We don't have to, right? If Job presses, let him run some tests. You're as baffled as me."

"You figured it out," he says. "Someone else could too."

I shake my head. "Mom told me there were seven stones. She said it confused her, her mother, and her grandmother. But that's not public knowledge."

"I wasn't aware the empresses knew. We believed it was a complete secret."

"Maybe it was," I say. "But we have Eve and Mahalesh's records. I think it was an obscure reference in one of those."

Noah sits up, but his brow remains furrowed.

"You want to call your dad, don't you? And warn him."

He bobs his head. "But I won't, not unless you allow it."

"We should probably open some kind of communication channel." I hop to my feet and pick up my phone. "Do it."

Noah dials. "Hello Dad." He gestures for me to sit next to him. I keep my volume set so low that you have to be right next to my phone to hear the speaker on the other end.

I scoot over next to him, cross legged on Mom's rug.

"—the nerve to call me," his dad's voice says.

"I am doing you a service," Noah says. "And I obtained permission to do it."

"Permission! You've forgotten who you are," his dad says. "You need to come home immediately."

"She knows, Dad."

Dead silence.

"I didn't tell her, just as you intended, I couldn't—not without your permission. You assumed she'd hate me for it, and kill me, or send me home. You don't know her at all. In fact, it's your absolute confidence that's your downfall."

His dad switches to Cantonese. "It's my arrogant, disloyal son who is my downfall."

Noah flinches.

I take his hand and he relaxes, marginally.

"What is the service you purport to be doing?" his dad asks.

"Chancery had an old text, from Eve herself, that mentioned the seventh stone."

The unbridled fury in his dad's tone scares me. Noah

206

may believe his father would never kill him, but I'm not so sure. "Is she with you *right now*?"

"She figured it out, Dad. She knows, but not because I told her. And if she puzzled out the truth. . ."

"The other idiots could, too." He growls into the phone. "If your girlfriend doesn't kill them all first."

"She had no choice," Noah says. "Her hand was forced."

"By her *fiancé*, you idiot. Are you not paying attention? Why are you still there, chasing a woman who doesn't care for you?"

"Because unlike you, I don't only love things for what they can do for me." Noah's fingers tighten on mine.

He could tell his dad that Edam and I broke up. He could argue that I care for him too. He could tell his dad that he's doing his part in this fight, in this effort to avoid utter destruction, but he doesn't say any of those things.

"I called to warn you, but nothing else has changed. I chose my side."

"You chose the wrong side," his dad says. "It broke your mother's heart, you know."

Noah freezes, his entire body completely still.

"You broke your promise to her. You betrayed her— which is worse than betraying your family. You'll never be forgiven. Never."

"One day," Noah whispers. "One day you'll thank me, for seeing what you were too blind to accept." He hangs up.

I don't ask about his mom, and he doesn't offer anything. There's no way for me to even know whether he can share. I'd hate to shove him back into convulsions on the floor. Noah stares out the window for several moments. Then he shakes all over, like a dog that has been playing in the ocean. "What's the next plate?" he asks.

Together, we work out a plan of attack, a ten-prong order for how to address the things that plague my efforts at sleep, that leave me unable to breathe in the middle of the night. "And for what it's worth," he says. "I have heard the same about the flood—that it was flooding, but that it hit the same time as a deadly virus. The two together eliminated the non-evian population of the earth. I don't think I've ever heard that it was intentionally spread."

"Have you heard of the Sons of Gilgamesh?" I ask. "Don't answer if it will cause seizures."

He laughs. "I haven't, but I'm willing to go hunting if you'd like."

I shake my head. "Actually, I already sent someone after it."

He closes his eyes. "Edam."

"Yes."

He catches my gaze. "That was brilliant, truly. With what people had seen, but given that you do still trust him not to betray you, I couldn't have advised better."

"And your assessment has nothing to do with the fact that his subterfuge requires us to not interact."

"Nothing whatsoever," Noah says with a straight face, but his eyes sparkle.

"I think it's time we share these plans with the Council."

When I open the door into the hall, Marselle is standing in front of it, her hand raised to knock.

"Is everything okay?" I ask. "I was about to call for a meeting."

Marselle's eyes are grim. "We've had a break in the investigation of your mother's killer."

Nereus. I practically lunge at Marselle. Why doesn't she just tell me what she's learned?

"What am I missing?" Noah asks. "This is great news. Right? Why do you look. . . pinched?"

"I think we should speak in private." She specifically does not address Noah.

"Come in." I shift so she can walk past me. "But Noah can stay."

Marselle frowns, but she walks past me.

I close the door behind her. "Okay, tell me why you look as if someone stabbed you in the kidney."

The head of my intelligence network holds up a thumb drive. "I was approached this morning, by a long time asset. They asked me for a favor." She swallows, the muscles in her throat working.

"And?"

"I agreed. I've brought someone onto Ni'ihau, under cover, without your permission." She waves at the window into my courtyard, and the door opens.

I blink as a hooded figure walks through the door. "My guards outside," I say.

Noah draws a sword and assumes a ready position.

"Your guards are fine," Angel says, drawing back her hood. "I darted them, but they'll awaken, unharmed, in less than half an hour. And I mean you no harm. I never have."

My mouth drops open.

"She surrendered herself," Marselle says. "But she did it on the condition that I would help her obtain a private meeting with you before we make her capture public. I didn't have time to consult with you first."

"I wanted the chance to plead my case before someone decapitated me," Angel says. "You're not going to like the information I'm bringing you, and you'll want to dismiss it."

I frown. "What information is that?"

"I went back in time," Angel says. "I located the prior shop of the dealer who sold poison to the individual who poisoned your mother. They noted the name of the purchaser as 'N' in the accounting log. Marselle informs me that you already knew this."

I nod.

"But I found a prior purchase." Her face is grim. "It was also noted under the log as being made by 'N.'"

My breath catches.

"It was purchased when your mother was pregnant with you in early 2002."

"Okay." At least we know why she was seen hovering around the site of the shop before. It makes sense she would work to clear her name, if she wasn't guilty.

"I found a video from the old shop location, taken by a camera on the corner, owned by a gas station."

I swallow.

"I brought it with me." She offers me a jump drive.

I take it.

"But I'll tell you what you're going to find." Angel's eyes soften, her mouth turning downward. "You won't like it, but the video shows that your sister Inara procured the poison that killed your mother."

It can't be, not Inara. I shake my head. "That makes no sense. Inara loved Mom. I know she did."

Angel steps backward. "Watch the video." She glances at Marselle. "You can take me now."

She doesn't fight as Marselle disarms her, or binds her hands, or guides her toward the door to the hall.

"And now that she has surrendered," Marselle says, "I should tell you both that my team located a video at the same gas station this morning."

Angel's features relax, tension leaving her eyes, her mouth, and even her shoulders.

"But," Marselle says. "The video we recovered doesn't show Inara purchasing that poison in 2002."

Angel freezes.

"It shows you," Marselle says, "old friend."

✃ 18 ✃

"I'm going to try both of them," I say firmly, meeting the gaze of every individual gathered in the Council Chamber one by one. "But I won't do it publicly. It's too sensitive, and the investigation is ongoing."

Balthasar frowns. "You'll allow the Council to watch."

I nod.

"Fine," he says. "Fine. And before you make any decisions, you should let us weigh in."

"I won't promise that," I say. "But as the trial progresses, I'll heed your counsel." Wondering all the time which of them might be in on it. Because if Inara and Angel are on trial, anyone could be involved.

"As Inquisitor," Judica says, "I—"

"You can't try your sister," I say. "It's too horrifying."

"You're issuing judgment on them," Judica says.

I sigh. "I am, and believe me, it's terrible. I won't force you to do that."

"Then I'd like to defend Inara," Judica says. "Represent her, argue for her."

That's not skewed at all.

"She wouldn't have killed Mother," Judica says. "I know

it. And I feel responsible for this dragging on. I had Angel in my grasp, and not only did she escape, she then captured me."

Someone has an axe to grind, and I don't even blame her. "Fine. Who will represent Angel?"

No one volunteers.

"She can represent herself." Marselle's hands grip the edge of the table, her eyes like flint. She didn't take what she considered to be Angel's betrayal of her trust in asking her to bring her in very well. "Did she think we wouldn't double-check her story? Every single feed for a two-mile radius around the purchase from a few months ago was wiped. But she didn't think to go back, and she thought I was too incompetent to pursue that lead."

"Two videos from twenty years ago," Noah says, "both showing a different purchaser."

"The same video," I say. "But one was tampered with and one is real."

"So either," Judica says, "Angel brought us a doctored video and Marselle's people recovered the real one."

"Or," I say, "Angel brought the real one and Inara planted the fake, after realizing it might exist."

"My agent said the main file was corrupted," Marselle says. "Probably by Angel."

"How did she recover the file, then?" Edam asks.

"There was a backup system in place," Marselle says. "My people scared Angel and she didn't have time to look for a backup, clearly. She put together the fake video and came here, hoping it didn't exist, or that if it did, we wouldn't find it."

"Can't we tell which one is real and which isn't?" Judica asks. "Don't we have tech people for just that issue?"

I push a button and turn on the video. "You should all see them, at least."

Every head turns toward the screen on the sidewall of

the Council Chamber. A woman approaches the front door of a shop. I squint to try and make out details. The lighting isn't great, and the video's a little grainy. It appears to be a shop for holistic medicines.

I've seen this dozens of times, but my heart still accelerates. Nothing here will change Mom's death. Nothing can bring her back, I remind myself.

The screen shows a timestamp in the bottom right. February 14, 2002. The woman who approaches the front door of the shop makes no effort to hide her face. Angel walks toward the shop and opens the door, disappearing inside.

To buy something that she hoped would kill me in utero.

A dear family friend, a mentor, a trusted confidante for my mother. She joked with Mom, berated Mom, chided me, and taught me cooking basics. Angel was always smiling. She made Mom laugh and smile and roll her eyes more than anyone else we knew. And the world is such a twisted place that I hope, right down to my toes, that this old friend murdered our mother.

Because when the second video plays, the face that approaches the shop door is Inara's, and that's even worse.

"We clearly need to analyze these two videos," Noah says. "Someone who is an expert with technology, someone you trust."

"Our top candidate for analysis has a strong bias," Marselle says. "Peteris has been instrumental in a number of instances, noticing the slightest details that flag a fake. He makes our fakes, when we need them for other families."

Oh geez. "And?"

"He worked directly under Angel for the last hundred years," Marselle says. "I'm not sure whether he'd be honest with us."

I close my eyes and pinch the bridge of my nose. "Fine, fine." I lick my lips. "Select your top three, Peteris among them, and we'll hear testimony from each."

"While they confer," Judica says, "I'll find out whether we have any information on the finger, and on the ashes," Judica says.

"I should probably tell you all this right now," Edam says. "I followed the leads on Tristan as they came in over the past few days, but one of the most obvious things in his history was that he was slated for execution for an inappropriate relationship with an operative from Shamecha."

"And?" I ask. "Why wasn't he executed?"

"Angel gave testimony that spared him. She convinced Enora to spare his life," Edam says.

He told us he incinerated and hid Enora's body, if it was Enora's, to repay past debts. Did he feel he owed his life to Angel, after that? Was he working for her all along? He was part of the team that conducted the autopsy on her in the first place. What other evidence did he destroy? Was it at Angel's direction?

"Bring Angel here in two hours," I say. "And the rest of you, gather whatever you can in that timeframe."

Everyone stands up.

"Marselle," I say.

She turns toward me.

"You'll be representing Angel. You brought her here, you felt some affection for her, at least as recently as earlier today, and she deserves an advocate."

Her lips compress. "Fine."

Judica returns with DNA evidence on both issues. "The sequencing was only ninety-six percent complete on the ashes, and ninety-one percent on the finger," she says. "But they're virtually certain that the ashes are from Mother, and the finger is Aline's."

I close my eyes. Melina still might be alive.

I wish the interrogation of Angel went as well.

"I did not kill Enora," Angel says. "And I would never have killed Melina, either. If she's dead." She chokes. "I felt that banishing her daughter was the worst mistake Enora ever made. Melina loved Enora, and she was banished for doing what was right. I would never have harmed either of them, never."

"Where were you on February 14, 2002?" I ask.

Angel frowns. "I was in the United States, dealing with details of the Olympics in Utah."

"Do you have evidence of that?" I ask.

She throws her hands up in the air. "Of course there are records on the jets taken. And the pilot, Ignacio, could corroborate."

"Salt Lake City is how far from Las Vegas?" Judica's voice is a little more aggressive than necessary.

"It's a few hours by car," Angel says.

She was a few hours from the shop where the poison was purchase on the day it was purchased. She could have driven out there, and unless the pilot was also her bodyguard, he would never know.

"So unsurprisingly," Judica asks, "you deny killing either of them. You further deny hiding Mother's body?"

"Why would I hide Enora's body?" Angel shakes her hands, rattling her bindings. "I loved her as I loved Alamecha."

"Why do you think Inara would have killed Mom?" I ask. "I believe she loved Alamecha, too."

Angel shakes her head. "I can't figure that out either. I never suspected her, not for a moment. And she loved Melina. I wish I knew something I could tell you that would help."

"Could there be another video?" I ask. "One that shows the real murderer? Because Inara can't even inherit the throne. Not without killing me and Judica too."

Angel shakes her head. "I recovered that video feed myself. The equipment hadn't been touched in years. We were lucky it was even there. I have no idea why, Chancery, but Inara killed Enora."

I question her for hours, but I get nowhere. She insists she wasn't on the island, she insists she couldn't have stolen Enora's body or even sent a message to make Tristan do it. In fact, she denies any interaction with him since she helped obtain his pardon. She claims she could never have murdered Melina's people, and she tears up when she hears the full list of how many died.

But as she's being escorted back to the holding cells, Job arrives, eyes darting left and right, hands closing and opening nervously. He glances at Angel as he enters the room, his look. . . almost apologetic?

"What is it?" I ask.

Angel digs in her heels and stops. I don't argue. She may as well hear what he has to say, as I imagine I'll have to ask her about it otherwise.

"I pulled a sample of the toxin Angel used on your guards, the paralytic."

I raise my eyebrows.

"It's the same as what we found in Melina's companions who were beheaded." Job frowns.

"Are you sure?" I ask.

"It's new," Angel says. "The shopkeeper's assistant told me about it when I went to interrogate her. I bought the very last of their stock, but you can ask them. They sold it to many, many people. Maybe to the real Nereus, too."

The proprietor is dead, of course, and can't tell me what Nereus looks like. I think about the list of wrongs inflicted by this person, either Angel or Inara. She killed Mom, she caused the shopkeeper's death, more than likely, and she murdered twenty-four people to capture Melina. "Take her back and lock her up."

"The analysis of the videos has been complete," Franco says.

I wave at the door guards and they bring Peteris inside. "They didn't confer?" I ask.

Franco shakes his head. "They were asked to analyze the videos in separate rooms."

"Fine. Proceed."

Peteris glances around the room, his eyes wide, his heart racing. "I've reviewed both files, and I can't find any of the normal markers that would indicate that either of them have been tampered with."

"Tell me about the methods you used," I say. "In as lay terms as you can manage."

"The digital footprint explanation will be hard to follow, but I brought some examples to show you of analyzing the video itself. The first is called motion tracking. When you freeze certain screens, you can see that the modified portion, ostensibly the face of the purchaser in this case, is slightly different, or perhaps blurred or far too sharp around the edge." He points at a screen and clicks a button to bring up a PowerPoint. "For example. Look at this video of Emma Gonzales. She's an anti-gun activist in the United States. She tore up a target here."

The video plays, showing a woman with buzzed hair, tearing a shooting target on screen, with several other women behind her.

"Now the video was modified," Peteris says, "only this time, notice it's not a target. It's the United States' Constitution, making her seem very anti-American."

It looks pretty real to me.

"But if you freeze frame it, and analyze the image, you can see that the Constitution is darker. See?" He zooms in and shows me some electronic pixel analyzers.

"I do," I say.

Then he blows up images from both Inara and Angel. "They don't show any markers."

I want to shred something now. "How can you not spot the fake?"

Peteris' mouth turns down. "The techniques employed have outstripped our capacity to debunk them, sadly."

"Which means you are no help at all."

He shakes his head. "I'm sorry." He stands up. "But I'd like it noted for the record that it's my professional opinion that Angel would never have done a single thing to harm your mother or Alamecha. She loved Alamecha over everything else and saw your mother as the epitome of all that it represented."

"Yes, yes." I hope the other two analysts will provide something Peteris doesn't.

But they say the exact same thing.

"So the video is a wash," I ask.

Heads of the Council nod all around.

"We have a finger, from Aline, indicating that she was dead, and her body disposed of in the water." I sigh. "We have ashes of my mother, disposed of by Tristan, seemingly, who stole Mom's body from her crypt to prevent anyone from discovering who fathered Enora's most recent daughter."

"I'm not sure those things point at either of them," Noah says. "After all, they both claim they'd never kill Melina or Aline, and we have no way to be sure that Tristan was doing it for Angel. At least, as far as we know, she can't have been the father of your mother's unborn child."

I frown at him for making a half joke. Not the time.

Noah clears his throat. "The timing on all of this is highly suspect. Angel turns herself in just as you find that video? Well, both videos?"

"Almost like she has someone on the inside, telling her

it's now or never?" Marselle lifts an eyebrow. "I hadn't considered that, but I agree, the timing is concerning."

"You're supposed to be advocating for her," I snap.

"I want the truth," Marselle says, "same as you."

"Inara has her own intelligence network," I say. "Maybe she knew Angel was going to surrender and made sure her false video was ready. Certainly, Angel hasn't been here, on Ni'ihau, to kill and destroy."

"But she does have the paralytic," Edam says. "And we searched Inara's room after we apprehended her. No trace of anything nefarious."

I think about Inara offering me poison to coat my blade before I fought Judica. "If she knew to make a fake video, she would have known to dispose of anything incriminating."

"So we are back to square one?" Balthasar asks.

"What if Inara drove Angel to surrender?" Noah asks. "They would have known one another quite well. Inara could have applied pressure for Angel to surrender herself, or she could even have promised to defend her, all the while knowing she had an ace in the hole. That you'd eventually find the video Inara planted that vindicates her and implicates Angel instead."

"Let's think this through," I say. "Assuming Angel is guilty, and she needs to pin it on someone. She picks Inara —who doesn't have a motive that we know of."

"But neither does Angel," Marselle says.

"Are we positive it's one of them?" I ask. "Because it seems to me that one of these videos is clearly falsified. Could they both be falsified?"

"A third, unnamed suspect?" Noah shakes his head. "So even the new evidence has gotten us exactly nowhere?"

I drop my head in my hands. "Oh, Mom. Why can't we just figure out what happened? Why weren't you honest with me about what was going on? Why hasn't whoever fathered your child come forward? Did he even know you were pregnant?" I want to collapse into a heap and bawl again, but I don't. There's no time for that.

In the absence of anything conclusive, we allow each of the women to present their case. Angel calls dozens of character witnesses, all of whom insist on being given the opportunity to defend their friend. "Angel cut off her hand to spare Alamecha." "She took a bullet in the lung and the thigh to defend Enora." "She nearly died herself when she insisted on tasting a dish that looked slightly off." And on and on and on. By the end of their testimony, I feel as if I should be giving Angel a medal of honor, not a sword to the neck.

But Inara has just as many compelling witnesses who testify of her innocence. She fought in wars, leading the charge for Alamecha. She ran operations I'd never even heard of—from the Bay of Pigs, to the Crush at Kashmir. She risked herself over and over and over. For my mom, for Alamecha, even for me and Judica. Hearing how she stopped not one, but three attempted assassinations against Judica brings tears to my eyes. And to Judica's, who has to take a short break.

"We should all take a break," I say. "I need to eat something, and we'll reconvene in half an hour."

Instead of one of the kitchen staff, Lark brings me a tray of food. She closes the door behind her and sets it on my desk.

"Is everything okay?" I ask.

Lark bites her lip. "Maybe."

"What is it?"

"Angel and Inara are both in custody, being closely watched."

I nod.

"And you're sure that they can't escape."

"Lark, what's going on?"

"Someone from the kitchens has approached me, and for that to be fully understood, you need to know that they obey me, but they haven't really accepted me."

"Okay."

"The fact that Helena came to me." Lark gulps. "She's terrified of Angel. Terrified."

"What did she say?"

Lark shakes her head. "She won't tell me anything, but she asked for an audience with you. She wanted me to promise her that if you discover that Angel is guilty, she'll be executed."

I don't mention that Balthasar wants to draw and quarter the guilty party. "And you did."

Lark gulps.

"Bring her to me."

I pace until Lark returns, completely unable to eat a single bite.

Lark walks in with a tray so heavy, she couldn't have carried it alone. A cover, so that anyone who saw assumes Helena helped Lark bring me food I requested. Smart.

"Helena?" I ask the second the door closes. "You have something to share with me?"

She won't meet my eye.

"You don't need to be afraid. If Angel has done something wrong, if she harmed my mother, she won't be around to hurt you."

"I'm not sure whether she did something or not," she says.

"Why do you suspect that she might have?" I ask.

Helena meets my eyes then, her light grey eyes wide, terrified. "Angel may be in a cell, but she's a powerful woman. She's got connections, and they won't disappear just because she dies."

"No one needs to know of your involvement," I say. "I promise."

She nods. "I saw her, more than once, sprinkling something onto your mother's food."

I hate how relieved I feel. "Are you positive?"

She bobs her head. "I saw it a few days before your mother passed."

"Why didn't you tell anyone?"

Helena takes a step backward, as if she's afraid I'll fling myself at her. "I mean, she sprinkles things all the time. She's a chef."

"But something about this was different." I don't move, I don't threaten, and I keep my voice steady and calm.

"She pulled something out of her pocket, and it was a liquid of some kind. I'd never seen her do it before."

"You didn't warn anyone?"

"She's the person I would have warned. I couldn't have gotten in to see your mother." Her eyes are wide. "But I watched her carefully, your mother I mean. She seemed fine. So when I noticed Angel doing it again the next day. . . I figured it was something special. A seasoning or a vitamin your mother wanted."

I nod. "Thank you for telling me." I order a guard to stay with Helena until this has been resolved.

"I appreciate the offer," Helena says, "but I think it would merely draw attention to me."

"Understood." I close the door behind her. "I need to see Inara."

"I can let them know to bring her next," Lark says.

I shake my head. "Here, in my room. I need to talk to her alone."

"Is that wise?" Lark asks. "If you suspect her?"

I sigh. "I can't kill Angel unless I'm certain she killed Mom. Evidence is so easy to manipulate, so simple to twist. I think that if Inara killed Mom, I will know it." When I open the door, Judica's standing in front of it.

"Come in." I nod at Lark and she leaves to deliver my request.

Judica shoots through my door and starts pacing right away. "I've been thinking."

"Okay."

"What if Angel found out Mother was pregnant, and she felt that Enora's pregnancy would throw things into turmoil, again? What if Enora told her you reacted to the stone, and confessed she was pregnant? Would Angel have worried Sotiris would derail the prophecy? Would she have killed Mother to protect you or the whole world?"

I tell Judica about Helena.

Judica swears. "You could execute them both, you know, if you're as conflicted as me."

My mouth drops open. "Would you really advocate that course of action?"

"Of course not," Judica says, "not under normal circumstances. But these aren't normal, and we can't have a traitor sneaking around behind us."

Her words send a shiver down my spine. Could she really decapitate our older sister on the chance that she might have been involved in Mom's death? Would Mom even want that?

"It's like that shell and pea game right now," Judica says, "only we haven't been able to figure out where the pea is trapped, and we can't lift the cups to find it. So we may as well smash all of them."

May as well. Casual. Easy.

"At least we've narrowed it down to two," she whispers.

"Inara is coming to see me."

"Aren't you worried she might kill you?" Judica's eyes are wide. "Because if it was her, only you and I stand between her and the throne. That's a motive Angel doesn't share."

I don't burst into tears. I don't scream at her either. She's giving voice to my own fears, to the deep, ashamed part of me that suspects Inara, in spite of all the happy memories, the moments, the history we share. If Inara killed Mom, if she has been hiding it all this time, then I don't know her at all.

I might prefer death to that discovery.

"I owe it to her to ask her face to face before I make my decision. I owe it to Angel, too."

Judica doesn't argue. She merely opens the door. "I'll be right outside."

Inara arrives a few moments later.

Her face was the third one I ever saw. It hasn't changed, not a bit. She has always been there for me, right behind Mom, protecting me from the world. When Melina challenged Mom to kill me, Inara protected me, she rocked me, and she changed my diapers. She fed me whenever Mom was caught up with something else, never annoyed at the prospect. She stood up to Judica on my behalf when the world collapsed. She has advised me, and supported me, and loved me.

Was it all some kind of elaborate lie? Why?

"Chancy," Inara says.

"Is it true?" I ask. "Are you Nereus?" My voice cracks on the name. A tear rolls down my cheek, unconcerned about my efforts to remain impartial.

"I am not Nereus," Inara says. "And I did not kill Melina. I did not ever want Mother to die."

"You were here, on the island," I say. "Angel wasn't here when Melina went missing."

"And I know Melina," Inara says. "She'd have opened the door to me and welcomed me inside."

My heart cracks. Why isn't she poking holes in the defense Angel built?

"But that's the precise reason I could never kill her." Inara's eyes well with tears this time. "I raised Melina. I love her, as much as I love you, as much as I ever loved our

224

mother. I would never have destroyed her. What would I stand to gain?"

I shake my head. "Melina and Angel were close. Angel says she told Melina about the video, and that's when she disappeared."

"And every single one of Melina's retinue was slaughtered, so they can't confirm or deny that story."

"Angel did call her right before," I say. "She has phone records to show that."

"Which could easily have been doctored," Inara says. "Or she could have called to threaten her, or to say anything at all. Those things would be much simpler to fake than her video. And think about this. If she did realize that we were pursuing recovery of the video, which Marselle will confirm she was, even before Melina died, Angel might already have been playing clean up."

"Where were you on February 14, 2002?" Oh please, please, be somewhere that makes a visit to Las Vegas impossible!

"Yosemite park," she says. "Climbing El Capitan."

I close my eyes. "Within a few hours of Las Vegas."

Inara swallows. "I'd say you could talk to my pilot who went with me, but David died."

I killed him—keeping the EMP from hitting China. Gah. I sit on the desk chair. "Inara, I want to believe you. I love Angel, like an aunt maybe, or a close family friend, but you're my sister. Give me a reason to spare you. Please."

Inara kneels in front of me. "I can't, because whoever wants me executed has made it too confusing. There are two believable videos. There's a code name. The trail is too old and too cold at this point. The evidence has been brushed and polished and obfuscated. But you know me, and you know I loved Mother." She chokes. "You know I've supported you, and I support you still. If you choose to execute me, I'll walk to the throne unresisting. I saw what these kinds of decisions did to Mother." She grasps my hands. "If you believe it was me, Chancy, order the execution and walk away. Don't watch, and never blame yourself. Promise me that."

I pull Mom's sword from my belt sheath. Inara offered me her sword when I went to fight Judica. She was tortured because she supported me while I was in New York, and now she's not even telling me I'm a fool for doubting her.

Inara inhales. "Kill us both. You know it has to be one of us. It's the only way to be sure, to know that Mother's killer is brought to justice."

It's the same thing Judica said. Our family is messed up.

"I could hold you both," I say. "And look for more evidence."

"I'm a liability, if I'm not an asset," Inara says. "And you can't keep Angel locked up. If it's her, she has someone helping her in the palace. She must."

If it's her?

"I'm trying to walk you through the logic. It's all I've done since I heard they found a video with my face on it. I've tried to understand how it all looks to you."

I hand her my sword. "If you killed Mom, and if you killed Melina." I bawl like a baby. "Then you must want this very badly. There must be some reason you need the throne. Kill me. Take it."

"Judica would never let me."

"You'd figure that part out," I say. "I'm sure. If this is what you want, if this is what you've been aiming for, do it. I don't even want to rule, if it means killing my sisters, my family. I won't do it. I might be stupid and weak, but it's who I am."

Inara bats the sword away. Mom's sword whams into the rug and slides to a stop. "I would never kill you, Chancery. Never."

I hug her so tightly that her bones creak. "And I could

never kill you. Tell me it was Angel. Tell me you're innocent, and you believe the evidence against her is solid. Tell me that I'm executing Mom's killer if I execute Angel."

Inara hugs me back, her arms as tight around me as mine are around her. "I don't want to believe it. I didn't back when Judica had her detained. I spoke to her then, you know. I wasn't convinced. You could hold her too, if you want. More guards, more vigilance. Dig for some kind of motive. She devoted her life to Alamecha. It doesn't make sense that she's suddenly turned—and torn out her master's throat."

"But I would expect her to make this last play," I say. "Angel has been in charge of intelligence for centuries, but she's also always held a cherished position next to Mom— on her right hand, even. Everyone respected her as Mom's chef."

"True," Inara says. "I think she saw this as her only way back."

"But I won't let her take you down in her bid to return," I say. "And I won't let Mom's death go one more day without being avenged."

"I'm sorry," Inara says. "You have no idea how sorry I am. From the beginning, this has been horrible for you, and you're so young." Her lower lip trembles. "You've always been so good, so kind, so generous. Don't let this destroy you."

I hold my head high when Inara and I return to the throne room. Inara drops to her knee beside me. I don't sit. I stand in front of Mom's throne, the seat that will probably never really feel like it's mine. "I am Chancery Divinity Alamecha. It is my ruling, as Empress of family Alamecha, that Angel Alamecha committed high treason by poisoning her monarch to death. It is my sentence that she will be executed immediately."

Angel, to her credit, never wavers. She doesn't cry out. She never even drops her gaze. "So be it."

Mom carried out most of her own executions herself, at least on royalty, but I don't think I can do it. My hands shake at the thought. "Zarsen," I say. "Will you please do the honor?"

Balthasar clears his throat, and I recall that I told him he could do it.

"Fine." I say. "Balthasar will do it."

Zarsen nods and steps back into his position, his axe still on his belt.

Balthasar's eyes flash as he walks across the room, his boots striking the ground sharply, his pace never faltering.

As I watch him move toward Angel, I scan the audience, noticing half a dozen young children. I wish I had asked for them to be removed, but Mom never did. It's our way. It's hard, but it's the truth. And as much as I love Inara, and as much as I usually heed her counsel, I ignore her this time.

I stand and watch, not averting my eyes, not flinching, not sobbing or crying or screaming in horror, while Angel kneels before the throne, and Balthasar lifts his broadsword over his head and then removes Angel's head from her body with one clean stroke. Justice. I really believe that it is justice.

It's finally done, but I don't feel better.

I feel worse. Much, much worse.

❧ 19 ☙

"There have been confirmed cases of SARS-COV-2 on every continent excluding Antarctica," Franco says. "But in those over which we preside, we have taken efforts to—"

"Is the death rate in Italy actually above ten percent?" I ask.

"Of those infected," Franco says, "yes. Front line workers have been hit especially hard."

What a way to start my rule. "Is it possible this was something Adika set up?" I ask. "Like the poisoned blade?"

Job shakes his head. "It has been around since at least late fall. Perhaps slightly before—long before your mother even contemplated changing her heirship paperwork, at least as far as the world knew."

Something that isn't my fault. That almost seems impossible. But of course, how we handle it from here forward, that *is* on me. "Walk me through the numbers on each scenario—widespread shut downs versus herd immunity."

"As we previously discussed, we followed one approach in the United Kingdom, to delay any social distancing and shut down protocols in favor of asking those most at risk to self-quarantine or shelter in place."

"And?"

"At the same time, the United States began more aggressive social distancing in both California and Washington state."

"But not in New York City." I frown. "I hear the numbers there are bad."

"To be fair," Franco says, "the numbers would have always been far worse in New York. Social distancing in a city of its population without large numbers of grocery stores, and humans living in such close contact." He shakes his head. "Without public transit, cabs are your best option, and without that, you're looking at sidewalks, which don't allow for six inches between pedestrians sometimes, much less six feet."

"There were unique challenges," I admit. "But what did you find?"

"The economy suffers either way," Franco says, "but the death toll spikes when contact and spread factors aren't suppressed."

"So we should have instituted the same protocols in the UK," I say.

He shakes his head. "There was no way to know that beforehand."

"And yet it seems Adora handled things better than we did without advance knowledge." I stand up. "What about a vaccine?"

Job grunts. He's not usually invited to Council meetings, but we've made an exception when we discuss the virus. "We're a year out, probably. Even with promising early candidates, you can't just test them on scores of humans. It must be carefully prepared and tested in advance. Then human testing, then we advance to production and distribution."

"A year?" I ask. "We can't fast track that? What about the evian blood? What are we doing with that?"

Franco frowns. "We tested it first in Germany, and it's very effective on infected members of the population, but we need quite a lot of it to make any difference. And the virus transmits so quickly, and many infected humans have no symptoms. They wander around, shedding the virus around anyone they see, completely oblivious to the chaos in their wake."

Job sighs. "Unless we can somehow share our DNA with the humans in general, it's a Band-Aid, not a fix. Think of it like this. The virus is a burrowing wasp. It can pierce the cells of the humans like the skin of an apple. It burrows in and destroys any resistance. But your cells aren't like an apple. They're like artillery shells. They repel the wasp without even trying."

"But my blood cures infected humans," I say. "And all of your blood does the same."

Job grunts.

"If we all donated blood every day—"

"You will have a full on revolt if you start making evians donate blood daily to try and save sick humans," Job says.

I scowl.

"Even the evians who have tolerated your human sympathy so far would be incensed," Balthasar says.

I'll revisit it once we're past the threat of war with two other families. "We need more people on this," I say. "Assemble more researchers, Job. More administrators, Franco. The whole reason a centralized leadership like this should be better is that we can expedite the solution. So do it. Even before we sent the blood I collected to Germany, I heard that Analessa was brilliantly handling the spread. Figure out who was in charge of that and bring them in." I glance at Edam, scowling a little, as though I blame him for Analessa not being here to contribute herself.

"Now that you have executed the individual responsible for your mother's death," Melisania asks from a screen on the wall. "Will you eliminate the position of Inquisitor and release Judica from her extra responsibilities?"

Melisania has been relatively quiet so far, only chiming in occasionally at the Council meetings. And it has been a tremendous relief, not needing to be involved in the day to day administration of her holdings. "I'll discuss it with her, but for now I am inclined to continue the process of vetting my people. Once I am satisfied with the Royal Court at Alamecha, I'll likely send her to other families to continue there."

"Send her here first," Melisania says.

"Really?" She wants us poking around?

"I have always been a fan of how your mind works." Melisania stares at Judica. "It would be my honor to host you, and it would fulfill your obligation of time for this year."

Right.

"She would, of course, also be welcome here," Moses says.

I hate all the screens through which we are now conducting Council meetings, but it can't be helped. We need boots on the ground in each place, and I haven't even sent anyone to manage Malessa yet. I have half a mind to send Edam. He might have more luck infiltrating the Sons of Gilgamesh if he's not right next to me.

But the thought of sending him away. . . I can't. Not now.

"Moses, how have—"

"Sir!" A bright faced palace guard bursts through the door.

Balthasar stands. "What is it?"

"We're under attack," he says. "Killian called and says

ballistic missiles just took out the Manifa Arabian offshore platform."

"What?" I ask.

Balthasar's phone lights up. So does Marselle's, and Edam's, and Inara's, and Franco's. Maxmillian's. Guards begin hailing Moses and Melisania.

"Your Majesty," someone shouts behind Melisania. "The Lula field platforms are under attack!"

I shout. "Everyone assess the damage and meet back here in fifteen minutes to formulate a response."

Fifteen minutes turns into an hour, but we finally compile a list. Adora and Shamecha hit forty-two of the world's largest oil producing sites—every single one owned by the first, second, third, and sixth families.

"What does that change about our oil capacity?" I ask.

"It's down by at least forty percent," Balthasar says. "I should have thought about that as an attack strategy. Especially given Melamecha's strength in oil production already."

"But it's surely phase one," I say. "That's not all they'll do."

Edam leaps to his feet. "Not if we engage them first, draw their attention away."

"How?" I ask.

"Adora is quite small, geographically speaking," Marselle says. "What can we do to put pressure on them? Close off their opportunity for trade? Blockades?"

Balthasar stands up. "You're focusing in too close. We need to think overall strategy at this point. They surprised us with step one, but we need to contemplate their next options before planning our counter."

Too many people talking, too many variables. Edam and Balthasar are already snarling, and Marselle is whispering with Alora in the corner. I haven't even brought Moses and Melisania in yet, and Analessa's holdings aren't even represented. "Balthasar is my Warlord," I say. "There's no reason for any of this nastiness. I named him for a reason. The rest of you will sit down and wait for him to ask your opinion."

The bellows and shouts and growls halt.

Balthasar meets my eye. "What's your directive?"

"Formulate plans A, B, and C. Work on the drawbacks and benefits of each. You've run simulations on this with Alamecha for years—I know factoring in the other families will be hard, but I have faith in your skill."

He bows.

"Consider that you have fireballs, EMPs, and kinetic blasts at your disposal where needed, within reason." I walk out.

Noah falls into step next to me. "You're not going to stick around, at least for a bit?"

I don't slow down. "I need to stop thinking about it right now."

"Because?"

I stop and stare at the toes of my boots. I thought that wearing black combat boots like Judica would help me channel my inner warrior, but it's not working. I resume my path and walk without speaking until I reach my room. Once I'm inside, I fling myself on Mom's bed.

My bed. I'm in the middle of a war, and Mom's loss still hits me, like a knife to the gut, at the strangest times. I wish she was here, even if she wouldn't take things away, handle the issues herself. I wish she was here just to tell me it will all be alright.

"Because," I finally say. "No one in there cares about collateral damage, but I do."

"And if they've read your proclamations, if they've paid any attention at all, they know that."

I slam my fists against the comforter.

"Whoa," Noah says. "Take it easy. You know, that silk coverlet isn't even fighting back."

I sit up and smooth the rumpled blankets. "How many people have to die, before we realize?"

Noah sits on the edge of the bed. "Realize what?"

My voice is small. Uncertain. Wobbly. "That maybe I'm the problem, not the solution."

Noah snorts. "Do you know how many wars there have been since Adam and Eve started popping out kids?"

"That's not very respectful," I say.

He sighs. "It's not, you're right, but this stuff gets *depressing* in a hurry. And I am sick of acting like the world can't be fun. So I make fun of everything, and the more nervous I become, the more jokes I make." He folds his hands in his lap. "I can stop, if I make a concerted effort."

I put a hand over his. "No. It usually helps."

"Look, my point is that you can control what you do. You can plan for what that might lead to, and you can do the very best you can to head off the worst stuff at the pass, but these skirmishes would have happened whether you seized the stones or not. I actually think you've accomplished a tremendous amount with very little bloodshed so far."

I haven't gotten a count on the lives lost today, but it won't be low. "There are worse things than dying," I say.

Noah lifts his eyebrows. "Like what?"

"If I sliced your belly open," I say, "and I yanked your intestines out of your body, you would be able to keep living, with them dangling out of your body, carrying them around in a little rucksack. But what kind of life would you have?"

He bumps my shoulder with his. "I worry about your brain sometimes, you know that? Usually you're all, like, 'Hey, sunshine and lollipops and save the cute little, fluffy humans!' And then the next second, you're like, 'I could yank your intestines through your nostrils and tie them in a bow on your head.' That is not normal."

I snort. "No one has ever accused me of being normal. Not here, among the vicious hyenas at court, and not in New York. I don't fit anywhere."

"There's a reason God chose you, and a reason he shaped you as he did." Noah turns until he can look me in the eyes. "I believe that. And I know that each death, each injury, each blow causes you pain, and I think that's what makes you right for this job. So when Balthasar comes back and he says, 'Here's plan A. We blow up half the world with nukes,' you will tell him no. And when he proposes a plan B that uses piles of humans as cover to smuggle in an evian Trojan horse, you'll turn that one down too. And when his plans C, D, and E are even worse, well, you'll think of something. I can help too. That's what we do."

"The easiest path," I say, "is already obvious. Only, no one has suggested it."

"Huh?" Noah bites his lip. "I'm like *super duper* smart, and nothing obvious has occurred to me."

"How did I beat Adika?" I ask.

"Well, technically, I'm the one who beheaded her."

I roll my eyes. "Personal combat. I took out the leader, and the regular rank and file from the royal evians down to the humans fall in line because they don't want war."

"True," Noah says. "And next you're going to mention Analessa, whom you personally defeated like ten minutes ago. But there's no way, after the Adika fiasco and the Analessa decapitation that's surely gone viral by now, that they'd ever agree to fight you, even if Melamecha is supposed to love her sword more than her Consort."

I close my eyes. Maybe this wasn't so obvious. "They originally refused my demand they surrender with identical denials. Then they declared war in carbon copy. I bet they'd agree to fight me. . . at the same time. Especially if I agree not to wear this." I slide Mom's ring off my finger and hold it in my palm.

Noah leaps to his feet. "Absolutely not. No. No way. I forbid it."

"Oh," I say. "I am so glad you said that, My Lord and Master. Now that I know you forbid it, well that's a weight off my mind."

"You may be God's chosen," Noah says, "but that's not a get out of jail free card. When you are cut, you bleed. That means you could die."

"But I just found out that there's another person on earth who can use the stupid, cursed, staridium stones." Before I can think about it, I hop up, cross the two feet separating us, and slam the stone into his palm, ensuring the stone meets his skin.

It flashes in his hand.

Just like it flashes in mine.

"And guess what that means?" I ask. "It means I'm not quite as important anymore, doesn't it?"

He drops the stone and it falls to the carpet, blackening in front of my very eyes. "I will *never* use that rock. Never. I want nothing to do with it."

"Huh," I say. "I feel the very same way. Only, I've been thinking about this. What if the Eldest *isn't* the older of two daughters? What if it's the older of two *people* who react to the dumb stone?"

He shakes his head so hard I wonder that his teeth aren't clattering. "No, it says *she*."

I shrug. "Transcription error. Some languages don't even have gender assignments. Tagalog doesn't."

"Stop it," Noah says. "You're scared and now you want to run, but you can't. I am not the person chosen by God to handle this. You are."

"Says who? Says my MOM? She's dead! Oh, and so is Angel! And Melina, probably, and Adika, Analessa, you name them, I've killed them. And now a whole kit and caboodle of other people are about to go down, so guess what? If I can murder two people, instead of *millions*, what kind of monster would I be not to take that gamble? Especially now that I know someone else can fill in for me with that stupid prophecy if this doesn't pan out?"

"Why didn't you ask the Council this? Make them the proposal." Noah crosses his arms.

"You know exactly what they would say." I fume. "And I can't even explain my reasoning, not without outing you. And they'd roast you for that, and insist on going after your dad too. This is our only play, and you know it. You come with me, and if I fail, you take them out with the stone."

"You should insist on wearing it."

I roll my eyes. "Right. I'm sure they'll agree to fight me with the volcano maker close at hand."

"So how would you possibly lure them out?" he asks.

"That's why I need the help of someone really *super duper* smart." I smirk. "Know where I could find someone like that?"

"Fine," he says. "I'll help you try and do this, but only because I think you can beat them, and I know that if I say no, you'll do it anyway, but without me."

I beam at him.

"You should know," Noah says, "that if Lainina and Melamecha don't kill you, Edam might kill us both."

"I think I'll take my chances," I say.

But I do worry that he might never forgive me for planning this without him, and I wasn't kidding when I said there are things worse than death.

❧ 20 ❧

"So plan A and B have both been refused?" Balthasar says. "Is that what you're saying?"

"I know you prepared them to finish this as quickly as possible, but the expected casualties are just too high. Look, battle is new to me," I say. "Since there weren't any huge ones during my lifetime, not fought by my mom anyway, and since I wasn't even her chosen replacement. . ."

"Understood," Balthasar says. "And we've prepared the presentation of these plans to take all of that into account. I have a few principles I'll need to explain first, but this third option is intended to mitigate civilian losses as much as possible."

"When your mother was fighting mine, long before my time," Edam says, "she perfectly executed the tactic of undermining the confidence and reliability of her enemy's army. She had thousands of 'sporting' texts printed up and disseminated at the front lines. The commanders believed their troops were reading about sports, preparing for post war times to return. But in actuality, these manuals explained how to fake illnesses that would allow them to be sent home."

I frown.

"Thousands upon thousands of healthy troops used the techniques to go home," Edam says, "weakening the German front line."

"And then," Balthasar says, "on the back end, when the leaders realized what was going on, they refused to send anyone home who complained of those illnesses and that resulted in sick soldiers staying on the front line, which spread disease among their ranks." His head shakes slowly, appreciatively. "Enora was brilliant at those ideas. Unparalleled, really."

"Okay," I say. "So do we have time to start printing books? And we don't really have an entrenched front line, so where exactly—"

"Edam had the idea," Balthasar says, "to search the Motherless and other refugees for the youngest sibling of both Melamecha and Lainina."

I close my eyes. Of course he did.

"If the men leading their troops have another option— someone else to follow, someone who supports you already. . ." Edam trails off. "It could have triple the effect of some manuals, and you laid the groundwork for it already, enabled by their sexist policies and practices."

"Most of the evian men are heartily sick of being treated like meat headed for the grinder," Balthasar says. "So Edam's right. And Afanasy was born just before Reshaka died—and he has no love for his sister, who has always refused to even acknowledge his existence."

"And Lainina? Did Esheth even have—"

Edam smiles. "Even better. Lainina's youngest child has been here all along."

I close my eyes. "We can't ask anything like that of Hikaru." I've known him my entire life, and he longed for the life he missed. He used to warn me that Judica was coming in notes he left inside of origami birds. Declaring himself as an enemy to his family, his mother, the life he would have chosen for himself, it would shred him. Hikaru shouldn't be crushed, not like this.

"He volunteered," Edam says. "He heard me talking to Afanasy, and he approached me."

"Fine." I sigh. "So prong one is to set up our own claim to the throne, other than my own demands predicated on my prophetic right. Hopefully that will split the focus and resolve of their forces. Maybe we'll even have some defection of intelligence assets."

Balthasar smiles. "Precisely. And for prong two, it's story time again."

"Okay," I say.

"Have you heard of the battle of Pelusium?" he asks.

I shake my head.

"It was 525 BC, so it's pretty far back. But it was one of your great great grandmother Meridalena's last huge losses —to the brand new ruler, Edam's great grandmother, Selah. Selah's army was dramatically outmatched, but she realized something. Meridalena loved cats. She surrounded herself with them. Panthers, lions, tigers, bobcats. Any exotic cat alive, she wanted them. That trickled down to the humans around her, and they worshipped cats, too. Cat statues, cat portraits, all of it. And it worked its way into designs, decorations, coffins, everything."

"And?" I ask.

"When Selah's Warlord Cambyses II attacked Meridalena's forces in the Battle of Pelusium, he had cats painted on all the shields."

I lift both eyebrows. "Seriously?"

"And he took thousands of cats with them. Every soldier had a cat. Large cats on leashes. Small cats were carried. Meridalena's army refused to kill the cats, or even attack the cats, and they fled." Balthasar laughs. "It was brilliant."

"Right, but what do both Shamecha and Adora citizens worship or revere?" I ask. "Are we going to attack them with iPhones held aloft? YouTube videos playing on portable TVs?"

"Hilarious," Edam says. "But no, we will be leading with *you.*"

"Umm, exactly no one worships me. In fact, my own people mock me incessantly."

Balthasar points. "But every evian alive is aghast at the power at your fingertips."

"Fingertops?" Edam asks. "Either way. You have, resting on top of your slender fingers, the power to convince them that they're on the wrong side—that their loss is inevitable, which will have them revolting, or defecting, or both."

"The humans will have no idea what they're watching, and we risk outing our existence."

Balthasar shrugs. "How? We control all media outlets. But beyond that, it may not matter anymore."

He's right. If the end is coming, our reasons for staying hidden: safety, convenience, and pride. . . they may be crumbling. "How exactly do you propose we affect this?" I ask. "Am I supposed to be on a chariot, holding up a torch at the front of our army?"

"We need to explain the other component first," Edam says. "So, your great grandmother, Corlamecha, got my great grandmother back—at Carthage, the Battle of Ilipa. Hannibal was brilliant, but Scipio Africanus." Edam whistles.

"The point?" I ask a little too sharply. Long journeys down the aisle of forgotten warfare aren't exactly my priority right now.

Edam's face shutters. "Both sides had their own legion-naires, strong, well trained troops, and were supplemented by Iberian mercenaries, but Scipio's forces were outnumbered by twenty to thirty percent, probably twenty thousand men. Both sides woke up every morning and threatened to fight. On the first day, and every subsequent day, Scipio Africanus positioned his troops so that his homegrown warriors were in the center, with the Iberians in the wings."

"And the Carthaginians mirrored him," Balthasar says.

"But then one day, Scipio Africanus woke early, fed his men, and reversed the order. He skipped the posturing and attacked—sending his men like wolves. The Carthaginians woke up and formed up out of habit, the strength in the center, the weaker fighters in the wings. Scipio's legionnaires mowed the Iberians down, and closed on the center before the Carthaginian legionnaires had even engaged. It was a complete and total rout."

"So we plan to feint, several times in the same way, and then move ahead quickly, but inverted?" I frown. "Which would be awesome, if we still fought with bucklers and shields in formations."

Edam sighs. "They didn't use bucklers."

"What are we doing?" I ask. "Get to the point."

"They took out our oil," Edam says. "They'll expect a reprisal there. Either seizing or destroying their assets. They'll be guarding them heavily. It's their upper hand right now."

"We'll feint there?" I ask.

Balthasar nods. "We will. But then we take out their largest food production facilities instead."

I frown. "Won't that harm their civilians, too?"

Balthasar throws his hands in the air. "It will, but not as badly as a pitched battle, or nuclear weapons, or even chemical warfare. Melamecha and Lainina know that you care about humans. It's patently clear. They will not hesitate to turn that knowledge against you, and our intelligence assets say that their next foray will be intended to cause maximum damage. Knowing you oppose that strongly, our priority is to end things quickly, but I can't do that with skywriting and flower bouquets."

"What about targeting Lainina and Melamecha?" I ask. "Like we did with Adika?"

"Too late for that," Edam says. "We used the strategy already, and they'll expect it."

"Which means they won't sit in place and wait for me," I say. "They'll be moving, running things from rotating locations."

Balthasar nods. "It's what I'd do."

"Fine," I say. "Prepare final details and we'll go with this option." I'm out the door and halfway down the hall before Edam catches up.

"Can we talk?"

"I need to—"

"You've made plenty of time for Noah lately," he practically whispers.

"Fine," I say.

Once we're inside my room, I walk to the window and grip the windowsill, watching the waves crash into the shore. I wish more of this was fake. "What do you need?"

Edam's voice comes from just behind me. He's always moved quietly, but I should've heard his heartbeat. I'm off my game. "Turn around."

My fingers tremble, and I still them. "Just tell me what's wrong."

His hand tugs on my shoulder, and I finally relent, spinning around ready for battle. But his eyes are soft, full of concern, maybe even fear. "I need a promise."

"What kind of promise?" I expect him to beg me not to kiss Noah, not to spend more time with him, not to trust him.

"I know you, Chancery. I'm sure you're planning something, even now."

"Huh?"

"You play innocent really well, and I might believe you, except no. You're contacting Lainina, or Melamecha. You're looking for a way to end this without any casualties."

My chin tilts upward. "And what if I am? Wouldn't that be a good thing?"

"Come on," Edam says. "You aren't thinking this through. Your mother was called Enora the Merciless. Melamecha, though, do you know her name?"

I gulp.

"The Sadist."

"People are always—"

"It's well earned," Edam says. "She loves hurting people and things. And Lainina, she relies on her Consort to fight for her. You know that, right? She won't fight you herself. She never does."

"Fine," I say. "So what?"

"Have you seen Rothgar?"

He's gargantuan. "I know he's fierce."

Edam steps closer. "He's massive, and I'm not even sure that I could defeat him."

"I guess I'm lucky that I'm God's chosen," I say.

"You aren't bulletproof," he says.

His words, almost verbatim what Noah said, send a chill down my spine. "I can't promise that if I find a way to end this at a risk only to myself, I won't take it."

"Why?" he asks. "Why, for once, can't you let someone else take the risk? Why can't you just do your part and let the rest of us do ours?"

"I didn't ask to throw my life onto the scales at our engagement party," I say. "That was your call."

"No," he says. "You did that. I challenged my sister, who ruled from a set of sexist, outdated laws. I was taking the risk on myself, and it was worth it to me, to know that if you and I wed, it was because you wanted to marry me, not because you *had* to do it."

"Well, your brave choice nearly killed me, and I've had nightmares ever since because I won. So while I appreciate your sentiment, I think I'll continue to do exactly what I want, since it's my life on the line."

Edam closes his eyes then, and a shudder runs through him. "You're right." He opens his eyes and steps back. "I can't undo what I did. I can't erase the pain it causes you. I know that."

"But you would if you could, I know."

"It's not fair of me to ask you to do something I didn't —to leave something alone. I know that Balthasar and I, we can end this, without you dying. We can. And sure, some people will die, but that's inevitable. And people will die of this virus, and the flu, and old age." He grits his teeth. "You can't save everyone in the world. Life is loss. Life is choices. And some of them are bad, and others suffer as a result."

"My job as a ruler is to mitigate that suffering."

"So you won't promise?" he asks. "Just give me two weeks. They'll be much more likely to accept some kind of wild offer once they've started to hurt, you know. If things get bad enough, I'll help you reach out to them myself."

"I'll think about it," I say.

The smile that dawns on Edam's face nearly knocks me over.

"But I can't promise yet," I say. "I was terrified, Edam, when I fought Analessa. I thought I might die then. I know nothing about spears, nothing about using a shield, and I thought that might be it."

"As scared as you were, I was—"

"When you challenged her, the thought of her killing you." My throat catches.

"Pretending to be angry with you," Edam says, "well. It might hurt less if you just stabbed me. Repeatedly, every time you saw me."

246

"I know it's a big ask, to act like you hate me, but I need information on that group," I say. "Badly. It seems like this organization has been around for a long time. They may be able to tell me what's coming, or they might even be the ones causing it."

"I think I've been approached," he says. "I'm not entirely sure."

"Oh?" I lift my eyebrows.

"Approached might be too strong a word, but one of your mother's former guards has been complaining. It started out mild, but Trevan asked me this morning how you could possibly be around an evian who pretended to be human. He asked how I could have ever supported your policies on granting humans rights."

"Could be nothing," I say. "Maybe he's just a bigot."

Edam shrugs. "Could be."

"Still." I put my hand on his arm. "It could be our way in, and that could change everything."

Edam's eyes drop to my hand, and suddenly I'm aware of him in a way I wasn't five seconds before. His breath on the top of my head. His heart beating steadily next to me. The heavy corded muscle in his arm. I should move my hand. I should step backward and press my shoulder blades against the solid wood of the window frame.

I know deep down in my soul that I can't meet his eyes. Bad things will happen if I do. Muddy things, messy things, confusing things. Even so, when his head slowly rises, I can't look away. I lose control of my limbs, my arms and legs languid, simultaneously heavy and weightless at the same time. His eyes, oh Eve, his eyes. They're fury and desire and need and desperation, and they'll consume me if I don't withdraw.

But I've already waited too long. Edam swallows, his lips closing and parting, his head moving down, closer, closer. But he doesn't kiss me. His lips veer past my face, stopping alongside my ear. His whisper is raw, as if it's being ripped from him. "I need you."

The bands around my heart snap and my fingers curl into his arm, hard. "Yes," I whisper.

That's all it takes. One little word. An acknowledgement that I've missed him in between every breath. That I've curled up against my pillow at night and sobbed, missing him beside me. That I've longed to touch his temple. Run my finger along his jaw.

Edam steps toward me, and I move backward reflexively. He grins, and my heart accelerates, my knees weakening. Luckily my back bumps up against the window frame like I knew it would. He lifts me then, depositing my backside on the windowsill, his hands flattening on either side. His mouth doesn't miss mine, not this time. His lips move roughly against mine, claiming me, and I revel in it.

For the first time in days, I feel safe, surrounded, anchored to the ground in a way I never am when he's not by my side. My hands fly to his jaw, the sharp angles I love so dearly, the scruff on his cheek abrading my palms. I push upward, my fingers tangling in his hair. He's overdue for a trim, and I love it. I yank him closer.

And he growls, deep in his throat.

Something inside of me catches fire, and my arms wrap around his shoulders, yanking him closer, still.

Of course, windows aren't made to withstand two hundred plus pounds of muscle, all shoved in their direction. I shouldn't be surprised when the window I'm basically slammed up against shatters, and we both tumble to the ground in the courtyard.

The guards stationed outside rightly sound the alarm.

Edam's smiling like a cat with his face in a bowl of cream, and I'm about to laugh when I remember the guard who was criticizing me. And how this story would kill that on the vine, if in fact he was feeling him out.

It pains me deeply, but I yank a dagger from my boot and press it to Edam's cheek.

The smile evaporates. "You aren't my fiancé, not anymore. I don't have to listen to anything you say. You better remember that, or you'll be removed from the Council, too." I hop up and gesture at the guards. "Get someone to clean up this mess. Now!"

Edam has to know the reason for my pivot, but the pain on his face isn't feigned. I finally understand what he means when he says lying about how he feels hurts worse. I don't even notice the gashes on my arms from the shattered glass until I'm out of the gate and halfway down the beach.

"Why do we have to tell anyone else?" I complain.

Noah snorts. "I may be a perfect specimen, but. . ." He gestures around the courtyard. "There is only one of me."

"Can you magic another?"

He rolls his eyes. "Not a corporeal one. It wouldn't help."

"Judica would stop me." It's a simple fact. She and Balthasar have been thick as thieves, and Edam has strangely gravitated toward her as he helps with her investigation of all security personnel.

"What about Inara?" he asks. "I feel like she could play a reasonably convincing sadist."

"She didn't kill Mom," I say for the twelfth time.

"You hope she didn't," he says. "That's not the same as knowing."

"You don't know that I didn't kill my mom."

Noah arches one eyebrow. "Now who's delusional?"

"Fine, not Judica, not Inara, who else can we trust?

Certainly not Edam. He wouldn't leave until I promised to wait and see whether the attack strategy is working."

"Was that before or after you shoved him through the window?"

Heat rises in my cheeks. Noah knows something happened between me and Edam—he's not an idiot. At least he doesn't press me about it. So far, he has just made snide remarks. "What about Alora?" I ask. "I hear she defeated Balthasar, and she's a melodics master. I could use someone who speaks my language."

"I learned a modified version of your melodics, you know," Noah says.

"It's the 'modified' that concerns me," I say.

"Ours was based on rhythms, not melodies and harmonies, but it's almost the same."

"You didn't answer," I say. "Alora?"

"What about Balthasar?" he asks. "He's tough, and he has trained warriors for centuries."

"If you think Edam won't let me go, you should see how fast Balthasar chains me up and throws the key into that somewhat burbly volcano."

Noah's eyebrows draw together sharply. "Wait, I thought you fixed the volcano."

I laugh. "Gotcha."

"Okay, look, we have to bring someone in soon, because we may have very little time to train. So go with your gut. Who?"

"Alora," I say. "She was always there for me, even when it meant defying Mom."

"Why didn't you suggest her originally?"

"Because she betrayed me, to you, if you recall." I put a hand on my hip. "You can't cast some light on that, can you?"

"Maybe." Noah's eye twitches a little, as he prepares for a possible seizure. "No harm in trying, right?"

"Very funny. I know that it could very literally harm you, but I need to know if there's some reason I can't trust her."

"Alora married my brother." Noah blinks. "Hey, I could say that. I wonder if I always could have, or if the vow shifts a little as you figure things out."

"The vow?"

He shakes his head. "That's definitely taboo. I'm sure. But let's see how far I can press. My brother's name is Isamu."

"Okay."

He smiles. "He was sent to integrate within Adora. He was supposed to marry someone there, and eventually, if he could trust her, bring her back home."

"So that's how you've survived. Your family poaches evians from all the other families."

He shrugs. "Not always, but sometimes."

"Okay, and he clearly didn't stay there."

"He did so well in Adora that they sent him on a mission."

"A mission?"

"Lainina didn't get along well with your mother. You surely knew that already, and Lainina felt that Eamon was making Enora even worse."

My dad.

"She planned to kill Eamon, your sister Melina, and hopefully your mother. She needed to know how Inara and Alora fell on the spectrum, politically speaking, and figure out which one might be easier to deal with."

"Isamu was supposed to suss out Alora's leanings?"

"As much as he could."

"And he did," I say flatly.

"He fell in love with your sister. He said she was the most brilliant, blindingly beautiful woman he had ever met. A north star amid a bunch of white dwarves."

I lift one eyebrow.

"Isamu is a huge nerd."

"Okay, so they got married."

"And they were happy," Noah says.

"Great," I say. "Although, I never met him, or even heard about him. So that's kind of strange."

"That's because he trusted her," Noah says. "So he told her everything."

I gulp. "Everything?"

"About our family, who we are, our purpose."

Things I don't even know.

"Isamu didn't have the same. . . restrictions that I have."

"What does that mean?" I ask.

"Mom and Dad trusted him more."

"Why?"

"It's a long story, and I doubt I can share it. Let's stay focused. Alora obtained permission from your mother to have him join the family and then tried to stay as far away from the spotlight as possible."

I shake my head. "That makes no sense."

"His cover as a former spy sent by Lainina wasn't great. If your mom pressed, she'd quickly find that Adora didn't know quite where he came from. Things would get dicier from there. So they stayed away from the center of everything, which was fine, until Mom and Dad needed something."

"What?"

"They wanted me to meet you, and they applied pressure accordingly."

"Pressure?"

"They called Isamu home, and your sister came, delighted to be invited at last. But when they arrived, our family guards restrained Isamu, and Mom and Dad told Alora they'd kill him if she didn't do what they said. It was a lot of drama."

"Your parents sound awful."

"Says the daughter of Enora the Merciless."

Fair point.

"Alora agreed to introduce us, and she set things in motion, inviting you to New York to live with her. But when your mom died, it expedited our introduction."

"Did she know what you intended to do with me?"

"Dad swore to her that I meant you no harm, that we were both involved in the prophecy."

"So she wasn't given much of a choice, but she also didn't believe meeting you would harm me."

Noah nods.

"I'm ready to invite her to join our training team," I say. "Assuming she can channel her inner sadist."

"Okay," Noah says. "But one more thing." He screws his face up in the way he has begun doing whenever he tries to say something he isn't sure he can say. "They haven't released my brother. Alora is still reporting to them."

I close my eyes. "So you're on my side, inasmuch as you can be, but if I press Alora about anything and she folds. . ."

"My parents could punish my brother." Noah's expression is grim.

"Fine, I won't let on that I know anything."

Noah follows me out the back gate and toward the front of the palace where Alora's staying. We've gone a hundred paces when Inara shoots out a side door of the palace. She pulls up short and glances from Noah to me and back again. "Nothing's wrong, is it?"

I shake my head. "Noah's been training with me, teaching me some things I never learned from Mom, since Balthasar and Edam are so busy."

"Is that the real reason?" Inara's eyes are kind.

I open my mouth to tell her the truth—that while things are strained, Edam and I are actually fine. Or, we will be, eventually. But before any words can emerge, an irrational sense of unease steals over me.

Which makes no sense.

After the trial, I struggled to sleep at all, and Judica went over and over and over Inara's life, turning up nothing that would throw her loyalty into question. I made the right call—sparing her and executing Angel. I know it, and yet. "It's easier," I say. "It's hard for me to be around him right now. And I think it's easier for him, too. I don't think he'd ever betray me, but I just can't look at him the same, not anymore."

"I understand that," Inara says. "I'd never be able to forgive someone for going behind my back either."

"It's hard enough," I say, "dealing with the war, the virus, figuring out who I can choose as a regent for Malessa." I shake my head. "I don't have the bandwidth to keep myself from hitting him with a fireball. Know what I mean?"

"If I could hurl fireballs at anyone who ticked me off, I fear the world would be a very charred place indeed."

I laugh. "I think if you actually could, you'd find far fewer instances justify it than you fantasize."

"Leave me to my imagination, then," Inara says. "And if there's anything I can do, tell me."

I hug her, and it's almost like I'm hugging Mom.

"Don't do anything rash," she whispers.

I pull back. "What?"

"When Melina—" She chokes up. "She competed in the Millennial Games. Did you know that?"

I shake my head.

"She competed in Weaponry, one on one combat. She nearly won. It's a dangerous discipline, and she always felt that whatever happened, God would keep her safe."

I blink.

"You have a prophecy saying you'll do certain things."

Inara cups my cheek. "I imagine that the weight of that, combined with the eagerness of youth, might make you feel like Melina did. Invincible."

I swallow.

"You're still flesh and blood." Inara's eyes are soft, caring, concerned. "Mom's not here to tell you this, so I will. Don't do anything rash. You aren't replaceable, but that doesn't mean you're invincible."

Geez, am I that obvious? "Believe me, you're not the first person to tell me to be careful."

She smiles. "I'm glad that you have people looking out for you. Truly."

So am I.

It takes us an irritatingly long time to track Alora down. She was out for an ocean swim.

"You've been looking for me?" she asks, wiping her face on a towel that was waiting on the beach. "I'm sorry. I didn't realize I was needed."

"It's fine," I say. "I hadn't realized it myself until a while ago. But I actually have a favor to ask."

"You want me to help you train to fight Melamecha and Lainina?"

I open my mouth, but no words come out.

"Or, Rothgar," she says, "technically."

"How," I ask, "did you have any idea—"

Alora laughs. "Everyone knows you're planning to try and challenge them somehow."

"Everyone?"

Alora shrugs. "We haven't talked about it, but we know you, Chancery. If there's any opportunity to spare the lives of your people, or anyone off the street you've never met, really, you'll do it. You haven't hidden that fact. That story I hear you told at Mother's funeral, I mean, that was more about you than about Mother. You wanted to save *birds*?"

"Birds whose mother had died," I say.

"Right. And no evian on earth has ever cared about the fate of baby birds. You're the first. So, of course you'd be raring to come up with a solution that will save the lives of thousands, tens of thousands, or maybe hundreds of thousands."

I'm the first evian to care about animals? Baby animals? Maybe I *should* let the world burn. Ugh. "Well, then you're on to me. I plan to issue a challenge to Melamecha and Lainina."

Alora shakes her head. "It's a waste of time. We all know that, too. Neither of them will ever accept."

"What if I'm willing to fight them at the same time, on their ground? Think they'll still refuse?"

Alora straightens. "You can't do that."

"That's why I need your help," I say. "Noah can't be two people at once."

"I won't help you kill yourself," Alora says. "Neither would Mother, if she was here."

"Well, she isn't here," I say. "Which is why I had to fight Judica, who everyone knew would destroy me. Only she didn't. And then, when I had to stop not one, but two nuclear warheads, well I did that without her too. And then, when I had to decide whether to kill not one, but two sisters, I did that alone. And I've killed two empresses myself."

"Technically, I beheaded Adika." Noah waves.

"Why are you waving?" Alora asks. "You aren't a tourist at Disney World."

"Oh man, that would be way more fun than being here right now." Noah sticks his hands in his pockets.

"I've always thought there was a screw loose in his head," Alora says, "but I feel like it's wiggling looser lately."

I laugh. "He does it for me. To remind me that even if

I've rolled in the mud, even if I'm murdering people, I'm still a person." I reach out and take Noah's hand in mine. "He reminds me to smile, and sometimes the only thing he can make fun of is himself."

"Oh no," Alora says.

"What?"

"I thought you loved Edam."

I drop Noah's hand. "It's complicated."

"And more importantly, I'm fine with it," Noah says. "So mind your own business, Miss I Know Everything."

Alora huffs. "See? Screw loose."

"But will you help me?" I ask. "Because if I don't make some plans, I really will die."

"I don't think it's going to help." Alora drops her towel in the sand. "And when I'm staring at your bloody corpse, and Mother is rolling in her grave, err, her remains are spinning around or whatever ashes do, I'm going to remember this moment, and I'm going to hate myself for this."

"That's a yes," Noah says. "The longest, most macabre yes I've ever heard." He mock whispers to me. "And she thinks I'm odd."

"You realize we will have to train in the middle of the night," Alora says. "Or everyone will figure out your plan in like one point one seconds."

I nod.

"And your guards might rat you out, even then." Alora quirks an eyebrow.

"I've got that one covered," Noah says.

"How, exactly?" Alora asks.

Noah squirms.

"You know what? I don't want to know." Alora sighs. "Meet me here, at this bend on the beach. Three in the morning. Everyone is asleep by then. We'll do our first training session by the light of the moon on unsteady ground."

And we do.

It's not very promising. And sand hurts almost as bad in an open wound as saltwater.

I slam into the sand, blood trickling down my thigh where Alora tagged me. Again.

"You suck at guarding when you're attacking," she says.

"Who taught you to fight two opponents at once?" Noah asks me.

"Edam!" I shout. "The guy who literally slices and dices people like they've been run through a food processor."

"And what did he tell you?" Noah says.

"That you can really only engage one opponent at a time, so your job is to rotate them so they can only come at you one at a time."

Noah shrugs. "And that works if you're in a box, or a ring, or you've got people following standard rules of engagement."

"None of which may be the case," I say.

"Right." Noah offers me a hand.

I kick him and stand on my own.

"What was that for?"

"You threw sand in my eyes," I say.

"I'm supposed to be making this hard. Otherwise we'd call it dancing."

"Get a room, you two," Alora says.

"Okay." I yank my sword out of the sand. "It's clearly not working for me to try and rotate until I'm facing one of you at a time. So what now?"

"I don't know," Alora says. "I've never been great at two-person combat."

"Don't look at me," Noah says. "I'm only two years older than you."

"Fine, let's do it again. At some point, something will have to click, right?"

But five minutes later, after Alora severs my spine

around T10, I realize something. Something depressing. No matter how badly I'd like to fight Rothgar and Melamecha and spare the world from the war that's coming. . .

If I fight them both at the same time, I'll die.

"What if you used my stone?" Noah asks. "I mean, I have no idea what would happen if you took it, but worst case, you like, knock me unconscious."

"Does the vow or whatever not work if you're passed out?"

He shrugs. "Who knows? I've never known what happened if I was unconscious."

"And then I could, what?" I ask. "Make Melamecha think I have two noses?"

Noah laughs. "It's not at its strongest in combat applications, that's for sure."

"Well Edam begged me to promise him not to challenge them anyway. So for now, I'm fulfilling the promise I refused to give."

"Is that why you threw him through window?" Noah asks.

"Getting closer," I say.

"Let's just hope Balthasar's plan works, and then we won't need to figure anything else out," Noah says.

"Because don't take this the wrong way, but last night did not inspire confidence."

We're three minutes early to the Council meeting, and we're still the last ones to arrive. I forget, for a nanosecond, that they're all here at my command, and worry that I've made them wait. It's still bizarre to be the empress, when a few weeks ago, I didn't even control the remote.

"Our first stage went flawlessly," Balthasar reports. "We've already begun to hear about defectors, mostly men, but surprisingly, not all. New Zealand, New Guinea, Iran, Turkey, Greece, they're all reporting a substantial number of defectors."

"And for every one who actually leaves Adora and Shamecha, ten more won't fight as hard, or will turn when the war is at its most pitched," Moses says. "Most of the people we're welcoming are telling us that their family would have left too, but they didn't feel it was safe."

"Which means it's time to start phase two," Edam says, "in which we begin the feints on oil production by targeted attacks that you are also heading."

Time to pay the piper. "What did you have in mind?"

"We need a dozen teams or more, all of them led by someone who Melamecha and Lainina will recognize as your direct commanders," Marselle says. "There can be no question in their minds that you are sending your best teams in, or they won't commit."

"Commit their resources, you mean?" I ask.

"Resources, personnel, everything," Balthasar says. "We need to be sending our legionnaires to these sites, remember?"

I nod. "Fine. So who did you have in mind?"

"More than seventy percent of India's oil is imported, and more than ninety-nine percent of Japan's is imported." Balthasar clicks a button and a map pops up on the screen. "I've marked the sites we need to hit tomorrow in red.

Each of you has been sent a dossier that contains the details of the operation you will lead. I have included several options that will denote your involvement."

"And where will I be going?" I ask.

"No offense to anyone present," Edam says, "but these Council meetings have gotten so big, and are broadcast remotely, so we won't talk about your locations until later."

"The point here is that Adora is relying on Shamecha to supply all the oil it doesn't have, now that it can't import from any of us. So if we scare them badly enough with this feint, it should be easy to drive a wedge between them." Balthasar clicks the map off.

"Divide and conquer," Edam says. "And let us know if you have any questions. Otherwise, we believe the rest should be discussed individually to mitigate the chance of espionage."

"Wise," Marselle says.

Which is why I barely have a second to see Judica before she's headed for the landing strip. Apparently, her location is the furthest away and to make the right rendezvous, she needs to leave immediately. I squeeze her until my arms hurt. "Be careful. Do you hear me? No running toward explosions or people holding guns."

Judica smirks. "I make no promises."

"The second this part is over, we are setting a date and planning your wedding," I say. "And you can't even object, because I saw you accept."

Judica blushes. My demonic, emotionally constipated sister *blushes* at the thought of planning her wedding.

"And you and I will choose the dress, and it will have frills of some kind. Or maybe just a lot of embroidery. Either way, you aren't going to pick it alone, and you aren't wearing anything black."

"It's my wedding," she complains.

"And as the Maid of Honor, I get veto power on

anything and everything."

Judica shakes her head. "It doesn't work like that, I'm almost certain."

"Maybe not normally, but your Maid of Honor also happens to be the boss of you, so it is what it is."

Judica beams then. "Fine, but you're telling everyone that you picked the super fancy stuff."

"Absolutely. No one would believe anything else. They've all met you."

She hugs me. "Please be careful. You can warn and chide me all you want, but lately the one jumping in front of bombs has been you."

"I know," I say, "but not this time. It'll be a simple operation: fly in, throw a few conspicuous fireballs, fly back out."

"You say that," Judica says, "but I have trouble believing it."

"Well, try harder," I say. "Because it's happening."

Judica's plane takes off without issue and is disappearing into the horizon when Lark and a team of forty others reach the runway.

"Wait, where are you going?" I ask.

Lark shrugs. "I guess it really is all hands on deck, even half-human hands."

I clasp her hands in mine. "As it should be. You're every bit as capable as the others."

"You're worried about who is going to bring you warm croissants while I'm gone, aren't you?"

My smile feels sheepish. "I have gotten used to them."

"Don't worry. I've got several people on staff who know how you like them. You really whipped them into shape for me, you know."

"They know they need to be chocolate croissants, right? Because I need my strength to lob full strength fireballs."

Lark hugs me even tighter than I hugged Judica. "I

know you're not my sister, but I love you as much as if you were. More, maybe, because I never had to compete with you."

My heart has been heavy lately, dark even, but Lark's words, the knowledge that the kitchen has shaped up, it fills me to the brim with hope. "We are making things better, right?"

She pulls back and meets my eyes. "You are making things better, every single day. I never doubted that you would, but this is beyond my wildest imagination, truly. So be careful, okay?"

"Geez. You'd think I was running around with a huge target painted on my shirt. I'm going to be careful," I say. "I swear."

Lark nods. "I know you will. I just want to make sure that when I come back as a conquering hero, you're here to knight me, or whatever."

"I'll do it now." I yank my sword out and pretend to knight her. "I dub thee Lady Croissant, and I encourage you to return quickly so that I will get fat and happy when this is all over."

She laughs. "Perfect. See you soon, then."

And then I watch as her plane disappears, too.

I'm on my way back to my room, where Edam and Balthasar are supposed to explain my assignment, when I'm stopped by Marselle. "Don't tell me you're headed off right now, too?"

She shakes her head and yanks me into a side room. Her voice is low, urgent. "I recently heard from a contact of mine in the Shamecha royal court."

My heartrate spikes.

"Lainina and Melamecha don't want a full-blown war. They can't take on the other four families. They know they'll be squashed."

"Are they willing to surrender?" I ask. "What are their

terms? I'm willing to be very generous."

Marselle shakes her head. "They are not, but you need to know that their plan, if it looks like they're losing, is to lock down in a nuclear shelter and bomb the entire world, or as much of it as they can reach." She inhales and exhales heavily. "Nuclear dawn."

"That can't really be their plan," I say.

Marselle's expression is grim. "They have one final offer, before preparing to do exactly that."

"If Edam and Balthasar hear about this," I say, "they'll—"

"They'll want you to bomb them immediately," she says. "I know. And I don't even disagree with them, but it won't be enough. We may strike first, but we won't get everything, and they'll take shelter. It'll be the utter destruction the prophecy predicted."

The veins freeze in my body. My brain throbs inside my skull. "You said they have an offer."

"They're willing to agree to a challenge, but the terms are ghastly. Completely unfair."

"I meet them on their stated location," I say. "And I agree not to wear my ring."

"They want the ring placed in a locked safe on site," she says. "Each side is only allowed to bring forty men. The place they propose is an abandoned island just large enough for a landing strip."

"Edam and Balthasar would never agree," I say. "Never."

She nods. "I know that."

"What's the timeline on their offer?"

"They'll give you three days to decide."

"Tell no one," I say. "I'll need some time to think." About whether there's any way I could win without just dying.

Although, if I'm being honest, it's looking like even my death would be a win at this point.

❧ 23 ❧

The flight to the drilling platform in Okhotsk, just off Sakhalin Island, is boring. Thousands of miles of water, and water, and more water. This deep out at sea, the waves are massive, and from this high up, even those are boring. I've never been on a standard commercial jet before, but I think this trip hardly gives me insight into what it's like, given that nearly every seat is empty.

"Should I be offended I didn't merit my own assignment?" Noah asks.

"Are you offended?" I ask.

"Not in the slightest," he says. "But I feel like perhaps I *ought* to be."

"Your brain is a strange wasteland," I say.

Noah sits down next to me and hands me a sandwich. The reason he got up in the first place. "Do you remember the last time we were on a jet, tasked to save the world?"

I roll my eyes. "Judica had just tried to destroy your entire family."

"A few warheads wouldn't have destroyed my family," he says. "We're tougher than that."

"And now, we're flying toward the end again."

"The end?" Noah asks.

"If Marselle is right, Lainina and Melamecha would destroy the world to keep from losing," I whisper. "And I only see one way to prevent it."

"You are all kinds of melodramatic," Noah whispers. "Those two families are made up of loads of people. Balthasar and Edam are doing their job—they're turning the tide of evian support against them. There are other ways to deal with this threat than a kamikaze mission. And believe me, I know kamikaze missions."

My head rotates until I'm facing him head on. "Kamikazes are Japanese. Are you about to claim you're Japanese now?"

He laughs. "Not at all. But I have studied them, and I'm an excellent student. So I know all about them. See?"

Oh my goodness. "Edam might have had a point."

"On top of his head?"

"No." I groan. "About you. You're exhausting."

He takes my hand. "You're tired. You meant to say charming."

Our fingers interlace. "Maybe I did."

"We saved China back then, when we had no idea who we were, or what we were doing. We will figure this out, too. But let's focus on one thing at a time. We have an oil drilling operation to destroy, and everyone needs to see you do it."

"Ugh."

"You're lucky that I'm handy with an iPhone," he says.

"I'm glad you're here," I say.

Noah doesn't have any jokes to make about that.

We land on Sakhalin Island without incident, and I check in with Edam. "Yes," I say. "The helicopter is ready."

"And?"

"Noah's with me, and everything is in place, just like you said it would be."

"The ground troops?" Edam asks.

"They're here. They said the path is clear."

"I hate that I'm not there," he says. "I hate it more than you can know."

"I think I get how much he hates it," Noah says over my shoulder.

"I'm not even mad that guy is with you," Edam says. "As long as he keeps you safe."

"Look at Edam," Noah says. "Growing up so fast. I'll hardly recognize you if you keep this up."

"Enough," I say. "I'll call back when we're done."

"Chancery," Edam says. "Remember the discussion we had about the guy who was super complain-ey?"

The Sons of Gilgamesh. "I do. Did you replace him?"

"I decided to give him another chance," Edam says. "I told him I'd talk to him later tonight, and let him explain his side."

He's meeting with them.

"Be safe today," I say.

"I'm not even taking point," Edam says. "Balthasar insisted I stay here to coordinate our efforts."

I know that's killing him, but I didn't mean today. I meant at his meeting tonight. I'm sure he knows that, too. But in case someone's listening. "Right. I forgot. Well, keep Ni'ihau safe."

"Will do."

Edam hangs up, and a profound sadness steals over me. I don't like being apart from him, and I hate faking that we're fighting. But it might not matter either way, soon, so I try not to worry about it.

Spring hasn't yet come to Yuzhno yet. We bank past a craggy mountain range and land. "Are there usually so few people out and about?" We flew commercial, on a regis-

269

tered flight, because it's probably the one method Melamecha would never consider taking herself.

Arafuto is already unbuckled and standing by the door, a Motherless raised in Russia. He claimed to have visited the island several times, so Edam assigned him to come along. "It is typically much busier," he says. "I fear the virus has shut things down here as well."

Late April, six months after it first popped up in Wuhan, and the stupid SARS-COV-2 virus has spread everywhere, even remote islands, it seems.

"Okay, there are three main drilling platforms, but the vast majority of the production moves via sub-oceanic pipelines," Arafuto says. "Which means very few people would be present to be injured."

I sigh with relief. "Right."

"We have a team of three helicopters and two boats," he says, "to make sure that we record every angle."

"I'm on a boat," I say. "Because it's better visibility for the video footage."

"Exactly," Noah says. "The people need to see your face. They need to know that you're who we know you are, that you are involved, and that you're a force to be reckoned with."

I hope showing them this doesn't remove Marselle's offer from the table. "And we're going to predominantly stick with fireballs," I say, "to stay on brand, and also to keep from showing them too much about what else I can do."

"Except you'll be using your kinetic ability to destroy their buried pipelines."

"Sure," I say. "Right."

I'm somewhat surprised that we don't encounter any resistance on the way to the new transports, but then again, we set up all the attacks to occur simultaneously for a reason. I call Balthasar. "We're here," I say. "Commercial flights worked perfectly. No one glanced at us a second time."

"It won't work on the way home," he says.

I laugh. "Which is why you have the jets tasked to pick us up."

"To provide cover for your departure, and to pick you up," he says.

"Cover I hope we won't need," I say.

He grunts. "You prepare for the worst."

Or at least, we're prepared for second worst. I don't mention the threat of nuclear war. Surely he's already fretting about the possibility.

"Are you in place?" I ask.

"Less than twenty minutes out," he says. "And I've heard from eight others. Same."

"Sounds like we are all set."

"You need to call me one last time, right before you attack," he says. "I want yours to precede the rest of us by at least two minutes. I want them to be hit on all sides at once, but I don't want them to have any warning you'll be there before you are."

"Understood," I say.

But as I board the boat, my companions spreading into another boat I insisted we bring for survivors, plus three helicopters, it feels more like a movie production than a military attack. As if she can read my mind, Varvara video calls me.

"What?" I ask.

"I needed to see, to make sure your hair still looks perfect," she says.

I can tell, by the image of myself in the top right corner, that it *is* disgustingly perfect, right down to the small tiara woven into the plaits around the top of my head. I groan. "I'm about to destroy three offshore drilling rigs and an underground pipeline. I'm not filming an action movie."

"An empress must always look her best," she says.

I hang up.

Noah puts an arm on my shoulder. "It'll be over soon."

"They're acting like it's all a game," I say. "It's infuriating. A lot of people are about to die."

"That can't be helped," Noah says. "And if Balthasar and Edam are correct, these moves will cripple Melamecha and Lainina. Maybe they'll surrender."

"Or perhaps, unwilling to yield in any circumstance, this will only harden their resolve to destroy the whole world if they can't win."

"Although they rule, there are a lot of people around them. What we're doing is for those people," Noah says. "To undermine their confidence."

But the nukes will fly at the touch of a single button, something those two alone are authorized to initiate. "Maybe."

The feeling of falseness, as though this is all just an act, persists as we fly across the water, the boat moving so quickly that it lurches and bumps as it leaves the surface of the water entirely. Nine hundred and four. That's the capacity of our two ships, once Noah and the rest of the crew have been picked up by the helicopters to rendezvous with the jets. That's how many people we can save, after inflicting maximum damage on this oil production operation.

"What are you thinking about?" Noah asks.

"After this is all over, it will take years for all of these oil wells to be rebuilt. Gas prices will skyrocket."

"That was already true," he says. "Thanks to Melamecha and Lainina's actions against us."

"But this will only make it worse. Think of all the families who won't be able to afford to drive to grandma's house. All the people who won't be able to fly home for Christmas celebrations, thanks to the price of tickets, or airfare. It's a shame, but our entire economy still runs on the price of oil."

Noah smirks. "But think what this will do for renewable energy. It might finally develop in substantial quantities."

"Oh good grief," I say. "You're like the font of all optimism."

He shakes his head. "It won't help for us to lament all the changes we can't stop, all the wrongs we can't right. We're better off focusing on the things that can improve, that will change for the better. That's what we can control, aid, and steer."

He's right, but sometimes I need a good wallow. So I give myself the next few moments, until the first platform comes into view, Mynginskoye. Four massive, circular concrete pylons support a fifteen-floor structure that could have been made using huge iron Legos. An unwieldy crane towers over it all, prepared to move anything that requires moving, apparently. Metal support beams are tacked on all over the place, seemingly without a significant amount of thought or planning. Four tall chimneys stick up into the air, but no smoke emerges from any of them. And a large rectangular protrusion ascends from the same side as the crane, with a huge opening at the top, for. . . I have no idea what.

We're starting with the farthest-from-land drilling site and working inward, so we'll be close to a location for the jets to rendezvous when we finish. My hands shake, my heart races, and my eyes tear up from the cold air and speed.

I wipe the tears, focusing now on the wells of power in my head, all entirely full.

I turn on my earpiece. "Okay," I say. "I'm starting with a warning shot. Prepare to video after."

The pilot turns on my megaphone and I shout into it. "Evakuiruyus!" I shout. And then I fling a fireball at the larger of the two cranes, the one on the drilling platform. It knocks it sideways, but doesn't destroy it. "Closer," I say into my earpiece.

The pilot brings me around, and I notice people pouring from the machinery. This time I shoot two huge fireballs, one at the base of the crane on the platform, and one on the barge.

The sound of screaming metal, the smell of char, the shouts and shrieks of more than two hundred people, it all happens at once, and then the crane from the platform plunges into the ocean. The crane from the barge collapses, crumpling inward on itself, swinging down onto the boat. I send a kinetic pulse to shove it the other direction, and it snaps off the base as well, sinking into the dark water.

The crew doesn't waste any time climbing into the emergency boats.

"Chancery, it's time," Arafuto says.

But people are still streaming into the boats, and they haven't been lowered into the water.

"We can't wait any longer," Gregory says. "We have two more platforms."

I swallow and wait another thirty seconds.

"Is there a problem?" Noah asks.

Only that I can see them, the men, with as close as we are, scrambling into boats, shouting, running, their hearts hammering. They don't heal, not like we do. And each one of them matters.

Noah's hand closes on my forearm. "Chancy, you know I want to save everyone too, but we're trying to prevent more. You have to focus on the big picture."

A tear streaks down my cheek, but he's right. I can't wait any longer. The first boat drops into the water, and then the second. And I release fireball after fireball, a dozen, then two more. Each one bigger than the last. Until the entire platform is burning, men diving into the ocean as I watch. Each one is another cut, another wound.

A huge explosion jolts our boat and sends two of the helicopters spinning. Luckily, they right themselves. But the captain of our boat spins us around and we begin to race away.

"You still need to destroy the pipeline underneath," Noah reminds me softly, gently, like I'm a frightened child.

I turn on the sonar locator and bring it up. There, it's there. "Stop," I say to the captain.

He does, and I waste no time. No men and women to escape, not this time. I focus on the image of the large rectangular manifold ninety meters down. It takes almost no pressure to pop it up and crush it like a tin can. Then I yank the pipes out, like shoelaces torn from a sneaker, and I pull up the well of clean, pure light. And I repair the hole in the earth, smoothing it over as if it never existed, to keep it from bleeding crude oil into the ocean.

"Done," I say.

And we speed away, the other boat lingering on my orders to help anyone who didn't fit in their rescue boats.

The Kirinskoye field is next, and this one goes almost exactly the same. Except near the end, my phone starts ringing. At first I ignore it, but by the time the well is destroyed, the underwater manifolds crumpled and torn, and the hole filled, I check to see who's calling.

Edam. Balthasar. Edam. Balthasar. Balthasar.

I call Edam back.

"Get out," he shouts. "Leave now."

"Why?" I ask. "Yuhzno-Kirinskoye is the biggest one, and I'm close." I signal the pilot.

"No," Edam says. "Listen to me, for once in your life, just listen. Marselle says they've retasked their jets. Everything they have is headed your direction, right now."

"We've been over this," I say. "That's one of the reasons

I'm way out here—I'm the closest to Ni'ihau, and the furthest from mainland Russia."

"They knew we were coming," Edam says. "At least, they did in several locations."

"What does that mean?" I ask.

"Everything is fine," he says. "The operations are alright, but you need to cut your losses and head home, right now."

"I can see the next oil platform." It's seven times as large as the other two. "I'll leave the second I've taken it out, no delays, no dawdling."

"Chancery! You can't—"

I hang up. I'll head home the second I've finished this last task. I don't quit in the middle, especially if this might change Lainina and Melamecha's mind.

"Do we need to abort?" Noah asks. "Because Judica and Edam are both calling me."

"Do you see the drilling platform?" I point. "Close enough." I fire off the first three fireballs, and one takes out the crane on the platform, and the other two knock the cranes on the two barges cleanly. I'm getting better. "It's fine."

Except this time, the men aren't scrambling for boats. They're grabbing something. I squint. Missile launchers.

I point at the pilot. "Sonar. Activate the sonar now." His eyes widen.

I don't wait, not this time. These men aren't acting like civilians. I rain fireballs down on them, and many of their weapons explode on impact. The blasts rock our boat mightily, and I grip the side. A missile makes contact with the ocean next to us, exploding a hundred yards away. Our boat flings to the left, but I use a little kinetic power to stabilize it.

If that was what Edam was worried about, a few armed workers, we'll be fine.

"Chancy," Noah says.

I look away from the destruction in front of me, expecting that he has located the manifolds that connect to the pipeline. When I look at the sonar, I see it and pull, crumpling it and patching the hole. I'm getting good at this. Three seconds, four at the most.

"Chancery!" Noah shouts. His eyes are wide, and he gulps. I didn't hear them, not over the cacophony of the explosions all around me, not with the shuddering air from the helicopters overhead.

"Tell the helicopter to lower," Noah shouts. "Pick us up."

"There's no time," I say. "Tell them to get behind me. Now."

Five jets, no six. Seven. All incoming. I dig down deep into my pathetically depleted well from Mom's staridium, almost empty thanks to the fireball light show, and fling everything I have at the fighter jets. The EMP that explodes away from me eclipses any I've ever released before, knocking them out of the sky like a grizzly batting at angry bees. They drop into the ocean almost immediately.

"How?" Noah asks.

I realize that, in my fear, I emptied my kinetic well of power at the same time, wiping out their electronics and slamming them all downward simultaneously.

"Hello?" Noah answers his phone.

"Get her out of there, right now!" Edam shouts so loud through the receiver that the men diving off the burning platform behind us can probably hear him.

As if they heard him too, a rope drops from the helicopter overhead. Noah's arms circle my waist and catapult me upward. I grab the rope and begin climbing, hand over hand. "Wait," I say, "I only got one manifold. Aren't there two?"

"Edam says there are a dozen more jets coming. GO!"

I gulp and practically race up the rope. Our helicopter doesn't wait for the others. The second Noah and I are both on, it shoots away. We're not far from the landing strip where our own jet is waiting, but that three-minute flight is one of the most agonizing hundred and eighty seconds of my life. But the helicopter lands, and we disembark.

Two hundred yards to the jet.

When another fighter appears on the horizon.

And I don't have any power yet. Noah glances my way and I shake my head.

We run for the Blackbird, practically leaping inside.

"Take off," Noah shouts. "She's on empty right now."

Sean doesn't miss a beat. The door slams shut and we haven't even buckled in to the jump seats behind the cockpit before he's taking off, my heart sailing backward into my spine. But when I hear him swear up ahead, I scan the horizon.

For the missile headed our way.

I have just enough to bat it away.

It flies downward sharply. And hits the helicopter below us, exploding into a million pieces. Oh, no, Ulysses and Oliver.

"Sit," Sean says sharply.

I do, and I buckle just before we hit Mach six, moving so fast through the air that I know the front of the jet has heated up to several hundred degrees Fahrenheit. I close my eyes and breathe. The flight home is significantly quicker and much less boring than the ride to the island off the coast of Russia.

The second I climb out of the jet, I stretch. The jump seats in the Lockheed SR-72 Blackbird are *not* made for comfort. And even from dozens of yards away, Edam's scowl makes the hair on my arms rise.

"I knew the last site was the largest," Edam says softly. "I drew up the plans."

I gulp, walking toward him slowly. "I survived," I say. "But I need to know who didn't."

"No one else on your team made it out," Edam says. "Not a single person."

Over a few hundred million barrels of oil. I'm an idiot. I'm a bullheaded, stubborn moron.

"But that's not the worst thing," Edam says. "And I know it's not a great time to share this. But there won't be a good time."

My eyes lock with his. "What?"

"Melamecha prepared well for an attack at several of the sites," he says. "She had anti-aircraft weapons in place."

My stomach ties in knots. My blood arrests in my veins. "Who?" I ask. "How many died, and who?"

"Melamecha took down two of our aircraft," Edam says. "Judica's and Lark's." He takes my hands in his. "Judica's recovering, and she's going to be fine."

"And Lark?"

Edam grimaces.

Oh, Lark. What have I done?

279

❧ 24 ❧

ased on their television shows and their movies, humans are obsessed with death. Dying kids, near death experiences, violence, explosions, and apocalyptic events dominate the stories they tell. But is it any wonder? They live a handful of years, such a brief span of time on this earth, facing the possibility of their demise from the outset. They're fragile, so easily broken. They can't resist viruses, infection, illness, and they heal so slowly that sometimes it seems like they'll never heal at all.

And yet in some ways, they're stronger for it.

My mom was invincible. She was larger than life. She could destroy *anything*, take down *anyone,* survive *everything.* I knew that she would be there for me in fifty years, just as she had been for the past nine hundred. I was utterly unprepared for her to die. It bowled me over, carved me out, gutted me. I was decimated by that loss, because she was everlasting.

But Lark was half-human.

Evians may live a long time, but we do not take care of ourselves, not in the ways that matter. We're careless with our power, and I've been so obsessed with Lark being just as *good* as a full blooded evian that I forgot that she's not the same. She wasn't invincible. She wasn't iron clad.

She was vulnerable, and I sent her into the crucible anyway.

What was I thinking? I order everyone to leave me be, and I throw my clothes into the incinerator. I step into my shower and turn the water to full heat, the spray burning my skin. The pain eases something inside of me, the steam mixing with the tears running down my cheeks.

Of course, the second the scalding water burns my skin, it heals. The same water that might maim Lark does nothing to me except to help me to feel on the outside what I already know on the inside.

It's my fault she's dead. Even more than with Adika, who Noah killed when I couldn't. More than with Analessa, who I slew with my own hand, Lark died *because of me.* I should have kept her safe, and instead I hurled her into the tempest, carelessly. Selfishly. Like every other evian in history, fodder for the cannons.

And now the entire world hangs in the balance, and it's up to me to decide, again.

I don't bother adjusting the temperature. I deserve the pain. I deserve so much worse.

I deserve to die.

If that's what it takes to save the world, the world I've broken now, beyond repair. Suddenly it becomes startlingly clear to me. Mom was so positive that I would *save* the world that she didn't realize it would be my fault that it needed saving. My egomania that led me to proclaim I would rule everything, my murder of Analessa and Adika, my deals with Melisania, my war against Melamecha and Lainina.

And the looming threat was. . . created by me.

I walk out of the shower and pull clothing on without

paying attention, annoyed that the burns on my skin have already healed.

Consequences.

I never face any, not really. I stole Judica's birthright, and she forgave me. I stole her boyfriend, and she forgave me. I follow Balthasar's desire to take over the other families, and without any plan, without any real justification, I do it. I blob the stones together and nearly wipe out the entire island with a volcano. I have no business doing any of this, and the fact that I've been acting like it was all for the greater good. . . that may be the worst part.

I'm disgusting. God's instrument? What a joke.

But I have this one chance to set things right. It's so clear, now, so obvious. I fought Noah and Alora over and over, and repeatedly I was decimated. There's no chance I can defeat two fighters with hundreds of years more experience, both of them determined and well matched. No, I'll be mowed down.

Sacrifice. So many people assume it means that someone loses something, but it's more than that. It's not loss. It's not hurt. I didn't sacrifice my mom; she was taken. Sacrifice is more—to truly be a sacrifice, I must give something up or accept an injury to myself voluntarily so I can benefit someone else.

I open my door and send for Marselle.

She appears moments later.

I sit at Mom's desk, not even bothering to meet her eyes. "Tell them I'll take the deal. Negotiate a place, and I get to bring as many guards as they have combined. I'll figure out how to get there."

"Are you sure?" Marselle asks. "We have contingency plans for this sort of thing, you know. They're probably bluffing. And even if they aren't, there are bunkers all over the world. They'll hold eighty percent of the evian population you control, maybe more."

My eyes slew toward her slowly. I don't ask her if she's lost her mind. I don't ask her if she knows me at all. I don't ask her how she could possibly think I might be willing to risk the entire human and mammal populations and all the flora of the earth. I just stare at her, with my dead, dead eyes.

"Okay, you're sure. I'll set it up. To be clear: you'll check the ring there, you can't wear it for the fight. They'll need to check their heirs, respectively. I mean, they need to put something at risk, too. And their Consorts, I should think. Or in the case of Lainina, her own physical person. You'll each provide surety."

"Sure," I say. "I trust you to work out the details of that." Not that it matters. I could save us all some time and just give them the ring. Then they can kill me, and not blow up the entire world. As long as no one from Alamecha feels the need to retaliate—which they shouldn't as long as the challenge looks legitimate.

Marselle swallows. "Okay, yes. I will."

"And you can't tell anyone, Marselle. Edam and Balthasar, Judica and Inara, they can't know. They won't understand. Not a word until I'm gone."

"Yes, Your Majesty."

Marselle has only been gone a few minutes when a food tray arrives. Old Chancery would have cried. She would have completely crumpled, her heart shattered in a million pieces, emotions overflowing.

I simply take the tray, thank Ines for bringing it, and force myself to eat every last bite. I can't give Edam and Balthasar any reason to question my health, my mental state.

A banging at the window into the back courtyard a few moments later startles me.

Noah.

I open the door and look around for my guards. "How did you?"

Noah shrugs. "You know how."

"What do you want?" I ask.

"I want to make sure you're including me in your plans."

"There are no plans," I say flatly.

He rolls his eyes. "Obviously you accepted their offer. You're going to the challenge."

I don't even bother arguing with him—I'll probably need his help to sneak away.

"Where are you planning? Tasmania?"

My jaw drops. "That's a perfect location. I mean, I haven't run Analessa for more than a few days. I have no strong ties, so it's almost like neutral ground. Centrally located, and it's essentially a game preserve."

"I know you like me for my looks, but my brain's not half bad either," Noah says.

I don't have the energy to fake a laugh or banter back with something like, 'it's not half good either.' "I'm counting on you to get me out."

"You're the ruler, you know that, right?" Noah asks.

I don't have the energy to fight with Edam, Balthasar, Judica, and Inara, and everyone else. I just don't. I collapse on the edge of my bed. "Doesn't feel like it."

Noah laughs. "Well, you're pretty young. I think everyone just wants to help."

"Is that why you're here?" I ask.

"I'm here because I knew what you'd do when you heard about Lark, and I want to make sure you're okay. I want to make sure you're doing this for the right reasons."

"To save the world?" I ask.

Noah sits next to me. "Are you sure it's not some kind of penance?"

"What are you talking about?" I count the inset boxes in the molding on the ceiling.

"After your mom died and you refused to kill your evil spawn sister, you left in a jet, alone, determined to spare the people of China from the bomb Judica sent."

"I was there." I huff.

"You did it because you were hurting."

"That's stupid. I did it to save them, and when I realized I could survive *and* save them, that's what I did."

Noah doesn't speak. He doesn't tell me that I'm hurting again. He doesn't say that he can see that I'm hurting all the time now. He doesn't tell me that he knows that my pain from Mom still throbs so badly sometimes that tears spring to my eyes for no reason. And he doesn't say that I can now add to it the guilt of murder after murder after murder. And the shame of allowing my best friend to die, for my cause, senselessly. If I had accepted this challenge before, called off phase two, or even just kept Lark home, but I didn't. I keep making mistake after mistake.

He doesn't say any of those things, but they hang between us all the same.

His hand shifts, bumping against my thigh.

And I slide mine into his.

He doesn't say a word, just lies on the bed next to me, counting boxes in the molding on the ceiling too, for all I know.

"One hundred and eighteen," he finally says.

"A hundred and twenty-six," I say.

He shakes his head. "You can't count the half boxes as full ones."

"You have to," I say.

"It's the wrong thing to do," he says. "Just like you can't go off to die."

"I can't go to win," I say. "It's not possible. That kind of stupid crap only happens in Hollywood."

"And we can't convince you not to go—to save the

world. But also because you think you deserve to be punished, for everything awful you've done."

"Yes." The word emerges as a broken sob. "I do deserve that."

Noah flips up on his side, yanking on my hand, shifting my entire body, forcing me to meet his eyes. "I almost came here tonight as Lark, you know."

"You wouldn't." My heart cracks open inside my chest, but there's nothing inside. No sorrow, no pain, nothing at all.

"I would, if I thought you'd believe her when she tells you what I'm about to tell you."

I close my eyes. I stuff my ears with wool. I wrap my heart in bubble wrap. I can't take any more.

"It's not your fault, Chancery."

The same thing I told Balthasar not that long ago. Except this time, the words are a lie. "I sent her," I whisper. "I did that."

"It could have been anyone," Noah says. "It was almost you who didn't make it."

I open my eyes. "I wish it had been."

"I won't help you, not when you're feeling like this."

"You will help me, because I'm ordering you to do it, and if you refuse, I'll take the harder way. I'll tell everyone, and use all my energy, my last hours, forcing them to let me go. And then they'll all watch as I march into that challenge —with the same exact result, but much more suffering. I thought Melamecha was the sadist."

"Oh, I think that word applies to you too, but stick a sado- on the front. You're only doing this to hurt yourself. To punish yourself, and that's all wrong. You don't deserve the penance, any of it."

I leap from the bed. "Who cares why I'm doing it—I don't see any other solution, Noah. They will drop their nukes, just like Analessa would have ordered her people to

286

hack as many of us up as they could. She would have killed all her people trying to defend her in a fight she could never have won, and you know Melamecha and Lainina are at least as bad. They're exactly the kind of lunatics who will burn the world to the ground if it means no one else gets what they stand to lose."

"I know."

"Then you know I'm doing what I have to do."

"And I would be holding your sword for you, if that was your only reason," Noah says. "I'm with you, to the end, wherever that is."

"Then stop being a pain in the butt," I say.

"The butt." Noah laughs and stands up. "You need me to be a pain, because Lark isn't here to do it. She would tell you what I'm saying right now. You need to go into this fight with a burning desire to survive. Because, as much as you wished that bomb headed for China was the end, it wasn't. As much as you wanted that to be the last hard thing you needed to do, it wasn't. You had more tasks ahead of you. And I know this feels like the end, too. Eve knows you deserve a break. But that's not how life works. We don't reach the finish line because the race has already been long. We reach it when the race is over."

"This is it," I say. "I caused the entire race—and now, I can end it. And whether I win or lose, the race is over."

Noah shakes his head. "I don't think that's true. I think that prophecy set all of this up, and you've got a long leg left to run."

My knees weaken. My head pounds. And suddenly, with the ferocity of a dam giving way, my hands begin to tremble and my eyes fill with tears. I collapse to the ground and bawl like a baby. "I can't keep running."

Noah sits next to me and inches toward me slowly, like a lion tamer worried he'll be mauled. Finally, he gathers me up against him, and I turn.

287

I sob against his shirt.

"It's not your fault," he says. "And I know it hurts. Sometimes it hurts so badly that it feels easier to walk away." He runs a hand down the back of my head. "Or surrender and let the pain terminate."

I can't stop crying. The tears, once they start, don't seem to have an end.

"But you aren't going to do that. Not to me, not to Edam, not to Judica, and Inara, and Alora, and Marselle. Not to your brother Moses, who has lost almost as much as you. Not to the people of this world. Because they need you to finish the damn race, no matter how long, no matter how painful."

But people keep dropping out of the race, leaving me to run it more and more alone.

"The Larks of the world, they still need you, Chancery. I still need you."

A few sobs later, something inexplicable happens. My tears dry up, and an inexplicably warm feeling spreads through my body. It's as if I've been stuffed with sunshine, a burning warmth confirming that Noah's right. That I'm not done. It's not the end yet. More is required, and I can do it.

"But how?" I ask. "You were there. I might be able to defeat one of them, but not two."

"I don't know the answer," Noah says, "but I think you'll figure it out."

Noah and Alora and I practice again that night and the next. Sometimes I get a few good hits in. Sometimes I come awfully close. I learn to sense both of them at the same time, using them against one another. But it doesn't matter.

I still lose every single time.

25

"You'll think of something," Noah says.

"She'd better think of it on the flight over," Alora says. "Because she's out of time."

"Speaking of," Noah says, "you need to go get ready."

Alora curtsies to me and ducks around the corner.

"It was a stroke of brilliance to name her the new Regent of Malessa," Noah says. "Because it gave us a jet, cover, and perfect timing."

"I am brilliant," I say. "Too bad that isn't helping me figure out how to keep from dying horribly."

"I'm not sure whether a warrior's death counts as horribly," Noah says. "I mean, it's not as if you're being eaten by snails. Or, you know, impaled a thousand feet below sea level by a huge tree, and nibbled on by huge-eyed shark worms."

"There were no shark worms," I say.

"I'm sorry, how would you describe that Gulper eel?"

"You didn't see one of those." I whack his arm. "Stop."

"I'm sure I would have, if I'd been conscious."

"Well, I'll be conscious for this."

"Maybe that's an option. You can pass out," he says. "Surely they won't attack an unconscious woman."

"I think they'll be all too happy to kill me, no matter my state of awareness." I think about how I defeated Judica— when she let me. I had no idea how easy I had it back then.

I bid Alora goodbye, waving and wishing her luck. And then Noah and I walk back down the hall. "I need to use the restroom." I duck into one of the hall bathrooms and sneak through the window.

Noah's already waiting just outside. "Done?" he asks.

"I didn't have to go," I say. "I said that to escape my guards."

"Good, because I hate to point out the obvious, but I didn't hear you wash your hands."

I would so kill him, if I didn't need him to sneak me back to Alora's plane.

"Okay, this is going to be strange," he says. "I haven't done this in years, but I know from when I was a kid, this only works if you're touching me at all times."

I nod.

And then nothing happens. We simply start walking around the corner and back out into the path that leads to the landing strip. Edam and Balthasar walk past us, arguing. They don't even spare me a second glance.

"Who are we again?" I ask.

"It doesn't change your voice, idiot," Noah says.

"Idiot?" I lift my eyebrows.

"Whisper, you royally wonderful idiot."

"What do I look like to you?" I ask.

"Exactly the same. So do I, right?"

I nod.

"But to anyone else, we look entirely different."

"I touched you," I say, my heart racing at the thought. "And you still looked. . . I can't explain it. Smaller. Less. . . imposing."

He smirks. "It's hard to project," he says. "I can't include you and exclude you—you just see what I see if I'm covering you. But it's almost second nature for me to make sure everyone sees me differently."

I shake my head. "Well, let's go. After all this is past, maybe you can teach me at some point."

Noah smiles. "I would really like that. I think after this is over, we definitely need to see whether you can take the stone from me."

"I wouldn't steal it," I say.

"I know," Noah says. "And you wouldn't have to."

We board the plane, with Alora welcoming us on, and take a seat. We wait until we've been in the air for a while before Noah drops the illusion.

"Whoa," Jaclyn, Alora's pilot, says. "What happened?"

"It's a long story," Alora says. "But it's also the reason for the stopover in Tasmania on the way to the bigger holdings of Malessa."

She gulps. "And your guards?" She glances over her shoulder.

Alora shrugs. "I left them."

Jaclyn blinks. "So we're flying to Tasmania, alone, to what?"

"We won't be alone. Marselle has arranged for forty soldiers to meet us there, which will counterbalance Adora and Shamecha's twenty each," Alora says.

"Uh, who will be supervising that?" Jaclyn asks.

"I've been in touch with the ground forces in Tasmania," I say. "Such as they are."

"And where am I supposed to land, exactly?" Jaclyn asks.

Alora walks to the front of the plane and reviews the details. I close my eyes and go over the plan in my mind again. When I tasked Marselle to set this up, I didn't much care how it went down. The result felt inevitable. But now, I very much care how it ends. Noah was right. If I'm not done, then the Larks of the world still need me. And maybe I was quick to assume that I was done, because I felt I deserved it. But only a coward would throw in the towel when there are millions, or billions, still relying on her.

I am many things: imperfect, impatient, rash, emotional, trusting, gullible, and naive.

But I am not a coward. Not anymore, anyway.

By the time the plane lands, I still have no plan, no solution, no reason to hope that I will survive this. Except for the utter calm that has settled in my chest.

"You don't look scared," Noah says. "But we're here. Right on time. You're about to surrender that ring and walk into a battle to the death against not one, but two epic warriors."

"I don't say this lightly." I raise one eyebrow. "Noah Wen, you give the absolute worst pep talks in the entire world. Reading me the prophecy would have been more helpful."

"All I'm—"

"Actually," I say, "reading me the back of a cereal box would have been more helpful."

Noah grabs my forearms. "Why are you so calm? I'm supposed to be the one making dumb jokes to help you relax."

I shrug. "I should be panicking. I should be a wreck, terrified that I'll fail you, Judica, my mom, everyone. But." I pause. "I'm not. Something about this feels. . . inevitable."

"Alright," Noah says. "Well. Alright."

I laugh. "Alright? Wow. You're still, like, epically bad."

"Well, I'm sorry. Next time I'll prepare a speech for when you're utterly, sociopathically calm."

"Next time." My breath catches in my mouth, and I drag Noah's head down to mine. I kiss him, short, sharp, urgent. "There will be a next time. Okay? Somehow, in a way that probably makes no sense, this is going to work. I am going to survive this."

"Okay," Noah says.

And he means it.

I walk to the appointed spot, right at the southern edge of Coles Bay, near the Freycinet walk, my feet sinking into the powdery white sand. My eyes feast on the pink granite peaks, the cerulean water, the exquisitely clean air.

It's not a bad place to die, if that does happen. Not a bad place at all.

"I'm here," I say, the guards Marselle chose lining up behind me. "And here are Alamecha's honor guards."

"I am Ella." A short woman with dark skin and dark hair stands in front of a glass cabinet, bolted in place on the ground, sunk into concrete and iron rebar. The bindings are also iron. It's impressive they were able to prepare this in a two-day period. Four sets of shackles are sunk into the ground two feet away, presumably to hold Lainina and Melamecha's consorts. Ella extends her hand.

I reach out my hand to shake.

She frowns and drops her hand. "I was of the understanding we would be taking surety and then signaling the others it was safe to arrive."

Duh.

I glance down at the stone on my finger. I didn't think much about the security it provides for me, not until I'm faced with the prospect of giving it up. In a place I don't know, on faith that the other families will honor the terms of our bargain.

For a split second, I doubt. I wonder whether I should have told Edam and Balthasar. Was this all a huge, epic, monumentally awful mistake?

"Chancery." Melamecha's voice is every bit as droll as I remember it. She has shaved her bright red hair on either side of her head and braided the center into a French braid that falls below her shoulders. It's much more severe, much more alternative than her usual style. It's actually pretty intimidating.

"I know I'm supposed to wait, but your family was always unfailingly *trustworthy.* I can't imagine that has changed."

Heat bubbles up in my chest when I see her, and I realize that like Mom before me, I hate her. I want to destroy her. And I could. She may not realize it, but right now, before surrendering my ring, I could split the ground beneath her feet, I could roast her into char, I could tear her limb from limb. Lark's face flashes through my mind.

Is this what I'm meant to do? Am I the whirlwind, the guillotine? The power in my mind surges, the wells trembling with my fury.

But no. That's not who I am: a liar, a cheat, a devastator. That is not me. I am Chancery Divinity Alamecha, daughter of Enora the Merciless. But unlike the world, I know that Enora knew mercy, and she taught me that there's a place for mercy and a place for justice.

I don't deceive, and I don't double cross.

But today, somehow, I will avenge. I hand my ring to Ella. "I am Chancery Divinity Alamecha. I am here to respond to a challenge issued to me by Melamecha Shamecha and Lainina Adora. I have chosen blades."

Ella's eyes don't blink as they take the stone, but her hands tremble, her eyes downcast. It blackens as she gently, reverently places it in a small glass case. "Bulletproof, shatterproof, but visible." She spins around and sets the glass case inside the secured cabinet and locks it all, employing titanium locks. Then she swallows the key.

"Um, I hate to be a downer here," Noah says. "But how exactly do you propose we get that key back, you know, after we've won?"

Melamecha's laugh is more of a bark than anything else.

"I'll slice her belly open to remove it, once I've separated your head from your body." She eyes me from my toes up to my face. "No offense of course. I'm even a little sad it's come to this."

"Excuse me?" I ask.

"You had a lot of potential," she says. "If only you'd been willing to be guided. But no, you've made a real mess of things."

She's not wrong about that.

"Your surety?" I ask.

Melamecha gestures and Venagra, her dark eyes flashing, and Michael, a vein popping in his forehead, both approach and extend their arms. Ella shackles them, arms and legs both, and then asks them to test the shackles. They might not withstand extended attempts to escape, but they should hold long enough.

"Lainina is always late. What a coward, wanting to ensure that any trap you have planned falls squarely on me." Melamecha spits. "I shouldn't have expected anything different from someone who doesn't even fight her own battles."

We only wait three minutes before Lainina appears, flanked by Ranana and Rothgar. Lainina may not be particularly physically imposing, but she certainly selected for that in a Consort, and she passed it along to her daughter, too. Ranana isn't as tall as her father, but she towers over her mother. All three of them wear their raven black hair down, flowing freely over their shoulders. They're so beautiful, it nearly hurts to look at them. Shining hair, unbelievably huge, dark eyes. It's easy to see where anime draws its inspiration.

"My surety." Lainina offers her hands to Ella to shackle and tosses her head at Ranana who does the same.

Rothgar, now that he's close, is probably the largest man I've ever seen. It's not so much his eight feet of height as it is the breadth and heft of his shoulders and the width of his chest. He smiles at me then, and it's feral. One tooth is twisted to the side, and it's jarring.

Evians are always perfect, from our hair to our toes. He must have worked for that imperfection. How had I never noticed it before? Perhaps because I usually headed in the opposite direction from wherever he was in the past.

"Shall we?" Ella asks.

Lainina's soldiers and Melamecha's line up on either side of the four shackled individuals. My soldiers encircle the glass cabinet.

Alora and Noah both smile at me, and if the smiles are a little forced, well, I don't blame them.

Ella walks calmly toward the water of the cove. "We agreed to fight here, and we've marked the bounds of the fight, as you can see." She gestures at the enormous concrete barricades, connected by metal cables. "It's roughly twice the size of a normal ring, to accommodate the addition of an extra combatant."

I unsheathe my sword, Mom's old blade, a gift from her first husband, Melamecha's brother. Evian life is incestuous in many ways.

"Anything goes," Melamecha says. "To the death."

"Well not quite anything. I did select blades," I say. "So we are each limited to two blades, of any length we choose."

"Yes, yes, of course," Melamecha says.

"The victor rules all six families," Lainina says. "That's the deal."

Whoa. My eyes shoot toward Noah's. Winner takes all? Which means—I thought Melamecha and Rothgar were here as allies, but if only one of them will emerge. . .

Ella counts us down.

And in the space between the numbers, I notice something else. Something I hadn't even considered. Melamecha failed to remove her ring. The staridium flashes gently on her hand. The hubris of it, demanding that I lock my stone away, and dangling one right under my nose, appalls me.

It's also the answer I've been searching for—the unbelievable gift I didn't expect.

The very second Ella reaches the end of the count, Rothgar's massive scimitars flash in the sunlight, arcing toward my neck and my waist.

I leap backward, and Melamecha scores a deep slice across my right hamstring. I drop to the sand, barely retaining my grip on my sword.

Not an auspicious start.

Rothgar beams, his crooked tooth taunting me. His scimitar swings at my neck, and I barely block in time.

But Melamecha slices again, this time scoring the back of my left arm. I'm holding my sword with just one hand now, too focused on healing my injuries.

"Not so fast, Rothgar," Melamecha says.

"I'm not like you. I don't enjoy playing with my food," Rothgar says.

I stand up, relieved at their squabble, since it bought me the time I needed to heal my leg and arm. But it's short lived, and I realize it was merely another step in Melamecha's game. She really does enjoy harming people. I try not to listen for her melody—because it turns my stomach.

Rothgar slams into me a third time, the shudders from blocking his attack traveling down into the soles of my feet, and again Melamecha strikes before I can recover, this time stabbing me in the kidney.

I fall forward and cough up blood onto the sand, but I haven't dislodged her blade. I don't have the strength to do it.

"Fine," Melamecha says. "If you're in such a rush, I suppose we can end this part, so we can focus on deciding which of us will walk away." Her eyes gleam, sizing up Rothgar, as she twists her sword, pulverizing my kidney, driving pain up the side of my body and down to my feet.

Rothgar knocks me forward further with the flat of his blade, my face colliding with the sand. They're going to finish me, right here, right now. Before I've had a chance to drive a wedge between them. Before I've even come close to Melamecha's ring.

As if she can't quite help herself, Melamecha reaches down and steps on my back, her hand fisting in my hair, yanking my head backward, breaking my spine, but it's low, below T-10.

Which means I can still use my arms. She laughs again, like a colony of sea lions barking with joy. "This was actually fun."

"You're sick," Rothgar says.

"I'm honest," Melamecha says. "And that scares you."

I slide my dagger down from my sleeve and into my right hand. And I while they're sneering over my broken body, I reach back, quick as lightning, and slice Melamecha's finger off. It drops to the sand in front of me, and I drop my dagger to grab it, surrounding the stone with my palm. Blood pours from Melamecha's hand over my head, dripping to the sand on either side of me, but she doesn't cry out, and she doesn't shout.

She swears, low and furious.

And she lifts her blade above her, ready to sever my head from my body.

I cast about wildly for the well of power in my head, the well I desperately hope will be there.

And it is. I reach for the power, and I feel it, the pulsing well of strength, just like the others, but also different, as they always seem to be.

I turn, as much as possible, throwing my shoulders sideways. My upper body screams with pain, but I ignore it.

What can this power do? I yank on it, pulling hard, and I feel it then.

It controls water. The ocean to my side beckons to me, ready to do as I bid.

Useless. This power is useless. I can't drown them. They'd hack me to pieces while I tried. Water power, I hate you.

Melamecha's blade connects with my neck, shearing tissue, shredding my body, my blood gushing from the wound.

And I realize.

We're all made of water.

I feel for Melamecha and for Rothgar, and I *squeeze*.

And they explode.

I dislodge Melamecha's blade from the vertebrae of my neck and heal the damage. My neck and then my back, and then I force myself to my feet, and I look down. The entire ring is covered in. . . a film. A pink film.

That used to be Rothgar and Melamecha.

Lainina is screaming, her eyes bulging. Ranana is utterly still. Michael and Venagra stare at me with identical looks of horror on their faces.

I walk into the ocean, letting the water rinse away the gore. I'm aware that it's cold, but it doesn't touch me. Maybe that means my brain is broken, or maybe I'm in shock. When I walk back out, I'm dripping with saltwater and dread. I wish I could wash away the image of what I've done as easily as I washed away the evidence on my body. I turn and walk toward the sureties and the guards.

"As you may have noticed, the stone I removed from Melamecha as she was attempting to behead me controls water."

I look from one end of the line of guards to the other. "You're all made of, well, mostly of water." I swallow. "All it takes is one little squeeze." All of them turn and sprint down the beach toward where they landed, stumbling over one another in their desperation.

"Now what to do with these four," I say.

"I vote you explode them," Noah says. "They'll just cause problems."

Alora's jaw drops.

She doesn't know Noah as well as I do—he's bluffing of course, which is good. It distracts me from doing what I desperately want to do—rushing back to the ocean to dry heave until I can blank the image of what I've done from my brain. "Or, we could take them back with us," I say. "Captives to ensure that their families behave."

"I'm with Noah," Alora says, catching on to his ploy to make them behave. "Easier to kill them."

Lainina can't rip her ring off fast enough. She throws it at me, in the midst of begging for me to spare her life. Of course, the flinching they do every time I move toward them, even incrementally, doesn't help me forget what I've done.

I may never forget.

Ella surprises me. She doesn't act afraid at all when I approach. "Congratulations, Your Majesty. That was an impressive win." She smiles, her white teeth nearly blinding. They remind me of Rothgar's twisted one. I wonder whether it is lying somewhere, in the sand, or floating in the ocean. I shudder.

"I assume you're not going to slice me open for the key?" Ella asks.

My mouth drops. I shake my head.

"I've taken a laxative and will shortly return with it," she says.

My lip curls, but I don't argue.

A few minutes later I watch as she washes the key in the ocean, thank goodness. Even so, I let her unlock the cabinet and the glass case. I rest easier once the ring is back on my finger. Easier, but not without guilt.

"You prevented the nuclear war that was imminent," Noah says softly, from next to me on the way home. "When you can't sleep at night, when you think you're a monster, just remember that. They were prepared to bomb the world out of existence. You did what had to be done to prevent that and nothing more."

I remind myself of that over and over the entire way home. And when I land, with two new stones in my pocket, and I hand the captives over to Balthasar, I remind myself again.

Somewhere around the hundredth time I repeat the words to myself, *you did what had to be done to prevent something far worse,* they cease to have much meaning.

Because what can be worse than exploding humans into droplets and teeth?

"Are you okay to be alone?" Noah stops at the door to my room.

I shrug.

Edam approaches from the other direction. "I need to talk to her."

Noah opens his mouth to argue, but I shake my head and he shrugs.

"It's fine."

Edam follows me inside.

"You have no idea how awful today was," I say.

"I wish I had known," he says. "I know you think I would have stopped you, but—"

"I can't," I say. "I can't talk about us right now. I'm barely a person."

Edam nods. "Understood."

"So if that's what you needed—"

"It's not," he says. "I wish it was."

I close my eyes. *What now?* "Please tell me that no one else has died."

"I'm officially a member of the Sons of Gilgamesh," Edam says. "And I could have waited and waited and finally been brought into their plans slowly."

I frown.

"But we don't have time for that."

"What did you do?" I lift one eyebrow.

"You don't want to know. You had a bad day, and I'll just say that you weren't the only one."

"Okay."

"But I have proof that the Sons of Gilgamesh released the SARS-COV-2 virus."

I lift my eyebrows. "But it's abating some, and many places are reopening—"

Edam shakes his head.

"What?"

"That was a trial run, to gather information about spread, timeframes, reaction from the local populations. The world has grown dramatically since the flood, apparently."

I gulp.

"They believe that there's a solar flare coming," he says. "It will boost the speed at which the human DNA breaks down. They believe the entire human species will cease to exist within the next twenty years. The onset of child cancer is the marker of the beginning of the end, in their opinion. According to them, the last time the humans dealt with something similar, the body attacking itself, cells growing out of control in children, was just before the flood. They claim that the virus that they released then was not to destroy. It was a mercy kill, to end things and reset the children of Eve in the most humane way possible."

I think about Mom's records. "And now?"

He nods. "Their reboot then worked beautifully, reset-

302

ting the world for evians. They plan to do it again now, and they believe that again, it's the merciful thing to do. They're releasing a new virus soon, and unlike SARS-COV-2, it has a one hundred percent death rate."

I shower, and change, and call for Noah. I hand him my phone. "Call your dad."

His eyes widen.

"We're out of time. I need to find the Garden of Eden, and I have a feeling he knows where I should look."

If you have a little faith in me, check out Inara's story, unRepentant. It's up for preorder, and as soon as I finish my current romance novel, I'll focus on it. I'll try and get it out early, but I can't promise anything. September 15, 2020 at the latest!

Destroyed, the FINAL book in the series, should be out by November 15, but I am struggling right now to get things written with all my kids home, so that may depend on how things go this fall!

If you're looking for something new to read while you wait for unRepentant, scroll past the appendix to check out a free sample chapter of my post apocalyptic series that starts with Marked! The entire series is in KU.

Finally, if you'd like a FREE full length novel, you can grab my standalone ya romantic suspense, Already Gone, if you join my newsletter at www.BridgetEBakerWrites.com.

❧ 26 ❧

APPENDIX

I . ALAMECHA: United States of America, England, Ireland, Scotland, Canada, Cuba, Puerto Rico

Eve

Mahalesh 3226 BC

Alamecha 2312 BC

Meridalina 1446 BC

Corlamecha 553 BC

Cainina 273 AD

Enora 1120 AD

Chancery 2002 AD

H. Judica 2002 AD

2. MALESSA: Germany, France, Netherlands, Switzerland, Norway, Sweden, Finland, Australia, New Zealand, Papau New Guinea, Iceland

Eve

Mahalesh 3226 BC

Malessa 2353 BC

Adorna 1451 BC

Selah 618 BC

Lenamecha 211 AD
Senah 1022 AD (Denah dead twin)
Analessa 1820 AD
H. DeLannia 1942

3. LENORA: All of South America (including Chile, Argentina, Brazil), Mexico, Spain, Portugal
Eve
Mahalesh 3226 BC
Lenora 2365 BC
Ablinina 1453 BC
Leddite 652 BC
Selamecha 379 BC
Priena 460 AD
Leamarta 1198 AD
Melisania 1897 AD
H. Marde 1987

4. ADORA: India, Japan, Korea, Indonesia, Thailand
Eve
Mahalesh 3226 BC
Adora 2368 BC
Manocha 1461 BC
Alela 590 BC
Radosha 192 BC
Esheth 638 AD
Lainina 1444 AD
H. Ranana 1967

5. SHAMECHA: Russia, Mongolia, Kazakhstan, Pakistan, Uzbekistan, Philippines
Eve

Mahalesh 3226 BC

Shamecha 2472 BC

Madalena 1639 BC

Shenoa 968 BC

Abalorna 299 BC

Venoah 333 AD

Reshaka 936 AD

Melamecha 1509 AD

H. Venagra 2000

6. SHENOAH: Continent of Africa, Saudi Arabia, Iran, Iraq, Turkey, Greece, Italy, Jordan, Afghanistan

Eve

Shenoah 3227 BC

Adelornamecha 2385 BC

Kankera 1544 BC

Avina 670 BC

Sela 467 BC

Jericha 135 AD

Sethora 399 AD

Malimba 708 AD

Adika 1507 AD

H. Vela 1990

❧ 27 ☙

SAMPLE: MARKED

I'm a big fat coward.

I've known this about myself definitively since one month before my sixth birthday. The night I lost my dad.

Case in point: I'm just shy of seventeen. I've been in love with the same guy for almost three years. Even though I see Wesley a few times a week, I haven't said a word. But tonight I have the perfect opportunity to do what I've always feared to try. Tonight, to celebrate our upcoming Path selections, all the teens in Port Gibson play a stupid, risky game.

Spin the Bottle.

I glance around as I walk toward the campfire in front of me. Only thirty-five kids turned seventeen in the past year, so of course I know them all. My best girl friend, Gemette, waves me over. I try to squash my disappointment at not seeing Wesley. When I played this scene in my brain earlier, I was sitting by him.

"You gonna scowl at the fire all night, Ruby?" Gemette pats a gloved hand on the slab of granite underneath her.

"You couldn't have saved us one of those seats?" I point

at the smooth, flat stumps on the other side of the fire. I sit down and shift around, trying to find a flat spot.

"I think what you meant to say was, 'Thanks, Gemette. You're the best.'"

Her straight black hair reflects the campfire flames when she tosses it back over her shoulder. It's against the Council's rules for hair to cover your forehead. Gotta make it easy to see anyone who might be Marked. Except tonight, no one's following the rules. Everyone's wearing their hair down, and Gemette's silky locks frame her face beautifully. I envy her sleek hair almost as much as I covet her curves.

"My bum's already hurting on this," I mutter.

"If you weighed more than eighty-five pounds soaking wet, it wouldn't bother you so much."

Instead of curves, I've got twig arms and a non-existent backside. I shift on the huge slab, trying to find a position that doesn't hurt. I arch one eyebrow, not that she can see it in the dark. "I weigh ninety-two pounds, thank you very much."

Gemette snorts. "That proves my point, you bony butt."

She leans toward the fire and picks up the glass bottle lying on its side. She tosses it a few inches up into the air before catching it again.

"Be careful with that." That bottle's the only reason I'm sitting here, sour-faced, stomach churning.

Slowly the remaining seats around the fire fill up. Wesley shows up last. There aren't any seats left, but before I can convince Gemette to squish over, he grabs a bucket. He turns it upside down and takes a seat a few feet away from everyone else. I guess that's fitting. His dad's the Mayor of Port Gibson and a Counsellor on the CentiCouncil, so Wesley's in charge by default tonight. He'll probably take over for his dad one day, which isn't as glamorous as it sounds since less than two thousand people live here.

He looks around the fire, and his gaze stops on me. He bobs his head in my direction, and I shoot him a smile. I'm glad he can't hear the thundering of my heart.

Although we're all huddled around a campfire, and I've known most of the kids here for years, we maintain carefully measured space between us. Tercera dictates our habits even when we're rebelling. Which we're only doing because it's a tradition.

Maybe Tercera's made cowards of us all.

"Are we starting?" Tom's sitting to my left. His parents are both in Agriculture and he's Pathing there, too. He has broad shoulders and tan skin from working outside most of the day. Gemette likes him, and it's easy to see why. Of course, he's nothing to Wesley.

I glance across the fire in time to see Wesley stand up. He straightens the collar of his coat slowly and methodically, like his dad always does before a town hall meeting. Wesley loves doing impressions, and he's usually convincingly good at them.

"I'd like to take this opportunity to welcome you all to the Last Supper." His voice mimics his father's, and he touches his chin with his right hand in the same way his dad always rubs his beard. Wesley himself is tall and lean with long black hair that he's wearing down, for once. It falls in his eyes in a way I've never seen before, and I feel a little rush. I want to touch it.

Wesley smirks. "I know you may be less than impressed with the culinary offerings for our gathering, but as I always say, Tradition has Value." He cracks a grin then, and everyone laughs. "Seriously though." He drops the impression and returns to his normal voice, which I like way better anyway. "I know the food sucks, but this whole thing started with a bunch of teenagers who were sick of rules and ready to throw caution to the wind for a night."

I look down at the three or four-dozen nondescript metal cans with the tops peeled back, resting on coals. Another few dozen are open but sitting away from the fire. Presumably they contain fruit or something else we won't want to eat hot.

Wesley leans over and snags the first can, his gloves keeping him safe from the heat. "I hope you'll all forgive me, but this was what we could find."

"This is a pretty crummy tradition." Lina reaches down and grabs a can with mittened hands. Her dark brown hair falls in a long, thick braid down her back, like it has every single time I've seen her.

"Traditions matter, even the silly ones. They help pull us together as a community, which is valuable when fear of Tercera yanks communities apart. We're stronger when we aren't alone. Thinking every man should look out for himself hurts all of us." Wesley takes his first bite right before Lina. I grab a can of baked beans.

The food really is as bad as it looks, but at least it's not spoiled.

Wesley talks while we eat.

"As you already know, we come from a variety of backgrounds. Before the Marking, Port Gibson housed approximately the same number of people, but not a single person who lived here before the Marking survived. We cleaned out the homes, burned some to the ground and rebuilt, circled the city with a wall, and made it our own. The Unmarked who live here are Christian, Muslim, atheist, black, white, Hispanic, Russian, German and Japanese. I could keep going, but I don't need to. Before the Marking, these differences divided humanity. Now, we know that what truly matters is what we all share. We embrace the traditions that bring us all together, because we're more alike than we are unalike."

I swallow the last spoonful of baked beans from my can and set it down on the ground by my feet. I'm almost the last one to finish eating, but several half-full cans are scattered around the campfire. A few people grab a can of fruit. I prefer the stuff my Aunt and I process and can ourselves, so I don't bother.

I rub my hands together briskly. Even in mittens, my fingers feel stiff. It's usually not too cold in Mississippi, even in January, but a late freeze has everyone bundled up. The Last Supper's supposed to be a chance to rebel, but I'm grateful that everyone's as covered as possible. It means I won't look as cowardly for keeping my mittens on. My aunt is Port Gibson's head of the Science Path, so I know all about how Tercera congregates first in the skin cells, even before the Mark has shown up on the forehead in some cases.

The wind moans as it blows through the trees, and we all huddle around the meager fire. Even though the flames have died down to coals in most places, it burns hot. My face roasts while my back freezes. The bottle lies stationary on the weathered flagstones by the fire where Gemette set it, light glinting off of the dingy glass at strange angles.

The quiet conversations die off and the nervous laughter ends. Eyes dart to and fro among the thirty something teenagers gathered.

"So." Evan's voice cracks, and he clears his throat. "Who goes first?"

"Thanks for volunteering," Wesley says.

I suspect no one else asked for just this reason. All eyes turn toward poor, gangly, redheaded Evan.

Evan gawks momentarily. Even though he and I work in Sanitation together, I don't know him well. I haven't been there long enough to guess whether he feels lucky or put upon. He sighs, and then leans forward and tweaks the bottle. It twists sharp and fast and skitters to the right, spinning furiously.

I really hope the bottle doesn't stop on me, and I doubt I'm alone in that thought. Evan's funny in a self-deprecating way, but he isn't smart, and he definitely isn't hot. I bite my lip, worried about what I'll do if it does stop on me.

It slows quickly and finally stops pointing to my left. I sigh in relief, which I belatedly hope no one heard.

Tom gasps, and then in a raspy voice says, "No way. I mean, you're nice and all Evan, but I'm not . . . I don't . . ."

"Yeah, me either. Chill, man." Evan laughs. "So, does it pass to the next person over?" Evan raises his eyebrows and glances at me.

I want to protest, but my throat closes off and I look down at my feet instead.

Evan stands up. "So Ruby . . ."

He may not have saved me a seat, but Wesley jumps in to save me now, thank goodness. "That's not how it works. If you get someone of the same gender, and neither of you . . . well, then your turn passes to him or her. Which means you sit down Evan, and you spin next, Tom."

"Who made these rules?" Evan grumbles as he sits.

Gemette smiles. "They make sense, Evan. I mean, it's not spin the bottle and pick best out of three. Your way, you'd basically pick someone in the circle who's close and kiss whoever you want."

Evan shrugs and glances at me again with a smile. "Sounds pretty okay, actually."

Tom snorts. "I don't hear Ruby complaining about Wesley's rules. I'd say that's your answer, man."

I look back down at my shoes, but not before I see Tom's wink. Jerk. Evan must feel idiotic, and I definitely want to sink into the ground.

I bite my lip again, this time a little harder. Tom's an

obviously good-looking guy, but I have no interest in kissing him. I hope his wink was a joke about Evan and not some kind of message.

Cold air blows past me as Tom leans forward to spin the bottle, his body no longer blocking the wind. One thing jumps out at me as he reaches for the glass bottle. In spite of the cold, Tom isn't wearing gloves. He must've taken them off at some point. He's either a daredevil or an idiot. I'm not sure which.

Tom spins the bottle less forcefully than Evan and rocks back and forth as the bottle circles round and round. His eyes focus intently on the spinning glass as if he can somehow control where it stops. I wonder who he's hoping for and look around the circle for clues. Andrea seems particularly bright-eyed. My eyes continue to wander. One gorgeous, deep blue pair of eyes in the circle stares right back at me. Wesley. I've looked at him a lot over the past few years, but this feels different somehow. A spark zooms through me, and I quickly stare at my feet.

No luck for Andrea tonight, or Gemette. The bottle comes to rest on Andrea's best friend, Annelise, instead. She and I were in Science together a long time ago. Her dark brown hair hangs loose, framing high cheekbones and expressive chocolate eyes. She frowns. Tonight doesn't seem to be going right for anyone so far.

"Now what?" Annelise's voice shakes. "We just kiss, right here in front of everyone?"

"No, of course not," Gemette snaps.

"Who made you the boss?" Evan frowns. Judging by his sulky tone, he's still mad about losing his turn earlier.

"Unfortunately, I'm the boss," Wesley says, "and she's right." He points to a dilapidated shed at the top of the hill. "You two go up there."

"Romantic." Tom rolls his eyes as he stands up. He rubs his bare palms on his pants. Gross. At least I know I'm not the only nervous one here. Tom and Annelise trudge a path through clumps of frozen brown grass toward the rundown tool shed.

What a special memory for their first kiss.

Gemette sighs and I pat her gloved hand with my own. I'd feel worse for her, but Gemette likes every decent looking guy in town, including a few boys a year younger than us. She'll recover from missing out on a special moment with Tom.

I glance again toward Andrea, an acquaintance from my time in Agriculture. She and Tom trained together for years. She may have liked him as long as I've liked Wesley. She looks into the fire while her foot digs a messy hole in the soil. I wonder how I'll feel if Wesley spins and gets Andrea. Or worse, Gemette. I'll have to sit here and twiddle my thumbs while I know he's in there kissing a friend. My stomach lurches. Coming tonight was a stupid idea. I clearly didn't think this through.

No one speaks to distract me from my anxiety. The shed isn't far. We could easily eavesdrop on them if the wind would shriek a little less.

"How long does this take?" Evan asks.

"Who the heck knows?" Gemette points at the bottle. "Impatient for another crack at it?"

Kids around us chuckle.

After another few awkward moments, Gemette grabs the bottle and gives it a twist. "No reason we have to wait on them."

"Sure," Wesley says. "Whoever it lands on can go next."

"Wait," Evan asks, "whoever it lands on goes next as in it's their turn to spin? Or goes next as in Gemette's going to kiss them?"

The bottle stops before anyone can respond, pointing directly at Wesley. His perfectly shaped brows draw together under disheveled black hair. Gorgeous hair. His lips form a perfect "o". His bright blue eyes meet mine again.

My heart races and the baked beans sit like a lump in my belly. I shouldn't have come. Of course Wesley will want to kiss her. Gemette's gorgeous, curvy, and smart. Ugh. Am I going to have to sit here while my best friend kisses the guy I like twenty feet away? This is all my fault. If I'd only told Gemette, she'd beg off.

I bite down a little harder on my lip and taste blood this time. I really need to kick this particular habit, especially with kissing in my future. Maybe. Hopefully. I'm such an idiot.

Wesley clears his throat. "I think I'm going to sit this game out. I'm more of a moderator than a participant."

"No," I blurt out. "You can't. You're here, you're seventeen, you have to participate." What am I doing? Why am I shoving him at my friend? But if I don't make him play, I'm flushing my chance to kiss him down the toilet. I want to cry.

"Well, then I guess it's my turn to spin." His deep voice sounds completely different than any of the other kids here tonight. My stomach ties in knots when I hear him speak, which is ridiculous because I've heard his voice a million times.

I glance at Gemette. She looks disappointed and I want to cry with relief, but I don't blame her. He could've kissed her but didn't pursue it. I imagine most any girl here would be disappointed. He glances up and his eyes lock with mine again. Caught. I start to shiver and try to stop it. This look is different somehow from any before, like something shifted. Wesley clears his throat, looks down at the bottle, gracefully reaches over, and snaps it between his fingers.

It spins evenly, not moving to the right or the left. It spins on and on, and I wonder if it'll ever stop. It slows, whirling a little less with each rotation, the butterflies in my stomach swooping and swirling with each pass.

Until it finally stops. On me.

My eyes snap up reflexively, wide with shock. Wesley doesn't even seem surprised. He simply stands and inclines his head toward the shed.

"Isn't it still..." I clear my throat. "Umm, occupied?"

"We can wait over there." He gestures at the hill to the right of the shed. One side of his mouth lifts in a smile and I feel an answering grin form on my lips. Which makes me think about what we're about to do with our lips.

Swarms and swarms of butterflies flutter in my chest.

"Sure," I say.

I stand up and without even thinking, I wipe my palms on my jeans. They aren't even sweaty and what's more, I'm wearing mittens! I really hope no one noticed. Okay, more specifically, I hope Wesley didn't notice. Gemette holds something out to me when I stand. I can't tell what it is from feel alone thanks to my thick mittens, and in the dark I have to squint to make it out at all. A tube of something. "What—"

"Lip gloss," she whispers. "A gift from my mom. I was going to use it, but looks like you need it more, you lucky, lip-biting brat." She winks.

I'm glad Wesley's still across the fire from me and that it's dark. Maybe he somehow miraculously missed both the palm wipe and her wink.

I walk as slowly as I can toward the old shed, partially to avoid tripping, but also so I won't look overeager. I try to hide my face while I apply the fruit-scented lip-gloss so that Wesley won't notice. It's dark, but I don't want him to be put off by dry, scratchy lips, or worse, dried blood. Gemette's a good friend. I feel guilty for overreacting earlier when I thought she might kiss Wesley. Not super guilty, but you know, a little.

Neither of us speaks a word, but I feel the eyes of the other teens follow us toward the shed. We're only a few crunching steps away when the swinging door flies open and Tom and Annelise barrel out. I jump when it bangs shut behind them.

Tom looks as ruffled as I feel, his eyes darting back and forth. He ducks his head and reaches down to take Annelise's hand. They walk out and away from the fire and the rest of Port Gibson's teens. I can't tell where they're headed, but somewhere far away from here.

"Did you know almost a third of the couples in town trace their start to the Last Supper?" Wesley asks.

"No way."

He shrugs. "We've only been an Unmarked town for seven years, so it's even more impressive. Not all of them are matched up from a bottle spin, but I think the game helps people realize how they feel."

A thrill rushes through me. Does Wesley feel the same as me?

My hand reaches for the door handle and collides en route with his. I'm wearing mittens, of course, and he's wearing shiny, brown gloves, but a thrill runs through me when we touch, even through layers. He doesn't move his hand away, but instead draws my hand in his and pushes the door handle back in one fluid movement. My heart skips a beat and time stops. When the door's completely open, he slowly releases my hand. I lower my eyes and step over the threshold into the rundown little building.

Although there's clearly no power, and consequently neither heat nor an overhead light, the walls at least cut the wind. It's at once both warmer and quieter. Two tall candles burn softly on a pile of rusted metal boxes in the corner. Someone prepared this dump, I realize. I wonder whether it was Wesley. The flames provide enough light that I can see his face. His dark brows are an even more startling contrast to his dark blue eyes than usual, accentuated by his hair falling in his face.

"So," I say. "Here we are."

Wesley looks at me from less than a foot away. The shed's small and crammed full of moldering farm implements. The air around us practically hums, but that isn't new. It's always like the moments right before a lightning storm when he's near. Supercharged almost, like the electrons around my body might fly off at his slightest touch. The difference is that here, away from the town's work projects, away from my family and his, it feels like anything really could happen.

Wesley's so close I can smell him, the same citrusy, woodsy smell I've secretly savored for years. It's even stronger tonight, like he put on more of whatever it is he usually wears. I breathe deep, and all the memories of him re-imprint on my brain. Scrubbing, sanding, painting, digging, cleaning, hammering. Projects his dad made him attend, but I suffered through to be near him. When I'm with him, I belong somewhere for the first time in a decade.

When we become adults next week, Wesley's mandatory attendance at work projects ends. Wesley steps into his role as an administrator, and I'll become part of Port Gibson's janitorial crew. It's now or never if I want to make any kind of permanent place with Wesley.

I never thought I'd be close to him like this, and I know I may never be again. I lean toward him and tilt my face upward, eyes closed, ready for what comes next. Maybe I'm even a touch impatient. I have waited for this for years.

Except I keep waiting, and then I wait some more.

Not a single thing happens. The trouble with being ridiculously small is that Wesley, who's on the tall side anyway, towers over me. Even with my face angled up, his lips are pretty far away. I can barely make out his expression, but it looks guarded.

Maybe he doesn't know how to do it?

No way. Wesley must know. I mean, it's not hard, right? You just push your lips onto the other person's mouth. Why isn't he doing anything? This is the moment. THE moment!

Until it passes. And then another moment falls on top of it, and another. All passing. Even the butterflies in my stomach get bored and go look for flowers elsewhere.

I'm not sure exactly how much time has elapsed, but the seconds drag, heavy with my growing frustration. Soon, someone will bang on the door. "You've been in there forever," they'll say. "Make room for the next couple."

I want to smack them in their eager faces.

I know I don't have much time, and I want to say something, anything. I need to tell him how I feel, say the words, take a gamble. But like it always does, my tongue shuts down. My throat closes off. The words stick inside my throat. Why am I such a coward? Our perfect moment withers and dies. Tears well up in my eyes, and I can't breathe.

Wesley isn't similarly affected. He steps back and says, "We don't have to do this, Ruby. It's not safe at all. I don't know why my dad even lets these dinners happen."

"Why'd you spin the bottle in the first place?" I hear the desperation in my voice, but the words pour out in spite of myself. "I know you, and you know me. How's it dangerous for us?"

He takes another step back, his expression registering surprise. "People get Marked, Ruby. It still happens. Every few weeks, in fact. Maybe I'm Marked. You don't know. It happens, even here, even with all our rules. It may take years to die once you're Marked, but it's inevitable."

I roll my eyes. "Well I'm not Marked, if that's what you're worried about." I point at my forehead. "See? Clear."

"We shouldn't be taking these risks." Wesley scowls. "Not now, not right before our real lives begin. This whole thing's supposed to be a time to say goodbye to being a kid, not act like an idiotic five-year-old, breaking rules for no reason."

Our real lives? Maybe he never thought it felt right, the time we spent, the way we are together. Maybe I never belonged with him at all. "Why'd you even come, then? Why follow me in here if you're not going to kiss me?"

Was he hoping for someone else? Was he stuck with me and looking for any excuse to bolt? Am I Evan in this scenario?

I look up, but I'm too close. The hair cascading over his face obscures my view. I want to touch his hair; I want to kiss him; I want to tell him I love him, and that I always have. My fingers and toes and everything connecting them zings in spite of the bitter cold, in spite of the indifference of his words. Energy spins round and round in my body, a closed circuit with nowhere to go.

"Look, Ruby, I don't know what to say . . . but the thing is . . ." He sounds torn, confused.

Suddenly, I don't want to hear "the thing," whatever it is. I've been talking to Wesley for years, talking and talking, and working alongside him, but I don't want to talk to him anymore. I know what I want and I'll never have a better chance to play things off as part of a game, if he feels like I now suspect he does. The notion of an excuse appeals to my cowardly heart. I can't speak the words, but I won't stand here and do nothing, not anymore, because he's the real life I've longed for.

I stop thinking and step toward him instead. He tries to step back and slams up against the back wall. I quickly take one more step and use my gloved hand to pull his head down to mine. I push my lips against his. In my haste, I push too hard and pull a little too fast. Our teeth smack into each other and my tooth knocks against my own lip, splitting it wide open again.

It's the opposite of magical.

I look up at Wesley instinctively. He has blood on his mouth, but whether it's his, or mine, I can't tell. And if it's not awful enough already, Wesley stiffens from head to toe like I mauled him, like I forced him into something torturous.

A tear rolls down my cheek and I inhale deeply. I won't cry over this. I can't, because there's no way I can play it all off as a game if I bawl my eyes out. I turn away from him. If I can't stop the tears, at least he doesn't need to see them. When did this go so wrong? I should be calm, cool, in control. I need to laugh it all off and tell him friends can't be expected to kiss well. Whoops.

Except my heart won't listen to the screaming from my head. I'm not calm. I'm the opposite of cool. I've lost all control.

He grabs my shoulder and tugs me around. I turn, but my eyes stay glued to the ground, too ashamed to meet his gaze.

"Ruby, look at me."

He puts two gloved fingers under my chin and lifts. His head comes down then, but slowly, too slowly. My heart stops pumping and I worry it might never beat again. His lips brush mine gently, then with more pressure. I ignore the discomfort of my torn lip and lean into him, connected to him in a way I can't explain. I need more air, but I want less, because that means more space between us. If this never ends, maybe it'll erase the moments that preceded it.

Suddenly, he lets me go and steps back. Emptiness fills the space where he stood. I reel again, sucking air in and blowing my breath back out to steady myself.

When I raise my eyes, our gazes lock. All my sorrow from before is gone, replaced with a feeling like I'm flying, soaring, floating on top of the world. His sapphire blue eyes reflect candlelight back at me. He's breathing as deeply as I am; he's as affected as me. I can't look away from his strong, almost hawkish nose, his square jaw, his flashing eyes and thick black lashes. I continue to stare as Wesley reaches up and brushes his unkempt hair away from his eyes.

I almost faint.

Such a simple movement. Small in the grand scheme of things, but also vast, earth shattering, all encompassing. My dreams crumble. My world spins out of control. He moves his hair off his forehead, and suddenly things make sense. His reticence to touch me, his skittishness, but also his quick recovery. Once he knew it was too late, he didn't hesitate to kiss me.

Because we'd already touched.

A tiny rash mars his otherwise perfect forehead. Before the world died, it wouldn't have mattered. Before the Marking, no one would have cared about a few bumps. It would be harmless: acne, a bug bite, or a reaction to hair product. It shouldn't matter that his forehead has a blemish. It shouldn't terrify me, but it does. Because that small rash means Wesley is Marked, and in under three years, he's going to die terribly.

And now, so am I.

G rab Marked here.

ACKNOWLEDGMENTS

I know I say this in every book, but my husband Whitney is just... as an author, I still struggle to find the right words. He supports me, he uplifts me, he inspires me. He is proud of me when I doubt. He is there for me no matter what. I couldn't do any of this without you.

My parents are right behind him in supportiveness—and that is really saying something. They come help out when I need it, and I think my mom buys the first ten paperbacks of every single one of my books. <3

My kids!! They have grown during my journey as an author and now they make dinner, they clean up, they care for one another. . . all so I can write. I am so proud of them, and they support me 100%. Eli and Dora are also my most eager readers. Their enthusiasm makes me grin ear to ear, even if they do love other authors a little better. . .

My content editor Peter Sentfleben is AMAZING. And my proofer, Mattie Davenport is also phenomenal. (Please feel free to blame any tenacious typos on her! Haha!)

And my readers—I doubt you understand the depth of my love and appreciation for you. When you leave me reviews, it makes me beam. When you send me messages, it warms my heart. And when you recommend me to friends, well, I can't even thank you enough for that. Truly, you're the only reason I am still doing this. Thank you, thank you, THANK YOU.

ABOUT THE AUTHOR

Bridget loves her husband (every day) and all five of her kids (most days). She's a lawyer, but does as little legal work as possible. She has two goofy horses, two scrappy cats, one bouncy dog and backyard chickens. She hates Oxford commas, but she uses them to keep fans from complaining. She makes cookies waaaaay too often and believes they should be their own food group. To keep from blowing up like a puffer fish, she kick boxes every day. So if you don't like her books, her kids, her pets, or her cookies, maybe don't tell her in person.

ALSO BY BRIDGET E. BAKER

The Almost a Billionaire clean romance series:

Finding Faith (1)

Finding Cupid (2)

Finding Spring (3)

Finding Liberty (4)

Finding Holly (5)

Finding Home (6) coming July 15, 2020!

The Birthright Series:

Displaced (1)

unForgiven (2)

Disillusioned (3)

misUnderstood (4)

Disavowed (5)

unRepentant (6)- coming September 15, 2020

Destroyed (7) - coming November 15, 2020

The Sins of Our Ancestors Series:

Marked (1)

Suppressed (2)

Redeemed (3)

Renounced (4) coming February 15, 2021

A stand alone YA romantic suspense:

Already Gone

CPSIA information can be obtained
at www.ICGtesting.com
Printed in the USA
LVHW051622051021
699598LV00011B/899